SPELLBOUND

SPELLBOUND

CRYSTAL J. JOHNSON
& FELICITY VAUGHN

w by **wattpad** books

W by **wattpad** books

An imprint of Wattpad WEBTOON Book Group

Published in Canada by Wattpad WEBTOON Book Group,
a division of Wattpad Corp.

36 Wellington Street E., Suite 200, Toronto, ON M5E 1C7 Canada

www.wattpad.com

First W by Wattpad Books edition: September 2022
ISBN 978-1-99025-940-1 (Trade Paper original)
ISBN 978-1-99025-941-8 (eBook edition)

Library and Archives Canada Cataloguing in Publication information is
available upon request.

Printed and bound in Canada

1 3 5 7 9 10 8 6 4 2

Cover design by Mumtaz Mustafa
Images © kharchenkoirina via Adobe Stock,
CURAphotography via Shutter stock

This book is dedicated to our mamas.
Thank you for nurturing our creativity, encouraging us to
imagine the impossible, and teaching us to believe in happily
ever afters.

PROLOGUE

People from all over the world flocked to the Reynard Hotel for one reason—ghosts. They charged their cameras, packed their families in minivans, and set off for a sleepy coastal town in Connecticut, exchanging the thrill of roller coasters and the excitement of meeting a beloved movie character for the chance to encounter the things that go bump in the night. People sacrificed the luxuries of fine hotels and crammed into small guest rooms with the hopes of catching a glimpse of the Hyde brothers.

The twin boys were rumored to haunt the grounds of the historic Reynard. Disembodied laughter, pounding footsteps, and glowing orbs of blue and purple had all been caught on video and attributed to the brothers. On occasion, keys and sunglasses would inexplicably fly across a room, and tapping would sound from inside the walls as the two souls cursed to live out eternity in the hotel made their presence known to the living.

Hazel Fox lifted a gnarled hand to the ruby pendant around her neck as she made her way through the empty narrow hallway. The light bulbs flickered, casting shadows over the golden outline of peonies etched into the peacock-blue wallpaper. With each step she took toward the staircase, the flowers appeared to sway with an unfelt breeze. Most would be unnerved by the groaning wooden floors and the squeaking of rusted hinges, but she found comfort in the settling of the colonial building. Especially on a night like this.

Winter Spirits was one of her favorite days of the year. For a single night, the brothers were free from the confines of the hotel's property. Legend had it they slaughtered animals and snatched babies from their cribs, but Hazel knew the truth. The twins wreaked havoc the way young men tend to do, but never with malice. So, when Hazel had taken ownership of the Reynard, she had dismantled the terrifying tales and turned the night into a celebration.

"Aunt Hazel! Wait!"

Hazel turned to find a blond, gangly preteen running toward her, buttoning her gray wool coat and skidding to a stop in her patent leather shoes.

"Someone looks ready for a festival." Hazel looked down at her favorite niece, and the brightness in the child's eyes filled her with pride. She hadn't had children of her own, so Gemma was the closest thing to a daughter she'd ever have.

"Yeah, but I was wondering if I could practice my ghost tour on you on the way out. You said I could lead them by myself next summer, remember?" The girl was practically bouncing on the balls of her feet.

"Of course. Show me what you've got," Hazel said, then stopped short, looking around the empty hallway. "Wait. Where's your cousin?"

Gemma didn't even bother to hide her eye roll. "Raven already went outside. She said she couldn't stand spending another minute in this creepy hotel, and the festival was the only reason she came." Hazel covered her mouth with her palm to hide her grin; Gemma's impression of her other niece was impeccable.

Where Gemma was free-spirited, Raven thrived on schedules and boundaries. One girl enjoyed her time at the Reynard, while the other saw the days there as nothing more than an obligation to spend time with her eccentric great-aunt. Gemma was open to all possibilities, but Raven was firmly grounded in tangibles. Which is why she would never be the one to cherish the Reynard as Gemma did.

"All right then, her loss." Hazel held out her hand, and Gemma wrapped her fingers around it. "I'm ready for the best ghost tour this hotel has ever seen."

"As the Fox family legend goes, it was the coldest night of 1886, and twin baby boys were left on the steps of the hotel. When they were found by Amity Fox, the hotel's first owner, they were blue, lifeless, dead. Their spirits are here roaming the halls of this hotel. Many see them in the form of the young men they never grew up to be."

"It's true. This is the only home Archer and Soren have ever known."

Gemma held her hands in front of her, brushing the air with her palms like she could feel their presence. She took big steps, lifting her knees to her chest and dropping her voice to a haunting whisper. "If you listen closely, you might hear them laughing in a hallway or knocking on the walls from the other side."

Hazel's big jeweled earrings dangled next to her cheeks, and her go-to fuchsia lipstick turned her thin lips into a wicked grin. She mimicked her niece's creepy stride. "The Hyde brothers never disappoint."

"They enjoy playing in the dark, and that's why every night at ten o'clock we turn out the lights and guide the ghost tour with nothing more than the light of lanterns."

Hazel couldn't fight her smile. While other girls Gemma's age were absorbed in social media accounts, celebrity crushes, and favorite TV shows, all of that fell off her niece's radar when she set foot in the Reynard. She spent every waking moment of her annual summer visits searching for the ghostly boys. Every year she begged her parents to book rooms at the hotel for Winter Spirits, and they compromised by bringing her every other January. Gemma's love for the Reynard was unquestionable.

"And where's the boys' favorite place to hide, Gem?"

Gemma didn't even have to think twice. "The bell tower. No one can go up there because the entrance is closed off. They like it there, because they're safe from curious eyes. But on this very night, they come out to play with all of Spelling."

Hazel squeezed Gemma's shoulder, proud that the girl clung to her every word. They would sit for hours in Hazel's suite, talking about the women in their family who had owned the hotel before her, and she gave her niece the necessary tidbits about the twins who were portrayed in a painting over Hazel's fireplace. Gemma studied the artwork and absorbed every story, eager to share the tales with those who wanted to hear them.

They descended the last flight of stairs and entered the lobby. Gemma skipped over the checkered tile and sat in the velvet wingback chair in the sitting room. She crossed her ankles and clasped her hands in her lap, staring at the fire crackling in the stone-carved fireplace.

Hazel rounded the antique mahogany counter, running her fingers over the hand-carved filigree along the edge. Her heart swelled at the sight of the girl so comfortably settled at the Reynard. It was quite the feat to gain Hazel's adoration; only two people had accomplished it before Gemma. Like them, her niece saw beyond the bright muumuus and collection of silver rings that adorned each of her fingers. She was one of the few who enjoyed Hazel's questionable humor and joined in with her boisterous laughter. Her niece loved her as she was, and Hazel adored her in return.

With the money from the register secured in the safe, Hazel stood and met the familiar gaze of a young man. A grin spread over her face; she would never grow tired of those unusual sparkling eyes, or how a dimple indented his right cheek when he smiled.

"Sun's just set. It's time for some fun, darling," he said, propping an elbow on the countertop.

His smooth voice, laced with a hint of mischief, echoed through the empty lobby and grabbed Gemma's attention. From the fit of his new slacks to the black button-down shirt, her wide-eyed gaze soaked in every detail. Hazel recognized the enthralled expression on her niece's face; it was the same one she herself had worn the first time she'd seen him.

"Is that—"

"It is," Hazel said to him.

"She's growing up."

"As are you, my friend." Hazel stepped out from behind the desk and held her hand out to her niece. "Come along, Gemma. It's time to celebrate with the spirits."

"Yes, *the spirits*," the boy repeated with a sly grin.

Gemma wrapped her fingers around her aunt's and tilted her head to the side, studying the boy through narrowed eyes. When they stepped out into the frosty winter evening, she asked, "Have you seen the Hyde brothers?"

He exchanged a glance with Hazel. A smile that held four life-times' worth of secrets pulled at his lips. "I guess you could say that."

"Do you think they're here now?"

Hazel didn't miss the calculated undertone of the question. If Gemma was anything, she was perceptive.

"I do. And I think it's quite probable that you'll run into at least one of them before the night is through," he said with a wink.

"Are you—"

"Let the young man be on his way, Gemma. There's so much to discover, and some only have this one night. And we have a tradition that awaits us."

Gemma followed her aunt down the hotel's front steps, eager to dance and play carnival games in the town square. "I hope you have fun tonight," she said, looking back at the boy, but her words fizzled when she found no one there.

"Where'd he go?"

Hazel put her arm around her niece's slender shoulders and led her toward the town square. "I'm sure you'll see him again."

The wistful look on the girl's face warmed Hazel's heart, and right then she knew—if anyone would be able to do what she herself couldn't, it would be Gemma Fox.

CHAPTER ONE

Of all the days for my chronic tardiness to kick in, it had to be today.

I crammed my keys into my purse and slung it over my shoulder. Slamming my car door, I caught my reflection in the dusty window. Wisps of golden hair broke free from my ponytail and crowned my freckled face like a lion's mane. I licked my fingers to tame the strands and cringed as it did little to better my appearance. With a sigh, I gave up and ran toward the sky rise.

Today was just another nail in my aunt Hazel's coffin. After years of battling breast cancer, my great-aunt had been in remission. Or that was the impression she'd given my family. It turned out Hazel had sugarcoated the truth in a thick, sticky glaze. She'd gone as far as concocting an active lifestyle of daily swims, Bunco every Tuesday, and a slew of renovation projects around the Reynard. When the disease claimed her, she had been alone, and I'd been living it up with no clue. Not only was I not at her side when she died, but I couldn't convince my family to forgo a traditional funeral. Hazel would have wanted a party to celebrate her life. Bright clothing, strong drinks, and cheesy '80s pop songs—a quirky gathering that she would have loved to have attended. Now, all that was left was this final meeting, which she would have hated too.

After the twenty-floor elevator ride, I burst into the attorney's office and asked the receptionist to point me to the conference room. My shoes beat against the tile floor, and I nearly tripped when I skidded to a stop in front of the double oak doors. Smoothing down my dress, I took two deep breaths to still my racing heart and walked in.

Everyone seated around the oval conference table fell silent. My skin prickled with embarrassment under their scrutinizing gazes. They were freshly pressed suits and designer shoes, and I was a broken-in pair of Vans and a red sundress from my senior year of high school. I avoided making eye contact, turning my attention to the window overlooking the Boston cityscape. It was bad enough that my parents and brothers were here to witness what I was sure they considered another irresponsible Gemma moment, but Raven's family was here too.

My uncle Kevin was the spitting image of my father, down to the silk ties and Italian leather shoes they wore to work every day at Fox Imports, the luxury-car empire they had built from the ground up. They weren't twins, but only eleven months sat between them, and they'd been inseparable since birth. The only discernible difference between them was their taste in women—while my aunt Deborah was pretentious and materialistic, my mother was a sweet, sincere woman, who was charmed by my father's charisma and stability.

"Nice of you to join us, Gemma," my father said, his tone dripping with sarcasm. His hazel eyes radiated disappointment—an expression I had grown to expect over the years.

My mom elbowed him, offering me a tight smile that didn't show off her new set of veneers, a gift from my father for their last anniversary. "Christopher, stop it. Come on in, honey, sit down."

I took the empty seat next to my brother Hunter. "You okay,

Gem?" he whispered, brushing his palm over the scruff on his jaw.

I appreciated Hunter's empathy. No one in this room understood just how much Hazel meant to me. She was just a kooky relative to them, a woman obsessed with ghosts who lived in a musty, old hotel. But Hunter was always sensitive to other people's emotions, especially mine.

I nodded, tears stinging my eyes. "Yes. I just—"

"I know today is hard for you. It'll be over soon enough," he said, squeezing my arm.

"That's right. I can finally shut down that outdated roach motel and do something useful with the profits," my cousin, Raven, said, flipping her long black hair over her shoulder.

Anger bubbled up in me, heating my cheeks and the back of my neck. Raven had always hated the Reynard, never wanted to spend the summer there, and never took the initiative to learn its history. Her ridicule and eye rolls were the only things I saw from her where the hotel was concerned.

"Raven, you can't—"

She shot me a glare across the table, and the air in the room seemed to chill. "I'm the oldest female Fox. I'll be able to do whatever I please."

Gritting my teeth, I clamped my hands down on the arms of the expensive leather chair, my pulse pounding in my ears. And I had no reply. None, because Raven was right. As soon as that will was read, everything I loved about being with my aunt Hazel would be in my cousin's hands. Hands that wanted to do nothing but destroy what our ancestors had worked so hard to build.

The door at the front of the room opened, and my great-aunt's balding, middle-aged lawyer, Mr. Cartwright, stepped over the threshold. "Are we all here now?"

"Sorry I was late," I said with a sheepish smile.

His face was warm and open, and he wore an expression that made me feel like maybe I wasn't the most irresponsible person ever to exist. "It's all right, Miss Fox." He sat at the head of the table and opened the folder in his hand, pulling out a packet of papers. The will.

"Let's get started. The will isn't very long, and it's relatively straightforward." He cleared his throat and began to read.

It was all the standard wording about sound mind and last will and testament. My thoughts drifted as he droned on, thinking, *This is it*. Hazel's will was her last act on this earth. Never again would she walk the halls of the Reynard or lead a ghost tour. We would never sit together in her hotel suite and talk about what it was like to own the hotel or our plans for the future. I would never pull her close in a hug and melt against her as she embraced me back. She was gone.

"'I hereby bequeath the Reynard Hotel and all its assets to my great-niece Gemma Diane Fox.'"

"Wait, what did you say?" I blurted out, snapping my gaze to Mr. Cartwright. "Did you say my name? That can't—"

"That can't be right!" Raven sprang from her seat and slapped her palms on the table. "For one hundred and fifty years, the hotel has been passed to the oldest girl with the Fox name. *I* am the oldest. Hazel can't break tradition."

It was my brother Trevor who backed her up. "She's right, there was only one incident when it didn't pass from an aunt to her oldest niece. What's going on here?" His dark, perfectly coiffed hair without a strand out of place only added to his *I'm better than you* attitude.

I shouldn't have been surprised at Trevor's reaction. He and I may have gotten along when we were younger—he used to take up for me on the playground when the older kids picked on me—but in our later teen years, he became more and more critical of me and my life decisions. He didn't like my friends, my boyfriends, my choice of extracurriculars. When I'd dropped out of college two years ago, he'd laughed and told me that I would never make it in this world. He had no mercy when it came to me, no forgiveness. He had become a carbon copy of our father.

"Hazel had every right to break tradition. She had no legal obligation to follow it, and she made no mistake in her wishes. We discussed it at length, and Gemma is the one she left the Reynard to. There's no question about it," Mr. Cartwright said.

"It doesn't make any sense; Gemma doesn't know anything about running a hotel," my father said, and my aunt and uncle grumbled their agreement. Of course they did. They wanted their daughter to inherit it so she could shut it down.

"I can learn," I started, but everyone spoke over each other, pushing me out of a conversation that had nothing to do with them and everything to do with me.

Raven raised her voice over the others, her attitude one of utter disdain and condescension. "Not to mention that I have my degree in hospitality and am currently the manager of a five-star luxury hotel in downtown Boston." Her eyes darted to me on the word *degree*, as if to rub it in my face that she had graduated and I hadn't.

"Hazel was very clear that even though Gemma is not the oldest girl, she was the one she wished to leave the hotel to as she showed the most interest in it throughout her life," Mr. Cartwright replied.

The attorney's words warmed my heart. Hazel had gifted me the thing that meant the most to her. The Reynard was mine because the oldest girl hadn't given a shit about Hazel or the hotel. The only reason Raven ever came to visit was because her parents saw it as an obligation. *I* was the one who took the time to get to know Hazel, helped her with ghost tours, spent weekends repainting the porches, and took afternoon tea with her when it seemed like no one else valued her presence. Hazel didn't care that Raven had her bachelor's degree in hospitality or managed a cookie-cutter chain hotel. She wanted someone to run the Reynard who *loved* it.

And that was not Raven. My cousin hated all things paranormal. Where I was intrigued by and open to the inexplicable, she was disgusted by it. I was the one who embraced it with Hazel. No one else in this entire world saw me like my great-aunt did. And I saw her too.

Mr. Cartwright held up a hand to silence everyone. "It is worth noting that the hotel will remain the property of the trust, as it has for over a hundred years. The person who it is handed down to will keep any profit made during the time it is under her care. If Gemma either does not want the hotel or is proven unfit to run it, Raven will take over, but there is a caveat."

"This should be rich. What outlandish stipulation did Hazel put in place for my daughter?" Kevin asked.

"Your aunt was not a foolish woman. She recognized that Raven has more experience in the industry. Therefore, Raven must put forth every effort to help Gemma learn to run the business. Christopher and Kevin, since you are the oldest surviving members of the Fox line, Hazel has given you authority to determine if Gemma is unfit to manage the hotel. You may check the physical state of the building and its finances at your discretion within the first year of her ownership. Once the first year has passed, the hotel and its assets will be fully assigned to Gemma in accordance with the terms of the trust. If you should choose to remove her, your reasoning must be based solely on her performance."

Trevor scoffed and said, "You might as well just give it to Raven now because Gemma isn't capable of tying her shoes, let alone running a business."

I glanced at my slip-on Vans, and anger and embarrassment heated my skin. "Shut up, Trevor."

"If we're done acting like children," Raven said, directing her attention only to me, "I'd like to understand what exactly is expected from me to fulfill our great-aunt's last wishes."

I fought the urge to roll my eyes. "Why? You couldn't even stay in the rooms by yourself. Every summer you threw a fit about going to spend time with Aunt Hazel."

"You know I was traumatized in that hotel as a child. Whatever is there liked to pick on me. It was evil."

"I know, I know. Things pulled your hair while you slept, and shadows chased you down the hall during a ghost tour." I gave in to the eye roll. "Funny, but it sounds like even the spirits never wanted you there. I had no problem."

"Whether you like it or not, Gemma, this is what Hazel wanted. When you fail—and you will—I want to be prepared to take over."

Raven couldn't care less about Hazel's final wishes. She wanted to get her perfectly manicured claws into what was left of our family legacy and rip it apart from the inside out. By the time she was done with the Reynard, the property would house an upscale boutique hotel. The guests would feast on caviar and schedule afternoon pampering sessions. All signs of Hazel and the Fox women before her would vanish.

"I'll schedule a meeting with you to discuss what actions you need to take to secure your place as owner if Gemma should forfeit or not meet the terms," Mr. Cartwright said, sliding a stack of papers across the table in my direction. "Right now, all I need is for Gemma to sign."

Deborah spoke up, her nasal voice piercing my ears. "There really is nothing else we can do? No recourse? Raven just has to wait for what is supposed to be her birthright?"

Hunter released a lip-rattling breath and ran a hand through his dark-blond hair. "Please. Everyone at this table knows that Gemma is the *only* one of us who gave a damn about the Reynard. And anyway, the will is final. Aunt Hazel is gone. Gemma is in charge of the hotel. Just let her sign so we can move on with our lives."

It amazed me how Hunter and Trevor were both my brothers but so different from each other in every way. Where Trevor couldn't get enough of insulting me, Hunter would always come to my rescue. I could have hugged him, but I settled for reaching over and squeezing his hand where it rested on the arm of his chair.

Mr. Cartwright handed me a pen, and my heart stuttered. This was the biggest kind of commitment I could make, and even I could admit that my track record wasn't exactly spotless.

"Can I—can I have some time to think about it?" I asked.

"Of course she can't make up her mind; it's just like ballet classes, piano lessons, and lacrosse." My father sat back in his chair and looked at my mother. "Libby, do you remember that summer she begged us to send her to space camp and then called us a week and a half into it to come and get her because she was bored learning about stars. What did she think *space* camp was going to be about?"

Just when I thought I couldn't feel smaller, my father knocked me down yet another peg. "We get it, Dad. I'm a total flake."

Before he could respond, Mr. Cartwright spoke again. "You

have seven days. The trust has some stipulations. Call me and let me know what you decide, and the two of us will meet again to go over the terms."

"Thank you, Mr. Cartwright. I'll give you a call this week." My skin was crawling with the need to get out of this room, away from my father's disapproval, my cousin's wrathful stare, and the final, stark realization that the one adult in the world who *really* understood me was gone.

When the lawyer dismissed us, I didn't waste a second, springing from the chair so fast I nearly knocked it over. I pushed open the heavy double doors and rushed to the elevator.

"Gem!" The pounding of footsteps came from behind me. "Gem, wait."

"What is it, Hunter? I just want to go home and forget that entire meeting ever happened. Especially the part where Dad made me look like an idiot."

Not only did Hunter and I look the most alike, but we were also the ones who didn't live up to our parents' high standards. The dark-blond siblings who didn't aspire for riches. We were the ones who preferred a beer over wine, and the wallflowers at the ritzy parties my parents threw for Christmas and New Year's. While they were talking politics and the stock market, we exchanged inside jokes and talked about trash reality TV. They were Gucci, and we were Target. And we liked it that way.

He pressed the Down button for the elevator, and we stepped on, trying to force the doors shut before the rest of our family could barge in. "He was just pissed things weren't going 'to plan,'" Hunter said, making exaggerated air quotes around the last two words.

"I wish he would pick on someone else for a change. Trevor

is long overdue for some parental humiliation," I said, earning a laugh from Hunter.

"Trevor is the golden child. You know that. Anyway, I was coming to offer my help. I'll go down to the hotel with you and take a look at it. With things having been worse than we thought with Hazel, there is no telling what you're getting yourself into."

I could use the extra set of eyes, especially when it came to the hotel's physical condition. While our father would have preferred that Hunter spend his days behind a desk and run his company from there, my brother enjoyed working with his hands and getting a little messy, and he had created a thriving construction business. I couldn't think of a better person to accompany me to the hotel for my first visit since Hazel had passed.

I bumped him with my hip. "I suppose I could use a passenger with impeccable taste in music during the two-hour drive."

"Just say it; I'm your favorite brother." He pulled me into a headlock and rubbed the top of my head with his knuckles. "Besides, I wouldn't let you drive your Honda; that thing is almost as old as you. You would just have to call me to rescue you from the middle of nowhere, and I have a date I can't miss this weekend."

I pinched one of his love handles until he yelped and let me go. Brushing my hair down with my fingers, I followed him to his brand-new truck with wheels so big that I almost needed a ladder to climb inside. Hunter turned on a playlist that the two of us had added songs to over the past few years, and I rolled down the window, kicked off my shoes, and watched the Massachusetts coastline fly by.

CHAPTER TWO

Spelling, Connecticut, had one main road with a single stop sign, but everything I loved most occupied that street. The redbrick storefronts with their enormous windows advertised palm readings and séances. Tourists flocked to the paranormal hot spots in the town—the bar where the spirit of a young man who was shot for cheating during a game of cards roamed the back hallway, the town museum where an entire family supposedly caught a mysterious infection and died holding each other in the living room, and the town's main feature: the Reynard Hotel.

The colonial hotel contained seventy-two guest rooms and sat on the very edge of seven acres, facing the street. The brick steps at the front led to double doors haloed by lilies etched into the stained glass. Deep-green shutters framed each of the countless windows, and on the second floor was a balcony that overlooked the town's shops. In the top center of the building stood the famous bell tower, which was depicted on Spelling's tourist brochures and welcome sign. The hotel—*my* hotel—was what kept this small community alive.

Hunter pulled his truck into a parking space on the side of the lot and turned off the engine. We sat in silence watching people come and go. At all hours of the day, those hoping to run into the hotel's resident ghosts roamed around with their cameras at the ready. The Reynard had even appeared in a couple of those ghost-hunting shows on TV. It was some spooky shit, and people came here chasing the thrill of it.

"This place has always attracted the weirdos, hasn't it?" Hunter asked.

I quirked my mouth and shrugged. "They're just curious. But weren't we the same way that first summer Mom and Dad brought us here?"

"You more than me," he said, opening his door and jumping out. "It was like you wanted to be creeped out by this place."

"I *was* creeped out by this place. I experienced my fair share of freaky shit over the years, and so did you. You just reasoned it away with the excuse that the hotel is old, but some things can't be explained."

"Here we go, you're already starting to sound like good ole Hazel."

I brushed off his snide remark and followed him to the entrance at the back of the hotel. A white wraparound porch housed several rocking chairs and two swings, overlooking a pool that looked like something out of *The Great Gatsby*. White stone statues with lifeless gazes stood on pedestals, guarding the calm blue waters. I never looked at them for long, fearing they would unexpectedly turn their heads or form real eyes.

A curtain shifted on the top floor just under the bell tower, and a face half cast in shadows peered down at me. I jerked my gaze away and counted the rows of windows leading back to the ground—five.

I looked up again, but the figure was gone.

"Hey, Hunt, I thought no one was supposed to be able to get into the bell tower."

"Yeah, they closed it off when they put in the speaker system and disabled the bells."

I was no better than an eager tourist wanting to come away with a ghostly tale. I was letting my mind play tricks on me and turning what could have just been a breeze rustling the curtains into something real. Perhaps it was my guilt eating away at me.

It ate me up inside to know that Aunt Hazel had died alone in this place, but she had held back the truth, denying us the chance to be there for her. That didn't ease my guilt in the least, though. It was something I'd never forgive myself for. Nights out drinking with friends or binge-watching the newest television craze could have waited. I should have visited her more often.

We reached the steps to the porch, and Hunter wiggled the loose railing before stomping a foot on the first step and finding it safe to bear our weight. "I swear Hazel was keeping this place standing with superglue and duct tape."

"It's old. Things are going to creak and jiggle."

"It never used to be like this. She must have really let things go when she got sick."

As I opened the back door, the smell of dust and old wood greeted us, and the dim, ornate fixtures in the hallway were just enough to light our path. The wood floor groaned under our steps, and the high-pitched voice of a frantic woman grew louder the closer we got to the lobby.

"I thought I could do it, but I can't! My bottle of water was just sitting there next to the bed, and then it flew across the room. I swear a dark shadow disappeared into the wall after that. It's just too haunted for me. I want my money back." A woman stood at the antique concierge desk with her brown hair in disarray and her clothes resting haphazardly on her thin frame.

"But, ma'am, you were warned that your room was one known for paranormal activity. You stated that you still wanted to stay there," said Larry, the elderly man working at the front desk. He ran his gnarled fingers through his wiry hair, making it look as if he had stuck his finger in a light socket, then patted the front of his black vest. Larry was just as much a staple at the Reynard as Hazel had been. I couldn't remember a single time when he wasn't here, helping guests and my aunt. He looked around as if he was waiting for someone to intervene. It was safe to bet that I wasn't the only one missing Hazel right now.

Hunter snorted next to me and whispered, "You really want to deal with this shit day in and day out?"

Ignoring his comment, I stepped up to the counter next to the woman and flashed a bright smile. "Larry! It's so good to see you!"

His bleary blue eyes lit up with recognition, and relief washed over his pale, wrinkled face. "Miss Fox, we've been expecting you! Do you have any suggestions as to how we can help Mrs. Harris here?"

My heart sped up and I took a deep, calming breath. If I had any hope of keeping this hotel and proving myself to my family, I couldn't fail my first customer-service test. Exuding more confidence than I felt, I turned to the woman and asked, "Which room are you in, ma'am? There must be some explanation."

She looked me up and down, taking in my beat-up sneakers and slightly wrinkled sundress. The curl of her lip spoke volumes; she was having trouble believing I was the owner of anything, let alone this moderately famous New England tourist attraction. "My husband and I were in room 109. And the only explanation is that my water bottle was thrown across the room. It slid all the way from the desk to the bathroom door!"

I put my hand over my mouth and nodded. "Well, that explains it! That room happens to be on the list to be worked on next, right, Hunter?" I turned to my brother, silently pleading with him to help me out. "It's got . . ." I had no idea what to say, but I prayed he knew where I was going with this.

Hunter's bushy eyebrow quirked upward, and I mouthed *Please*, hoping he'd be able to think faster than I could under these circumstances.

My brother stepped to my side. He kept his voice low so as not to ruin the experience for the rest of the hotel's guests. "We don't talk about this often for business purposes, but the foundation is shifting a bit on that side of the hotel. That room has borne the brunt of the imbalance, and sometimes that causes things to roll and items to fall and slide, even all the way across the room. But I assure you, the room is safe. This building has survived a century and it will continue to stand for many more." One of the reasons Hunter believed strange things happened in the hotel flowed so smoothly from his mouth that he almost had me convinced.

Mrs. Harris leaned into my brother and said, "I can understand why you wouldn't want people to know things like that, appearances and all. I appreciate your honesty, and don't worry." She slid her index finger and thumb across her lips and twisted them like she was locking her mouth shut. My brother had a gift for charming people, including the previously irate Mrs. Harris.

"We really want you to stay for the rest of your vacation and enjoy your time in Spelling. Please, allow us to move you to"—I glanced at the key hooks behind Larry's head—"one of our king suites on the third floor at no extra cost."

Mrs. Harris looked from Larry to Hunter to me and nodded, her wild brown hair bouncing against her shoulders. "That would be delightful. But if there are any other ghostly issues, I will demand a full refund."

"Absolutely!" I grabbed a key for room 315 and pressed it into Mrs. Harris's palm. "And please, call down later and order a drink for you and your husband from the bar. One of the servers will bring it up to you. On the house."

"Why, thank you," she said, and all trace of anger was gone from her face. "I appreciate that, Miss Fox."

"My pleasure. Your comfort is our business at the Reynard." I recited the motto Hazel had printed on stationery, business cards, and coffee mugs like I'd said it every day of my life. When the woman was out of earshot, I let out a massive breath and leaned against the counter.

Looking up at Larry, who appeared as frazzled as I felt, I said, "Please, Larry. Call me Gemma."

Larry smiled and held out his hand. "It's a pleasure to see you again, Gemma. You must have picked up a thing or two from your aunt during your visits here, because you handled that just like she would have. Thankfully, most of our guests are looking for a little mischief and find happenings like that more exciting than terrifying, but it's not for everybody."

I shook his hand and my heart warmed. It was a boost to my self-esteem to know I had handled something the way Hazel would have. It was all I'd wanted growing up—to be just like my aunt. She not only ran a thriving business, but she didn't give a damn about societal norms. Hazel lived for the things that made her happy, and I desperately wanted what she had. But most importantly, I wanted her to be proud of me.

"It's good to see you again, Larry. Thank you for being here with Hazel through everything. I know how much she cared for you." His cheeks tinged with pink as I continued. "My brother and I were stopping by just to check the condition of the place. Is there anything you think we should take a look at?"

"I hope you've got some time, because I've got quite the list for you. Starting with the room that our permanent residents did a number on last week."

Hunter furrowed his brow. "You're not talking about—"

"The boys have been restless since your aunt's passing."

When I was younger, I'd heard the two identical boys roaming the hotel at night, laughing and horseplaying, but I remember interacting with them only once. Or at least I think I spoke to one of them. It was the unearthly color of the boy's irises that had left me enchanted—blue or purple? I had just found the courage to ask him if he was who I thought he was when he disappeared. I searched for him and his brother every chance I got, but I was left with nothing more than tapping on the wall and disembodied laughter. As time passed, I began questioning my belief in the paranormal. Had I really encountered supernatural beings in the hotel, or should I just chalk it all up to a child's overactive imagination?

"Who were you talking about?" I blurted, and Larry and Hunter turned toward me in alarm as if they'd forgotten I was behind them.

Larry lifted his brows and cocked his head to the side. "What's that, hon?"

"Just a minute ago, when you said, 'The boys have been restless since your aunt's passing.' Are you talking about—"

"The boys who live under the bell tower. Well, I suppose they're more like men now."

Hunter and I locked eyes, and he lifted his hand to his temple and slowly moved his index finger in a circle. I swatted it down just as the older gentleman stopped in front of the room at the end of the hall.

Larry slipped a key in the door, wiggled it, and said, "Rumor had it, Hazel spent years renovating a space for them. Out-of-state lumber companies would drop off the supplies on the fourth floor in the middle of the night. Of course, those who claimed to have seen the piles of wood and drywall could never prove it. The hallways always appeared normal the next day. She said the boys needed a more sophisticated space since they were older. Grown or not, they're still prone to getting emotional over the loss of a loved one just like us."

The room was a wreck—the mattress flung off the bed frame, the dresser shoved onto its side, and holes the size of fists in the wall.

"Larry, it looks like you had someone with a rock star complex in here," Hunter said.

"Jesus," I mumbled, stepping into the room and turning in a circle. Not only was the main area of the room in disarray, so was the bathroom. A fist-sized crack sat in the center of the mirror over the sink, the shower curtain had been torn from its hooks, and the towel rack hung crookedly from the wall. Someone had lost control, and this room had taken the brunt of their anger.

"What happened in here?" I asked.

Larry looked at me like a kindergartner who hasn't quite learned to listen yet. "I told you. They're grieving the loss of the woman they saw as their sister and caretaker. They don't have any other way to let out their aggression, so—"

"Larry." I lifted my hand to stop him. "You're telling me that those two boys are actually here?" In more recent years, I'd almost let myself believe that the twins I'd seen in the painting in Hazel's room were figments of my imagination. Now, the idea that they were real was a touch alarming, yet oddly reassuring.

Larry nodded, leaning against the doorway with his arms over his chest. "You may think you rationalized what Mrs. Harris witnessed in her room with the water bottle, but even she knows she saw one of those boys. She just liked your explanation better."

"Well, can we go to their room?" Hunter asked.

"No, none of us knows how to get up there. Hazel said they deserved their privacy."

"Of course she did," I said, running my hand through my hair. The idea that all my aunt had had in her life were two supernatural beings and a couple of hotel employees as companions made my chest burn. Maybe my family was right; Hazel had had a fragile state of mind. She'd spent her entire life in this hotel and mostly conversed with strangers about the spirits she lived with. She'd needed real interaction with real people.

I stole a glance at Hunter, who shrugged his shoulders and said, "Well, this room is easy enough to fix. Let's continue the tour."

By the time we got back to the lobby, we'd seen no fewer than a dozen things that needed to be repaired, some small, some that would be more costly, but one thing had become abundantly clear: I owed it to Aunt Hazel to keep this hotel running, to keep her legacy alive. I intended to see it through.

Larry retreated to the desk to help a customer, and I turned to Hunter, determination swelling within me.

"I want to do this. I want to keep the hotel."

"You and Aunt Hazel are two birds of a feather then."

"That's not funny, Hunt. I want to continue to build upon what she was doing. This place was her life, and it has a lot to offer," I said, sweeping my arm toward all the people coming and going in the lobby. Every single one had a look of awe on their face. Some were blown away by the mahogany staircase, the intricate designs carved into the ceiling and crown molding, or the focal point of the sitting room—an elaborate fireplace big enough for most to stand in. Others enjoyed learning about the hotel's historical roots and how it was the first woman-owned business in the region. But most were fascinated by the stories of the unexplainable.

Hunter puffed up his chest and let out a long breath. "All right, if this is what you want, let's do it."

"You're going to help me?"

"Do you know how to patch those holes in the wall?"

"Of course not. It's just another item in a long list of why you're my favorite brother."

After saying goodbye to Larry and letting him know I'd be back, I dug my phone out of my back pocket and called Mr. Cartwright. Two hours later, I sat alone with him in his office with a stack of papers set before me.

The attorney straightened his suit jacket and cleared his throat. He turned to the first page of the trust document. "Hazel had three strict stipulations that the new owner must follow. First, the annual Winter Spirits festival is to proceed as scheduled every January twenty-first, without fail."

"Easy, I love Winter Spirits," I said with a shrug.

"Second, renovations may be made to the hotel to keep it up to code, but the main structure has to remain in its current design. It cannot be relocated or demolished. It comes *as is*, for lack of a better explanation."

"Done."

"Lastly, it cannot leave the ownership of the family."

I laughed at that one. "All those big plans my cousin had for turning it into another cookie-cutter chain?"

"They were nothing more than pipe dreams. It can't be sold." Mr. Cartwright held out a pen. "In all the years I knew your aunt, she spoke of nothing the way she did about the Reynard. This is a big commitment, Gemma."

Commitment. The thing I feared the most, my Achilles' heel that my family loved to throw in my face—but for my favorite aunt, I would conquer my fear. I'd never forgive myself for not being there with her until the very end, but this, this I could do. I sat up straighter in my seat and said, "I know. I want to do it and make her proud."

I took the pen from him and signed my name to the paperwork, my excitement uncontrollable as I let my mind imagine all the new possibilities that managing the Reynard would bring.

✳   ✳   ✳

The next forty-eight hours were a whirlwind of activity—packing all the stuff in my apartment, cleaning out my desk at the office where I'd been temping after my last job went awry, and promising my mom I'd come back to visit. But I was more than ready to get back to the Reynard and start this new chapter of my life.

When I fumbled with the hotel's lobby doors, Larry rushed to my side. He took my heaviest bag, even though it looked like it weighed more than he did. "Thank you, Larry," I said, setting my cosmetics bag on the counter.

"You're welcome. I'm so glad you're here to stay. What about that brother of yours, will he be joining you?"

"Yes, but not until tomorrow. He had some loose ends to tie up back home."

"I'll make sure to have a suite ready for him when he arrives. Do you want him to be on the same floor as Hazel's—I mean your—suite?"

A pang of sadness hit my chest like a lightning bolt. I should've been prepared for this; it was reasonable that Hazel's suite would become mine. It was the nicest one in the hotel and the one most outfitted for permanent residence. But the idea of being in there without her ignited the burning emptiness I'd experienced since I'd gotten the phone call that she was gone.

"Yes, the same floor would be great. He'd appreciate a king suite if it's available."

"You got it, boss."

The term of endearment brought a tight smile to my lips; that was what Larry had always called Hazel. It made me believe, if only for a moment, that I could actually do this.

Larry rooted through a drawer behind the counter and held out a large skeleton key on a silver key chain. "Here you are. Let me help you with your bags," he started, but I shook my head as I grabbed a luggage cart from beside the front desk.

"I got this," I said, piling my bags onto the cart. "You just stay down here and man the desk. You've been such a help already."

He looked at me with a dubious expression but finally nodded. "All right. Be careful on that elevator. The luggage rack's wheels tend to get stuck in the gap at the threshold."

I raised my eyebrows as my fear of the ancient lift flooded back. The elevator was up to code, so I had no real reason to worry, but the creaks and groans that contraption let out were like something from a horror film. Every time I rode it, my imagination conjured morbid scenarios of cables snapping and me falling to my death in the antique metal box.

I rolled the cart into the elevator and pressed the button for the fourth floor, the anticipation of seeing Hazel's suite turning to lead in my stomach. It was the place I'd spent so many nights with her, listening to ghost story after ghost story, hearing tales about Spelling, and eating freshly baked brownies until we were ready to bust.

I reached my floor without incident, pushing the cart toward the end of the hall where Hazel's—my—suite waited for me. Reaching the white door with a gold 400 above the peephole, I pulled the skeleton key from my pocket and took a deep breath before slipping it into the lock.

I swung the door open and just as quickly had the urge to shut it again. "Oh, Hazel, you were one more stack of papers away from ending up on *Hoarders*," I murmured, taking in the environment that my aunt had called home.

The room wasn't much different than I remembered. The living space was furnished with antiques—a roll arm sofa and matching armchairs, a dark walnut secretary desk against one wall, while across the room was an enormous Victorian dining table that seated eight. The suite had no filth, nothing was dirty. But the clutter—piles of papers and books scattered around the room. Just stuff. Everywhere. It would take me weeks to get through everything she'd left behind.

The kitchen was impeccably clean, testifying to how much she'd enjoyed cooking. It had the same ancient feel as the living room, but the antique appliances were modern impersonations. The single bathroom housed a massive claw-foot tub and a separate open shower. But it was Hazel's bedroom that took my breath away. The memory of it rushed back like a raging river, overwhelming my senses. The four-poster bed was covered with a homemade quilt, and a little reading nook was tucked in across from the wood-burning furnace. I ran my fingers along the tall dresser and looked inside the empty walk-in closet.

"Where had you been staying before you died, Aunt Hazel?" I whispered. This room looked like it hadn't been used in months.

I returned to the front room but stopped dead in my tracks as I took it in from this new angle. When I'd entered Hazel's suite, I hadn't given much attention to the fireplace. It was beautiful, hand-carved with an ornate floral baroque design on each side, but it was the painted portrait above the mantel that sent my heart racing. Hazel had said she was the artist, and I'd spent hours staring at it while she regaled me with stories about the hotel.

The subjects of the painting—two teenage boys—were identical: dark-brown hair, plump lips, tan skin, and defined jaws. The only difference between them was the shade of their jewel-toned eyes. One boy was sprawled casually in a high-backed chair, and the other stood beside him with his arm propped on the back. They couldn't have been more than fourteen years old. I hadn't seen this painting in years, but now I wondered how I could've forgotten even the littlest detail.

They were the hotel's ever-present residents—the reason people from all over the world flocked to Spelling. The men who, according to Larry, were still here and mourning the loss of the Reynard's prior owner. And now, the haunted legacy of the Hyde brothers was mine to share with every person who set foot in my hotel.

CHAPTER THREE

"Psst."

"Shh!"

My eyes snapped open, goosebumps covering every inch of my body. Without moving, I cut my gaze up and to the side, toward the whispers.

There, at the foot of Hazel's bed, barely visible in the strip of light bleeding underneath the bathroom door, were two dark shadows, staring down at me, heads bowed like they were trying to figure out if I was awake.

Squeezing my eyes shut, I pulled the blankets over my head and tried to control my breathing. A quiet thump came from down the hall, and when I peeked out over the top of the blanket, the shadows were gone.

"What the fuck?" I whispered, sitting up and flipping on the stained glass lamp on the bedside table.

I flopped back onto the mattress and stared at the antique light fixture hanging from the center of the ceiling. Was my imagination getting the better of me, or were the unearthly men my aunt had made friends with visiting me? As she was a woman who valued her privacy, I couldn't picture her having an open-door policy that extended into the middle of the night.

After my breathing slowed and my body stopped shaking from being startled from sleep, my brain sorted through the problems Hunter had found with the hotel and what we needed to fix first. Anything to redirect my wayward thoughts from my uninvited visitors.

The long list of repairs gradually morphed into thoughts of my family. They weren't being totally unfair regarding their concerns about me taking over the Reynard. I had a history of starting things and not finishing them, as my father had so kindly pointed out at the will reading. But considering my brain didn't work the ways theirs did, that wasn't a surprise.

My teachers in middle school said I had ADHD, that I couldn't focus for longer than a few minutes, definitely couldn't multitask, and had trouble following multistep directions. My mother and father hadn't taken me to the doctor, claiming the disorder wasn't real. They rejected the idea of medication and swore that if I had an official diagnosis of ADHD, it would just be an excuse for me to be flaky and irresponsible. Their refusal to take me to see a specialist didn't change the fact that I'd struggled with every aspect of school, from academics to self-discipline.

Luckily, I'd had a teacher in high school who saw my struggle and taught me ways to cope when it came to my schoolwork and impulses. I'd managed to graduate with a 3.0 and get into college, but the fact remained that emotionally, I was still impulsive. No matter how many years passed, commitment remained an issue for me. I'd never stayed in a relationship longer than nine months, I couldn't seem to choose a career path, and I gave up nearly every project I started, from knitting a scarf to keeping a journal.

But this time would be different. People were depending on me for their livelihood; this *town* was depending on me. And I loved the hotel and would do whatever it took to keep it successful. I'd do it for my aunt Hazel and to prove my family wrong.

With a sigh, I punched my pillow a couple of times and flopped to my side. I closed my eyes, hoping to not hear any more bumps in the night. The heaviness of sleep drew me in, and my body relaxed into the mattress.

The brass doorknob to my bedroom rattled, and I bolted upright, glaring at it and holding my breath. The knob twisted to the right and then the left.

I jumped out of bed and flung the door open. The heavy wood crashed against the wall, and I scanned the suite hallway.

No one was there.

The distinct creaking of the front door set me in motion. I raced down the hall and skidded to a stop in the living room. Everything was how I'd left it except for the security chain swinging back and forth, the door ajar. Peeking out into the hallway, I looked both ways only to find the corridor empty.

"How did that happen?" I muttered, stepping back into the suite. I stopped short of clicking the door back into place when a dark shadow accompanied by footsteps flashed in my peripheral vision.

"Hello?" I whispered, not wanting to wake any sleeping guests.

Muffled voices came from around the corner, and I tiptoed toward them. It dawned on me that maybe I was walking into something questionable, supernatural or not, and if so, how would I defend myself? I scanned the passage for a weapon, considering the candleholder on the accent table beside me, but it would be too hard to hide. A tray with used dishes sat outside of a suite, and I snatched a clean fork from it. Holding it next to my ear with the prongs out, I moved forward again.

Spearmint and citrus lingered in the air the closer I got to the voices. A light flickered behind me, and I spun around, my heart racing. I held my weapon tighter as perspiration formed on my brow. My breathing was erratic as I leaned against the wall and looked into the next corridor. Nothing but dim lights and silence awaited me.

"Gemma, come on. Get your shit together," I muttered, turning away to head back to my room.

I felt like an idiot, wandering around the hotel after hours, chasing creepy sounds like Nancy Drew. When I reached my room, I grasped the doorknob and pushed. But instead of giving way and swinging open, I was met with resistance—a locked door.

"What the hell?" I looked down at my white cami and green snowman pajama shorts. Even though I had no pockets, I patted around my waist for a key that was most definitely inside the room. I'd forgotten to grab it before I'd darted out to ghost hunt. This wasn't a problem; I would make my way downstairs and grab the spare.

I looked over my shoulder all the way down the hallway and the spiral staircase. A part of me wanted to spot something supernatural and confirm I wasn't out of my mind, but the other part was terrified. If the Hyde brothers were up to their old tricks, they showed no qualms about entering my suite. The thought of creepy night stalkers in my bedroom wasn't the least bit appealing to me.

When I got to the lobby, Larry was puttering around behind the desk and humming a familiar TV-show theme song. I wasn't ready to confess my blunder. Every time I locked myself out of the room, Hazel would have me chant a simple phrase before she fetched me the spare. *Never leave your room without the key.* I needed a moment before I went to him with my tail between my legs.

Soft jazz music drifted from an open door opposite me. Since I'd been underage during my summer visits to the Reynard, I hadn't been allowed to spend time in the hotel's bar. But the clinking glasses and contagious laughter had me sneaking peeks through the double doors. I'd always wanted to be a part of the adults-only party.

The lights in the bar were low, the entire room dim with candlelight. Only a few straggling guests remained, nursing whiskeys and absentmindedly eating peanuts from the little glass bowls in the center of the tables.

The bartender was around my age, with short turquoise hair and brown eyes framed with long, dark lashes. Her skin was a rich brown with a beauty mark under her left eye. She wore a tight black vest that clung to her ample breasts and displayed her defined biceps.

"Good evening." I looked for a name tag, but she wasn't wearing one. "What's your name?"

She grinned, her smile warm despite her edgy exterior. "I'm Skylar, but you can call me Skye."

This girl might be the only relatable person in the entire hotel. She appeared out of place against the vintage furnishings but comfortable among the bottles of Jack Daniel's and Jose Cuervo. By the way she moved around the bar, filling glasses and popping the tops off bottles, I got the feeling that she'd found her place at the Reynard. She was owning her position as barkeep, and I admired her for that.

"It's really good to meet you, Skye. I'm Gem—"

"I know who you are. It's nice to finally meet you, Gemma. I've heard a lot about you; your aunt adored you."

A pang of sadness hit my heart at the mention of Hazel, but I just smiled and said, "I miss her." My attention jumped to Skye's turquoise spikes. "I bet she liked your hair, huh?"

Skye grinned. "She did. She told me she wanted me to dye hers purple, but . . ." She sighed and changed the subject. "What can I get you?"

My heart leaped in my chest, excited to finally get to partake in the hotel's bar. "How about your favorite beer on tap?"

"Coming right up."

I looked down at my pajamas and remembered my lack of pockets. "Oh, crap, wait. I don't have my wallet on me to tip you."

"Don't worry about it. This one's on me." A deep, rich baritone from right next to me caught my attention, and I jumped in my seat, turning to look at the person it belonged to.

The man had to be one of the most gorgeous humans I'd ever seen in my life. His dark hair was perfectly styled, except for one strand falling on his forehead. A black button-down hugged his biceps, and his skin was flawless in the flood of candlelight. But what stood out more than anything else were his eyes. His irises were the deepest shade of purple, like the predawn sky.

"Th-thank you, but you don't have to do that."

His gaze raked over my skimpy sleeping attire. "It looks like you're having one hell of a night. It's the least I can do."

I crossed my legs and pulled my shirt up to cover my cleavage. My cheeks must have been as red as the wallpaper covering the small barroom.

"What was your first clue? My out-of-season pajamas or the random fork I'm still holding?" I muttered, tossing it onto the bar with a resounding clatter.

"Neither—it was the bedhead that gave it away." He reached to a wavy strand of hair next to my ear and playfully tugged it.

"How do you know this isn't the way I *wanted* my hair to look?"

"Don't get me wrong; the night-of-passionate-sex hair looks good on you, but seeing as you're alone, I'm guessing this is more of a tossing-and-turning look."

"Well, *that* is definitely not a style I get to rock very often these days," I muttered.

My flirtatious company took a step back from the bar as Skye approached with my drink. He leaned in toward me, and his breath was warm against my ear when he said, "I hope one day soon you get to remedy that."

Every inch of skin on my body burned as Skye set my beer on the bar top and gathered the dollar bills left on the other side of me. I turned in my seat to thank the man or perhaps ask him to join me, but he was gone. I stretched my neck, scanning the far corners of the room, and turned back to the bartender. "Did you see where that guy went?" I asked, gesturing with my thumb toward the empty space beside me.

Skye scrunched her perfectly sculpted brows and slowly said, "I have no clue what you're talking about."

I hummed and brought my beer to my lips. Something told me she absolutely knew what I was talking about.

The beer from the Reynard's bar helped ease my tension after the mysterious drink-buyer disappeared. But the alcohol did little to slow my racing mind. I returned to my room and dredged up every reasonable explanation for where he could have gone. And just as the first sunrays lit the sky, I finally told myself that I was overthinking the entire thing and fell asleep.

Morning came too soon, and I hit the snooze button, releasing a sigh. There was nothing like working through a busy day with minimal sleep. But I'd be damned if Hunter got here before I was up. I swung my legs over the side of the bed, and my phone pinged with a text message.

"Ugh, Hunter, I'm coming," I grumbled, but when I unlocked my phone, I rolled my eyes so hard it hurt.

Raven.

> I know you are floundering without my guidance. When can I come and help you so I can secure my inheritance?

I shot my middle finger at my phone and threw it facedown on the bed. No way was I answering that. I would rather walk over hot coals, gouge my eyes out, and play in traffic before I asked her for help. She was out of her mind if she thought I was going to give her an easy path to take the Reynard from me.

Contrary to what our parents had hoped, Raven and I never got along. We attended the same pretentious private school and had a few classes together, but more often than not she pretended that I didn't exist. I wasn't smart enough or involved enough in extracurriculars to be a part of her friend group. Our contradicting life choices put us at odds.

Not that I needed her; I made friends with the people who appealed to me. I had a group to eat lunch with, and people who cared about my problems. She was an afterthought until she began belittling me in front of anyone who was paying attention. Raven found joy in loudly pointing out anything from a rogue zit on my forehead to my latest failed biology test. It didn't take me long to learn I could never count on her for anything unless it involved mortifying me.

I ignored her text with the hope that my lack of engagement

would annoy her and started my day. While my coffee brewed in the single-cup machine, I couldn't stop thinking about my cousin. It was only a matter of time before I had to give in and accept that Hazel wanted her to help me. She was bound to step into the hotel and impress everyone with her hospitality know-how. Raven was pressed pantsuits and sleek updos, and I was a green Reynard polo shirt and ponytail. I might not look the part, but I planned on working my ass off to be what this hotel needed.

With my coffee in hand, I headed downstairs.

"Good morning, Gemma," Larry said, pulling an envelope from under the leather-bound guest registrar. "I found this in the key drop box this morning. It looks like our guests were extremely happy with their experience here last night."

I took the letter from him and read the comment card. They were pleased with all the bumps in the night and a never-ending conversation that took place between two male voices that kept them up. The bottom of the note was signed and marked with a room number just down from my suite.

"I'm glad they enjoyed their stay. It's nice to know *someone* likes having their sleep interrupted all night." I handed the letter back to Larry. "When my brother gets here, will you let him know I'm on the back porch?"

"Sure thing, Miss—Gemma," he said sheepishly.

Shaking my head, I stepped onto the balcony and sipped my coffee, enjoying the light morning breeze. Even after being here for twenty-four hours, I still couldn't quite believe the Reynard was mine. Mine to run like Hazel would've wanted, to do all the things she wished she could have done, up until the end.

The door behind me creaked open, and I jumped, spinning around to see my brother standing with his bags in his hands.

"You okay, sis?" he asked, resting his duffel bag on top of his rolling suitcase and watching me with concern in his eyes.

"Last night was rough," I said, gesturing for him to go back inside the lobby.

"What happened?"

I could tell Hunter what I saw in my room and heard in the hallways, or about the disappearing drink-buyer, but why? He'd just tell me that my imagination was out of control. "Just the first night in a new place and all. It's never easy to get settled for the first week or so."

His dubious gaze rested on my face for a moment, but he didn't push it. "Well, maybe having your favorite brother here will help."

I bumped him with my hip as I plucked the key to his suite from my pocket. "I hope so. You're just down the hall from me."

We shuffled onto the elevator with Hunter's bags in tow, and I pressed the fourth-floor button. We rode in silence until the doors dinged open.

"Larry said you're staying in Hazel's suite."

I nodded and held the elevator door open as he passed. "Yeah, I figured it was the smart thing to do."

"I agree, I just wanted to make sure you were okay with it. I know how much she meant to you, Gem." Hunter's brows pinched with concern, and it warmed my heart. He may not have had the same kind of relationship with our aunt as I did, but he cared.

"Thank you. But it was nice, actually. I felt close to her. The only thing that sucks is how much clutter she had. It's going to take a while to go through all of it."

"I'll help you do anything you need me to; you know that."

"I do. Just help me with the maintenance stuff, and that will be *more* than enough." I placed my hand on his arm when we reached his room. "Seriously, Hunt. Thank you for being here for me through all this. I couldn't do it without you."

He grinned and tousled my hair. "Sure you could. You can do more than you think, Gem."

His faith in me was endless, and I was going to do everything I could to ensure it wasn't misplaced.

CHAPTER FOUR

That night, as I tried to go to sleep, the covers felt too heavy, like bricks were crushing me. I kicked the blankets to the bottom of the bed and huffed out a breath, staring at the ceiling.

I had so much on my mind—the intimidating task of organizing Hazel's suite, learning the ins and outs of managing the hotel, the run-in with the handsome man at the bar, and the strange fact that Skye claimed she hadn't seen him. And his purple eyes, they just added to the intrigue. I was so captivated by them and his charm that I didn't even consider that I'd seen that color many times before.

It wasn't until I returned to Hazel's suite and glanced at the painting over the mantel that it dawned on me: I'd had an up-close encounter with a Hyde brother.

Giving up on sleep, I sprang out of bed and marched into the living room. I needed to work off some of this excess energy, and I knew just where to start.

If I wanted solid answers about what was going on at the hotel, I had to figure out how to get to the room Larry had alluded to on the tour. Others may say it's irrational to believe in the supernatural, but I couldn't deny that something strange was happening. I had to confirm what deep down I'd always believed to be true.

I spun in a circle, unsure where to start looking for answers. Papers, so many stacks of papers. I sorted through a pile of magazines, tossing them into the trash can next to the desk. Tabloid, lifestyle, travel, and fashion, Hazel must have subscribed to every monthly publication known to humankind. I stopped short of tossing a thick home-improvement catalogue when the bright-blue words on the cover caught my attention—*The Blueprint to a Successful Renovation*. What if I could find the hotel's blueprints? Wouldn't the room have to be on them? Even if it was a secret from everyone else, it still had to be designed, right?

I pulled a chair up to the desk and rifled through the stack, careful not to damage anything. Most of the papers were already fragile and yellowing with age. There were receipts for big purchases, small purchases, letters, invoices, greeting cards, but no blueprints.

I rooted through the cabinets in the kitchen, figuring that Hazel wouldn't keep something as important as the hotel's blueprints in a likely place. It wouldn't have surprised me to find them hidden behind her champagne flutes or stuffed inside the freezer. After checking the bathroom, I made my way to the bedroom. Getting down on my hands and knees, I peered under the bed. Against the wall, a large metal box caught my attention. I stretched my arm as far as it could go and swept the box toward me. Sitting cross-legged on the floor, I turned the latch, but nothing happened. I crammed my fingernails between the lid and base and pulled, but all I had to show for it were aching fingers. The hole for a key stared at me, mocking my failed attempt to break in.

I glared at the ancient keyhole. It reminded me of the ones found on each of the hotel room doors, including this one. Unlike the other keys that sat on hooks behind the lobby counter, Larry had pulled this one from the safe. Hazel had taken extra care with the key to her quarters, and I had a feeling it opened more than the door to the suite.

"You think you're so smart," I grumbled, scurrying to the dresser and retrieving the key. The lock popped, and inside were a few more papers, Hazel's Social Security card and birth certificate, and several velvet boxes containing large jeweled rings, but underneath was the jackpot. Several pieces of paper were rolled together, the curled edges giving me a peek of the precise lines printed on them. Blueprints—I'd seen them a million times at Hunter's jobsites.

I rushed out into the living room and swiped well-worn drink coasters, stacks of old mail, and several paperbacks with cracked spines off the coffee table onto the floor. From the end table next to the sofa, I lifted a bizarre wooden statue and a huge marble paperweight and placed them on the corners of the plans, and I set to work studying the hotel's layout. The first sheet was stamped with a date of November 20, 1863. It showed simple rooms without restrooms, totaling 116. I flipped to the next set of plans, which were from the early 1900s and included the current consolidation of the rooms to accommodate bathrooms and the addition of the bar. But it was the design from the 1960s that captured my attention. The plans for a new floor—a fifth floor that sat right under the bell tower, just above this room.

With fear and excitement pumping through my veins, I jumped to my feet and opened every single door in the suite, hoping one would lead to a stairway. If I was ever grateful to be alone, this was the moment. I must have looked like I'd lost my damn mind, opening coat closets and feeling along the back and side walls for another doorknob. I even tore the canned food out of the small pantry. Yet again, I found nothing. This was an ongoing theme of the Reynard—vanishing men, empty hallways, and missing entrances to secret rooms.

I rushed back to the coffee table and flipped to the next set of plans. This time I found myself puzzled by the layout. A series of mazes—passageways, running between rooms and winding from floor to floor. Every room in the hotel had a secondary entry. Starting under the bell tower, I traced the only passageway down to the fourth floor. It ended in the hallway just outside my room.

Minutes ticked by as I contemplated my next move. Did I really want to see what Hazel was hiding up there? I knew deep down that it had something to do with the boys in the painting, but was I ready for those answers? I didn't know for sure, but I did know that all the mystery was about to drive me up the wall. It was the knowledge that I had the tools to figure all of this out that propelled me forward and forced me to my feet.

I grabbed the wooden statue from the coffee table for protection, because who knew what I would run into in those dark passageways? Better safe than sorry.

With several deep breaths, I crept into the hallway. Every step I took sent the old floorboards groaning under my weight until I reached the middle of the corridor where the passage was supposed to be. I ran my palm along the wall, but nothing was out of place.

Moving away, I studied the dual-toned wall while rhythmically swinging the statue back and forth. Each section had a sconce and was separated into framed panels, dark wood on the bottom and beige on the top. I stepped forward and grasped the brass bottom of the nearest light and squeezed the statue in my other hand. My muscles coiled as I counted to myself.

One.

Two.

"I wouldn't do that if I were you."

I spun around with a yelp and lifted my weapon above my head. The air left my lungs as I came face-to-face with Mr. This-Drink-Is-On-Me. Except it wasn't. This man was identical, but something was off.

I studied his face for a moment, trying to ignore the fear spiraling in my belly. *What is it? What's different about him?*

He raised an eyebrow and cut his eyes from my face to the statue in my hand.

And that's when it hit me.

The guy from the bar had those strange violet eyes. This man had eyes I could only describe as cerulean, my favorite crayon in the sixty-four pack my mom bought me in elementary school. They were bright, electric . . . mesmerizing. Eyes that I'd seen more than once and never forgotten. Swallowing hard, I lowered the statue to my side but didn't loosen my grip on it.

"Are you who I think you are?" I managed, holding my voice as steady as possible.

He cocked his head to the side and crossed his arms. The muscles in his biceps flexed, and the way his T-shirt clung to them fascinated me. I don't recall ever seeing a simple cotton shirt look so good.

"What a strange way to greet someone you think you may know. Is it a habit of yours to bludgeon to death harmless hotel guests with a carving of a woman giving a man a—" He finished by clearing his throat.

I looked at the object in question, and my eyes went wide. All color drained from my face, and I shoved the statue behind my back, like hiding the damn thing was going to magically wipe away my mortification.

"I wasn't going to *bludgeon* anyone. And it so happens that I am the owner of this establishment, so I think I have the right to know who's roaming the hallways in the middle of the night."

"It looks like you share the previous owner's questionable taste in art." He leaned against the wall across from me. The smirk on his face spoke to how entertaining he found this moment, and all that was missing was the popcorn.

"Who are you? How do you know my aunt?"

"I guarantee you that I knew Hazel better than anyone. From the homemade quilt on her bed to each ring on her finger, I knew the story behind them all." He pushed off the wall and ran his hand through his hair.

My lip curled, and I put my free hand on my hip. This guy had been in Hazel's room before. My aunt hesitated to let family in her suite, opting to entertain personal guests in the ballroom or bar. I remember the first summer I spent alone with her and how honored I felt when she invited me into her home and let me see a side of her so few got to witness. I was the one person in our family who understood and appreciated her quirky ways, and she deemed me worthy to invade her space. The thought that someone else had been on the same level as I had been left me fuming.

"I know you're related to the guy I met at the bar last night."

"Am I?"

I knew he was; after all, the men were identical except for the eyes. But I needed to hear it from his mouth. This was the solid proof I had searched for as a child—the confirmation that two brothers really were cursed to spend eternity in this hotel. I'd never wanted anything the way I wanted him to admit that every story surrounding the Reynard was true.

"You look exactly like the guy who bought me a drink last

night. Only he had purple eyes and was a lot more pleasant."

"Do you normally take drinks from strangers? That's so dangerous. If it weren't for your choice in weaponry, I would have taken you as a bit smarter than that. Next time, get the name of the weirdo offering you drinks."

"I took the drink straight from the bartender, thank you very much. I'm not a *total* imbecile, contrary to popular belief," I muttered. "If you're done berating me now, I think I'll just go back into my aunt's suite—that's *mine* now— and get away from creeps that wander this hotel at night."

"Make sure to lock the door and sleep tight with your fellating sculpture, Gemma."

"How did—"

"I told you. I knew Hazel better than anyone, and that includes details about her family." He turned his back to me and strolled down the hall. "I know all about you, Gemma Fox."

My jaw unhinged, and I stood in stunned silence before marching back to the room. Since I couldn't think of a way to clap back at him, I settled for slamming the door instead. Leaning against it, I took several breaths, my gaze trained on the painting of the two boys. The men I met were a far cry from the thin twins dressed in dated suits. They were now defined muscles and chiseled jawlines. But I couldn't mistake their blue and purple eyes.

Every doubt I'd entertained over the years vanished, and a slew of questions flooded my brain. Only two beings could give me the answers I needed.

I pivoted on my heels and jerked the door open. The section in the wall I had been examining before I was interrupted slid into place with a click. I ran to the sconce and wrapped my fingers around the curved metal at the bottom. It wiggled from side to side, but when I pulled down, nothing happened. Did I really see the wall move? I must have, because if not, the mysterious dickhead had just vanished like a ghost.

Which wouldn't be surprising after the last couple of nights. In this place, nothing was impossible. Case in point, not only had I met one of the infamous Hyde twins, I'd met them both.

CHAPTER FIVE

After skimming the pool of fall leaves, I hung the net from the hooks on the fence and checked my watch to see that I was ten minutes late for my lunch with Hunter. I rushed for the back porch and stopped short when the hairs stood up on the back of my neck. I lifted my gaze to a figure standing on the balcony right below the bell tower. He gripped the iron railing with both hands and stared down at me. I fought the urge to flip him off, scared it might be the wrong brother. So, I gave him a half-hearted wave before taking the steps two at a time and going inside. I might as well play friendly with my new neighbors, even if the blue-eyed one was an arrogant prick.

Hunter waited for me in the dining room at a round table in the corner. I zigzagged through the lunch crowd and took the chair across from him. We ordered our lunch, and as soon as the server left, I told Hunter about the blueprints I'd found in Hazel's room.

"Oh, for real? I'd like to see those," he said, eyes lighting up like he was a kid who'd just gotten an epic visit from Santa Claus.

"Yeah, anytime, just come get them."

"Did you find anything interesting?"

"Actually, yeah. Did you know the hotel has secret passages?"

He laughed. "I'm not surprised. All the haunting stuff makes sense now. I'm guessing Hazel used them to make this place seem haunted. I'm sure she sent good ole Larry through them to bang on the walls and shit."

I cocked my head to the side and rolled my eyes. "That's not it. I saw—never mind. You won't believe me anyway."

"Believe what? That you met a ghosty here when we were kids and now you've found his lair? No, I don't. I love you, Gem, but your belief in the supernatural is a little alarming."

My brother was a lot of things—compassionate, hardworking, and witty—but also skeptical as hell. I decided not to push it; maybe when I had concrete proof, he'd hear me.

"*Anyway*, I saw the entrance to the room under the bell tower on the blueprints, and I'm going to try to find it tonight after work."

He sat back in his chair and eyed me with trepidation. "Maybe you should wait for me to go with you."

"Why? You don't believe in ghosts, so what could go wrong?"

"No, but I do believe in potentially rotting floors in dark places where it'd be easy for a klutz to trip and break her leg, and—"

"Okay, okay, I get it, but I'm still going up there tonight, *and* I'll be careful."

"Fine. It's not like I can stop you. Why do you want to go up there anyway?" When I didn't answer, he let out a huff. "Are you serious, Gemma? You really believe there are twin ghosts under the bell tower ready to socialize with you?"

"I just—I want to see the entire hotel, that's all. Shouldn't I be familiar with every part of it?"

"Whatever you say, sis. Just don't get lost and fall into a pit where some creep who lives in the walls keeps you for the rest of your life."

❋   ❋   ❋

I didn't fall into a pit, but I did get lost. Even with the blueprints and a satchel of necessities, I quickly got turned around in the cold, pitch-dark corridor. The flashlight I brought must have had batteries in it from the '90s because it did little to nothing to ease away the inky darkness. At least I could make out some of my surroundings in the dim light. The passage was surreal, like something out of the French catacombs. The walls and floor were made of stone, the surface cold to the touch. My skin prickled with unease the further I walked, but I was determined to satiate at least a little of my curiosity surrounding the hotel layout and hopefully find myself underneath the bell tower.

I wondered what the purpose of these passages was. It made no sense to have a secondary way into the rooms when the hotel guests usually let the cleaning staff inside. Why would someone need to sneak around behind the scenes? Maybe Hunter was right; maybe Hazel and the employees had run around back here scaring people. What a clever way to ensure that guests left with a spooky story.

But I knew the truth; it was instilled in me as a kid, and it still rang true after being here for only a week. Something was up with this place, and the Hyde brothers were behind it. I was going to figure—

I collided with another solid form, and the shriek that left my throat was both unexpected and unearthly.

"Jesus Christ, be quiet!" a voice commanded, and a palm was gently placed over my mouth. "I'm not going to hurt you."

"Oh, like I should just believe you," I grumbled, my voice muffled against his skin. I didn't have to shine the flashlight on him to know who it was.

One of the twins.

"Is it that I left you in the bar or that you had a run-in with my brother that makes you suspicious of me?" He cupped my elbow and guided me through the darkness.

I jerked my arm away and shone the flashlight in his face, causing him to squint and shield his eyes from the beam. "I mean, it could be both. Or maybe the fact that I don't even know your name, and I'm meeting you in a fucking secret passage in a million-year-old hotel. There are several options here, sir."

"Archer." He placed his hand over mine and lowered the beam. "My name is Archer Hyde."

I almost came back with a smart-ass reply, but I needed information that only he would be able—or willing—to give me. "Good to meet you. I'm Gemma. Sorry for the reception, I'm just a little bit jumpy these days." I cleared my throat. "And yeah, I was a little put off that you left me in the bar. I didn't even get a chance to thank you."

One side of his mouth quirked up in an effortlessly sexy smile. "Do I get to choose the reward?"

Despite myself, my cheeks heated, and I was glad the light wasn't pointing at me. "I don't know. I guess that depends. What were you thinking?"

He held out his arm. "Walk with me. I could use the company. Soren has been in a mood lately, and I could use a nice conversation that doesn't consist of grunts."

I raised my eyebrow and linked my arm through his. "Soren? Is that your brother's name?"

"The one and only."

"It's good to know he isn't just an asshole to me."

Archer snickered, not at all offended by my comment. At least one of the twins had a good sense of humor.

"Would you mind if we exited the labyrinth? I'd like to be able to see you while we talk," I said.

"We can do that." He led me through the narrow passages, every step he took certain, like he had walked this route a million times. And maybe he had; he was strolling through the passageways without much light. We stopped, something clicked, and we walked out into the rose garden at the side of the hotel.

The sun sat low in the pinkening sky; I must have been wandering the passages longer than I thought. Shadows from the bushes and trees seemed to reach toward us as we meandered through the garden. The crisp air was infused with the scent of dying roses and burning wood from the fireplaces of nearby houses. It was the epitome of a perfect autumn evening.

"So, Gemma, what would you like to discuss?"

Are you immortal? Are you a ghost? What the hell are you? I couldn't ask any of those questions, at least not outright, so I stayed quiet for a moment. As we walked, my eyes were drawn to his like a moth to a flame, and I couldn't resist the allure they exuded. Contrary to the fear I'd harbored just moments ago, I felt like I could trust Archer.

"How did you know my aunt? I mean, besides the fact that she was the owner of the Reynard."

"She was an old friend."

"Then you knew her your entire life."

"No."

My eyebrows dipped and I pressed, "Okay, then when did you meet her?"

Archer stopped walking and released my arm. "Are you sure you want to know this, Gemma? If I tell you, you'll never be able to go back. It will change everything, even you."

Never go back and change everything? I hated absolutes. But even more than that, I despised not having the full story on these men, Aunt Hazel, and the hotel.

"I'm sure; tell me everything."

Archer placed his hand on the small of my back, sending an electric shock through my veins, and guided me forward through the darkening garden. "I knew your great-aunt all of *her* life."

He didn't look a day over twenty-five, making him old enough to be Hazel's grandson. It wasn't feasible for him to have known my great-aunt her entire life. Hell, he shouldn't have known her *half* of her life. But wasn't that the beauty of the Reynard? Nothing was impossible around here.

"Were you good friends with her?" I asked.

"With Hazel? Yes. But I also knew every woman who has owned the Reynard."

"You were friends with all of them?"

A bitter laugh escaped his lips, and his violet eyes darkened. The muscles in his jaw ticked, and his fingers along my spine grew rigid. "No, not exactly."

"But if you're telling me that you knew them all . . . Well, there would be a whole lot of problems with that claim. For instance, your stunning good looks—not even men who have been around only twenty years look as good as you," I joked, trying to lighten the mood.

He looked at me with amusement, and I breathed a little easier at the smile that crossed his face. "My brother and I age differently than you."

I rolled my eyes. "And apparently you're invisible too. It all makes perfect sense."

"We're not invisible, more like hard to see."

"So, you're saying you *are* ghosts?"

He laughed, and the sound was like warm honey on a summer day. It made me want to lean my head against his shoulder and feel the warmth of his skin. Whatever Archer was, my body was reacting to him in magical ways.

"We aren't ghosts, but we aren't human either."

"You look pretty human to me. What are you then, an elf? Werewolf? Vampire?" I shook my head and lifted his arm closer to my face. "Nah. Not sparkly enough."

"Would that be the book you're referencing, or the movie?"

"I didn't realize that supernatural beings were into pop culture, and you're changing the subject."

"You'll find that I'm full of surprises, but give me some time, Gemma." He flashed me a heart-melting grin, and when I didn't return it, he blew out a breath that rattled his lips. "Do you really need to know all my secrets tonight? Isn't it more fun when you take the getting-to-know-each-other stage slow?"

Something told me he was telling me some semblance of the truth; too many things had already added up to the conclusion that he and his brother were not of this world. I was fascinated with him. But he didn't have to know that.

"Touché." After a second, I added, "Well, fair is fair. Do you want to ask me anything?"

He didn't hesitate before asking, "Who were you having lunch with earlier?"

I smirked at the quickness of his question until I realized he'd been watching me. I didn't know whether to be flattered or freaked out, but what I wasn't going to do was let on that he was getting to me. "Jealous?"

He shrugged and crammed his hands in his pockets. "Perhaps."

"Don't be. It was my older brother, Hunter. He's a contractor and is helping me fix up the hotel."

We fell silent for a moment, and I mulled over the fact that I was walking side by side with someone who wasn't from this world. It was easy to believe; Archer was beyond handsome. Not even stone sculptures could compete with his strong jaw and high cheekbones. His tall frame was all lean muscle and tan skin, and his hair . . . God, I wanted to feel the dark, silky locks glide between my fingers.

"Would it be too bold of me to ask you to join me for dinner tomorrow night? I could cook."

My heart skipped a beat, and I jumped at the opportunity to get more of my questions answered. "Not at all. I'd love that. Your place?" *Under the bell tower?*

"If you recall, I have a brooding brother who makes a terrible dinner guest. How about I meet you in Hazel's room?"

"It's actually my room now," I said. "But yes, you can come there."

"That will be perfect." Archer pressed his lips to my knuckles, and every cell in my body buzzed to life. Such a pure gesture had me weak in the knees. "Until tomorrow night, Gemma."

"Good night, Ar—"

And just like that, he disappeared.

I twirled in a slow circle, looking for any sign of him. But he was gone.

"Definitely a vampire," I muttered under my breath.

"Definitely *not* a vampire."

I whipped my head toward the deep, somber voice. Leaning against the side of the building was Soren, his arms crossed and dayglow-blue glare cutting through me.

I stepped closer to him, resting a hand on my hip. "Then what are you?"

"Dangerous. Keep your distance, Gemma. If you know what's good for you, you'll steer clear of both me and Archer."

My body heated, and my hands shook with the irritation coursing through me. The other thing I hated more than absolutes was someone who had no authority over me telling me what to do. It might be petty, but Soren telling me to stay away pretty much guaranteed that I wouldn't. At least not from Archer.

"No problem. I will keep as much distance from you as humanly—or inhumanly—possible."

He grunted and pushed away from the wall. "Keep away from my brother, run the hotel, and stop fraternizing with the things that go bump in the night. You have your job, and we have ours, so let's keep it strictly business."

Each of his warnings only firmed my resolve. My date with Archer would happen if it was the last thing I did.

"Like you said, you and me, we're business. Less than business. In fact, don't ever speak to me again, and we'll be good to go. Got it?" I asked.

He stalked toward me, and I took a step back before planting my feet and lifting my chin. He stopped with only inches between us and shoved what I thought at first was his hand into my chest. But when I looked down, I was gripping a heavy gilded book.

"You have the key to open it. Read it. Learn what we're all about, and then decide if you want my brother to warm your bed." I opened my mouth to snap back at him, but he stepped around me. "And whatever you do, don't try to take it off the property."

I spun around, but he vanished, leaving me in the same mysterious fashion his brother had.

The book Soren gave me lay heavy in my arms as I walked inside and down the hallways. His claim that I would find answers to my questions about him, his brother, and this hotel was enticing. I'd spent hours contemplating what was going on inside these walls. But as I got closer to my room, it was Archer's warning that played the loudest in my mind. *If I tell you, you'll never be able to go back. It will change everything, even you.*

It was a simple decision when I was standing in front of a gorgeous, mysterious man. I wanted to unwrap all his secrets, but having all the answers cradled in my arms with no one to talk me through them was a burden I wasn't sure I wanted. I'd learned a long time ago that something was to be said for remaining blissfully ignorant when it came to family matters, and I wasn't ready to commit to that type of heartache.

I set the book on top of the dresser when I entered my room and occupied myself with getting ready for bed. The hot water from the shower relieved the tension in my shoulders, and it felt good to have my body scrubbed and shaved after a long day. I had almost forgotten about the book until I fell across the bed and opened my favorite social media app.

The glow from the screen illuminated the cover, its bronze clasp catching the light and beckoning me to look inside. But something about it terrified me, and I was torn between facing my fears and pretending the damn thing didn't exist. Tossing down my phone and throwing back the covers, I pulled my hoodie on over my pajamas and crept out of my suite.

The hallway was void of any mumbled conversations or creepy shadows, but that didn't stop me from speed walking. I tapped on the door three down from mine, placed my mouth close to the doorjamb, and stage-whispered, "Hunt, are you still awake?"

Bare feet hitting the wooden floor and the creaking of a mattress filled the silence. Two voices hissed an exchange of words before the handle jiggled, and my brother stood before me in nothing but joggers. He propped an arm up on the doorframe, blocking me from seeing into his room.

"What's going on, Gem?"

"I was having a hard time falling asleep and thought we could talk. Are you busy?"

"Yeah, I was kind of in the middle of something."

"I can tell. Just meet me in the morning for coffee and we can talk then. I won't keep you from who—whatever you're doing right now," I said with a wink before turning to go back to my room.

"For Christ's sake, Hunter, let your sister in." My brother was nudged aside, and a familiar face peered out at me. Hunter's high school best friend and on-again-off-again boyfriend, Caden. "She is clearly having a moment, and you'll have no problem getting it up again."

Caden grabbed my arm with a dark-brown hand and pulled me into the room as my brother mumbled his disapproval and shut the door.

"Long time no see, Gems; what have you been up to?" Caden asked.

I looked away as he bent his bald head into the mini fridge Hunter had set up in the room, and his bright-orange briefs strained against his round ass. "Oh, ya know, just running a hotel, getting asked out on dates by strange men, trying to prove to our family that I can do this. I'm just a little bit stressed." I took the bottle of water from him and smiled as I unscrewed the lid and gulped down a quarter of it in one swallow. "Sorry, that was a whole lot."

"Oh, Mommy and Daddy Fox issues, my favorite." Caden sat

his muscular frame on the edge of the bed, crossed his legs, and propped his chin on his knuckles.

"It's not even Mom; she tries to take up for me when Dad gets going on one of his tirades. Which he did at the will reading, effectively humiliating me. He is so overbearing, so critical, especially now, with me taking over here." I took another drink of water and continued, "But that's not what's really bothering me."

"That's surprising," Hunter mumbled.

"Stop being a dick to your little sister," Caden scolded, pulling my brother down beside him. "What's troubling that pretty little head of yours?"

Caden was the type of person who just exuded trustworthiness and empathy. He was so easy to talk to; I'd always been comfortable spilling my guts to him, more so than to Trevor and even Hunter at times. But how much could I really tell him, especially with Hunter sitting right there and being already annoyed with me? I decided to tell an amended version of the truth.

"I met this guy down at the bar last night. I didn't have my wallet, so he paid for my drink. Then, he just ghosted. Completely disappeared." Skipping the part about his identical twin, I continued, "But then I ran into him again tonight, and we talked for a while. He asked me out for dinner tomorrow night, and I just—I don't know if he's my type. We come from two different places, and we might not be compatible. But he's drop-dead gorgeous *and* single? Something must be wrong." I laughed and shook my head, running my fingers through my hair. "Am I being stupid?"

"Yes," Hunter and Caden said at the same time.

Hunter bumped Caden with his shoulder and said, "If you want to go on a date with the guy, then do it. It's not like the two of you are getting married. Have a little fun, Gem. This place is going to take a lot out of you; it sounds like it already is. Remember to take a moment for yourself."

"Your brother is saying that sometimes you just need to get laid to relieve a little stress. Take it from me, fucking a hot guy never hurts."

"I better be that hot guy."

Caden's lips turned up in a sly smile. "Oh, you will be."

I smacked my palms on my thighs and jumped up. "And that's my cue to exit. I hope the two of you have an eventful night."

Hunter gave Caden a lingering peck and said, "We will."

I closed the door and made my way back down the hall to my suite. When I crossed the threshold into my bedroom, all I wanted was to pass out facedown on the bed and sleep for hours. But that book still beckoned me from the dresser. With a heavy sigh, I trudged over and picked it up, plopping down on my bed to take a peek. It was thick, with hundreds and hundreds of pages, and the two decorative strips of metal that supported the binding bit into my palms. If Soren was telling the truth and it held all the answers I was seeking, it would take me forever to read it all.

I crossed my legs underneath me and inspected the lock on the front. I tried prying the leather from the clasp with my fingernails, but it wouldn't budge. Tracing the keyhole on the front, I remembered Soren saying I had the key, but I didn't know where it would be.

Reaching into my hoodie pocket, I pulled out the skeleton key that opened my suite and the fireproof box. Could it be that easy? I slid it into the lock, and it opened with a click. I had to hand it to Hazel; she may have been a little scatterbrained, but she was consistent.

I slid my finger in the back of the book and lifted the countless pages. Ever since I was a kid, I'd had a bad habit of picking up a book and reading the last page. I figured if I didn't like the very last sentence, it wasn't worth my time. And the same held true for this monstrosity.

The final page was blank.

"What the hell?" I murmured, my brows furrowing as I flipped forward a page.

Blank.

I grabbed several pages at once and let them slide through my fingers. Nothing was written on any of them. Was this some kind of corny life lesson where Soren was trying to tell me that I held the answers and needed to write my own story? Fuck that.

"Thanks for nothing," I muttered, dropping the book on my nightstand with a thud. Pulling the covers over my head, I squeezed my eyes shut and, attempting to forget about Archer and Soren, gave in to my exhaustion.

CHAPTER SIX

After my late-night conversation with Hunter and Caden, I decided I'd shove the book in the nightstand for a while and "forget" about it. I *did* deserve to have a bit of fun, and Archer was the first guy I'd met in months who truly piqued my interest. I'd be damned if I let Hunter be the only Fox having a good time.

On a regular day, I had trouble concentrating on whatever task was at hand, but today, I'd been spacing out since I'd stepped behind the front desk. Daydreams about what tonight would be like flitted in and out of my head with every passing minute, and more than once, Larry asked me if I was okay.

Oh, I was more than okay. The thought of spending time with Archer in such a private setting was both intriguing and arousing. As much as I tried telling myself that I was letting him come over only to learn more about what he and his brother were, the ache in my core told a different story. The last guy I'd dated had been a total asshole who wanted to come over and fool around whenever it was convenient for him and never took my feelings into consideration. Being in a long-term relationship might not be my forte, but recognizing when it's not going to work is. He finally pushed me too far, and I told him to get the hell out of my apartment. That was nine months ago. I was getting restless, and Archer seemed like the perfect cure for what ailed me.

The last thing I'd done before getting ready was straighten up the suite, making sure it was presentable. I figured Archer had been inside before if he and his brother had been as close with Hazel as he'd claimed. I didn't want to tarnish that memory with a messy kitchen.

Standing in front of the closet, I debated what to wear. It would be my first date like this—staying in and cooking instead of going out. For the guys I'd dated, going to the club was the preferred location for a night out, surrounded by sweaty bodies and thumping bass. Apart from the aforementioned asshole, that was the last date I'd been on.

I had only brought a fraction of the clothing I owned with me when I moved in, but when I remembered the burnt-orange fit and flare dress that accentuated my legs and waistline, I shoved everything else aside and snatched it from the hanger. Slipping into it, I cinched the satin ribbon around my waist and rested my hands on my hips, admiring the two parts of my body I didn't mind drawing attention to. My blond hair fell in natural waves around my shoulders, and while I was already losing my summer tan, a smattering of freckles remained on my nose and cheeks. I looked pretty good considering I was working with limited resources.

I stood over the bathroom sink, reaching for my makeup bag when a knock sounded at the door. Archer was early, leaving me to go au naturel. Pressing my palm to my forehead, I exhaled sharply before examining my bare face and all its flaws—the scar under my chin from the time I got in between one of Trevor and Hunter's wrestling matches and landed face-first on the coffee table, a couple of scattered chicken pox scars, and the pink marks along my hairline from teenage acne. I kind of liked the idea of not hiding my flaws. If Archer hung around after an up-close-and-personal encounter with them, then he was worthy of my time.

Another knock interrupted my appraisal of my "natural beauty," and I groaned, crossing the room and sliding the chain from the door before swinging it open.

Archer was a sight to behold, his hair brushed back from his face and a powder-blue button-up rolled to his elbows. He held a bouquet of vibrant tropical flowers in one hand and a bag from a nearby grocer in the other. His gaze traveled my body from my feet to the top of my head, and he smiled. "Good evening, Miss Fox. You look beautiful tonight," he said, handing me the flowers.

A warm flush crept from my chest to my neck and all the way to my forehead. "Thank you. I'd say this is a vast improvement from my snowman pajama shorts," I said, holding my arms out to my sides and spinning in a circle. When my back was to him, I mouthed the words *Oh my God*. He was drop-dead gorgeous and ready to spend a night with *me*. "You look pretty good yourself."

He lifted a brow and cocked his head to the side. "Are you going to invite me in, or should I figure out a way to cook the chicken Florentine out here?"

For fuck's sake. I did a mental head slap and stepped aside. "Sorry, I've never done something like this before. I mean, I've been on dates, but the whole inviting a guy over is new to me. Not that a guy hasn't ever come over, it's just that—"

"You've never had a man make you dinner before."

"Yeah," I confessed, following him into the kitchen.

Archer motioned for me to take a seat on a chrome and vinyl stool in the corner, and he began to unload the food. I was impressed that everything he removed from the paper bag was fresh. Even the chicken was wrapped in butcher paper. He moved smoothly around the kitchen, pulling out pots and pans, like he had spent many hours in this very space.

"So does your kind frequent the grocery store often?" I asked.

Archer paused, and a smile pulled at one side of his mouth. "Gift cards, online shopping, and delivery go a long way in this day and age. I can't say it's always been this easy."

"Did you cook for Hazel a lot?"

He finished washing his hands and used the dish towel hanging from the oven to dry them. "She insisted that we have a family dinner every Sunday night, and no meal could be the same unless we were celebrating a holiday. She said it made every meal with her special, and it did."

My eyes filled with tears at the thought of Hazel having a routine with Archer and Soren, and my guilt flared. I should have been the one sitting across from her during family dinners. Instead, she spent her Sundays with two beings who, by their own admission, weren't even human.

"That's really sweet. I—" I cleared my throat before continuing. "Thank you for being here with her. That means a lot to me. She was the only one who really understood me, but I spent too much time trying to please my hypercritical father over the past few years. I feel terrible that I wasn't here more often before she . . ." My voice cracked, and I swallowed back tears.

Archer looked up from the skillet where he was seasoning the chicken. "You don't have to thank me, and you don't need to feel guilty. Your father is Christopher, correct?" When I nodded, he continued, "She told us about him and the extravagant life he leads. She said it was surprising that he raised a daughter as well-rounded as you. I know she was excited to see you step out from under the expectations he and your mother had for you and start living your own life. Never feel bad for doing the things that made you happy; I promise you that Hazel was doing the same until the end."

His words stunned me into silence, and not only was I proud that Hazel felt that way about me, but the fact that Archer seemed to agree with her after knowing me for only a couple of days made me feel warm all over. "Thank you for saying that." I chewed the inside of my cheek and jumped off the stool, suddenly desperate to lighten the conversation. "Can I help you do anything?"

"Can you slice that loaf of French bread in half?"

I surveyed the knife block, unsure of which utensil to choose, but I settled on the big one with a smooth-edged blade. After removing the bread from the packaging, I began sawing at the soft loaf.

Archer's laughter filled the kitchen. "Stop, stop," he said, taking a knife with a serrated edge from the top of the block. He moved behind me and took my hands in his. "If you keep hacking away at it like that, we're going to be left with nothing but breadcrumbs." He exchanged my knife for his and placed one of my hands on the top of the loaf as he guided the other in smooth strokes down the middle of the bread.

My eyes fluttered shut, and I inhaled his woodsy scent laced with citrus undertones. The heat from his chest pressed against my back was calming. As I watched his hands, my skin tingled with the desire to feel them on me. When in the hell did *slicing bread* start turning me on?

"Nice and gentle always does it," he said against my ear.

An electric jolt, much like the one I'd felt last night in the garden, shot straight to my core, and I inhaled sharply. I stared at the counter, not daring to move, and whispered, "Is that so?"

"Well, there's always a time and place for everything. I'd be happy to demonstrate after dinner."

I would be perfectly fine to get a demonstration now and just forget about eating. But he'd worked hard on this meal, and I owed it to him to eat it. I plucked a piece of bread off the counter and turned around to face him, popping it in my mouth. "In that case, let's eat."

Eat we did. We sat across from each other at the massive dining table, exchanging quick remarks between bites of pasta and chicken. I wanted to pick his brain and learn more about him, but I couldn't stop eating. Archer was one hell of a cook. The only thing that consumed my thoughts more than the savory meal was what he had implied as we'd sliced the bread.

I'd be happy to demonstrate after dinner.

Was I ready to take that next step after knowing him for only a couple of days? No doubt, I was attracted to him. The way my heart raced and the throbbing between my legs when he was close were proof enough. We had an undeniable chemistry. So why should I hold back? I was a grown woman with needs too, for fuck's sake.

I took the last bite of chicken Florentine and finished my wine. Crossing my legs under the table, I jiggled my foot and folded and unfolded my napkin. "That was delicious. Thank you. I haven't had a home-cooked meal that good in a long time. My mother isn't exactly Betty Crocker, and I can barely boil water."

"I'm glad you enjoyed it. I miss cooking and having a nice dinner. For the first time since Hazel died, I feel a sense of normality." Archer stood and gathered the dishes from the table.

I jumped up and put my hands over his. "Stop. You cooked all of this; let me at least clean up." He opened his mouth to argue, but I put my index finger over his lips, feeling a pull in my lower abdomen at the softness of them. "It'll only take a minute. Just sit down." I pointed at the same place I'd sat while he'd cooked.

He obeyed and kept his eyes on me as I loaded the dishes into the dishwasher and put the bigger pots and pans into the sink to soak. Washing my hands with the lemon soap Aunt Hazel had loved, I dried them on a towel and tossed it on the counter. "See? That didn't take long."

"One might think you're looking forward to what comes next," he said, standing and crossing the kitchen. He stopped just short of reaching me, and his gaze trailed down my body. My heart thumped in my chest, and every inch of my skin heated. "Are you excited for what comes next, Gemma?"

I thought about acting coy, but I couldn't hide what he was doing to me. My breathing came in quick pants, and I couldn't stop drinking him in. I wanted him to quench this all-consuming thirst for more. "Yeah, I am."

"Me too." Archer cupped my face and tilted my chin up. "I've wanted to do this ever since I laid eyes on you." He brushed his lips over mine, sending my stomach into giddy somersaults. His second pass over my mouth was bolder, capturing my bottom lip, the warm tip of his tongue gliding over it.

I laced my fingers into his hair and pulled him closer, giving in to my desire to taste him. He stepped forward, and I moved back until the curve of my spine met the edge of the counter. My insides melted as his hands curled around my waist and hoisted me on the top. Guiding my knees apart, he created a space for his hips between them.

Archer never stopped kissing me, and my chest was heaving as the passion between us grew wild and hungry. He was taking my breath away, and I was seconds from running out of oxygen. I couldn't have imagined a better way of surrendering my last breath.

He pulled back just as I felt light-headed, and I grabbed the front of his shirt, tugging him closer. "Where are you going?" I teased, pushing his hair off his forehead.

"Obviously nowhere," he said with a chuckle and placed his hands on my knees. "As if I would want to be anywhere else." His hands slid up my thighs and under the hem of my dress. "Except for maybe here." He brushed a knuckle over the damp center of my panties, and my hips lifted from the countertop, applying more pressure to the spot where I ached for him the most.

Archer moved in slow strokes against me as his other hand tangled in my hair, raising my face to his. His gaze never left mine as he slid the lace at the juncture of my legs to the side and dipped his fingertips into my wet center.

"You feel like heaven," he whispered, brushing against the bundle of nerves, making me bite my lip to stifle a moan.

"Please," I breathed, fighting the urge to throw my head back. "Please don't stop."

Something about the way he touched me was unearthly, like his body was made to pleasure mine. I tightened around his fingers, pushing forward with more force than I intended, embedding him deeper within me. A moan escaped my lips, and he tugged on my hair in response.

His thumb worked in time with the rest of his skillful fingers, sliding over the most sensitive part of me, the part that hadn't been touched by another in far too long. I gripped the front of his shirt as my body tensed and the euphoric release I was chasing was just within my reach.

Archer ran his lips over my jaw and when they arrived at my ear he whispered, "Come for me, Gemma."

With a whimper, I let go of the last shred of my control, the fear, the stress, the constant pressure to be perfect. I let go and just allowed Archer to treat me like I was the only thing that existed. The ecstasy his touch sent through my body was nothing like I'd ever felt before, and I was happy to lose myself in it.

When I finally stopped shaking, I leaned into him, resting my head against his chest. "Oh my God," I murmured, my voice muffled by the soft fabric of his shirt.

"That may have been the sexiest thing I've ever seen," he said, removing his fingers and righting the lace between my legs.

I missed Archer's touch the second he pulled away. His fingers were magical. Not only had he brought me to a much-needed release, but he'd also eased some of the tension from my first week as a hotel owner. It was fitting that it had been the sexiest thing Archer Hyde had ever seen because it was *definitely* the sexiest thing I'd ever experienced, and I hoped it wouldn't be the last with him.

And based on the searing good night kiss he gave me, this was only the beginning. I had a feeling we were destined to have other moments that were as out of this world as the Reynard itself.

CHAPTER SEVEN

Almost every day since our dinner, I had found myself in a compromising position with Archer somewhere in the hotel. It was a risk to be so bold in the middle of my workday, but it was also a great stress reliever. Not to mention that sneaking around like two hormone-driven teenagers gave our rendezvous an added thrill.

Yet we hadn't taken our physical relationship to the next level.

It was more my choice than his; a little nagging voice in my brain kept telling me to slow down. We had spent every day together for the past three weeks, but there were still so many unanswered questions between us. I couldn't fully give in to my desire when I didn't know exactly who—or what—he was. But I couldn't deny my growing need for him either. I indulged just enough to sedate the nagging ache that resided low in my abdomen, even in the middle of my workday.

I pulled the hem of Archer's shirt from his jeans as he pressed me into the back corner of the third-floor hallway. His tongue brushed over mine while his hand slithered under my polo shirt and cupped my breast. He worked the button of my jeans open and tugged down the zipper, his fingers dipping under the top of my panties. I hitched my leg over his hip, giving him better access to touch me; his fingertips danced over my center, twirling over the place that sent my entire body into a state of euphoria.

I rolled my hips over his hand as I tangled my fingers in the hair at the nape of his neck, gripping it at the roots. "God, yes, this is exactly what I need," I murmured, running my tongue down the cord of his neck to his shoulder.

"I aim to please, Miss Fox."

"It's unfair of me to leave you to do all the work," I said, my voice going breathless when he eased a finger inside of me.

"This is all play." He kissed me and drew my bottom lip between his teeth, sending a lustful surge through me. "Besides, I like the way you feel and sound. This is a job I'd happily do all day."

I pulled his hair harder and pushed against his hand, the pressure building between my thighs. "You're definitely hired, Mr. Hyde. Your task completion rate is one hundred percent," I teased, nipping at his earlobe.

"I'm working for a bonus."

His thumb worked in tandem with his finger. Each stroke tightened the coil low in my stomach, until it was on the verge of snapping and filling me with pure bliss. My skin prickled with anticipation, and my breathing matched the thrumming of my heart. I arched my head back, ready to lose myself in the endorphin rush.

"Gem, you down here?"

My body went rigid.

"Gem?"

I pushed Archer away and fumbled to fasten my pants. "Do the weird vanishing thing. My brother can't meet you like this."

Archer shook his head and smiled. "The man is eventually going to figure it out."

"Not today. Go!"

Hunter rounded the corner just as Archer vanished into thin air.

"Who are you talking to? You're starting to worry me with the constant disappearing and talking to yourself," he said, crossing his arms.

Straightening the hem of my shirt, I squared my shoulders and said, "I don't know what you mean."

"Something weird is going on with you. Does your odd behavior have anything to do with that guy you told me about?"

My heart stopped for a second before I answered, "No. Seriously, Hunt, I have no idea what you're talking about. What did you need me for anyway?"

My brother narrowed his eyes. I didn't know why I was lying to him. He could tell something was up, but he also knew when to let it go. I never gave up my secrets until I was ready.

"You asked me to remind you about your meeting with the permit officer for the back porch. I didn't want you to forget that it's today at eleven."

"Thanks. I'll be down before they get here."

Renovating the porch was the first of several projects Hunter had proposed to improve the hotel. He wanted to start with the outside, fixing rotting wood planks and repainting the green shutters. Once everything appeared aesthetically pleasing from the street, he suggested revamping the bar. He had drawn up an amazing concept that would keep the original decor but open the space to tourists passing by on the sidewalk. Hunter had an eye for small details that made a huge impact, and I was ecstatic to have him working on the hotel.

"If the permit officer has any questions about the plans, give me a call. But I'll leave the rest up to you, Miss Hotel Owner,"

Hunter said, patting me on the shoulder before heading back the way he came.

"Will do. Thanks for the reminder."

I leaned into the wall and released a lungful of air, annoyed at the interruption. Archer had been so close to giving me what I needed, and I could have used the stress relief before my meeting.

"It could have been worse. At least he didn't catch us," I murmured, moving to follow Hunter's path.

"You're so worried about getting caught with my brother that I bet you still haven't read the tome I gave you. Your priorities are a little fucked, Gemma."

I whirled around, my ponytail whipping me in the face, and I swatted it over my shoulder. Glaring at the blue-eyed twin, I said, "Shut up, Soren. How about you mind your own business like we discussed? And who the hell says *tome*?"

He stepped forward. "How about you quit acting like you don't care about what's going on here and pull the *book*, *journal*, *diary*, whatever you want to call it, out of your goddamned nightstand? Make no mistake, the man you are messing around with is not human."

A chill, unlike the ones Archer sent through me, rattled my bones. *Not human*. "Stop being a creeper and going through my room." I crossed my arms over my stomach, matching his smug, arrogant stance. "And it just so happens that I tried to read the *tome* right after you gave it to me. And just call it a book, for Christ's sake."

"You *tried* to read it? What does that mean? Was it not in English? Or were the words too big for you?"

"Actually, it wasn't in any language at all because it was blank. Just a bunch of white pages in fancy leather binding. So, thanks for all the 'answers.' They were very helpful," I drawled, pushing past him. His fingers closed around my wrist, and he spun me around to face him.

I yanked my arm away and snapped, "What the hell?"

"What do you mean, it was blank?"

"Just what I said. The pages didn't have any words on them."

"That's—that doesn't make sense."

"Looks like there aren't any easy answers after all. I guess I'll just keep messing around with your nonhuman brother," I said with a smirk.

"Gemma, this isn't the time to—"

"Look, your brother and I enjoy spending time together; we're having fun. Maybe you should try it; you might feel better if you released some of that excess energy and stopped sticking your nose in my business!"

"Don't pretend to know my agenda or my brother's. And who do you want me to have a good time with? You? I'd rather ram a hot poker in my eye."

I let loose a maniacal laugh. "Please, I've no desire to do anything with you. I am a hundred percent sure the superior twin is taking care of my needs. And even if the book did have the answers in it, I don't know why the hell it matters to you."

I rushed past him, anger coursing through my veins. Soren Hyde was rapidly becoming the bane of my existence—snooping through my room, telling me what to read, and putting in his two cents regarding my relationship with his brother. I had enough stress in my life, and I didn't need him adding to it.

I turned back to tell him as much, but he was gone. The only evidence he was ever there was the lingering scent of spearmint and salty sea breeze.

CHAPTER EIGHT

Last night's conversation with Soren replayed in my head as I filed invoices with Larry, handing the older man paper after paper as he placed them in their respective folders. I had to admit that while Soren and Archer appeared to be human, something was absolutely otherworldly about them, and I wanted to know what it was. There had to be something in that book. But how could I figure out how to read it when even Soren didn't know? *And he thinks he knows everything*, I thought with a scowl.

Watching Larry's gnarled hands organize the papers gave me an idea: What if he had some answers regarding the twins or the book?

"Larry?" I asked as he closed the filing cabinet.

"Yes, Miss Fox." I glared at him, and he said sheepishly, "Gemma."

"I have a question about the boys."

He leaned against the counter and crossed his arms over his stomach. "Soren and Archer."

"Yeah. I— How much do you know about them?"

"Well, they've been here since I started this job, and I watched them go from teenagers to adults. I reckon I know a decent amount."

"What—what are they?"

Cocking his head to the side, Larry regarded me with curiosity. "Why? Have you seen them?"

"Am I not supposed to be able to see them?"

"You can, but they've become experts at staying hidden. So, if you've had a run-in with them, it's because they wanted it to happen."

My face reddened, and I chewed the inside of my cheek before saying, "You could say I've come across them. And now I'm curious. I mean, they live in my hotel; I feel like I should at least know a little bit about them."

Larry pushed off the counter and pulled on his jacket before taking off his name tag and putting it in the drawer of the front desk. "I'd tell you if I knew, dear. But I don't. Hazel never told me, and while I've known about the boys all along, watched them run around the hotel and then saunter about like they owned the place"—a warm, nostalgic smile spread over his face at that—"I've never actually had a conversation with them. I'm sorry, Gemma, that I can't tell you what you want to know."

My heart sank, but I gave Larry a smile. "That's okay. Have a good night, and be careful. It's foggy out there tonight."

He grinned as he moved toward the front door. "Just the kind of evening Hazel would've loved," he said, and with a tip of his hat, he stepped into the cool night.

If only my aunt were here to give me the answers I needed. Once again, I kicked myself for not being around when she was still alive. She'd come so close over the years to telling me more about the paranormal legends surrounding the hotel, but she'd always stopped just short of giving me any real answers. I was left with tiny tidbits that were nowhere close to painting the entire picture for me. I already knew Archer and Soren were not from this world, but I needed the missing pieces. My curious nature wouldn't let me rest until I knew the whole truth.

I closed out the cash register, propped the OPEN AGAIN AT 8:00 A.M. sign on the desk, and forwarded the calls to my cell in case of an emergency. Archer was nowhere to be found tonight, Skye had her hands full at the bar, and my brother was out with Caden. My restless mind wouldn't quit racing, and I wanted more than ever to be close to my aunt. Since that wasn't possible, I decided to do the next best thing.

Think like her.

Larry had said that Hazel would've loved a night like tonight. So why not go out and enjoy it? I hadn't gotten to explore Spelling since I'd been back, and this seemed like the perfect time for it.

I wished a good evening to a small group of tourists and pulled my jacket around me as I strolled down the foggy sidewalk. The town center was quiet, with the occasional guided group of ghost hunters roaming from one haunted landmark to the next.

People believed that Spelling sat on a portal that led to the life after this one. Every soul was meant to use the passage to leave this world, but some got lost in the process, trapping them in our dimension. Like any doorway, spirits could come and go, causing every questionable death or disaster that took place in Spelling to be attributed to malevolent spirits. Learning about the town's sordid past was big business, and the Reynard was at its center.

I passed under hand-painted signs that hung from the eaves of the redbrick storefronts, advertising the antiques and souvenir shops. Every store had a name that alluded to magic—Enchanted Creamery or Voodoo Hot Dogs. Mannequins stood in storefront windows wearing bright T-shirts that read *I Was Spellbound in*

Spelling, Connecticut or *Spelling, Connecticut: Where Magic Lives.* The likeness of the young twin boys was even printed on shirts. It was bizarre to know people were walking around with Archer and Soren on their chests.

The fountain that sat in the middle of the main intersection came into view. Water jetted out from the pool, forming a tall arch illuminated by color-changing lights. Locals claimed that it was a symbol of the portal and that the same energy found in the passage was also in the water.

I moved onto the next block, where gaggles of tourists were often found at this time of night. Old colonial houses lined the street with neon signs in the windows. Palm readers, shamans, mediums—if you were looking for those who conversed with spirits, you would find them on Charmed Street.

"I can tell you're troubled," said a deep voice with a Southern drawl. Sitting on the steps of a small house covered in ivy was a man in a top hat. He watched me with beady eyes as I passed the walkway to his stoop.

I believed in the paranormal, but I wasn't a fool. The people who made their living telling fortunes and talking to the dead had spent years perfecting their craft. They were convincing, saying the things that others wanted to hear but giving them just enough that they returned to pay a heftier price for more.

"I have the answer you seek," he said in another attempt to draw me to him.

Every rational instinct told me to continue walking, but something about his words made me stop. I gripped the top of the picket fence surrounding his yard and glared at him. I was desperate for answers but fearful of coming off as a gullible idiot.

"Do you know anything about magic 'tomes'?" I asked.

"I'm sure one of the spirits has the answers you need."

I shook my head. "I'm not looking to talk to spirits; I do that on a daily basis now. I need someone who knows about magic books with blank pages."

He cocked a bushy brow and tilted his head to the side. It was official; even *he* thought I was out of my mind. "That's not my specialty."

"But do you know someone who can help me?"

"I do, but—"

"It's going to cost me." I dug around in my jacket pocket and pulled out a crumpled twenty-dollar bill.

The man stood, his back hunched as he shuffled over to the gate. He eyed the money, and before he could imply it would cost me more, I said, "It's all I've got on me. Take it or leave it."

He snatched the bill with a gnarled hand. "Four doors down. Wanda Willow. If anyone around here knows about magic books, it's her."

"Thank you," I said, rushing down the sidewalk to the house he'd indicated before I could chicken out.

Wanda Willow. With a name like that, she was bound to have some answers. In fact, the more I thought about it, the more familiar the name sounded. I was certain I'd never met her before, but I wondered if I'd heard Hazel talk about her. I could only hope.

I stopped in front of a small but magical-looking cottage. Night-blooming jasmine snaked up the side of the house, purple shutters hung haphazardly from the brick, and smoke puffed from the chimney in big black plumes. Unlike the other houses on the block, this one didn't have a sign advertising paranormal services. All I knew for sure about Wanda was that she might have the answers I'd been seeking. Climbing the steps up to the creaky porch, I took a deep breath before tapping on the door. The hinges whined, and a cluster of metal chains swung back and forth against the splintered wood on the inside. The door inched open, and withered brown eyes framed in purple and green eye shadow scanned me up and down through the crack.

"I'm not too sure about you," the woman I assumed was Wanda said, her voice shaky but stern. "Your aura is putting off some bad vibes—worry, disbelief. Are you confused? Damn tourists." She shut the door, and the chains slid free one by one. When the woman reappeared, she was dressed in a leopard-print silk robe with fur trimming and fuzzy house slippers, and her black hair was rolled with pink curlers. "If you're looking for the Reynard Hotel, it's around the corner," she said, speaking loudly and pointing down the street.

"No, ma'am. I'm looking for you. I'm actually the new owner of the Reynard." I held out my hand. "I'm Gemma Fox."

"Hazel's niece. I remember seeing you around the hotel a time or two. But you were younger and not so . . . voluptuous?"

"Puberty will do that to a girl," I replied with a grin.

"So will a few too many boxes of doughnuts. What can I do for you?"

I should have been offended by her remark, but it was so matter-of-fact that I found her sort of charming in an insulting way. Besides, she knew Hazel, and my visit was looking promising. "I wanted to ask you about the Hyde brothers and a strange book I received."

Wanda opened the door further and stepped to the side. "Come on in, and let's see if I can help you, girl."

I stepped over the threshold, and as soon as I entered the small foyer, the overwhelming aroma of incense filled my nostrils. But that didn't seem out of the ordinary for a woman named Wanda Willow. I half expected to find a table with a crystal ball and a deck of tarot cards, and maybe even a raven perched on the top of bookshelves overflowing with old, leather-bound books.

While the inside of Wanda's home was dark and a little gloomy, it was also cozy and comfortable. Long black curtains reached the floor, and the violet walls were covered with paintings of various gothic and shadowy scenes. Upon closer inspection, I noticed the initials H.F. in the bottom corners of most of them. A lump rose in my throat; this woman wasn't just an acquaintance of my aunt's, she knew her well enough to have her art hanging in her living room. The sofa was black with purple stripes, and when Wanda invited me to sit while she went to get us some tea, I sank so far into the cushions that I had to heave myself up straight before she came back into the room.

Setting a tray with a teapot and two steaming mugs on an octagonal coffee table, Wanda settled in the wingback chair adjacent to me. She sipped her tea, watching me with eagle eyes, waiting for me to speak.

Wanda seemed like the kind of woman who appreciated candor, not a beat-around-the-bush kind of person, so I just blurted it out. "Why would Hazel believe a book with a bunch of blank pages was important enough to give it to questionable people for safekeeping?"

"She wouldn't. If there is one thing I knew about your aunt, it was that she did nothing without purpose. Everything she did around that hotel took those boys into consideration."

I sank into the couch, relieved to hear Wanda talk about the Hyde brothers as real people. Dancing around their existence would have made this difficult conversation harder.

"One of them gave me a book that he claimed came from Hazel. He has no reason to lie, so I assume it was hers. But all the pages are blank. He was shocked when I told him that but had no idea what to do about it. It's really important that I figure this out. Do you have any idea how to go about reading it?"

Wanda laughed, the hearty, rich sound vibrating through the house. "Did you try opening it up and starting from the beginning?"

"I told you, the pages were blank."

"You aren't answering my question, Gemma. Did you start from the beginning?"

I swallowed the knot of embarrassment growing in my throat. "I have a habit of reading the end of a book first."

"I thought so. Spells and magic are not about the rules we put on them. They are their own entity that most of us struggle to understand. Hazel had an innate knowledge of the paranormal; every woman who owned the Reynard before you did. So, to answer your question, the rules are found in the natural order of things."

The natural order of things. The phrase hung between us, and something about the way she said it told me it was the answer I was seeking. "I think I understand."

Every woman who had owned the Reynard before me had an innate knowledge of the paranormal. And once again, I was the odd one out, the family member who didn't meet the standard.

"Are the Hyde brothers ghosts or spirits or something that was once alive and now dead?" I asked.

Wanda sat forward and clasped her hands in her lap. "No. That is their story to tell you, girl. Even I don't have all the details on what exactly brought them here."

"Did Hazel practice witchcraft?"

"She dabbled in spells once. Like I said, she had a connection to things outside the understanding of this world. It was something she was born with."

Hazel was special, I never doubted that. But to have it confirmed by someone who truly knew her made me giddy. Every snide or belittling remark about her from my father and uncle no longer mattered. She was extraordinary, and only I saw that. The rest of my family had missed out on the most magical person they would ever meet.

"Do I have some kind of dormant magic?" I asked.

Wanda's gaze softened, and the deep lines on her forehead vanished. "You have a calling, Gemma. It is not the same as Hazel's or any other Fox woman before her. You may not cast spells or understand the paranormal, but you are extremely special. Your choices will be life changing."

A mixture of emotions brewed inside me, making my stomach churn. I was dying to hear that I was just like Hazel—unique, strong, a force to be reckoned with. Instead, Wanda confirmed that I didn't need to be like Hazel to find my worth because I was already invaluable. It had been a long time since someone had made me feel that way.

I stood, not wanting to tarnish this moment with more questions. "Thank you for your time, Wanda. If there's anything you think I need to know about the Reynard or any advice you can give me as its new owner, I'd be eternally grateful."

"You're welcome. And I'm sure our paths will cross again. My door is always open to the great-niece of Hazel Fox."

Optimism burned inside of me as I left Wanda's house. I was going to return to the hotel, open the book, and finally get the answers I wanted about the Reynard and the men who lived there.

CHAPTER NINE

As soon as I got back from Wanda's, I sat on the sofa in my suite and crossed my ankles under me, covering my legs with Hazel's favorite crocheted blanket. The fireplace roared, warming the drafty suite as I lay the volume on my lap. I took a deep breath and held it before bringing the key out of my hoodie pocket, sliding it into the keyhole, and opening the latch. This time, instead of flipping to the back in my usual manner, I lifted the front cover.

A gasp escaped me when black ink moved across the page in sweeping loops and lines, revealing each word one at a time.

The True History of the Reynard Hotel.

I slammed the book closed and opened it to the back pages— they were blank. The paper fanned through my fingertips, and I took special care to study the second page of the book as it flipped by. Nothing was written on it.

I read the title again and turned the page. Swirling, beautiful letters that looked as though they were written hundreds of years ago graced the yellowing paper.

The spiritual advisors in Spelling warned us not to build the Reynard on this land. But James did not heed their warnings.

I was hell-bent on finding the vortex and proving to him that it existed. My obsession came at a great cost to my family. If I had never opened the vortex, Celestia would have never stepped through it. If she had never left her dimension, I would not be in the position I am in now.

Something is wrong with my boys. Robert and Gregory are not developing like they should. And their eyes. They were born with milky brown irises, and now, Robert's are a strange violet color I have never seen before, and Gregory's are a brilliant shade of blue. It makes no logical sense.

And I know it is her. I know she has done something to them, because the odd colors of their eyes match hers. One of hers is violet and the other blue. That cannot be a coincidence. I do not know what she has done, but I am determined to figure it out.

—Amity Fox, April 7, 1886

I slammed the cover of the book, my eyes wide with horror. The boys that Amity was describing sounded an awful lot like Archer and Soren.

But that couldn't be right because Amity was my great-great-great-grandmother, which would make her children my distant aunts and uncles.

Bile rose in my throat, and that horrific idea was enough to have me turning the page to read more, desperate for a different explanation.

April 22, 1886
I knew it. I knew it was her. These are not my boys at all. She took Robert and Gregory and replaced them with these inhuman creatures—her children. She has promised that my boys will be

safe in her care, and she will return them when the threat to her twins is gone. I do not understand why anyone would harm precious, small beings, and she would not go into the reasons.

How can I trust her with my boys after she tricked me? This is the ultimate betrayal by a woman who befriended me at a fragile time. I considered her my best friend. I should have known better than to trust a being from the kobold realm.

All I want is my sons returned to me unharmed.

I gingerly pushed the book off my lap and ran my hands over my face. Swapped babies and vortexes and dark powers—it was all too much. But at least I wasn't related to Archer. That would have been the piece of information that I would *not* have been able to handle.

But the rest of it was bizarre, to say the least. Archer and Soren's mom switched them out with Robert and Gregory Fox. But why? And nothing in those entries explained *what* they were. And what the hell was a kobold?

I snatched my phone off the side table and did a web search for *kobold*. Two images popped up, one more horrifying than the next—an anthropomorphic reptile with a lizard tail and a canine face followed by a little green goblin man with a big nose and ears that looked like something out of my worst fantasy nightmare.

"Oh Jesus, what the fuck?" I yelped, throwing my phone facedown onto the cushion beside me.

I needed a reprieve from the madness before it got to me. Setting the book on the coffee table and marking my place, I pocketed the key to my suite and headed downstairs and into the bar.

"Tough night?" Skye asked, placing a cocktail napkin in front of me as I hopped onto a barstool.

"More like a roller coaster of a night." I leaned on the bar top and propped my chin in my hands. "Tell me, does working at this place ever get to you, Skye?"

Her laugh echoed through the bar as she pulled a glass out. "Like any job, it has its moments. But overall, I enjoy being here. The people are nice, and the stories are enough to keep me entertained. Why do you ask? Feeling a bit overwhelmed?"

"I'm not exactly the business-owner-slash-star-entrepreneur type. I can hardly commit to a new shade of lipstick. To say I am overwhelmed is an understatement." I tore the corners off the cocktail napkin and looked back up at her. "What can you tell me about the boys?"

She finished pouring me a drink in a tall glass and set it in front of me. I took a sip and almost choked. Skye clearly thought it was the kind of night where I could use a strong drink, and she was right.

"The boys are harmless. They mostly pull pranks on the guests, but it's all in good spirits. Their shenanigans have fueled the legends the locals like to share about malicious acts happening inside these walls. The stories hold no truth and are mostly told to pique tourists' curiosity." She pointed to my glass. "Keep drinking and I promise you'll sleep like a baby tonight."

I did as she asked with the hopes that it would keep her talking. I needed basic details about Archer and Soren. Namely, what the hell they were. I could keep reading, and I would, but it would be nice if someone living could tell me something about them.

I gulped down another couple mouthfuls of the amber liquid. It burned my throat and made my eyes water. When I caught my breath, I asked, "What's the backstory on them? When I led ghost tours here as a teen, I was told to say they were just abandoned children who froze to death on the front steps." I lifted the drink to my lips and finished it off.

Skye raised an eyebrow as she swapped out my drink for a fresh one. "As far as I know, your aunt always thought the real story was too risky to share with the tourists. They would either run off screaming or want to rip this land to shreds to uncover the kind of power it holds. Either way, it would destroy the Reynard."

The alcohol soured in my throat. "What do you mean by power?"

I had an inkling of what it was that Hazel thought people couldn't handle, but I wanted to hear someone else say it. If she'd shared what was in the first pages of the book with others, it must be true.

"Your aunt was reluctant to give too many details. I think she was scared that the truth would spread and kill business. All she ever said to me was that a curse binds the Hyde brothers to the property, and their only opportunity to leave is once a year when they can roam through the entire town. She was the one who made the Winter Spirits festival so popular. Before her, the town was quiet that night, and everyone locked their doors to keep the 'evil spirits' of the twin boys from entering their homes. Some of the older folks still aren't fond of the celebration, but I, for one, enjoy it."

I shook my head and slung back the rest of the drink. I was prepared to hear about the vortex or a portal to another dimension. I knew the legend behind Winter Spirits; it was another myth that brought people to Spelling. What I didn't expect was learning that the brothers were cursed to stay in the hotel. I always thought they were here because spirits haunted places of importance to them. But they weren't spirits—these living, breathing beings were here because someone bound them to the property.

Something even darker than betrayal and swapped babies

made up the real history of the Reynard. The pages of the journal held the answers, and I was terrified to learn them.

"I'm going to need another of those concoctions," I said.

Everything I learned tonight was too much to process, so I took advantage of what was right in front of me and kept drinking. In the two years I'd spent at the university, I'd built up an impressive tolerance, but whatever Skye was mixing had quite the effect on me.

"Are you sure, Gemma? I don't usually serve that drink in a glass that big. Most people would be falling off the barstool by now," Skye cautioned, wiping her hands on a white cloth and tossing it onto the bar top.

"Yes, I'm sure," I slurred, leaning toward her and nodding vigorously. "I can handle it."

She glanced at the clock and raised an eyebrow. "I'm not known for being a rule follower, but you know last call was ten minutes ago and we close in thirty."

I crossed my arms and stuck out my lip in a petulant pout. "But, Skye," I whined, "I'm the owner of this establishment, so don't you think it's fair I get just *one more drink*?" I held up an index finger to illustrate my point.

With a sigh, she turned her back to me and set to work.

"Come on, I think you've had enough," said a warm voice in my ear as strong fingers curled around my biceps.

I jumped in my seat and whirled around to see Archer right in my face, his breath minty and eyes a deep, dark amethyst. I hopped off the stool and pressed myself against him. "How long have you been standing here? Just let me grab my drink, and we can go back to my room." I wiggled my eyebrows and ran a finger down the center of his chest.

"I'll come back and get your drink when it's done," he whispered.

His hand engulfed mine, and he led me out of the bar despite my whimpered protest about my abandoned cocktail.

Archer stopped in the narrow walkway between the lobby and bar. Countless black-and-white photos covered the wall, each memorializing a moment in the hotel's history—the ribbon-cutting ceremony after the first renovation, a ghost tour on Halloween night, and my great-great-aunt Betty, who was married in the sitting room. He pressed the corner of a picture frame, and the wall swung back enough to give us entrance into the secret passages behind it. Archer guided me through the dark, and I stumbled behind him as everything around me tilted and spun.

"Shit," I mumbled as I stepped on his heel and fell against him, gripping his waist to stop myself from hitting the ground. "Sorry, Arch." I righted myself and bunched his shirt in my fist to keep my balance, taking a deep breath and closing my eyes to stop the spinning.

"Not a problem. Here." He took my arms, wrapped them around his neck, and grabbed my thighs, hoisting me onto his back. "Just don't vomit on me, please."

I rested my chin on his shoulder and kept my eyes shut, my mouth close to his ear. "I've never been *that* drunk. I just need to lie down."

"You also haven't drunk Skye's sleeping potion before. In her short time as the bartender here, her signature drink has gained quite the reputation. Rest assured; you *will* be vomiting tonight."

Archer maneuvered through the stone and concrete maze with ease. His steps were nimble, and he didn't so much as grunt with my extra weight added. He was *definitely* not a normal guy who would have cried like a big baby at having to overexert himself in the name of chivalry.

"Do you have night vision or something?" I asked.

A low chuckle vibrated through his back and rattled my chest. "No. I've just navigated these passages for years upon years. I could lose my sight and never get lost on any inch of this property."

"And exactly how many years would that be?"

"I've always been here. Always."

"*Years*, Archer. I'm not in a position to do math."

He released my legs, and the wall gave way. The light from the hallway flooded my sensitive eyes, but I could still make out the somber expression on his face. "Just short of one hundred and forty years."

I released his neck and stumbled back against the wall. "Ex-excuse me? I know I'm a little boozy, but did you just say a *hundred* and forty years? Like the eighteen hundreds?"

"Maybe this is a better conversation for another time," he said, helping me upright and to my door.

I shook my head and pulled the key out of my pocket, taking too long to slide it in the lock. "No way. You're coming in." I grabbed his hand and yanked him through the door, closing it behind us. "I need to lie down, but you have to tell me more," I said, leading him to my bedroom and collapsing onto the mattress. I patted the blanket next to me and wiggled my eyebrows. "Join me?"

Archer didn't say a word, lowering to the mattress and crossing his arms over his abdomen. Ignoring the spinning sensation, I flipped to my side and bent my elbow, propping my head in my hand. "What's a kabbel?"

"A cowbell?"

"No! You know, the people on the other side of the vortex. The lizard men. The koolads."

"The kobolds?"

I snapped my fingers and pointed at him. "That's it! The kobolds. The little green trolls."

He raised his brows and slid his tongue over his teeth. "Legend has it that they are a type of sprite who like to take knickknacks and swap human children for their own."

I barked a laugh and sat up, my knees brushing against his thighs. "You say that like it's no big deal. I guess you don't believe they're real, huh?"

"Sprites—little green fairies with pixie dust? No."

"But couldn't they, like, take on some other form or something? Like Transformers?"

He glanced at me from the corner of his eyes and smiled. Turning onto his side, he took my hand and placed it on his chest. "Do I feel like a Transformer to you?"

I slipped my fingers between the buttons on his shirt and gently scratched his skin. "Not at all." I swallowed, not taking my hand from his chest before whispering, "Are you trying to tell me that's what you are?"

"I'm trying to tell you I'm here and very real." He guided my hand down his torso, over the waist of his jeans, and onto his very real erection.

All thoughts of kobolds and drinks and ancient books flew from my brain, and I scooted toward him and slung one leg over his, squeezing him gently. "Well, well. It would seem you are," I whispered, gripping the front of his shirt with my free hand and pulling him up to face me. "What would you like me to do about that?" I breathed against his mouth before licking at his bottom lip.

"I can think of several things, but mostly I would like to see that pretty mouth of yours wrapped around me. But only if that's what you want."

I sat back on my heels and grinned, sliding my hand down to his waistband, unbuckling his belt in one fluid motion. "Yeah, that's what I want," I said, unbuttoning his jeans and sliding the zipper down. He lifted his hips toward me as I lowered his pants and boxers, a gasp escaping my lips as I took in the sight of him for the first time. *If he really is a kobold, well, at least I now know they are well-endowed.*

I leaned down, flipping my hair over my shoulder, and took him in my left hand. Dipping my head closer to his lap, I closed my mouth over him, swirling my tongue around in smooth strokes. I added the motion of my left hand, sliding my right up his chest and gripping the fabric of his shirt.

My gaze traveled to his face, where he bit his lip while watching himself disappear into my mouth. He gathered my hair into his fist, and the muscles in his stomach flexed as his hips joined the pace he set.

"Fuck, Gemma," he hissed. "That is so perfect; *you're* so perfect."

A chill ran down my spine, ending in a delicious throbbing between my legs. I pressed myself to his thigh, moaning against him as the friction between us flooded my nerve endings. I kept rhythm with his hips, my tongue gliding up and down the smooth skin, squeezing him firmly in my hand. I spiraled back to the tip, tasting the salty evidence of his desire, my eyes never leaving his.

Archer's breathing quickened, as did the thrust of his hips. I nodded, letting him know that it was all right for him to find his release. His jaw went slack, and my name flowed from his lips. Even when his fingers freed my hair, I showered him with my tongue for a moment longer until every muscle in his body sank into the mattress.

He took my hand and guided me up his body and into the crook of his arm. Kissing the top of my head, he said, "That was amazing."

I held back my laughter; that compliment always felt so trite to me. I wasn't familiar with an orgasm that wasn't amazing in one way or another. Wasn't that the point of them?

"I'm sure you've said that more than once in your one hundred and forty years," I teased, laying my palm against his face and running my fingertips over his smooth skin, tracing his cheekbone with my thumb.

Archer looked down at me, and the corner of his lips tilted up. "Maybe once or twice, but it doesn't make it any less true."

I snuggled against him, resting my head in the crook of his arm and gripping his shirt. "Don't leave, okay? I don't want to wake up alone."

"I promise; I'm not going anywhere."

CHAPTER TEN

Archer was right—Skye's sleeping potion was not meant to be drunk by the gallon. In the middle of the night, I found myself hugging the toilet. I was grateful that Archer didn't wake up to witness my humiliation. I must have spent two hours in there caught between regretful tears and dozing off with my head on the seat. I woke up just before dawn, brushed my teeth, and snuck back to bed like nothing had happened.

When I woke up again, the sun beamed through the lace curtains, scorching my retinas and aggravating my pounding head. A tinge of disappointment ran through me when I found the space beside me empty. Perhaps it was my drunken haze last night, but I thought he would be different from the normal hit-it-and-quit-it kind of guy.

"God, I hope I brushed my teeth well enough last night and didn't stink him out of my bed," I croaked, my imagination running wild with pictures of Archer awakened by my foul stench and sprinting from my room.

I shuffled my way to the bathroom to do a full dental inspection—including brushing, flossing, and gargling—and the rest of my morning routine before stepping into the living room. To my surprise, Archer was sitting on the couch, his arm draped over the back and his feet on the coffee table as he watched the flat-screen TV that I had temporarily placed next to the fireplace.

"Good morning, Gemma. I think there's still some coffee left in the pot if you feel up to it, and I set two aspirin next to the sink for you."

I rubbed my temples with my forefingers. I had been so caught up in the notion that he had left that the pounding in my head had just been an annoyance until now. I mumbled a thank-you and padded to the coffee maker to wash down the aspirin with black coffee—one of the only things I'd learned from my father.

Hugging the mug between my cold hands, I sat down next to him on the couch, leaving a decent amount of space between us. Stumbling out of the bar, giving him a blow job, and then spending time up close and personal with my toilet had me feeling a little self-conscious.

"Your brother was here this morning, knocking on the door. I'm guessing he's wondering if you're planning to show up to work today," Archer said, rubbing my knee.

It would be a typical me move to get drunk and call out the next day, claiming I'd come down with a stomach bug. But I didn't want to be that person or for the staff to think I was. This was the new and improved Gemma, the woman who showed up to work on time and tended to her responsibilities.

I got to my feet and took a deep breath. "I better get down there. I know what he wants to talk about."

"What's that?"

"The budget. Running this place costs far more than I could've ever imagined."

"Hazel never mentioned having financial problems. Everyone was paid well, and she kept the lights on in this place."

"Right, but she cut some corners, and Hunter has found some things that he's scared will give us problems down the road. We're going to have to squeeze every penny just to get them done. Besides, getting by is not what my parents care about." I lifted my hand and rubbed my thumb against my other fingers in a circular motion. "They want the business to turn a bigger profit. We have to figure out how to do that, or they're going to claim I'm incapable of running this place and hand it over to my cousin." I leaned down and gave him a peck on the cheek. "And trust me, Raven is not as fun as I am."

"You *are* a good time." He pulled me into his lap and kissed me.

Every time his mouth met mine, it was full of passion and longing. It was like I was the sole possessor of what he wanted most.

Even though it was the last thing I wanted to do, I pulled back from him and ran my hand through his hair. "I have to go. Hunter is patient enough with me; I can't stand him up. But I'd love to see you later. Maybe we can *explore the grounds* a bit," I said as I slipped my shoes on and led him to the door.

"I'd like that."

He kissed me again, and I pressed my body to his and glided my tongue over his lip before stepping away. We turned to walk out of my suite but skidded to a halt.

Soren stood in the hallway glaring at us.

I hated that look: the judgment in his gaze and the way he clenched his jaw like he was holding back his words. Why couldn't he just leave us to make our own choices and keep his attitude to himself?

He eased the passage door closed behind him and nodded at Archer. "Brother."

"Good morning, Soren. Have you had the pleasure of meeting Gemma?" Archer's question held a chipper tone, a sharp contrast to his brother's.

"You know I have." Soren's blue gaze darted to me. "I see you are still choosing to disregard my suggestion."

"Wow, you're a quick one," I snapped, holding tight to Archer's hand. "And I thought I made myself clear the last time we spoke. Stay away from me."

He shifted to the side and slid a hand in the pocket of his black jeans. "You don't see me chasing after you or trying to warm your bed. I *am* minding my own business."

"It doesn't appear that the hotel's new owner likes you much, brother. How long did it take you to get under her skin, two minutes?"

"Give or take."

It irked me that he didn't even care that I disliked him. What kind of person or non-person was all right with being despised? And what was it about me that made him act like an asshole? Was he blaming me for Hazel's death and taking over the hotel? Surely he was more intelligent than that.

I squared my shoulders and glared right into Soren's mesmerizing blue eyes. "Speaking to me about who I do or do not spend time with doesn't seem like minding your own business. So, why don't you just keep walking next time? And for the record, I wouldn't ask you to warm my bed if I were sleeping on a goddamned glacier."

"No worries, I couldn't get it up for a frigid woman anyway." He turned on his heel and threw his hand up, saluting the air. "Both of you should follow my advice before you fuck everything up."

I cast Archer a side-glance and asked, "What was his advice to you?"

"Soren has a tendency to lean toward theatrics. I wouldn't bother putting any credence in what he says. What did he say to you?"

"He told me to stay away from you. To stay away from both of you."

Archer threw his arm around my shoulders and flashed a wide, dimpled grin. "Brooding asshole. I told you he enjoys a good dramatic episode."

Something didn't feel right about Archer's explanation. Soren was adamant that I read the book, and it didn't come across as overdramatic. I couldn't shake the feeling that there was more to his foul mood than either brother wanted to admit. And the more it ate away at me, the more I wanted answers. Whatever was driving Soren was something other than just an attempt to stifle his brother's happiness or mine.

Both of you should follow my advice before you fuck everything up. I needed to know what exactly he believed Archer and I were in the process of fucking up.

✳ ✳ ✳

I canceled my dinner plans with Archer, claiming that Skye's sleeping potion was still wreaking havoc on me. In truth, I was eager to read more of the heavy gilded book that supposedly held the answers to all my questions about the Hyde brothers. Now that I'd figured out how to make the words appear on the pages, I needed to discover what was behind Soren's warnings.

Sitting on my bed and pulling the comforter around me, I hauled the book into my lap and picked up from where I left off.

December 24, 1886

For months, I have sat outside the vortex, waiting for Celestia to return with my sons. I grow more bitter with each passing day. Her "children" do not age as our own. They appear to grow at a rate much slower than ours. I fear that I am losing my patience with the children, and James is questioning their mental state. They should be sitting up and crawling, but both boys are as small as they were the day they were switched with my own. If their mother doesn't return for them soon, James will have nothing to do with the babies, and I hate to imagine the effect this will have on our own sons.

Archer and Soren, the names Celestia gave the boys, are in the nursery, taken care of by a member of the staff who has been sworn to secrecy. They are difficult children who become inconsolable when touched by certain people. They are probably starved for attention; they are given plenty of milk during the day and have their diapers changed when necessary, but the love that would be given to them by their mother is absent. I am aware they are just children and have not done anything wrong, but I simply cannot give them the affection of a mother. Not when my own babies are lost to me.

It is Christmas Eve, and all I can think of is Robert and Gregory and where they are tonight. I hope whoever has them is less inattentive than I.

Thinking of the twins as babies, locked away in a nursery and receiving only the bare minimum to survive, made my heart ache, even for Soren. I begrudgingly turned the page, and my head swam with the misery of it all.

March 2, 1887

Today I began the trying task of learning to close the vortex. Once my boys are brought back to me, I will ensure that this never happens to another family in Spelling. The kobolds will remain in their dimension and our children will be safe.

On a brighter note, I have discovered what makes the kobold children so fussy. They have an odd reaction to gold. Just setting my wedding ring on their backs renders them immobile. I've ordered the staff to remove all golden jewelry when tending to them, hoping to bring them some peace during their time in my care.

"An aversion to gold. That's bizarre," I mumbled.

I kept reading, and with each passing month, Amity's mental health appeared to decline. Entire entries were nothing more than her sons' names written repeatedly or fragmented sentences about how much she loved and missed them. In her more coherent entries, she went on about her plans to close the vortex and her desire to ensure her twins were never taken from her again once returned. She dove into dark magic, learning spells to bind people to objects. She planned to tether Robert and Gregory to the hotel when they returned, releasing them from the spell only when they were old enough to venture out on their own. After the trauma she'd endured, I don't believe she would have ever let them leave.

May 17, 1887

They are gone. My handsome baby boys are dead.

Celestia promised she would keep my sons safe, but her enemies killed them as if they were her children. She took what was mine away. I never got to hold them or kiss their sweet,

round cheeks. I didn't know their cries or even the color of the
downy hair on their heads. And she will never know the same
of her sons.

I shoved her back through the vortex the moment the words
left her mouth and closed it. And if she finds a way to return,
she will never take her children from this property. Soren and
Archer are bound to the Reynard. As my sons died on her land,
hers will die on mine.

Amity did it; she cursed Soren and Archer to the Reynard
for the rest of their lives. They didn't belong here, yet this was the
only home they would ever know. My heart ached and my vision
blurred with tears, distorting the words. I was dizzy with emotion,
so much so that the book slipped from my hand, hitting the floor
with a thud before I surrendered to my exhaustion.

CHAPTER ELEVEN

A shrill ring screamed once, then twice, and I bolted up in bed. I squinted against the sunlight glaring through the blinds in my bedroom. Diving under my comforter and patting the mattress, I searched for my phone, desperate to answer it and stop the obnoxious ringtone I had chosen. I found it faceup on the floor with a picture I had assigned for the front desk lighting up the screen. Bent over the edge of the bed like a contortionist, I snatched the iPhone and accepted the call.

"This is Gemma," I said, my mouth dry like I'd chewed on cotton all night.

"Sorry to bother you, Miss Fox, but I have a woman here claiming to be your cousin. She insisted that I inform you of her arrival," Larry said, his voice void of its normal chipper tone.

"Raven is here? Right now?"

"Yes. She said you were expecting her."

"Shit. I'll be down in a minute."

I scrambled out of bed, pushing back the hair plastered to my forehead and blocking my vision. The call ended and the time jumped out at me. 10:30 a.m. I was over an hour late to work.

I rushed to the bathroom, cursing myself for falling asleep

early and not checking to see if my alarm was set. I was always at the desk to check in with Larry no later than nine. Of course it had to be today that Raven showed up.

I pulled my hair into a quick braid and grabbed the first clean clothes I could find. Shoving my phone and charger into my purse, I ran downstairs in record time, not bothering to wait for the elevator.

Skidding into the front lobby, I stopped short, and dread filled my gut when I saw Raven behind the desk, bossing Larry around with an iron fist and sharp tongue like she owned the place.

She lifted her gaze from the computer I'd bought to update the hotel's reservation system and took in my rumpled polo shirt and jeans. She scowled, wrinkling her perfect button nose like I was yesterday's garbage. "Nice of you to make it to work. Do you usually come rolling in at nearly eleven a.m.?"

"Uh, good morning, Raven," I said, stepping behind the desk and dropping my purse on the stool in the corner. "I didn't know you were going to be here today."

"Obviously."

Larry shot me a sympathetic glance. Now that he understood who graced us with her presence, I'm sure the memories of her had come flooding back to him. Raven had been a demanding child, expecting the staff to wait on her hand and foot. The summer after her thirteenth birthday, she didn't accompany me to the hotel, and to this day, I recall the relief on everyone's faces.

"I'm usually here at—" I stopped and pushed my braid over my shoulder before turning around and fiddling with some loose papers on the desk. It didn't matter what I said; she'd made up her mind about me a long time ago and that wasn't going to change. "What are you doing here, Raven?" Like her, I didn't bother disguising my irritation.

"Hazel's wishes were very clear. I'm supposed to help you learn how to run the hotel, so here I am." She flashed me her fake, toothy grin.

I wanted to tell her to leave, that I had this under control, that this was *my* hotel. Hazel had left it to *me*. But I couldn't. It wouldn't be fair to honor Hazel's wishes only when they were what I wanted.

"Fine. I already know how to use the computer system. I installed it myself, so I don't really need help with that. What else do you have to offer?"

Raven stepped out from the desk, her sensible black heels clicking on the mosaic tile. Unbuttoning a blazer that matched her pencil skirt, she said, "Well, let's start with the checklists you're using to make sure the staff is on task and that the rooms are meeting sanitation standards."

My jaw went slack, and I silently begged Larry to jump in and save the day. The complaints I'd received were standard—guests wanting more towels or pillows, occasionally a sock found under a bed that the housekeeping staff had overlooked. Everyone understood their jobs, and I didn't see a reason to micromanage them.

My cousin crossed her arms and clicked her tongue. "Gemma, how are you ensuring that your staff is on task if you're not putting procedures in place? For all you know, your pool boy is lounging in a cabana searching online dating apps."

"*I'm* the pool boy," I said.

Raven gave me a judgmental once-over. "Well, I guess perusing dating apps is a given then."

My cheeks flamed, and I clenched my hands into fists at my sides. Having ADHD presented a host of difficulties for me, and one of them I'd had to work the hardest to control was my anger.

When I got mad, the impulse to punch something was always strong—the brick wall at school, my pillow, my cousin's face. And right now, the urge to act on that last one was strong. But thankfully for me *and* for Raven, Archer came strolling around the corner, looking like sex on a stick in perfectly tailored black slacks and a red button-down with the sleeves rolled to his elbows.

My heart sped up, my usual reaction to his presence but multiplied by ten due to the current situation I was facing. My anger was overshadowed by the all-consuming desire I felt whenever he was near.

But I played it cool, refusing to fawn over him in front of my cousin. "Good morning, Mr. Hyde. I hope you're having a pleasant stay."

His purple eyes sparkled, and one side of his lips quirked up. "Miss Fox. Thank you for asking. I didn't wake up in the best of situations this morning, but I'm hoping things get better as I roam the hotel today."

I cocked an eyebrow and let my eyes trail up and down his broad form before saying, "I hate to hear that; is there anything I can do to improve your stay here at the Reynard?"

"I was thinking—"

"Raven Fox, manager of hospitality," my cousin said, darting her hand between us and gripping Archer's. "I'm sorry to hear that your stay hasn't been exceptional. Could we perhaps move you to another room?"

Archer shook Raven's hand and said, "If I'm being honest, I quite enjoy my accommodations. My bed was a little on the cold side this morning, but I'm sure that can be easily remedied."

The flush on my face deepened, and I said, "I'm sure you're right."

Raven looked between Archer and me. "If there's nothing

else we can help you with, Mr. Hyde, I have a few things to teach Gemma this morning."

"I wish you all the best, Miss Fox and Miss Fox. I'm sure Gemma will catch on quickly to your valuable expertise." Archer took Raven's hand and lifted it to his mouth. His gaze landed on the gold rings wrapped around her fingers, and he released his hold. Without missing a beat, he took her other hand and lowered his mouth to her knuckles, winking at me. "You ladies have a wonderful day, and I look forward to seeing you around."

I narrowed my eyes. Did he have the nerve to put his lips on my cousin's skin right in front of me? I wished he'd kissed the hand with the ring and that it had burned his perfect lips right off. Not that the book said that would happen, but I could always hope. I didn't know why I was feeling jealous. It wasn't like Archer and I were exclusive or anything. We weren't in a committed relationship, and what we had together was purely physical. But glancing at Raven looking up at him, batting her perfect long eyelashes over her almond-shaped green eyes, I realized why I was jealous.

If Archer had pulled that move with anyone else, I probably would have found it charming. But this was my cousin. The person I loathed the most in this world, the person who could make me feel an inch tall in two seconds flat. I didn't want her anywhere near him.

Snapping myself out of my thoughts, I said, "Can we go ahead and get started with this? I have other things to do today, like making you a name tag for the new role you just randomly assigned yourself." I rolled my eyes so far back I thought I saw a glimpse of my frontal lobe.

She sauntered past me and picked up a black leather satchel sitting on a pile of luggage. "Thank you, I'd appreciate that before you try your hand at more failed attempts at scoring a date with hotel guests." I wasn't given the opportunity to clap back as she directed her attention to Larry. "I'll require a room on the fourth floor, preferably one with a balcony that overlooks the woods. I'd like my things placed in the closet and not left in the middle of the room."

"Yes, ma'am," he said, walking around the counter with his shoulders slumped.

"Gemma, let's discuss the future of this hotel in the dining room."

With a tight-lipped smile, I mouthed an apology to Larry and prepared to experience hell on earth.

※　※　※

Sitting with Raven and listening to her berate me and my management skills for two hours was *not* how I wanted to spend my morning. Finally, she excused herself for her afternoon yoga session, and I breathed a sigh of relief as I trudged up to my room to grab a bite for lunch.

When I turned the corner to my suite, a familiar form stood in front of my door, leaning against the wall with his arms crossed over his chest.

"Hey, Gemma," Archer said sheepishly.

I narrowed my eyes and brushed past him as I unlocked my room and went inside, leaving the door open so he could follow. "Good afternoon, *Mr. Hyde*. I trust you've found someone to warm your bed tonight?" I asked, unable to keep the bite out of my tone.

"Did charming your cousin not put her in a good mood? I was hoping she would take it easy on you."

I stalked to the kitchen and threw open the cupboard, rattling the drinking glasses inside. I grabbed one and slammed it on the counter and moved to the refrigerator. "I don't know that it's possible to make a good time out of designing spreadsheets and setting a budget. Not to mention that she is putting up a fuss about the changes Hunter suggested for the bar."

Archer grabbed my elbow and spun me around, pinning me between his body and the counter. He dipped his chin so our eyes were level and asked, "Are you jealous that I didn't kiss *your* hand?"

"Why would I be jealous? It's not like you're my boyfriend or something," I said, reaching behind me and gripping the edge of the countertop with both hands. "You can kiss whoever you want."

He leaned in, brushing his lips against the sweet spot under my ear. "And if I want to kiss you in places other than the back of your hand?"

I melted just a bit and let him touch me. "I'd allow it, but only because my bed was pretty cold last night too," I teased, pushing his hair off his forehead.

His fingers inched up my shirt and caressed my lower stomach. "And is there a place you want me to kiss more than the others?"

My breath hitched as he popped the button of my jeans and lowered the zipper. His hand slid down and played with the waistband of my panties. I widened my stance, giving him room to take things further. After the morning I'd had, all I wanted was to get lost in the sensation of his touch, but ignoring the reason Raven was here wouldn't make things better.

"I don't think you understand how serious this is, Archer."

He bit my neck and then soothed the sting with his tongue. "I think I do, and that's why I'm trying to make it up to you."

I cupped his face and lifted it away from me. "I'm talking about Raven. Yes, she's here to satisfy my aunt's wishes, but she is preparing to take the hotel if I can't run it. All she has to do is prove that I'm incompetent, and it's hers. Do you understand what that will do to me if she gets her way? What it will do to the hotel?"

Archer sighed and moved his hand to my waist. "Hazel wouldn't have put you in charge if she didn't think you can handle it. This was her life's work, the possession she loved the most. Have a little faith in yourself, and stop thinking you are not as good as Raven."

I slid my hand into the hair at the nape of his neck and gripped it, keeping my eyes on his. "Do you really believe that? That I can make Hazel proud?" Archer was one of the only other people my aunt trusted, one of the only ones she let in to see who she really was. If he believed that, then maybe it wasn't so impossible.

"I do, Gemma. It's hard for me to understand why you're so shocked by someone believing in you. Have you never experienced that before?"

I chewed the inside of my cheek and shook my head, pain from somewhere deep within me rising to my throat. "Not really. Only with Hazel and my brother."

The smile that crossed Archer's full lips made me tingly all over. "Well, looks like that's something we have in common."

"At least he's not a colossal dick to you too," I said, standing on my toes and pressing my lips to his. "Thank you, it's nice having another person on my side."

"So, does that mean you're ready for that kiss now?"

I nudged him with my shoulder and slid out from his embrace. "As amazing as that sounds, I'm going to have to take a rain check. I have to get back to work and prove that I can run a hotel. How about tonight?"

"I promised Soren some brother time. We're having dinner together. You want to cash in tomorrow night?"

"I will *definitely* cash in tomorrow night."

And I would. After another day working with my cousin, I was going to need the distraction, but for tonight, I'd settle with substituting Archer's kisses with answers I could find only in the book.

CHAPTER TWELVE

I sat curled up on the couch with a fire crackling in the fireplace. To some, it might look like a lonely Friday night, but this was where I preferred to be if not with Archer. He'd invited me to meet him and Soren in the bar after their meal, and I'd gladly declined. I'd found more solace in deciphering the past than in dealing with a *man* whom I couldn't have a civil conversation with.

As I continued to read, I felt more and more sorry for Amity Fox. I didn't like how she ignored the twins, and her efforts to care for them were lacking. She wasn't cruel, but distant. They missed out on the love a mother shows her children. And Amity's affection for not only them but her own children was stunted as well. The situation was painful for everyone involved.

December 25, 1910
It is the twenty-fourth Christmas without my baby boys, and I have not been able to truly accept that they're gone. Some days, I sit in the lobby in front of the fireplace and wait for them to come through the door, fully grown and handsome. But they never do.

I am glad I am closer to the end of my life than the beginning. My surviving children have families of their own, and I have things not of this world to look forward to. Maybe in the next realm, I'll see Robert and Gregory again.

I wiped a tear from my cheek and fanned the hundreds of pages I'd already read. For years, Amity had used this book to journal the pain of her loss and the love she had for the twins she'd never met. Her beautiful swirling script had become flat and thin, like the weight of her words was too heavy. She was flatlining before my very eyes, and it broke my heart.

My eyelids drooped. But I kept reading. Nothing short of Archer bursting through my door and taking me to the bedroom could stop me. Toward the end of Amity's life, her anguish had morphed into apprehension. I breathed through the tight ache in my chest as I read what I suspected to be her last entry.

August 8, 1928

My days are dwindling to an end. The cancer has eaten away at my liver until there is nearly nothing left. It is time to give my dear daughter, Maybell, the Reynard and everything that comes with it. Her life has been blessed, and she has raised children of her own, and as she is past the prime of her life, I've made accommodations for Archer and Soren in the woods behind the Reynard. They behave as seven-year-old boys, and that constant energy will be too much for her to bear; Maybell has always been a fragile, sickly thing. The one-room cabin is comfortable, and they will have everything they need delivered to them by a hotel employee. It is the best I can do for them and for their new guardian.

Robert and Gregory, I love you more than you can imagine, even though I hardly had the pleasure of knowing you. I pray I will see you in the next life.

—Amity Fox

A cabin in the woods? Soren and Archer were basically living *alone* at seven years old? While I understood Amity's thought process, I didn't like the idea of them out there raising themselves at such a young age.

I reached for the steaming mug on the coffee table and took a gulp. Each entry of the book enthralled me, yet the emotional roller coaster was taking a toll. Every muscle in my arms, legs, and neck was fatigued, like I'd spent the night training for a bodybuilding competition. I was tired but refused to give in, pressing on to Maybell's first entry.

September 8, 1928

It has been a month since my mother died and left me ownership of the Reynard and guardianship of Archer and Soren. I am not one for keeping a diary; nothing appeals to me about writing down my every thought.

I am going to take care of these boys the best way I can. I am fifty and my health is declining. My father passed down his bad heart to me, and I do not have the energy to keep up with young children. Soren and Archer will have everything they need, and I will ensure that they are well-fed and have books and toys to entertain them. Once a week, I plan to visit them and teach them how to read and write as they need to be able to communicate for themselves.

Per my mother's wishes, I will fulfill my responsibility to make sure they are taken care of.

—*Maybell Fox-Jones*

Maybell was the only owner of the hotel who didn't inherit it from her aunt, and she wasn't kidding when she said she wasn't one for journaling. However, she appeared to like photographs.

On the next page began a scrapbook that brought a smile to my face. Every January until she passed, Maybell took the boys into town to have their photo taken. Archer and Soren always wore crisp brown suits with ties and somber expressions. And I enjoyed every photograph of them as kids. It rattled me to see the years increase while they remained caught in time—same faces rounded by baby fat, same height, same tiny hands.

Not only did Maybell use images to record their growth, she also left a handwritten chart. She estimated that for every six human years, the boys aged one. When I reached the end of the scrapbook, Archer and Soren had aged three years at best. She spent nineteen years with the twins before her bad heart got the better of her, and she passed the Reynard down to her great-niece, the next woman in line born with the Fox name, Betty.

Where Amity had been a victim of a cruel betrayal and Maybell had done her best, Betty Davenport was a heinous bitch who I would have loved to have slapped on sight.

January 17, 1947

This godforsaken hotel is ruining my life. Just last month I was a twenty-two-year-old housewife with a husband and two sons, living a quiet, peaceful life, when out of nowhere I am left the Reynard Hotel in my aunt Maybell's will. Not only do I have to take control of it and keep it open, but I must also play guardian to the two spectral beings that have haunted the place since it was built. As if that weren't enough to send me into a frenzy, my brother Frank and his wife were killed in an automobile accident, and I was lucky enough to be the godmother to their four-year-old daughter, Hazel. Lucky my foot. I begged my sister, Phyllis, to take the girl and let me raise our brother's older boy, but the stubborn ass refused to budge. Now, I have my husband, my sons, the hotel, the kobold boys, and my pain-in-the-neck niece to take care of.

—Betty

The entries just got worse from there. As soon as Hazel was old enough to work, Betty forced her into indentured servitude. The only good thing that came of that was Hazel's blossoming friendship with the boys. It was my great-aunt's responsibility to take them their meager daily rations and tidy their cabin, which was falling victim to the weather. Betty showed no kindness to Hazel or the twins, and her resentment for the three was displayed in the cruelest ways.

April 9, 1950
One day, those boys will learn. I caught them once again trying to sneak out of their cabin into the hotel. And Hazel was helping them. After tonight, I don't think that will happen again.

I took Hazel with me to their cabin and stripped their beds of the sheets and blankets. I sat them down and told them why they must stay where they are told, and to make sure they understood, I had them lie on their soiled mattresses while I draped a gold chain over both of their bare torsos. After making Hazel listen to their wails and the punishment she helped cause, we left them for the night. I will have her go remove the chains in the morning.

Maybe this time they will learn their lesson.

My stomach turned, and a wave of horrendous nausea swept over me. Betty was a terrible, abusive woman. No matter what dickish things my dad said to me or how complacent my mom could be, they would never treat me so heartlessly. Compared to Betty Davenport, my parents were angels sent down from God Himself.

As if on cue, my phone rang, and when I looked at the screen, my heart sank. It was my dad. If I didn't answer, he'd just text me or call me back until I gave in, so I took a deep breath and tapped the green button. "Hello?"

"Gemma," my dad said in a formal tone that had always grated on my nerves. My father insisted on speaking to me as if I were a business associate. And not a very respectable one.

"Hi, Dad. How are you?"

"A little worried. Raven called and told me about your conversation from the other morning," he said without so much as an inquiry about my well-being.

"Why are you worried?" I asked, an edge of annoyance to my tone. "There's nothing to worry about. It wasn't a big deal."

"Raven said the hotel looked a mess when she arrived, the old man working the front desk is practically senile, and you were *late* to work. What are you thinking, Gemma?"

My blood heated, and I clenched my fist against my knee. "Larry does an excellent job. The hotel is not a mess, and yes, I was late, but—"

"No excuses. This is embarrassing, and if this is how you are running things, it won't look good on the quarterly report Kevin and I plan on turning into the attorney. Get it together."

"But—"

"Have better results for me next time I call," he barked, and the line went dead.

Unable to sit still for a moment longer, I slammed the book

shut and took a ragged breath. The air in the suite was stuffy, and I felt trapped in my own skin. I needed out before the walls closed in on me.

I struggled to pull a sweater over my head, my arms weak like wet noodles. The state of my legs wasn't much better; they trembled beneath me as I rushed through the hotel and out the back door. Pushing down the roiling in my gut, I ran into the crisp fall evening. I wasn't sure where I was headed; I just knew I had to get away—from the book, my dad, Raven, from all of it.

Hazel's childhood must have been horrific. She never spoke much about her relationship with her aunt, choosing to share stories about growing up at the Reynard. I spent hours listening to her talk about climbing the trees behind the hotel and describing her favorite guests. Not once did she make me believe that her days here were anything but magical. She was the kindest soul I knew and didn't deserve an ounce of the animosity her aunt had directed at her, and neither did two young boys.

No matter how badly Soren irritated me, thinking of him and Archer living in some little shack in the woods made me ill. It didn't really matter what they were or how they got here; it wasn't right to treat a living being like that.

I felt so disconnected from the women who came before me— I'd never experienced a loss like Amity's, and for all my faults, I wasn't a heartless bitch like Betty. Even with a good chunk of the book to go, and unanswered questions, I still wasn't sure how knowing all of this about my ancestors was supposed to affect me.

The maple leaves crunched beneath my feet. The air was chilly, and my arms, even under the sleeves of my burgundy sweater, broke out into goosebumps. It was too quiet, like even the woods behind the hotel were in shock after the horrors they'd seen over the decades. The hotel and the lights that illuminated it disappeared, leaving me to navigate by nothing but the moon and stars. Trees towered over me, their branches like bony arms reaching for the sky. I couldn't tell if the rustling around me was from the leaves rattling in the breeze or hungry forest animals. I pivoted with the intention of heading back when a dim light drew my attention.

Narrowing my eyes, I crept toward the yellow orb. My heart banged against my chest and my brain screamed at me to turn around. I was the stupid girl in every scary movie who ended up hacked to pieces by a guy wearing a flesh mask.

The trees thinned, giving way to a clearing, and my racing heart fell to my feet. A dilapidated wooden structure that could barely pass for a shed sat in the center. Rotting planks of wood made up the sad excuse for walls, and the tin roof was rusted. A lantern sat on the grass, lighting a well-worn path to the front door. And sitting on the steps with his elbows resting on his knees was Soren.

"I've been waiting for you," he said.

"Wha-what do you mean?"

"I knew you'd find it eventually when you started reading the to—the journal. Betty took so much pride in remodeling our lovely cabin in the woods. I've never read her entries, but I'm sure she described it with fantastic precision. She was sadistic like that," Soren said, his electric gaze locked on mine.

"She did, and she was. Aren't you supposed to be at dinner with Archer?"

Something flashed over Soren's features, but it was gone in an instant. "It's way past dinnertime," he said with a wan smile.

"Right."

"I have to admit that I was starting to give up on you. You come off as the type that won't comply just to prove a point."

"You might be right about that, but my curiosity got the better of me. And once I dove in, I couldn't stop."

"And? What did you discover?" he asked, picking at a dead blade of grass near his foot.

Something about the way he was sitting tugged at my heartstrings; maybe it was just because he was on the front step of this shack where he'd suffered abuse at the hands of my great-great-aunt, but the pity I felt for him in that moment superseded the loathing.

"Do you mind if I sit down?" I asked.

He shrugged and gestured to the space next to him. "Be my guest. You own it."

The last thing I wanted was to stake claim to this shitty hut, but I did want to know what he was thinking. I dropped to my butt on the narrow wooden step, keeping my distance as much as possible. "How did you know I'd come out here tonight? Are you psychic too?"

A small smile played at his lips, but the worry line between his brows didn't fade. "No. I come out here every night," he admitted, looking up through the trees at the moon hanging low in the sky.

"Why?"

He shrugged, continuing to pick at the blade of grass. "To remind myself what Hazel did for me and Archer. That as soon as she could, she got us out of this fucking shack. Treated us like we were worth something. No one loved us the way she did."

My heart squeezed in my chest, and I swallowed over the lump in my throat. That sounded just like Hazel. She had a way of taking the most miserable situation and turning it into something joyful.

"I'm sorry."

"For what?" he asked, his head snapping toward me in surprise.

"Not for anything *I've* done," I clarified, holding up my hands. "For the way Betty treated you and Archer. There was no excuse for that."

Soren rubbed the side of his face, staring into the woods. "Pain has a way of making us do unspeakable things. I certainly had my moments with her. I tried my damnedest to make her pay, but it did little to heal the damage." He turned to me and asked, "How far did you get?"

"Just to Betty's entries. I read some of them, but then I couldn't stomach another syllable. She was horrible not only to you guys, but to Hazel too. I loved Hazel with every piece of my heart, and the thought of the person she was supposed to count on as a parent figure loathing her very existence makes me physically ill." I clutched my stomach, wrapping my arms around my waist, the roiling rising once more. "No wonder Hazel built you your own room, treated you like her own. She knew the hell you'd gone through, and what it was like to have a guardian who hates you. She'd never want anyone to feel that pain, and God knows she did her best to shield me from it too." I took a deep breath and shook my head, blinking away the tears forming at the corners of my eyes. "Sorry, I get a little bit passionate when it comes to the people I love."

"I know the feeling. Besides my brother, Hazel was the only other person I deeply cared for. She was the best of us."

She was the best of us—the very best. A traitorous tear fell down my cheek, and I brushed it away, hoping Soren didn't notice. Whatever moment we were having here, I didn't want him to see me cry. "She really was. And now here I am, on the verge of 'fucking everything up,'" I quoted with a side-glance at him. "That's the part I still don't understand. It was disturbing to read about my family's neglectful and abusive nature, but that hardly changes my entire life. I also don't understand why I need to stay away from Archer, which, by the way, I still don't plan on doing. If anything, reading those entries only made me care about him more."

"That's not surprising, and"—the corner of his mouth quirked up—"very Hazel of you. As far as the answers go, you have two choices: keep reading or ask Archer. I have a feeling one will be more forthcoming than the other."

I opened my mouth to ask him to explain, but the edges of my vision went blurry, and my neck couldn't hold the weight of my head. My entire body tipped to the side, my head landing on Soren's shoulder.

"Gemma? Are you okay?"

His voice startled me, and the mist clouding my mind dissipated. "Ye-yeah, I'm fine." I sat up and continued talking as if nothing had happened. "I've read almost half of the book, like you've asked me to, and I just want you to tell me one thing. The kobold, that's what Amity called your—" I stopped, chewing on my bottom lip. Did Soren and Archer know the entire story of how they came to be at the Reynard? That their own mother left them? If not, I sure as hell didn't want to be the one to spill that tea. I took a second to gather my thoughts and continued, "That's what Amity called your people. Is that what you are?"

"That's what we've been told. It was only under Hazel's watch that we were allowed to research our people. This"—he gestured to his body—"isn't our original form. Hence, we age differently. Among other things."

"Like disappearing."

"We don't really disappear; we shrink and fly fast."

"You *fly*?"

His lips pulled into a lopsided smile. "We fly *really* fast. And when we are emotionally charged, we glow."

I raked my fingers through my hair and blew out a breath that rattled my lips. "This is crazy. I've heard of elves, goblins, nymphs, fairies, werewolves, imps, whatever, but I had never heard of a kobold, and when I researched it, what I found looked nothing like you two."

Soren flashed me a rare grin. "That's the myth; we're the reality. The legends about my people are few, mostly found in small villages in western Europe. Kobolds are a type of sprite known for playing pranks, causing mischief, but most notably, switching their young with human children. It's said that their realm is inhabited by creatures that crave the taste of newborn kobolds, so to protect them, they leave them here. But those are just stories. Archer and I don't remember anything about the kobold realm or anyone who lives there. Our information comes from what little Hazel knew and what we could find on the internet, which obviously isn't always accurate."

"Well, no one in the book went into even that much detail, so thank you for filling in the blanks. One more question, and don't tell me to read the journal, because the answer won't be in there. What is it that you have against Archer?"

"Nothing. I love him with every fiber of my being." He shook his head. "It's just that you need the entire story, Gemma. I don't care how you get it. And just because you know what we are now doesn't mean you have all the information you need."

"I don't understand, Soren. Why can't *you* just tell me, if it's so damn important?"

He pursed his lips, causing his jaw to tick. "Because Hazel deserves to tell you in her own words. I respect her too much to take that from her."

God, I wanted to be like my aunt. I wanted the adoration, her bravery, her self-confidence, but I was a shadow of the woman she was. And I wasn't the only one who knew it.

Standing up, I brushed the dirt off my jeans and turned to face him. "So, this is it. You drop confusing hints about everything, hate me, and I pretend not to care?"

It could have been a play of the lantern light, but I could have sworn he flinched, until his words confirmed otherwise. "If that's what it takes, then yes." He jerked his chin toward the hotel looming in the distance. "Good night, Gemma."

"Remember, Soren, there's a reason Hazel wanted me to know all this and to take care of the hotel."

"Let me know what it is when you figure it out."

"Good night, Soren." I rolled my eyes and was about to pivot to head back the way I came. Nausea twirled within me, gathering the contents of my stomach into a deadly wave that traveled up my throat. I doubled over and vomited onto the toes of Soren's black leather boots.

Soren jumped back, thrusting a hand out to steady me, but I slid through his grip. My palms and knees hit the ground, narrowly missing the mess I'd just made, knocking the breath from my lungs. I gasped, pushing through my burning airway to breathe. The edges of my vision blurred, and my thoughts were a gooey, chaotic mess before it all went dark.

CHAPTER THIRTEEN

"What did you do to her?"

"Nothing, asshole. She passed out and her heart rate is low."

As the conversation between two familiar male voices carried on around me, I fought to open my eyes. The world swayed back and forth, and something firm pressed into the backs of my knees, bending them so they swung with the motion. My cheek rested against soft, warm fabric, and a steady beat thumped against my ear. Someone was carrying me.

I urged my eyes to open again, but my eyelids weren't cooperating; it felt like I had five-pound weights lying on top of them.

"Okay, what did you say to her?" Archer asked.

"Nothing but the truth."

"You shouldn't have sprung this all on her. Let her figure things out on her own, Soren. Why the fuck do you feel so compelled to meddle with everything?"

"She is figuring out things on her own. Nothing I said would have upset her enough to make her pass out. Stop jumping to conclusions."

The muscles against my cheek flexed, and I was lowered onto a plush cushion. Relief washed over me, my stomach grateful that the swaying had stopped.

"I think we should get her brother; she might need to see a doctor."

I battled against the grogginess, scrambling to stop them before they made a big deal about all of this. I had enough to worry about without fending off my brother's questions. Hunter would demand answers not only about what happened, but about why two strangers were taking care of me. It was best if my episode stayed between the three of us.

"Stop," I croaked, holding my head and prying open one eye.

Archer and Soren stood next to the couch. Their matching faces were inches apart, blue and purple battling for dominance. The Hyde brothers were seconds from coming to blows in my living room. Soren was the first to look away, and they dropped their gazes to me.

I gripped the back of the couch and pulled myself upright. "Don't fight in my home; I don't want to clean up after you Neanderthals."

Archer eased down next to me and pulled me into his side. "How are you feeling?"

"I'm fine," I said through chattering teeth, snuggling closer to his chest.

Soren grabbed Hazel's favorite hideous afghan, the one I'd been curled up with earlier, and handed it to Archer. While he wrapped me up, his brother turned to the abandoned book on the chair and ran his fingertips over the lock. "How much of this did you read tonight, Gemma?"

"I don't know. A lot. I told you, I was on a roll. I would have tried to finish it tonight, but Betty made me want to throw up." My skin heated, and I closed my eyes before saying, "Which, I did. Sorry you had to see that."

"You don't need to apologize," he mumbled, stroking the worn leather like it was something precious.

Archer shifted and furrowed his brow. "Why are you acting so weird about a book?"

"Because Gemma said there wasn't anything written in it at first."

"I found someone to help me understand how it worked. It turns out I was reading it wrong." Both brothers cocked a brow, and I realized how stupid it sounded out loud. Yep, good ole Gemma couldn't even figure out how to read a book.

My cheeks burned as I quietly confessed, "I like to read the end of a book first and see if it's worth my time before I start it."

Archer laughed and pulled me closer to his side. "My kind of girl; she goes straight for the good stuff."

"Yeah, I hate a sad ending. I want to know that everything the characters go through is worth it."

"Why am I not surprised to learn that you would rush things?" Soren asked flatly.

I curled my lip and shook my head. "*Anyway*, I flipped to the end of the book and made my way forward, as usual, and it was blank. Then one night, while I was walking around town, I found this old friend of Hazel's, and she explained that it was important with magic to do things in the right order. When I started from the first page, the words appeared." I wrapped my hand around Archer's and placed our entwined fingers in my lap. "I know that sounds crazy, but it's the truth."

"No crazier than the past hundred and forty years in this hotel," Archer said with a gentle squeeze.

Soren squatted in front of the book and opened the cover. "Fuck!" He snatched his hand back, shaking it like he was trying to put out a flame. "It's the same spell that keeps us on the property."

"It couldn't have hurt that bad," Archer snickered.

Soren sneered at his brother and carefully lifted the book. He set it on my lap and said, "Open it."

"Is it going to . . ."

"It won't hurt you unless you take it from the property. The purpose of the book is for you to learn from it while you're at the Reynard."

I gingerly slipped my index finger under the corner and lifted it open with no problem. The title page looked as it did when I first read it.

"There's nothing written in it," Archer said.

"Yes, there—"

Archer moved to touch the page with his finger, and the book buzzed under my hands like a cell phone. Just like his brother, he drew back as if he'd been burned. "Son of a bitch, it is the same spell, just not as painful."

Soren shook his head. "Why would you do that after you saw what it did to me?"

The brother next to me shrugged his shoulders. "Because you're kind of a pussy, and I wanted to see if maybe that was the issue."

"You're such a dickhead." Soren turned his attention to me. "Gemma, do you see something on the page?"

"Yes," I said, finding it hard to believe that they couldn't see what I so clearly could. It was the first time in my life where I could recall having one up on someone. And it felt good.

"It's spellbound," Soren said.

"Like cursed?"

"Not necessarily, but I'm guessing only the owner of the Reynard can read it, and that magic requires energy in order to work."

"You think it's draining her?" Archer asked.

Soren shrugged one shoulder. "Think about it. How long can

you be in your kobold form? It's paranormal to this dimension, so it requires more energy to maintain it. The magic placed on the journal isn't any different."

"Wait, so you're saying that reading this is what made me get sick and pass out?" I asked, lifting the book toward him with both hands. He nodded and took one step back as if he were frightened of the open pages.

Archer's arm tightened around me. "Is it even safe for her to read?"

"I think so, but there can't be any more binge-reading. You need to be careful, Gemma."

"Maybe you need to lay off the reading for a bit and occupy your time with something a little more fun," Archer hissed in my ear, sending a quiver down my spine.

"Or she could make sure she understands everything that her ancestors thought was important enough to pass down," Soren countered, heading toward the door.

"Or *maybe* she could just continue to steer clear of people who enjoy brooding and having a stick up their ass," Archer retorted.

Soren whirled around. "Fuck off."

"Don't you worry about my fucking, brother."

"I couldn't care less about your sexual escapades, Archer."

The men glared at each other with jaws flexing and fingers balled into fists. The tension between them was thick, suffocating. At any moment, one of them was going to snap, and I feared my aunt's antique furniture was going to fall victim to their fury.

I released Archer and stood on wobbling legs, hoping my fragile state would stop them from pummeling each other.

"Whoa, Gem, what are you doing?" Archer said, immediately sitting up and gripping my hips. "You need to sit down."

"You guys are stressing me out with your bickering. I don't feel well as it is; I just want to go to bed and sleep for twenty-four hours." I walked toward my bedroom, planning to just leave them to duke it out and damn the consequences, but I lost my balance and nearly fell to my knees.

Archer sprang to his feet to catch me and held me close to his chest, glaring over my head at Soren. "See? Look what you did, worrying the hell out of her over that damn book, and now she can't even walk straight."

Soren rolled his eyes. "Oh for fuck's sake, Archer. She wasn't feeling well before that. I had nothing to do with it. Perhaps she's nauseous from your constant doting. I get a fucking toothache just—"

"Guys. Please. Just go," I said, attempting to break free of Archer's grasp.

Soren spoke up and walked back to the door. "I'll go, but let your annoying lover stay with you. You're still dizzy, and you'll end up tumbling ass over head trying to walk around by yourself."

I was stunned by Soren's concern. He cared enough to want me to be safe, and that felt like a change after he had basically told me that we were enemies. Nothing about this felt hostile—his attention to detail about the book, his warning to take it easy reading it, and his clear animosity toward his brother where I was concerned. Was he jealous that I'd connected with Archer first?

Squeezing my eyes shut, I shook my head. This was not the time to inflate my ego because I had a fleeting thought about being the third point of a brother love triangle. As hot as the possibilities were.

"No, I just want to be alone. Please, I promise I'm fine," I said, dragging Archer toward the door and flinging it open.

I waved both of them into the hall, Archer still protesting even as I leaned against the doorway, feeling my strength wane again.

"Wow, Gemma. It's a little late to be entertaining male visitors, don't you think?"

My cousin's eyes swept over the three of us, Soren's hair mussed from the raking of his fingers, Archer's shirt rumpled from cuddling me on the couch, and me looking like I was about to pass the fuck out.

"Raven," I said, meeting her disparaging gaze without hesitation.

"Looks like the three of you had quite an evening," she said, her attention locking on Archer for a second too long. "I'm surprised your guests are fully dressed as you push them out of your room, Gemma. I'm sure most would be tripping over their pants as they stumble down the hall."

I didn't even bother to correct her; Raven was going to believe whatever she wanted about me, and no one could change her mind.

Archer clicked his tongue and shifted closer to me. "Actually, we were just starting our pregame; would you care to join us? I'm sure my brother would be happy to lick your cu—"

"I have standards," Soren cut in. "The beautiful but bitter type always leaves a sour taste on my tongue."

"Come now, there is something to be said for a little sour with the sweet," Archer said.

Raven's full lips stretched to a smile. She was eating it up, and I didn't blame her. Even if the boys were only trying to get a reaction out of her, they were paying her attention. That was what she thrived on—the lingering stares and not-so-subtle hints that she was beautiful. Everything they were saying was feeding into her already inflated ego.

I bit down on my lip and closed my eyes, taking several deep breaths. "Should I leave the three of you to it? I can grab some pillows, have Larry bring up a cot." I glared at my cousin. "Does your species self-lubricate, or should I have him bring some coconut oil?"

Soren and Archer snorted and rubbed the backs of their necks in a casual attempt to hide their faces. I would have laughed at their mirroring mannerisms if Raven hadn't sucked all the joy out of my life.

Soren cleared his throat and took a step forward. "I appreciate the offer, Gem. But I have an adverse reaction to coconut oil. And unlike some"—he glared at Archer—"I don't like mixing my spices; it makes it difficult to savor the natural taste."

Archer brushed his fingers over the back of my hand. "I've never cared for the bland, and that's why I find myself in better company than you. You need to learn to indulge in the finer things, brother. But I suppose that's a lesson for another time."

"I'll pass on acquiring your adventurous taste." Soren gave me a curt nod and strolled past Raven without so much as batting an eye.

"Gemma, it's always a pleasure." Archer kissed my cheek. "Raven, I'm sure I will see you again." He squeezed her shoulder as he passed and followed his brother around the corner.

I waited until his footsteps faded and said to my cousin. "Have a good night, Raven. We have a lot of work to do tomorrow, so I suggest you get some rest."

She pursed her lips and cocked her head to the side in that condescending way that only she has mastered. "Speaking of a lot of work, you do realize you have two weeks until Halloween, right? I hope you've started planning. I'd hate to see the hotel set a precedent proving that it's floundering without Hazel. We could lose a lot of money in the future if one of our biggest nights is a flop."

Shit. Between getting used to Raven being here, the journal, and Archer, I had totally spaced on Halloween. And she was right; it was the most lucrative time for us. It was also Hazel's favorite day aside from Winter Spirits. The first one without her needed to be epic.

"Of course I have. What do you think I've been doing? This Halloween is going to be the best this town has ever seen," I said, hoping my confidence was believable.

Raven regarded me with suspicion. "Right. I look forward to seeing your plans on paper tomorrow." And with that, she flounced away toward her room, leaving me in the state of irritation that only she could conjure.

I had to make Halloween the absolute best it had ever been. This was my gift from Hazel, my time to shine. It was my turn to make my mark on the Reynard, earn the respect of my family, and prove to everyone that I was the Fox woman for this job.

CHAPTER FOURTEEN

The morning after I barfed on Soren's designer shoes, I met with Raven as planned. We sat across from each other in the hotel dining room, my hands folded on top of a notebook. Written on the pages inside was nothing more than a sad heading—*Halloween at the Reynard*—and random pen marks. I fought to stay up all night and plan the festivities, my heavy eyelids drooping until I jerked awake to try again, but the book had drained my energy. Not to mention, the exchange in the hallway between my cousin and the Hyde brothers hadn't helped.

I didn't bother coming up with excuses for the lack of planning; Raven knew I'd forgotten. She forced me to sit with her for over two hours while she picked apart every idea I had. Her least favorite was inviting Wanda Willow to do a séance. Raven didn't take kindly to tampering with spirits, fearing we would unleash the wrath of the *ghosts* who had terrorized her as a child. For a woman who wanted to take my "haunted hotel" from me, she was very against the idea of what she termed "fraternizing with the occult." But once I pointed out that we could charge guests to participate in the event, her desire to make more money won out. She gave in and agreed that Wanda was one of my "better ideas." I took that and ran with it; I called a couple of local tarot-card readers, palm readers, and fortune-tellers complete with crystal balls.

With a rock-solid plan for Halloween night in place, Raven left me alone, turning her attention to the cleaning staff. She was hell-bent on teaching them to fold the towels and the ends of the toilet paper into origami-like designs. "It's the little touches that will make guests feel like they've had a luxurious experience and come back for more," she had told them. For someone who knew so much about hotel management, she seemed to overlook the Reynard's main selling point. Unless she was slowly attempting to erase it.

The rest of my day was spent in the hotel lobby, greeting guests and answering questions about the hotel's history. I hoped engaging with others would distract me from thoughts of the journal, but it lingered in the back of my mind. It didn't matter that it was eating my energy to fuel the magic necessary to reveal the writing inside; I needed to know more.

Soren had clearly told me everything he was willing to share, even as he insinuated that there was some big secret, some monumental thing I was on the verge of fucking up. That left Archer. I hadn't pressed him for any details past that night when I'd drunkenly asked him what a kobold was. If I was being honest, this had more to do with my libido than a lack of curiosity. Every time we got together, I intended to gather more information, but we always ended up groping in an alcove or getting tangled on my couch. What could I do? His hands and kisses were distracting! But I was determined to make tonight different. I *would* get answers.

At ten o'clock, Larry and I were counting the register and making sure all customer requests had been fulfilled when Archer peeked out from behind one of the columns in the lobby.

I grinned and discreetly wiggled my fingers in a wave, mouthing, *Almost done.*

I wasn't sure why the twins felt it necessary to hide from the staff. Larry and Skye were both very in tune with everything going on in the hotel. Skye would regale bar patrons with every sighting for the past week, and Larry could recall occurrences from decades ago. Plus, Larry was the one who bought and delivered their monthly allowances in the form of gift cards to their mail cubby in the back office. It wasn't like either Larry or Skye had any qualms about their existence. Another question I was eager to get the answers to tonight.

"Any big plans this evening, Gemma?" Larry asked as we stepped out from behind the desk, startling me from my daydreams about just what Archer and I could do after he gave me all the answers I was seeking.

My cheeks flushed and I said, "Oh not much, just going to relax in my room, maybe—"

"Have a friend over?"

I glanced at him, finding an unmistakable twinkle in his blue eyes that told me ole Larry knew more than he let on.

"Well, I guess you never know," I said with a smile that turned up one corner of my mouth as I locked the security door leading behind the desk. "Have a good one, Larry." When he was out the door, I sauntered over to meet Archer behind the column. "Fancy meeting you here. Did you get off creep patrol early?" He—or Soren, I wasn't sure which—had wandered the passages and knocked on the walls all afternoon. I'd been especially entertained when a group of thirty-odd bikers hightailed it out of the lobby like Satan himself was chasing them.

"Creep patrol? Is that what you're calling it now?"

"Isn't that what you spend your days and nights doing?"

"I'm restricted to seven acres of land, and most of that is trees; I have to entertain myself somehow. Thankfully, I came up with a better way to spend tonight." He leaned in and brushed his lips against mine. "You've been sulking around here all day. What's bothering you?"

"Raven just got under my skin again today while we were planning for Halloween, that's all."

"She does come off as a bit evil." A mischievous grin spread across his handsome face. "You should let me put some different wicked thoughts in your head."

A delicious shiver traveled up my spine, and I captured his bottom lip between my teeth. "I would like that. A lot."

"You pick the room, and I'll make it happen."

I tapped my fingers on my chin and hummed. "Let's see." An extremely naughty thought entered my head, and before I could stop myself, I held my finger to his lips and said, "Be right back."

Slipping back behind the desk, I snatched a key from its hook and tugged him up the spiral staircase to the third floor. When we reached the door to the billiards room, I peeked in. A middle-aged couple was playing at the pool table. I held up a finger, cautioning Archer to stay where he was and stepped inside.

"Excuse me, good evening, folks," I said in my best customer service voice. "I hate to ask you to do this, but I need you to exit the room; we're spraying for bugs." The woman's hot-pink lips curled, her nose crinkling, but I held up a hand. "Don't worry. This is a preventative measure. It's the reason you'll never see a bug in our lovely hotel."

The man nodded, his thinning gray hair bouncing against his forehead, and replaced the cue stick. "No worries," he said and took his companion's hand. "I'm sure we can find something fun to do in our room."

They brushed past me, her giggles echoing in the hall.

"Care to join me for a nightcap?"

I jumped, not expecting to find Archer sitting on a stool at the mini bar. He must have done the disappearing act—shrinking act—turning-into-a-kobold act. Now that I understood what was happening, I wanted to witness it. How big was he exactly? Did he glow this time? And how long had he been sitting at the bar waiting for me to notice him? The questions kept piling up.

I weaved my way through the four cherry-wood pool tables, running my fingers over the unusual dusty-rose felt tops as I passed. I always loved this room. It made me feel like a grown-up to pretend that I knew how to play pool and was sipping whiskey instead of Coca-Cola. I'd spent hours in here with whoever was willing to play with me.

"I'll make the drinks and you set up the game?" I offered, handing him the ball rack from under the table.

"Deal."

I removed two glasses from the overhead rack and unlocked the liquor cabinet. While I poured us both a Jack and Coke, Archer set up the table to play eight-ball. His jeans hugged his round ass, and his biceps nearly bulged out of his slim-fit jade T-shirt. He was exquisite, and I could easily be content staring at him all night.

But gawking at him would have to wait; I had questions to ask.

Walking to him, I held out the drink and leaned against the pool table. "Do you know what would really get my mind off my terrible day? If I got some more answers about you and the hotel."

He brought the glass to his lips and eyed me over the rim. "Is that so?"

"It is. I'd keep them simple to start."

Archer took a second to size me up, his gaze lazily traveling over my body. A tinge of irritation knotted in my stomach. Magic books and cryptic answers weren't satisfying; I was tired of jumping through hoops. But he wasn't going to make this easy. I needed him to let his guard down before I pressed him for what I really wanted to know.

"I don't know if you've earned any answers yet," he said playfully. "Let's play a game of pool first."

Progress. "All right. You should break. It's not my strong point," I said, offering him the semblance of control before I swooped in.

With a nod, Archer removed a cue stick from the wall. He stretched his tall frame over the table, his eyes trained on the cue ball and his muscles coiled. With a crack, the multicolored balls scattered around the surface, two of them dropping into pockets.

"Impressive break, Mr. Hyde."

He moved next to me and leaned in again. "Solids," he called, taking another shot and missing. With a wide grin, he stepped back. "I figured you should have a go before I clear the table."

"How generous of you."

I positioned myself with the stick over my outstretched hand as a guide. My elbow bent back and stopped, ramming into a hard body. Archer bent over me, mimicking my stance. He ran his hands over mine, and his warm breath brushed the shell of my ear.

I glanced over my shoulder. "What are you doing?"

"I thought I could give you a few pointers to up your game against me."

I raised an eyebrow, my lips turning up into a smirk. "Oh, is that right? Well, why don't you let me show you what you're working with so you know how to proceed?"

With a nod, he stepped back and held his arm to the side. "I'm watching."

I repositioned myself, fingertips steady against the soft felt. Drawing the cue back through my steepled fingers, I released it, slamming the end against the cue ball and sending it crashing into a cluster at the end of the table, sinking two stripes into pockets on opposite ends.

With a smug glint in my eyes, I said, "Now, what did you want to show me?"

He stepped behind me again, wrapping his arms around my waist. "A lot of things, none of which have to do with pool."

"I can tell." I wiggled my ass over the taut fabric between his legs.

"We should up the wager and make this fun for all involved."

"Strip pool? It sounds a little juvenile, don't you think?"

"The things it will lead to are far from childish," he whispered, dragging his mouth up the side of my neck.

I stepped out of his embrace and my body immediately missed his touch. My tense muscles and skin yearned for the stroke of his fingers or a swipe of his tongue. He could alleviate the day's stress and make me feel good again. But my brain knew better and didn't release its hold. I needed long-term solutions, not a temporary fix.

"Tempting," I said, moving around the table and placing it between us. "I think you're right; we should up the ante. Unless you think you can't beat me."

Archer narrowed his gaze and licked his lips. "I've got over a hundred years on you. I'm confident in my skills."

"How about for every ball we sink, we get to ask the other a question? And you have to answer truthfully. If your skills are so good, you'll sink all the balls before I even get a chance to ask, right?" I said, holding his amethyst stare with mine.

"Take your shot and pray you sink it."

I squared my shoulders and aimed for a ball sitting on the edge of the bottom left pocket. With a gentle hand, I knocked the cue ball toward it and hit true. Without hesitation I asked, "Why do you and Soren keep your distance from the staff? They know you're here and have a hunch that you aren't ghosts."

"I thought you were going to take it easy on me."

"I'm not wasting my chance for real answers."

Archer lifted his drink and downed what was left. He stalled by wiping the back of his hand over his mouth and placing his cue stick on top of one of the high-topped tables. "We kept our distance for the sake of the hotel and Hazel. If the staff became friendly, we risked them letting their guard down. Their stories about encounters wouldn't be as convincing, and they would want to carry on conversations with us. Not to mention that they would talk to others about their time working here when they were no longer employed. It would ruin the legends we created. Unlike the other Fox women, Hazel didn't have a husband to support her. This was her only income. If the hotel went under, she would be homeless and hungry, and we would be confined to a decaying building. So, we limit our interactions to Larry, and those are mostly simple exchanges, nothing substantial."

That actually made sense. Not nearly as juicy of an answer as I'd been hoping for, but it was sincere. "Okay, fair enough." I lifted my cue, positioned it between my fingers, and shot again. But this time, the ball veered too far to the right, and I missed. "Shit," I grumbled, looking up at him. "Your turn."

Archer grinned, took aim, and sank a solid ball before turning to me. "How old were you the first time you had sex?"

My cheeks flushed, and I cleared my throat. "Damn, bringing

out the big guns on your first question. Would you believe me if I told you I was a virgin?"

"No way, beautiful. Not after that blow job the other night."

"Touché. I was sixteen. The first boy I ever really loved."

"Even better for me. I enjoy the know-how of an experienced woman in bed." He moved around the table, searching for his next shot.

I needed to get back in control of the game so I could get to my real question. Moving into his line of sight, I slid down the zipper on my jacket as soon as he took aim, revealing a thin white cami with a red push-up bra underneath. "It is so *hot* in here," I said a little too loudly.

Archer's eyes darted in my direction and the stick slid through his fingers. The tip nicked the cue ball and it rolled like it was on a casual stroll over the felt, waving to each ball as it passed.

"Oh, now you're going to play dirty?" He smiled and reached for my glass, taking a long sip. "It was worth it for me, though."

I winked and stepped up to the table, surveying my best chance to sink a striped ball. "I won't miss this one," I promised, lining up the shot and sinking the 9-ball.

"Get on with it."

I moved in front of him and leaned against the table, lifting my glass to my lips. "I'll play nice. This time. How old were you when you first had sex?"

"In human years?"

I laughed. "Yes."

"Eighty-nine. But to be fair, I had the body and mentality of what equates to a fifteen-year-old human boy."

"Damn, you had to have broken a record for world's oldest virgin," I joked, and when he pretended to lunge at me, I held up my hands and said, "Kidding, kidding. Now let me sink another ball so we can get back to the juicier questions." The ball rolled in just as I wanted. "Do you think Soren doesn't like me and wants me to leave?"

Of all the questions that boggled my brain, that was the one I chose? I could have asked what life-changing information he thought was in the journal, or if he was invested in what we had going on. But I chose to talk about his brother.

Archer fell silent and paced the length of the table. "No, he doesn't want you to leave. I think my brother has experienced his fair share of heartache, and his disagreeable attitude is a defense mechanism."

I nodded, raised the cue, and sank another shot. "Why is he so insistent that I stay away from you—from both of you?"

"Remind me again why we aren't playing strip pool?" I raised an eyebrow in warning, and he threw up his hands. "I don't know, Gemma. You're an outsider, and he doesn't trust you. Or maybe he doesn't trust us around you."

"Why wouldn't he trust you around me?"

His expression darkened, and he crossed his arms over his chest. "What is that supposed to mean? Have I ever given you a reason to question my motives?"

"No, you haven't. But you have to agree that it's odd that a complete stranger went out of his way to tell me to stay away from you. If you're right and he doesn't actually loathe me, why would he be pushing that if it weren't true?" I blew out a breath and put my palms on his cheeks. "I am clearly missing a vital piece of the puzzle here, and since it involves me, I have the right to know everything. Especially if you two are hiding something that could cost me this hotel."

"I wish I could tell you that I understand my brother's motives, but I don't." He gripped my hips and pulled me closer. "All I know is that I'm happy being with you. And it's been a long time since I felt this way."

A nagging voice in the back of my head didn't believe him. It could very well have been the part of me that feared the complication and commitment of a relationship. The part that didn't want to fully open up because if I did, he'd just be another person I disappointed.

However, my intuition wouldn't relent. It didn't agree that this was my normal fear of commitment. Archer knew far more about Soren's objections than he was letting on. Before I could say anything, he lifted his hand to the back of his collar and pulled his shirt over his head, letting it drop to the floor. It was hard not to stare at the way his jeans sat low on his hips and the dusting of hair below his navel that disappeared into the waistband. Despite my growing doubts, just seeing him half-naked had me squeezing my thighs together.

The sound of longing from low in my throat was involuntary, and I ran my fingertips over the chiseled muscles. "The sight of you never gets old," I admitted, lifting my gaze to his and meeting violet flame.

Archer eased his hand under the hem of my cami, dragging it up my torso with each sweep of his wandering fingers. My heart sped up, skin rising with goosebumps, and his breath against my ear made me weak in the knees. Knowing he was withholding information from me made me nervous, but before I could call him on it, he was pulling the shirt over my head. He licked his lips and reached for the strap of my bra, sliding it down my arm. His fingers worked their way back up, over my shoulders, and across my collarbone until they brushed along the skin just above the cup of my bra. "I want to take all of this off and lay you out on top of this table."

The tone of his voice said it all—he wanted more from me tonight. He wanted *everything*. And I couldn't give it to him. Not like this. Not when a small part of me didn't trust him.

I took a step back. "I'm not ready, Archer."

The flame in his eyes dimmed for a moment as he said, "I don't want to do anything you don't want to do. If you need some space—"

"I'm not looking for space from you. This—the hotel, Raven showing up, your brother—it's a lot, and I'm doing my best to wrap my head around it. You're my one reprieve from it all, and I don't want to lose you."

Archer pulled me into his arms, his warm skin melting mine until every inch of me was pressed to him. I breathed him in, citrus and juniper, and exhaled the stress that plagued me. Even my doubts about him slid to the dark corners of my mind. I couldn't give Archer up, not when he was the only one holding me together.

CHAPTER FIFTEEN

Archer pulled me against him on the couch, and with a giggle, I gripped his hands and tugged him to his feet. "You have to go. Hunter is coming over to review the final plans for the bar."

"I'm starting to feel like your dirty little secret. The stunning man you keep hidden under your bed," he said, wiggling his eyebrows.

It wasn't my intention to keep him hidden; he did that well enough on his own. And as far as my bed went, I hadn't invited him to so much as sit on the edge of it since that night in the billiards room. I liked things the way they were. Heavy petting and playful exchanges suited me just fine for the moment.

"I'm not hiding you; I just don't want to endure my older brother's relentless teasing. And he's so nosy; he's going to ask a hundred questions, and I just can't deal today."

"Come on, Gem. It's not that big of a deal. Hunter's here all the time; I might as well meet him. I won't embarrass you, I swear." He held up his pinky as a sign of the ultimate promise.

His eyes were so bright and his expression so hopeful that when Hunter knocked at the door in the next breath, I couldn't bear to ask him to do the shrinking thing.

"Fine," I hissed, hooking my pinky with his and tugging on it, bringing our faces within an inch of each other. "But do not say anything weird. Hunter doesn't believe in anything he can't scientifically explain."

"Scout's honor," he said with a solemn smile, holding up two fingers and pressing them to my lips.

I nipped at them and snorted as I crossed the room to the door. "I have a feeling you were not a Boy Scout." He winked in response and his smile morphed into a smirk. I rolled my eyes and flung the door open. "Good morning, Hunt," I said, grinning at the familiar pink box in his hand. "Are those chocolate cream–filled doughnuts?" My stomach growled at the thought of the melt-in-your-mouth mousse.

"Yes, ma'am, from Put a Spell on You. I know it's your favorite bakery, and they actually weren't packed this morning." Hunter set the box on the counter before his eyes landed on Archer standing on the other side of the kitchen, getting a bottle of water out of the fridge. "Oh, you have company," he said, and the dip of his eyebrows told me he was about to tease me. I tried to cut him off before he could start. "Hunter, this is Archer, my . . ." I searched for the best label to put on us, but in the end chose the lamest one possible. "My friend. Archer, this is my brother Hunter."

Archer held out his hand. "It's nice to finally meet you. I feel like I practically know your sleeping habits."

I shot Archer a wide-eyed glare over my brother's shoulder and mouthed, *Behave.*

Hunter shook his hand. "Funny, I didn't even know you existed until this moment."

"I hear that all the time."

I clapped my hands and stepped between them, snatching

a pastry from the box. "Everyone, take a doughnut." I turned to Archer. "These are the best doughnuts in the whole world; when I was little—"

"Gem." Hunter snapped his fingers in front of my face. "Focus. You're already off track, and we haven't even started yet," he said, gesturing to the tube of papers he'd brought in with him, motioning for me to follow him to the couch. He unrolled the parchment and pushed the centerpiece to the edge of the coffee table. He reached for the gilded book, and his eyebrows dipped. "What's this?"

"Nothing, it's just a book I found in the study. History of the hotel and stuff like that."

"Sounds like a snooze fest." I breathed a sigh of relief as he set it on the corner of the plans with a *thunk*. I didn't want to explain why it might send him into flames if he tried to open it. "We'll use it as a paperweight."

"That's the most use that book has ever been," Archer mumbled, looming over us and biting into a glazed doughnut.

"I'm sure that could be said for half the junk in this suite. Our aunt was clearly sentimental and had an affinity to projecting feelings on objects."

"It became worse with age."

I shot Archer a warning glare. He was walking the line of a man who knew Hazel too well. I couldn't explain to my brother why our seventy-eight-year-old great-aunt had been hanging out with someone who looked fifty years younger than her.

"I mean, it's common for the elderly to cling to things as they draw closer to death," Archer said, strolling to the dining table and easing into a chair.

"Moving on from Hazel's odd collection of things, let's see what this bar layout is going to look like," I said in a hurry to change the subject.

After we inspected new cabinetry for the liquor, the addition of a patio, and a small stage for performers, I gave the plans my stamp of approval. Hunter slapped his palms on his thighs and stood. "I guess I better get out of your hair," he said, eyeing me with that look on his face again. "I'm sure you two have a busy day ahead of you."

My cheeks burned, and I nodded toward the pink box on the counter. "Thanks again for the doughnuts, Hunt."

"No problem. Have a good day. Just make sure you're *careful*."

"Oh my *God*, Hunter, stop!" I said, shoving him toward the door. He just laughed and disappeared into the hallway.

I shut the door behind him and leaned against it, shaking my head. "For fuck's sake, the two of you could work me into a panic attack."

Archer propped an elbow on the dining table and flashed a sly grin. "I'm taking it that my 'meet the family' skills need some work."

I laughed and pushed away from the door. "You could say that."

"I have other skills I promise are more refined."

I crossed the room and stood between his legs, placing my palms on his shoulders. "Is that right? Do you want to elaborate?"

"I'd rather show you what I can do."

Archer slid his knuckles up my stomach, leaving a trail of pebbled skin and a steady pulse thrumming at my center. His hand glided higher, and my shirt followed until my abdomen was bare. He pressed his mouth to my sternum and gripped my hips, holding me in place. I couldn't look away from his lips, the dusty pink mesmerizing against my freckled skin. Small open-mouthed kisses left a glistening trail from my navel to the underside of my bra.

My heart raced as he wedged his legs between mine and lowered me to his lap. He eased my shirt over my head, tossed it to the floor, and returned to toy with the transparent lace that covered my breasts. "I want to take all of this off and touch you. I've spent days thinking about my mouth and hands on your skin."

"So have I," I murmured, tangling my fingers in the hair at the nape of his neck. "Put your hands on me, Archer."

With a low groan, he reached behind me and unhooked my bra, letting it fall to the floor. He slid his hands up my rib cage, and his thumbs grazed the hardened peaks, drawing a sharp breath from me.

"Is this okay?" he asked, leaning in and planting kisses across my collarbone.

"More than okay," I whispered, hooking my finger under his chin and tilting his face up toward mine. "I like the way your lips feel against my skin."

Archer moaned and his palms glided up my legs. His fingertips brushed against my sex as his other hand rested on my lower back, pulling me to him. Goosebumps rose along my arms and legs when his mouth brushed the sensitive skin below my ear, and his fingers pressed the place that throbbed between my legs. Every stroke over the sensitive bundle of nerves was sweet torture—not enough to satisfy me, but enough to make me want so much more.

He kissed his way down my neck, over my collarbone and to the swell of my breast. As his fingers traced slow circles against my core, he drew my nipple between his lips. I hissed, arching my back against his fingers, relishing the warmth of his mouth on me.

"God, Archer." Pushing my hips forward, I tangled my fingers in his hair and tugged.

He pulled away from my breast with a pop of his mouth. Cool

air mingled with my heated skin, and a whimpered protest spilled from my lips. Archer grinned as he lowered his face to my other breast and showered it with the same attention. My hips kept pace with his skilled fingers playing over the soft fabric covering the apex of my legs.

"Touch me. Feel how badly I want you, Gemma," he said, biting my nipple.

My heart pounded a relentless rhythm against my chest. I reached between us and snapped open the button on his pants, slid the zipper down, and slipped my hand inside. Gripping him in my fist, I lifted my head and sucked at the skin below his ear. "God, you feel so good."

Archer pressed his lips to mine in a hungry kiss as he rocked his hips. He glided in and out of my hand in long strokes that matched the way his tongue caressed mine. "I need you," he panted.

I was so close to giving in, but I couldn't. I couldn't compromise my principles for a few minutes of ecstasy. And I knew it would be ecstasy with Archer Hyde.

"I'm right here," I murmured against his lips. "I want to make you feel good." His fingers quickened their pace on the most sensitive part of me, working over my leggings. I moaned into his kiss as I continued the up and down motion of my palm against him. "Keep doing that. Don't stop."

He tipped his head back, his pulse beating at the side of his neck as he thrust into my hand. "Fuck," he called to the heavens, and his thumb pressed into me the way I needed.

Our bodies shuddered together, ripple upon ripple of euphoria. It was addicting, and I continued to chase it until it was physically impossible to go on. Out of breath, I fell into him and kissed his jaw.

"Thank you," I whispered. "That was exactly what I needed."

"You're welcome," he replied with a squeeze to my hip. "If your hand feels that good, I can only imagine what it would feel like to be inside you."

The butterflies in my stomach lurched to a stop. The idea of sleeping with Archer should have thrilled me, made my toes curl. But it just rattled my nerves. I didn't know if I'd ever be ready to give him everything. The two of us had fun together, he was sexy, he made me laugh, and he was a great stress reliever.

But I'd never completely given my body to a guy I didn't trust. Even though the relationships hadn't lasted, I had trusted them at the time, and that was crucial to me. And right now, I didn't fully trust Archer, and I didn't know if I ever would.

I nuzzled his neck and kissed the corner of his mouth. "I have to go to work. See you later tonight?" I tried to keep my voice steady, but my nerves were winning that battle.

Archer dipped his head, placing his face in my line of sight. "Did I do something wrong?"

"No, you did everything right. The results are favorable on my side," I said, moving to my feet and contorting my face into a wide, and hopefully convincing, smile. "I have a busy day ahead of me, and you have taken up a good portion of my morning. But like I said, we can hang out again tonight."

"I'd like that." He wrapped his fingers around mine and brought my knuckles to his lips before he slipped out of my suite.

Again, my stomach nosedived, and my mind flashed with the image of him kissing Raven's hand. The nagging voice that had taken residence in my head was on a rampage. *Listen to me! Something is off; you have to figure it out.* I tried to stifle it—shove it in a locked box and push it to the far corner of my brain—but it persisted. It screamed at me while I finished getting ready for work and taunted me when I locked my suite door. The damn voice even echoed in my head as I took the stairs toward the lobby.

I reached the second landing, where two angry voices carried down the hall. Both hushed but intense, like whatever the argument was, it was extremely important. Unable to ignore it, I moved closer to an alcove at the end of the hallway, and the voices became clear.

"This isn't how this is supposed to work, Archer," Soren hissed, his tone laced with venom.

Flattening myself against the wall, I squeezed my eyes shut, listening intently. It didn't matter how wrong eavesdropping was, my curiosity held me in place.

"Why do you think you know so much about how it's supposed to work? Have you done this before? No. It's what needs to be done," Archer snapped.

"You have no clue of the damage you are going to do! You know someone will end up heartbroken if you do this."

"Oh, get off your high horse, brother. If you had a chance to do the thing that once seemed impossible, you'd do it in a second. You're just jealous that I'm bettering my chances," Archer said in a contemptuous tone.

"No. No, I'm not. You're going about this the wrong way, and you know it. If Hazel could see you, you would break her heart."

"I suppose no one understands that better than you."

"You're fucking impossible, but better than this. I wish you would act like it," Soren said, and footsteps moved in my direction.

"Shit," I muttered, ducking into the shadows of another alcove. My heart hammered in my chest until I was certain they were both gone.

What had they been talking about? What was it that needed to be done? Why was Soren so against whatever it was? How could I get the answers to all these questions?

The book, my conscience said, the constant harping replaced by a firm, clear voice.

My fingers trembled, and a knot twisted in my chest. The thought of reading until I got sick spiked my anxiety. I was eager for the answers and fearful that I wouldn't stop until I got them. But I couldn't continue to ignore it. I was going to have to face my fears and dig deeper into the past, all while executing the most phenomenal Halloween the Reynard had ever seen.

CHAPTER SIXTEEN

I'd always loved Halloween, but this year, it was my salvation.

Planning the festivities was keeping my mind off all the things that plagued me—Raven, my dad's doubts about how I was running things, Archer and Soren's bizarre conversation. But as all the plans began to come together, I was running out of things to do. I still needed answers, so I reluctantly turned to the journal.

I'd decided to take it with me when I worked the front desk. If the fear of puking on a guest didn't help me pace my reading, then the constant up and down of taking care of them would. After days of reading entry after entry about how much she hated the boys, Hazel, and the hotel, I was finally reaching the end of Betty's entries—thank God—and was excited to move on to Hazel's.

After lighting a fire in the sitting room, I unlocked and pulled back the gate from around the front desk. Raven hated that I closed the desk at night; she strongly suggested that I hire someone for the graveyard shift. I refused to budge on the matter. Since the hotel's opening over a century ago, the owner had handled any late-night crises. Besides, it made for good stories from our guests when they roamed around the dark first floor during the midnight hours.

The crackling fire popped throughout the quiet lobby, and

the early-morning sun shone through the stained glass above the front door. Colorful fragments of light danced over the lobby floor, reminding me of the countless pictures posted on the internet of this room with the tiny orbs floating over the entry and resting on the furniture in the sitting room. Everyone believed they were spirits, but I now had a feeling they were kobolds trapped on this property.

I looked up toward the stairwell, expecting to find an orb. "Jesus Christ," I yelped, placing my hand over my speeding heart.

Soren was leaning against the grand staircase's banister, watching me, one long leg crossed over the other.

"Don't you ever sleep?" I mumbled, taking a sip of the coffee I'd brought down with me from my room.

"You didn't know? Ghosts don't sleep."

"Funny. Is there something I can help you with?"

He pushed away from the mahogany railing and followed me to the desk. "I actually came down to ask you the same thing. Hazel would always ask us for a few extra creepy favors on Halloween, just to keep the guests talking. Do you want us to do the same?"

"Actually, yes. I was hoping that when I cut the electricity, maybe you and Archer could ramp up the spooky just to scare the shit out of them."

Soren raised an eyebrow and rubbed his palms together. "Sounds like a good time. Are you still doing the séance?"

"Of course. Hazel would turn over in her grave if I didn't. I'm even bringing in Wanda Willow to lead it. It's going to be supercreepy. So, you're in?"

"Yes, I'll do it for Hazel. She'd want the first Halloween without her to be spectacular."

The repeated mention of Hazel brought the conversation I'd overheard between Archer and Soren to the forefront of my mind.

Something shady was going on, and Soren was adamant that my aunt wouldn't approve, determined to make sure his brother didn't hurt her even in death. I thought no one loved Hazel as much as me, but Soren might be a close second.

"You cared about her a lot," I said.

"I would have done anything for her."

The compassion and sorrow in his blue eyes spoke to his bond with my aunt. It was easy to see that her death left a gaping hole in him, the kind that ran deeper than just a caretaker and her charge.

I shuffled a stack of papers. "Were you and Hazel ever . . ." I cleared my throat and ran my fingers through my hair, doing everything in my power to not make eye contact.

"Lovers?" He set his elbows on the desktop and cocked a brow.

"Yeah."

"No. Our relationship for the most part was platonic in nature."

"For the most part?"

He clicked his tongue behind his teeth and knocked on the book resting on the desk. "Check back with me when you're finished, and we can discuss."

"Seriously, Soren?"

He turned on his heel and said, "Get to work, Gemma. You have a busy day ahead of you and a good chunk of that book still to read."

"Thanks, asshole!" I called back, but I couldn't hide the amusement in my voice.

The man had an effortless way of getting under my skin and then making me smile. I liked that he didn't hide his more flawed qualities from me. And although his habit of telling me exactly what he thought annoyed me, it also earned my respect.

I could handle his bossy nature knowing that it was driven by good intentions.

Between reading the book every chance I got and checking in guest after guest, my day passed in a flash. And surprisingly, Raven wasn't there. I figured she'd be lurking around, micromanaging every move I made on a day like today. But she was nowhere to be found, even at 6:00 p.m., when I left the front desk responsibilities in Larry's capable hands.

I returned to my suite to put on the form-fitting black lace dress I'd found in the back of Hazel's closet. Matching the dress with a velvet cloak, I twisted my hair into a waterfall braid, letting it flow over my shoulders. The ensemble was very Morticia Addams meets Belle from *Beauty and the Beast*, and it made me feel like I was worthy to stand in my aunt's place tonight. And I was. I could safely say that tonight's festivities wouldn't be nearly as elaborate if it weren't for me.

I descended the grand staircase, careful not to disturb the fake spiderwebs woven into the banister. The lobby was packed with witches, goblins, and superheroes. Many were lined up to take pictures with the life-size animatronic werewolf and vampire guarding the hotel's front door. Others played with the battery-operated lanterns they received upon check-in. And the smiling faces and exuberant chatter said they were all excited to be there.

Larry approached and handed me Hazel's real lantern, the one she'd used during all the ghost tours. "She would want you to have it."

"Thank you," I said with tears pooling in my eyes. I pictured Hazel standing behind the counter in a bright dress and big, ugly earrings and smiling as the torch was passed from one owner to the next.

"Oh my God, Gemma, you look stunning!" Skye said, clunking out of the hallway that led to the bar in towering platform boots. Green makeup covered her face, and her turquoise hair was spiked in a mohawk.

"Thanks. And I'm guessing you're the punk-rock version of Frankenstein's monster."

"Or my normal self, just painted green. I mostly dressed up to piss off your cousin. I knew she would have a conniption seeing me out of dress code. Speaking of the she-devil, I see she's in the running for tonight's scariest costume award—grumpy hotel manager."

I laughed and skimmed the cheerful faces around the lobby, stopping on the one person who appeared disgusted with the gathering. Skye wasn't wrong; Raven hadn't added so much as a pumpkin brooch or skeleton earrings to her crisp skirt suit. Leave it to my cousin to try to suck the fun out of the room.

The door swung open, letting in several brown and red leaves, and Wanda Willow entered. The lobby fell silent as the medium sauntered in wearing a skintight zebra-print dress and lime-green boa. She pulled a fuzzy pink rolling suitcase behind her and met each stare with a stoic nod.

Stopping in front of me, she fluffed her curls and asked, "Where would you like me to summon the spirits at, Miss Fox?"

"The sitting room." I waved her in that direction. "All the furniture has been moved aside to give you and the guests room," I said as we crossed the threshold. "We have twenty people who paid extra for the séance, plus myself and our bartender." I smiled at Skye; I definitely wanted her to be a part of the festivities.

"Very well. The departed souls are pleased with the ambiance. Tonight, we will open a gateway to the other side," Wanda said in an ominous tone. Despite the fact that I had invited her here myself and was prepared for the creep factor, a chill ran down my spine.

"Perfect," I said, glancing at Skye, who just grinned.

Wanda got to work setting up her accoutrements for the séance, and before I walked back to the lobby, she stopped me with a hand on my wrist. I jumped at the frigid temperature of her velvety skin.

"Have you found the answers you were seeking when you came to visit me weeks ago?" she asked, her eyes gleaming with curiosity.

I cleared my throat and shook my head. "No. Not all of them. There are still a few questions I don't think I'll ever have the answers to. I'm three quarters of the way through the book, and I still have questions for Amity. I don't think those will be answered by my great-aunt's entries."

"No, they won't, but I believe they *will* be answered."

With a quick nod, I returned to the front of the hotel.

Larry was gathering those who paid for the ghost tour, which included a trick or treat for the kids. I almost wished I hadn't handed the responsibility of retelling the hotel's creepy history to Raven. I'd miss watching the wonder in the guests' faces as they strolled the dark hallways. Not to mention the eerie feeling that rolled in my stomach as the start of the séance grew closer.

"If you're ready, I'm going to flip the breaker," Larry said.

I glanced back at the sitting room, where Wanda had placed dozens of white candles on the fireplace mantel and in the center of the floor. "I think we're good."

Larry disappeared through the door that led to the basement. A sudden bang came from the second floor and then the lights went out, casting the hotel in the amber glow of the lanterns. Several of the guests shrieked and then giggled nervously—a sure sign of the adrenaline pumping through their veins. Soren was already at work setting everyone on edge.

The tour ascended the stairs, and Wanda stepped out of the sitting room. "Come, everyone, let's invite the dead to our party."

My heart leaped into my throat, and my nerves were unsteady as I followed Skye. In the past, Hazel's séances were always just her pretending she knew what she was doing; sometimes she even used a Ouija board. Everyone was aware that it was just for fun, but this felt different. Darker.

"Please, everyone, sit in a circle around the items on the center of the rug," Wanda said as she settled directly in front of the fireplace.

I raised an eyebrow and looked down at Hazel's dress. No way was I sitting on the floor in this getup.

"I don't know if I—"

"If an old lady like me can do it, so can you."

Wanda Willow single-handedly proved the existence of a god that night. It was a miracle that she got down on the floor in her dress. I just prayed the Almighty would show me the same mercy. I swallowed and managed to settle on the floor next to Skye with my legs awkwardly bent to the side.

"Excellent," Wanda said, waving her hands over the flickering candles and burning incense. "Everyone, join hands and close your eyes. Open your minds and let the worries of this world leave you."

Before I closed my eyes, I watched to make sure everyone was participating. When I was satisfied, I let my eyelids flutter shut and listened to Wanda's words.

"The spirits are here tonight. The air is charged with the aura of their presence," she said, and something began to stir within me. "We welcome those who have passed from this life to the next and grant you precedence in this place. Come and share your message with us."

Something lit up in my belly, and it traveled to my chest, my throat, and the top of my head before I was thrust into pure darkness.

"I feel your energy, so much sadness and regret. Who is in this room with us?" Wanda asked.

When my mouth moved, I couldn't stop it. But even more strangely, I didn't remember opening it to begin with.

"Amity Fox, the first owner of the Reynard."

My voice was mine, but not—it was raspy, throaty, and somewhat disembodied.

"And what business brings you back to this place, Mrs. Fox?"

"I've come to have my story heard, to fill in the missing pieces for my kin."

I scrambled to gain control of my body, but I couldn't. Something strong and frightening bound me to a dark corner of my mind, holding me back as it took over. The movement of my hands wasn't my own, and I was helpless to do anything but hear the words that weren't mine.

"We're listening," Wanda said.

"Even in the next life, I have never forgiven Celestia for what she did. For taking my boys and leaving me with hers. I fear I will never feel content if I do not tell the whole story, and my living relative here at the Reynard needs to know the truth. Maybe if I release all this hate, I can finally be at peace."

"Go on," Wanda said, her voice gentle.

"The boys cursed to this place, Soren and Archer—they are more than just an ordinary set of twins. They are the last of their line, and without them, their people will never know peace. But I struggle to be at peace when my boys never knew this life at all."

A new surge of energy flowed through the room, this one light and full of warmth, and another voice cut through the tense, heavy air. "I have been reunited with my brothers in the afterlife."

"Who else enters this place?" Wanda asked, her head snapping in the direction of the voice.

"My name is Maybell, daughter of Amity Fox and the second owner of the Reynard," the voice replied, and my heart stuttered even as Amity spoke through me.

"Daughter, is it true? You have seen Robert and Gregory?"

"Yes, Mama. They are at peace. We want you to be as well. And it is time for the cursed to go home. Until their king returns, their people will remain at war, never agreeing on who should sit on the throne."

King? Throne? My brain was short-circuiting, and I couldn't think straight. Was Maybell saying Soren and Archer were kobold royalty? Was there a way for them to go home?

"Aunt Maybell, hold your tongue," said a venomous voice as harsh, cold fingers gripped my arm.

Betty Davenport had taken residence in Skye's body.

My blood ran cold at the mere thought of Betty's spirit in the same room as me.

"Betty, do not tell me to hold my tongue. You made those boys' lives miserable. You thought that we could not see from beyond? We could. It was not fair, the way you treated them. Now that they're grown, the least you can do is let us help them."

Betty laughed, and the sound was laced with contempt. "Do not speak to me about fair. Those boys ruined my life. Just like Ha—"

"Just like I did?"

My heart stopped and my gaze cut to the left. Unlike the

others who were possessed, a spark of terror was not evident in Wanda's demeanor. She was at ease with the spirit of my great-aunt flowing through her body. Hazel commanded the room in a way the others didn't. I'd known they were here just by what they'd said. But Hazel—I could feel her all around me. Her warmth, her love, even her eccentricity.

In this Halloween séance meant to spook the guests, I was truly seeing the other side.

Skye pointed a finger at Wanda and hissed, "You were a life-sucking leech, Hazel Fox. I should have raised my sons and lived a full and happy life, but I was burdened with you, this wretched hotel, and those *things*. May this family burn in hell for what it did to me."

"You were always a hate-filled, miserable old bat, Betty. The only one of us who will *always* remain at unrest. The curse on this place will unravel with love."

Right then, Amity's spirit retreated, and it was like a seven-ton boulder lifted from my body. Wanda's dark-brown eyes moved from Skye to me and softened in a way I'd experienced many times. Even in another's body, her adoration for me shone through. "You are on the right path to finding the answer that will free them, Gemma. Trust your instinct and open your heart. Their freedom could be your happiness."

I extended my hand toward Wanda, wanting to be closer to my aunt, but in that instant, the spell was broken. Skye was shaking her head as though waking up from a dream, another woman across the circle looked dazed, and everyone in the room was struck silent by the events that had transpired. A couple of people scrambled to their feet and fled like the devil was on their heels.

"What the hell just happened?" Skye asked, breaking the silence as a nervous titter of laughter rippled through the crowd.

Wanda blew out the candles closest to her. "You just experienced a true communication with the dead."

My heart galloped at the speed of light, and Skye's jaw dropped. "Excuse me? You're saying that was really—"

"Every previous owner of this hotel? Yes. That is what I'm saying," Wanda said, regarding Skye with wry amusement.

"That's—that's impossible."

I gaped at her. "Skye, Betty was speaking through you."

Her eyebrows bunched together. "What? No, no, she wasn't."

"She was. I saw it. Amity had taken me—"

"Wait, you mean you actually saw me talking? And *you* were talking?"

"Yes. And Wanda, she . . . Hazel was here," I choked out, tears filling my eyes.

Wanda crossed the room and stood before me, her downturned gaze a mixture of amusement and warning. "Of all the spirits that have passed, your ancestors had the most important message to share. Take heed, child; it appears not only does their freedom hang in the balance, but so does your future."

Before I could respond, she squeezed my shoulder and strode into the lobby and out the double doors into the brisk night.

Skye scooted to my side and looped her arm through mine. "Are you okay, Gem?"

I blinked the tears from my eyes and nodded. "Yeah, I'm fine, I just—I need some time to think. I know it's going to be crazy with the adult after-party, but do you think you can handle the bar without me?"

She patted my forearm before saying, "Don't worry about a thing. You go on upstairs and get some sleep. Larry and I got this. If you need me, just shoot me a text."

"Thank you, Skye. Call me if anything goes wrong."

She winked and made her way over to some guests gathering at the front desk, greeting them in that bright, sunny way of hers.

Even with all the confusion and emotion flowing through me, I felt like a success for once in my life, and as I listened to the guests share their paranormal experiences with others, tears sprang to my eyes once again. I'd wished so many times that my aunt could be here to see how I was doing, to tell me I was going to be okay, and tonight, she was here. She confirmed I was on the right path. But to what? I had never stopped to consider that my path would be so tightly woven with Archer's—or Soren's.

When I reached the second floor, it was eerily empty. Most of the guests had congregated downstairs at the bar for half-price cocktails and dancing. Halloween had always sent a shiver through me, but after what happened during the séance, I was downright creeped out. The light from my lantern stretched down the hallway, the flicker sending shadows racing in front of me. All I wanted was to retreat to my room, but first I had to case each floor to make sure no nonregistered guests were wandering where they shouldn't be.

Reaching the third floor, I turned down the long corridor when the wick in my lantern faded out. Lifting the rusted metal to my ear, I shook it, and fuel sloshed inside.

"What the hell?" I whined. It would be impossible to make it to my suite and find a flashlight in the dark without falling on my face. I inched my way over to the wall and placed my palm against it as a guide. The hairs on the back of my neck stood on end, and sweat beaded at my brow.

Drumming steps and a breeze rushed past me, ruffling the bottom of my dress.

"Archer? Soren? This isn't funny." My voice echoed off the walls, and no one answered.

A tickling sensation fluttered across my cheek, and I swatted at it only for it to move to the outside of my ankle. "It's just your cloak," I told myself, moving further down the hallway.

I had taken no more than two steps when something brushed against my earlobe and then the bare space where my neck met my shoulder. I jumped and turned around, straining to see through the pitch dark. "What the fuck? Stop it, Archer, you're freaking me out!"

Nothing. Not a chuckle or one of his token flirty remarks. Everything was silent.

But I could feel it; a presence was watching me scurry in the dark. I spun around to head back the way I came when I crashed into a solid form. I opened my mouth to scream, and just as swiftly, a hand clapped over it.

"It's just me." The low humming sound of a male voice vibrated through my body.

I gripped his wrist, pulling his palm away from my mouth. "Damn it, Soren! You scared the shit out of me!"

"You scared the shit out of me. I ran up here to see why you were yelling."

My heart softened, and I looked up at what I assumed was his face. I imagined him watching me with his stoic blue gaze. "Oh. Well, thank you." I paused and then asked, "Did Archer not hear me yelling too?"

"I don't know. We split up about two hours ago. Do you need help to your room?"

"Yeah, but first, can you help me check this floor and make sure no one without keys is roaming the halls?" I glanced down and realized I was still holding on to his wrist. I dropped it quickly as my cheeks flushed. "Sorry. I can't see my hand in front of my face. Do you think you can get me a flashlight from the janitor's closet?"

"Yes. Give me the key."

I placed it in his palm, and he looped my arm through his, walking me in the general direction of the storage room. The doorknob rattled, and he released me, saying, "Stay right here."

Holding on to the doorframe, I listened as he banged around in the supply room before a beam of light swept over the shelves and brooms hanging from the wall.

"Thank you," I said.

"You're welcome."

We walked side by side in silence, our hands occasionally brushing against each other. Soren swept the beam of light back and forth, checking every nook and cranny for people attempting to stay in the hotel all night. Not only had tonight's activities been a huge hit, but every room was booked. Halloween was a true success.

"Hazel would have been proud of you," Soren said.

My jaw went slack. He was on a roll with acting civil, charming, and even sweet. "Thank you. It really did go off without a hitch, and—"

We rounded the corner, and the beam from Soren's flashlight was harsh, but what it revealed in the cover of darkness was harsher.

Archer jerked his head, squinting against the light. Manicured nails tangled in the hair at his nape, and a slender leg wrapped around his hip, just as mine had been so many times before.

My stomach knotted as familiar green eyes met my gaze.

Raven.

CHAPTER SEVENTEEN

"What. The. Actual. Fuck?" I spat, taking a step backward and bumping into Soren, who steadied me with a hand on my waist.

My chest heaved with unsteady breaths, and my blood reached boiling point, searing my veins. My body quivering with rage, I balled my fists at my sides.

"Gemma, please—"

I held up my hand and shook my head. "No, you don't get to fucking try to make excuses right now, Archer. Just be honest. What in the hell is going on here?"

"I think it's pretty obvious what's going on here," Raven said in a sickly sweet voice, batting her eyelashes.

"I wasn't talking to you," I barked.

Soren bunched my cloak in his fist, gripping it like a leash. I would have turned on him, but I was grateful he held me back because all I wanted to do was plant my fist in the center of her smug face. No one, not one damn person, ignited violent anger inside me the way she did. I closed my eyes and inhaled, then exhaled three times, grounding myself and focusing on the feel of Soren's grip on me.

Archer stepped toward me and calmly said, "Gemma, we

both know what we had was just for fun. You weren't looking for anything serious."

I take it back. Raven wasn't the only person who could ignite violent anger inside me. "That doesn't mean you get to just go fucking around with my *cousin*! Of all people, you had to choose her. You *knew* how badly that would hurt me, Archer! What, did I not give you everything you needed? Because I wouldn't fuck you?"

"You clearly didn't want to take our relationship to the next level."

"And since when are you looking for something serious?"

"I was always looking for a woman to fall in love with me."

"For fuck's sake, Archer," Soren groaned from beside me. "I understand the desperation you feel, but I didn't really think you'd act on it."

Archer shrugged. "You shouldn't have underestimated me, brother."

I cut my eyes toward Soren. "What are you talking about?"

Soren shook his head but kept hold of my cloak. "Nothing. My brother is just a fucking idiot."

I frowned, but decided to let it go for now, my gaze turning to a glare as it settled back on Archer. "I was never going to fall in love with you. Maybe you'll have better luck with her."

Raven took his hand and flashed a winning smile. "Face it, Gemma; he chose the better cousin, and you know it."

"Oh fuck you," I growled, taking a step toward her in spite of Soren's grip on my cloak.

"Gem, don't," Soren said, pulling me back. "She isn't worth it. None of this is worth it. Let me walk you to your room."

"I don't want to see either of you ever again. If I'm walking the halls, you turn the other way. You"—I pointed to Raven—"will put your time in and then get the fuck out of my hotel. The only way you will *ever* lay a finger on this place is by prying it from my cold, dead hands." My eyes darted to Archer. "I'll find a way to get you out of here, because I'll be damned if I look at you for the rest of my life. What you did, I expected better of you, and I'm sure Hazel would feel the same."

Archer dropped his head, his purple eyes dark with shame. He drew in a breath, filling his lungs until his chest expanded and strained the buttons of his shirt. Lifting his chin, he said, "I have no regrets."

Raven gripped his biceps and said, "And you shouldn't, baby."

I rolled my eyes and marched down the hall.

The end of my relationship with Archer had been looming for days. I wasn't feeling a deep-seated connection with him. We were never meant to be more than what we were, but he had moved on with my cousin, my adversary, the woman who wanted to take this place away from me. He didn't even have the decency to break things off with me first.

If he'd wanted more so badly, he should've just told me. Why go behind my back and juggle both of us? If it had been anyone but her, I probably would've been able to blow it off. But she wanted to take *everything* from me.

"Are you okay?" Soren asked as he matched my long strides.

"Yeah, I'm fine," I said, glancing at him from the corner of my eye. "I'm glad you were with me, or I might have ripped someone's face off."

"It's understandable."

We continued to the fourth floor in silence, making our way to the stretch of hallway we shared. I dug my keys from the pocket in my cloak, and Soren paused in front of the portion of wall that housed the hidden passage to the bell tower.

"Hey, Gemma?" I glanced back at him, and he continued, "I know I don't have the right to ask you to do anything, but just imagine it's coming from Hazel."

"Okay," I slowly replied.

"Don't get so caught up in the drama of my brother and your cousin that you miss out on all the other amazing things going on around you. You're meant to be here more than anyone."

Warmth spread through my chest. This was the first piece of advice from Soren that I had no intention of ignoring. And truth be told, I shouldn't have brushed off his other warnings either. If I'd simply listened, Archer would have never had the opportunity to betray me. But as much as I'd tried to keep a barrier up, he'd weaseled through my defenses. I had relied on him to take away my stress and create new happy memories with me in this place.

Now I needed to rely on myself. And after tonight, even with all the bullshit with Archer, I knew I could.

"I am actually pretty proud of how Halloween went, despite how the night ended."

"Good, because you did this. You made tonight memorable for all those people. I—Hazel would want you to bask in your accomplishments." Soren's lips tilted in a timid smile, and with that, he yanked on the light fixture and disappeared into the walls.

I sighed and shut the door with a click, leaning against it and exhaling deeply. I wasn't going to be able to sleep after all that, and I sure as hell didn't just want to sit here by myself staring at the ceiling.

I walked into my bedroom, unclasped my cloak, and draped it over the chair in the corner. After unzipping my dress, I hung it back in the closet, grabbed the book from the top of the dresser, and settled into bed.

Hazel had said I was on the right path, and the only thing I could do that might benefit Soren and Archer was finish reading the journal. I dreaded what was left of Betty's hateful entries, but if this is what my aunt thought I should do, I couldn't deny her—or the pain and unrest I'd felt from Amity.

She was in limbo, paying for keeping Soren and Archer from Celestia. The kobolds were suffering without a ruler—a position meant for one of the supernatural beings in this hotel. Amity was existing in tormenting guilt, and all she ever wanted was to reunite with the baby boys she'd seen only once. As the owner of this hotel and the only one who could read the book, it was up to me to save her and free Soren and Archer. I would endure the upcoming entries to learn how to release everyone from the curse.

February 14, 1954

I caught Hazel making a Valentine's card today. She was in her room, drawing hearts on a red sheet of construction paper. At first, I just thought she was doodling, but when I looked closer, I was horrified.

It was addressed to Soren.

Hazel is in love, or at the very least infatuated, with him.

This cannot come to fruition. First of all, I won't have her cavorting with a creature that isn't even human, but more than that, I did not spend years ensuring these boys had a miserable life just for Hazel to fall in love and make one of them happy.

She will be watched closely from here on out, spending no time alone with the boys. I will have one of the help take them their meals from now on.

These boys will never know love—not on my watch.

The book slid from my lap as the realization dawned on me.

Aunt Hazel had been in love with Soren.

Did he love her back? He said they were just friends, but he implied more. *Our relationship* for the most part *was platonic in nature.*

I scrambled to pull the book back to my lap, desperate to read more.

February 28, 1954
I am giddy with the knowledge that Soren does not love Hazel. Not only because I do not want him to experience the feeling, but because it is entertaining to watch her suffer.

I curled my lip in disgust, slamming the book onto the mattress with an unsatisfying plop. I could only stomach a couple of Betty's entries at a time; the book didn't even need to use its magic to make me sick when it came to her. And damn, if she didn't have a lot to write about. The woman loved to jot down every event that veered from the normal. Almost every day, she added a new entry, proving what a hideous monster she was. And her rants—I was embarrassed for her. She was so narrow-minded and wished the most problematic things upon the twins and Hazel. She was a creature of her time in all the worst ways, and I was ashamed to be related to such a reprehensible bitch.

My hate for Betty was outweighed only by my heartbreak for Hazel. It was hard to imagine a single reason Soren wouldn't return her affections. Hazel wasn't timid when it came to her looks; she would be the first to say she was "quite the looker back in the day." And she was correct; I'd seen the pictures of her as a young woman. She had been classically beautiful, like Grace Kelly or

Audrey Hepburn—sleek hairstyles and awe-inspiring tea-length dresses. Not to mention that she was fun, smart, creative, and so funny. No one could make me laugh like she did.

Soren had to be out of his mind not to fall in love with her.

Or maybe he wasn't. Maybe I hadn't considered an easy explanation until this very moment. This was one question I wouldn't find the answers to in the magical pages of the book. I'd have to go to the source to learn why he broke my sweet great-aunt's heart.

CHAPTER EIGHTEEN

The ladder wobbled under me as I stood on my tiptoes to pull down the fake cobwebs stretched in the corner of the lobby. I yelped, grabbing for the wall and sending the container filled with the decorations I had already removed crashing to the floor. Not even a cup of steaming pumpkin spice latte could make up for the mess I'd made.

A warm hand rested on my back, steadying me on my feet. "Let me do that before you break your neck."

I looked down and found Soren holding out his hand. I hadn't seen him since the other night when he'd dropped me off at my room, and thankfully, I hadn't seen a trace of Archer. But there he stood in a burgundy sweater and dark jeans, looking like he was on his way to go bobbing for apples at a fall festival.

I took his hand and stepped off the ladder. "Thank you," I said as he climbed the rungs and pulled the remaining cobwebs from the corner. I took advantage of his distracted state to soak in the way the denim clung to his firm, round butt. The man might be imperfect with his moody disposition, but his body had been carved by the gods.

He stepped down and brushed his palms together with a

satisfied twinkle in his eyes. "That was easy; no need for you to end up in the hospital over it."

I scratched my neck, pretending that I wasn't just ogling his ass, but I couldn't hide my burning cheeks. "Yeah, yeah."

"Can I help you with anything else?"

I could name several ways I'd like to see him get his hands dirty, but none of them had anything to do with transitioning the hotel's decor from Halloween to autumn. It had never been lost on me how attractive Soren was; he and Archer *were* identical after all. But I'd never had enough space in my head to compare the two. Archer and I had connected so quickly, while Soren and I had had a tumultuous relationship for a few weeks there. I'd spent the last couple of nights reflecting on how he'd changed, how he'd given me a glimpse of who he really was. Despite his earlier attempts to push me away, he now exuded nothing but sincerity and gentleness. It was so obvious now that the first Soren I'd met had worn a disguise, a mask that had, over the past few weeks, melted away to reveal his true nature. Now, there was something about Soren Hyde I couldn't shake.

"That was the last of the decorations." I tilted my head toward the bar, which wasn't due to open until five o'clock. "I was thinking about rewarding myself for my first successful Halloween." I chuckled before adding, "And celebrating the fact that Raven is in Boston for the next week and out of my hair. Would you like to join me?"

"Lead the way."

The bar was dim, lit only by the emergency lights. Soren slid onto a stool at the counter, and I moved to the cabinet along the back wall, pulling out a bottle of red wine. After grabbing two glasses, I sat next to him and poured our drinks.

"I didn't get the chance to thank you last night. Larry and Skye told me the Halloween regulars said that the only sign of Hazel's absence was that she wasn't there to greet each guest as they came down the stairs or walked through the front door."

"You're welcome. Here's to many more successful Halloweens," he said, clinking his glass with mine and taking a measured sip. "I overheard some guests talking about the séance. It sounded eventful."

I gulped down half my wine and cleared my throat. "You could say that. I spent the night listening to my dead relatives go back and forth about the curse."

He placed his glass on the bar top and folded his hands. "Did you learn anything interesting?"

I pursed my lips and took another sip of wine. "I—yeah. Hazel was there." It sounded unbelievable to just say it like that, but I continued when Soren didn't question me. "She—she told me I was on the right path. That I was the key to your freedom. I just don't know what the hell she means by that."

"You know what I'm going to tell you."

"Keep reading."

He nodded.

"I did learn something that wasn't in there. So, your precious enchanted book doesn't have *all* the answers." He topped off my glass, and I took it as my cue to continue. "Did you know that the kobolds are at war over who should be ruler?"

"Before her death, I overheard Amity discussing the turmoil she caused by keeping Archer and me here, and Maybell always called Archer and me little princes. It wasn't until we were older that we assumed there was a connection."

"What she said implied that there's a way for you to go home." He opened his mouth, and I held a finger to his lips. "I know, I know. Read. I've been working on it."

His lips were full and soft beneath the pad of my finger, and I pulled my hand away before I could do something stupid like trace the shape of his mouth.

"I did read more last night. I know Hazel was in love with you, and you didn't love her in return."

He shifted in his seat and took a long swig of his wine.

"Soren, I don't mean to pry into your personal life, and not that it matters, but do you . . . *enjoy* the company of women?"

He choked and wiped the back of his hand over his mouth. "You're right; it doesn't matter, but yes"—his gaze swept over me from bottom to top—"I very much enjoy the company of women."

Warmth ran through my body, and it had nothing to do with the wine. I crossed my legs, quelling the throb between them. "Well, Hazel was a catch, so I just thought that maybe, you know, she just wasn't your *type*."

"My affections ran deep for Hazel, but I never looked at her in a romantic way. She was my savior, my confidant, and everything I needed her to be. A lover wasn't what I was looking for during that time of my life."

I took another sip of my drink, and before I could stop myself, I asked, "And what about now?" Blood rushed to my cheeks, and I shook my head, pushing my hair out of my face and looking at the ceiling in horror. "Oh my God, I'm sorry. You don't have to answer that."

The question didn't seem to ruffle him, and he answered without pause. "Now, I'm just coming to terms with my fate. There are many things I'm destined to never have."

He radiated such sorrow and regret; I couldn't help but feel like he thought he didn't deserve any better. What could he have done to think so poorly of himself? Hazel clearly found him worthy of her love, and I'd found no fault in him so far.

"You don't think you're destined to have love? Or even intimacy? I know it doesn't really matter what I think, but you're wrong," I said, my voice nearly a whisper.

"You don't know the damage I've caused, Gemma. I don't think you can make that call yet."

I'd like to blame it on the alcohol, because against my better judgment, I stood and moved in front of him. My leg grazed his, igniting the heat low in my stomach. I didn't pull my gaze from him as I said, "You tried to warn me about your brother. You gave me the book that holds the answers I need. I can't speak for whatever you've done in your past, just like no one can judge me for mine. But in my eyes, you deserve anything you want."

He swirled the rest of the red liquid around the bottom of his glass, watching it dance in circles. When his gaze returned to mine, it was dark with regret.

"What about you, what do you deserve? An old, drafty hotel and two wards who should be able to care for themselves? What are you looking for, Gemma?"

I raised my hand and brushed his fingers with mine. "I'd like to feel needed," I whispered, not meeting his eyes this time.

"Well, if anything, you're needed here, more than you know." He swallowed the last of his wine, which seemed to embolden him to squeeze my fingers. "And you deserve so much more than this place can offer you in return."

"We'll see about that. Do you want to walk with me up to my room? I wanted to grab the book so I could read at the front desk."

"I—yes, I'll go with you."

Taking our glasses, he washed them in the small sink behind the bar and set them to dry before offering me his arm. When he headed for the elevator, I contemplated following him into the small space, but my fear for the death trap got the better of me, and I pulled him toward the staircase.

He laughed and said, "It's perfectly safe. I've only heard of a handful of faulty episodes, and those were decades ago."

I laughed. "I don't know if that makes me feel better."

"You don't think I could save you if it all went bad? Maybe I have some superhuman powers you don't know about."

"Oh, I have no doubt you could save me. Superhuman powers or no. I mean, you've already saved me from breaking my neck today. Why not from a crashing elevator?" His comment resonated in my head. "Wait . . . *do* you have superpowers?"

"If you consider turning into a sprite a superpower, then yes."

I laughed despite myself, my skin still warm from the wine and his hand on me. "Do you have a bag of dust that can make me fly?" I teased.

He shook his head and rolled his eyes. "Tinker Bell was a pixie."

"That doesn't answer my question, Mr. Hyde. Can you make me fly?"

He patted my hand where it rested on the crook of his elbow. "If I give away all of my secrets now, how will I keep you entertained for the next sixty years or so?"

I should have been horrified by the idea of spending the rest of my life in one place. My spirit was wild, restless; it refused to settle. But instead of the desire to run, a calm washed over me. I wanted to stay here and keep the hotel alive. Bubbles of joy burst in my stomach when I imagined the future of this place. For the first time in my life, I was ready to conquer my fear of commitment and dedicate myself to something I truly loved.

CHAPTER NINETEEN

Nothing good ever starts with a knock in the middle of the night. I sprang up straight in bed, startled awake. Three rapid knocks reverberated throughout the suite. I jumped to my feet, wrapped my short silk robe over my barely there pajamas, and rushed to the door.

After peeking through the peephole, I swung it open to find my night maintenance technician, Victor. He tipped his green Reynard hat, giving me a peek of his balding head, and kept his brown eyes respectfully on my face as he said, "Deepest apologies for interruptin' your sleep, Miss Fox, but we have a major problem in the basement."

I stepped outside into the hallway and crossed my arms over my chest, my heart already sinking at the mention of yet another issue to deal with. "That's all right, Victor. What's going on?"

"I went down to the basement to gather some more cleanin' supplies when I heard a rushin' sound. I could guess what it was, and when I took the first step down, I knew I was right." He held out his legs one at a time to show they were soaked to the knees. "Water-main break. The entire basement is flooded. Water risin' as we speak. Kenny is tryin' to get the flow to quit, but you may need to call your brother."

I gripped my hair and clenched my jaw. This was bad—really bad. "My brother is in Hartford for the weekend. Larry and Skye are gone for the night. What am I gonna—"

"We'll help." Soren stood shoulder to shoulder with Archer at the end of the hall. They looked like some creepy, sexy twins from a porn spoof of *The Shining*.

We? I slowly turned my head and smiled at Soren and, in the same split second, cut my eyes to Archer with a scowl that I hoped made him feel like the shithead he was.

"Thank you, Soren," I said.

Archer shook his head and rolled his eyes as if I were being childish. "You're welcome, Gemma."

"Let's go see how bad the damage is," I said, breezing past them, shoulder-checking Archer with a little more force than necessary.

It was worse than I could have imagined. The water was rising quickly and already almost to Soren's and Archer's thighs as they trudged across the basement to help Kenny. I waited just above the waterline on the stairs, clenching my robe around me and shivering from the cold, damp air. The lights in the underground room were flickering like they were ready to blow at any moment and add a fire to the hotel's problems.

"I'm going to have to cut off the water to the hotel," Kenny said. "The leak is bubbling up through a crack in the concrete."

"I know where the valve is," said Soren, making his way back to me, his eyes dropping to my chest for a split second before returning to my face.

Kenny seemed unfazed by a "stranger" knowing the ins and outs of the hotel. Like the rest of the staff, he pretended that it wasn't peculiar that two twentysomething men were always hanging around while not paying for a room.

"Archer, call around and see if we can get a plumbing company out here that has an industrial sump pump. Don't bother with a local company; go for the bigger cities," Soren said, raising his voice over the sound of the water sloshing around his legs.

"I'm on it."

"You're going to have to evacuate the hotel, Gemma," Soren said, the side of his mouth kicked up in a sad smile. "Hopefully, we can get someone out here before the water does too much damage to the foundation. But until we know, this isn't safe for your guests. Not to mention we can't leave them with no running water."

I rested my head against the cool stone and closed my eyes, gritting my teeth so hard that my jaw ticked. Why could nothing be easy for me? Just when I'd gotten Raven out of my hair, a catastrophe had struck. And it couldn't be something small that I could slide under the rug and quietly fix on my own. It was the Second Great Fucking Flood that would leave everyone questioning if I could manage the hotel. Because of course it would be my fault that a pipe in the basement turned into Old Faithful.

I opened my eyes and met Soren's gaze, hoping to find some answers there. "Where am I going to send them? What am I supposed to do? I don't know how to handle this!"

"How many guests do you have right now?"

"Ten rooms are occupied right now. Thank God it's the middle of the week."

"That's not bad, Gem. Just call one of the big chains over in New London. It's only fifteen minutes or so from here. They'll be able to take them in, and you can pay them over the phone. You can give either refunds to the customers or vouchers for a free stay. Larry can help you with all that when he gets in." He squeezed my arm. "It will be all right. I hate to leave that all to you, but I've got to get this water shut off."

"Go. I've got this," I said with more certainty than I felt.

Soren nodded and trudged back through the water, calling out to Kenny across the room. I ran back upstairs to the front desk to wake up my guests and break it to them that they'd have to leave.

Hours later, Larry and I sent the last couple off to the Holiday Inn in New London and filled out the last voucher. The hotel was empty except for the employees. Slipping out to the back porch, I collapsed into one of the Adirondack chairs. Now that everything was quiet, the weight of the night's events crushed me, and tears fell down my cheeks.

How did I go from booming success on Halloween to total disaster in less than a week? I was finally feeling like I was getting the hang of running the hotel, and now this? How would I ever dig myself out of this hole? Half of the Halloween profits were gone after sending all the guests to another hotel, not to mention the money I'd lose on the vouchers, which I didn't regret handing out; it was what Hazel would have done.

If Raven could see me now, she'd have the Reynard in her name before Archer moved on to the next girl.

I pulled my knees to my chest and rested my forehead on them, my tears soaking my bare skin. I hadn't had time to change out of my pajamas, even though I probably should have for professionalism's sake. But that had been the last thing on my mind.

Thankfully, I didn't have to handle everything on my own. Larry and Skye were calling the guests scheduled to be here this weekend, and Hunter returned just after dawn to meet with the insurance adjuster. Even Soren and Archer had helped people with their luggage.

My phone rang, joining the birds' morning song. Hunter's name flashed on the screen, and I slid to answer. "You are literally in the hotel. Why are you calling me?"

"I just wanted to keep you in the loop. The insurance money may take a while to come through due to the holidays. We need to get this water fixed sooner rather than later."

Panic rose in me, making it hard to breathe. "Okay, well, what do we do?"

"You could always ask Mom and Dad for the money."

"Uh, no. There's no reason for them to know about this at all." As if Raven would keep her mouth shut.

"Well, you'll have to say *something* to them, because they're coming for Thanksgiving," he mumbled.

My eyes widened, and I threw my head back, banging it on the chair. It took every ounce of self-control not to scream. "They're coming for *Thanksgiving*? That's in three weeks, Hunt!"

"Yeah, I know. And Gem, it's not just Mom and Dad. Uncle Kevin and Aunt Deborah will be here with Raven."

"My God, Hunter! What were you thinking telling them yes?"

My brother laughed, and I could practically see his scowl through the phone. "Do you really think Dad posed it to me as a yes-or-no question?"

I blew out a breath that rattled my lips. "Why can't we just have Thanksgiving at Trevor's place?"

"Because he, Kelsey, and the kids will be here too. And I invited Caden."

Jesus. "That's a lot of family. Are we going to be able to have things back to normal by then?"

"I'm afraid we won't if you don't ask them for help. Listen, I gotta go and finish the claim, we'll talk later."

"Okay . . . thank you, Hunt. Bye," I said before dropping my phone to the arm of the chair and exhaling heavily, resting my forehead against my knees again.

The screen door creaked and slammed, and footsteps sounded on the weathered deck. "Hey. They're setting up the pumps now. How are you holding up?" Soren asked, sitting in the chair next to mine.

I lifted my head and met his gaze, my eyes no doubt red and swollen, my cheeks tear-stained. "What do you think?"

"I think all your guests are safely relocated, your staff is working hard to get things cleaned up, and the insurance company will move as fast as a snail. All in all, we can be grateful for two out of three." He smiled, and it was annoyingly contagious.

"You're right. It's just—my whole damn family is coming in three weeks. What if it doesn't get cleaned up before then? It'll all be over for me," I said, my teeth chattering.

Soren stood and shrugged out of his wool coat. He draped it over my shoulders before squatting in front of my chair, a hand on each arm. "Look, I've watched this place go through ups and downs, and every time it came out all right. And to be honest, most of your relatives before you were fairly incompetent people when it came to running shit. The Reynard is in good hands with you, so don't let the high expectations of your family set you up to fail now."

I slid my arms into the sleeves of his jacket and pulled it closed. "Thank you, Soren. For helping me. I don't know what I would've done if you hadn't shown up."

"You're welcome." He squeezed my knee, his hand lingering, warm on my skin.

Soren watched my mouth, and I focused on his eyes. The

energy between us was a minuscule spark that rapidly snapped the closer we got. I licked my lips, tasting the air to see if it was coated with that same sweet electricity. It sizzled through me, pushing the breath from my lungs.

"I should go," he whispered, letting go of the chair and putting some space between us.

A strangled noise released from the back of my throat, and I nodded with a fake smile to try to cover my mortification. "Okay," I murmured, running my fingers through my hair and looking down at my feet, my cheeks heating to an uncomfortable temperature.

"Gemma, I—"

I shook my head and stood. "It's fine. Thanks again for everything." I shrugged out of his coat, pushed it to his chest, and slid around him. Yanking the door open, I stepped inside before he could say another word.

When I was out of his sight, I leaned against the wall in the hallway and ran my hands over my face. It was weird—me wanting to kiss Soren so soon after Archer. But it didn't soothe the sting of knowing he didn't want to kiss me in return.

CHAPTER TWENTY

Raven paced the length of the lobby, her hands clasped behind her back and high heels clicking on the checkered floor. She held her pointed chin high and her sharp nose in the air.

"Let me get this straight," she said, stopping in front of the counter. "I leave for one week, and you've managed to empty the hotel of guests?"

I propped my elbow on the desktop and turned a page in the journal. "If that's what you got out of the entire story, then sure."

"This isn't funny, Gemma. We're losing money."

"I'm aware of that."

She slapped her palms down in front of me, and I raised my eyes from the book. "You should have improvised. Found rooms that have higher water pressure and rented them out for double the price."

I took a deep breath and puckered my lips to slowly exhale. Closing the book, I said, "It was the main waterline. There's no water pressure, and I've been taking *very* cold showers under a drizzle. Hunter's friend owns a company that specializes in this sort of thing, but it could take two or three weeks before the hotel is safe for guests. Now tell me again where I'm supposed to put people?"

Her nostrils flared, and instead of just giving it up, she doubled down. "You could have found another way, Gemma! You have to use your imagination and get creative." She laughed. "Look who I'm talking to. It takes intellect to use imagination."

My face turned scarlet, and I opened my mouth to answer when a familiar voice spoke from behind Raven, "You know, Miss Fox, you really should get your facts straight before you come into someone's place of business and berate them."

Raven spun around on her heel and crossed her arms over her chest. "Why don't you just mind your own business, *Mr. Hyde*?" she sneered. "This is between me and my incompetent cousin."

Soren laughed. "Incompetent? Were you here to watch how Gemma reacted to a shit situation? No? Well, I was, so allow me to explain. Gemma was awakened from a dead sleep and pulled into an unfamiliar, disastrous situation. She immediately got on the phone, making calls to figure out where to put the guests, dealt with the company who cleaned up the water, and made sure every guest left satisfied. She did all of that on her own until Larry got here and helped with the last of it. She was nothing short of amazing," he said, his gaze meeting mine and running down my body before settling on my face.

"And yet, she found a way for you to stay behind. How convenient."

I rolled my eyes. "They insisted on staying and helping since it's more convenient for their jobs. So don't worry, my sloppy seconds is still around here for you to grope in the hallway."

Raven curled her upper lip. "You're so crude, Gemma. Besides, you can't possibly believe that he still thinks about you. Ever." Turning her attention back to Soren, she said, "Since you have Mr. Hyde so convinced that you have things under control,

I'll leave you to deal with this mess on your own." She sauntered toward the stairs. "And don't worry, I won't tell your parents. I'd rather be around to see the disappointment on their faces when you tell them you've failed yet again."

"I'd rather deal with ten 'disastrous situations' than one more second with you. Enjoy your stay. If I have anything to do with it, you won't be here much longer," I said before turning back to Soren.

Raven flung her hair over her shoulder and laughed as she jogged up the stairs toward her room, and I breathed a sigh of relief when she was no longer in sight.

I met Soren's eyes and said, "Thank you for standing up for me."

"No problem. I mean, really, she seems like a peach. If a peach were overly polished and had a nasal, obnoxious voice."

I giggled and added, "If a peach wore four-inch heels and a fake smile."

"If a peach pulled her hair back so tightly, her eyebrows were at the top of her forehead."

Never in my life had anyone turned my sour mood around after dealing with my family so quickly. It was strange; Soren had been such a heavy presence when we first met. Even the weight of his stare had bogged me down. And now, he was like the sun and fresh air and all the things I needed most when I felt caged in with no one to free me. The thought was odd since I was the one who Hazel thought could release him from his prison.

I jumped behind the counter and wrapped my arms around a big box that had been delivered today. "This came for you this morning," I said, stumbling over to him.

He chuckled and took it from me, setting it on the counter.

"What are you guys always ordering?"

He studied the cardboard and then gave it a light shake. "I think these are new pillows for my bed."

"You order pillows?"

"Yeah. Haven't you ever ordered something online?"

"Well, yeah, but not pillows. How do you know if you'll like them?"

"It's not like I can go to the store and try them out there." He went silent for a moment, his blue eyes darting back and forth. "Is that what you do? Do you put them on the floor at the store and try them out?"

I snorted and covered my mouth with my palm, attempting a straight face before removing it and saying, "Not exactly. But I can at least squish it and fluff it and make sure it's soft enough for me. And why don't you just use the pillows that the hotel buys?"

His expression turned wistful, like he was daydreaming about warm cookies and milk or snowflakes melting on the tip of his tongue. "Do you know what my favorite part of Winter Spirits is?"

My eyebrows knitted together. *What do pillows have to do with Winter Spirits?*

"No, I don't. Tell me. What's your favorite part of Winter Spirits, Soren?"

"I don't need to rely on this hotel. I fill my wallet with money, and I'm just another man walking the streets of Spelling. I can sit at the bar on the corner of Main and Folkner and not a soul knows who I am. Strangers strike up a conversation, and they never ask me if I've had an encounter with a ghost. I'm real, like them." He pulled the tape from the top of the box and removed a pillow in its plastic wrapping. "Those gift cards that Larry puts in the mail cubby for me every week? I *earned* those to buy this pillow. Granted, my job is to knock on walls and roll water bottles around hotel rooms, but it is a purpose. Hazel gave me the means to care for myself, to be my own being."

My heart constricted, and I felt an immense amount of admiration for him. It would have been easy for him to just live off of the hotel with zero responsibility. But he cherished the purpose he had here, and he didn't take the little things, like buying a new pillow, for granted. I couldn't say that for many of the other people in my life. Soren Hyde surprised me every time he opened his mouth, and I enjoyed delving deeper into who he really was.

"Then I will make sure that I give you more work to do," I said with a wink. "That way you never run out of gift cards for fluffy pillows." I squeezed the one he held in his hand. "You like them exactly how I do, by the way."

He leaned in and his voice dropped to a whisper. "The key to buying pillows online is to read the reviews."

My laughter filled the lobby, joined by his. I liked the way we sounded together, my high cackle and his rich chuckle. Even the expressions of our happiness complemented each other.

I checked the clock and said, "Larry will be here in a few minutes to watch over the phone and the lobby for the rest of the evening. What are you doing tonight?"

"Ordering pizza with you and watching your favorite movie?"

"That sounds even better than what I was going to suggest."

"Which was?"

"Throwing darts at a picture of Raven in the billiards room."

Soren grinned and shoved his hands in his pockets. "There's always tomorrow night."

And that was the beginning of the next week and a half.

Soren and I spent every evening together after work, doing anything from binge-watching Netflix in our pajamas to playing gin rummy in my suite. The friendship we'd begun to forge on Halloween was easily my most cherished relationship. We hadn't mentioned the almost-kiss we'd shared, but that spark of electricity I'd felt between us that day hadn't gone anywhere.

The night before my family arrived for Thanksgiving, I was spending a rare night alone when I picked up the book, eager to find out more about Hazel's earlier years. Between getting the hotel back in order and hanging out with Soren, I hadn't had much time to read.

I was so engrossed in an entry that I hadn't even noticed Soren come into the bedroom until he slipped behind me, pulling me between his legs and resting my back against his chest. He draped his arms over my shoulders, careful not to touch the book.

Warmth pooled in the pit of my stomach, and I glanced up at him, brushing his palm with my index finger. "Well, hello there," I said with a grin.

"I see you're reading again," he said, propping his chin on top of my head.

"I am. Since *somebody* still won't give me any info," I teased, reaching back and tickling his ribs.

He squirmed behind me. "That's right. You have to figure this stuff out for yourself."

"Yeah, yeah."

I returned my attention to the page and continued reading. Long gone were the sadistic ramblings of Betty; I was now enraptured by the inner thoughts of my sweet aunt Hazel. The current entry was about Soren, and I was fascinated to learn what she'd thought about him. And grateful for the spell that made it impossible for Soren to see what was on the pages as I read.

It's clear that Soren is never going to feel the same way about me as I do about him. He insists that the only reason I love him is because I'm never around anyone else and have never really known any other men besides his brother. That's totally untrue, but he won't have it. He is incredibly kind to me, but being in his presence is becoming physically painful. I know he'd never hurt me on purpose, but it's just so hard to be near him knowing that he'll never love me.

I stopped reading and opened my mouth to ask Soren about the entry but quickly changed my mind, letting my eyes drift back to the page. The next few entries were devastating; if I could've skipped them, I would have. Her heartbreak was excruciating. I raised my hand and placed it over his, running my thumb across his skin as I continued reading.

I thought I never would, but I've gotten over Soren. Well, I've grown out of him, so to speak. I'm getting older and older, and they're aging at such a different pace, so at this point I look at Soren and Archer as little brothers.

But now something bigger is plaguing me. These boys are stuck here forever as a result of decisions made before they ever had a chance to make them for themselves. I have to find a way to give them a chance, to reverse the spell binding them to the Reynard.

To do that, I think I must delve into the same dark magic my ancestors participated in. I'm not sure if this is such a good idea, but it's the only way to find a solution for the boys.

With a gasp, I tossed the book to the mattress and turned

around to face Soren. Putting my hands on his thighs, I leaned forward and asked, "There's a way to break the spell?"

He cocked a brow and his lips quirked—the expression he'd given me every time I'd asked a direct question about what I was reading.

I was resenting that look at the moment. If there was hope of undoing the curse, I needed to know. I had to try to fix it for Soren if I could, no matter what it took. And didn't he want that too? It couldn't be easy living in the same place, looking at the same scenery day in and day out. But even batting my eyelashes and flashing a cheesy smile didn't change his mind. He wouldn't budge.

I sighed and flopped back down between his legs. "You could save us a bunch of time if you would just tell me. Maybe I could break it. Fix what no one else has been able to."

"And live with the guilt of disobeying one of your aunt's dying wishes? I don't think so. This is your journey to take with her, not mine."

With another heavy sigh, I returned my attention to the withered pages and resumed reading. I was already feeling queasy, and if I didn't put the book down soon, I might find myself passed out on top of Soren. My body heated at the thought; every day we spent together, we pushed the boundaries of being "just friends," and the more we touched, the closer we crept to the edge.

But I would not cross that line; it was for the best. I shouldn't think about Soren like that anyway, not so soon after Archer, and maybe not at all—I mean, wasn't the bro code, like, doubled when they were brothers, and tripled for twins? I didn't want to be the girl who wedged herself between them, the bad memory they brought up during dinner twenty years from now.

More importantly, I didn't want to screw up my friendship

with Soren. I adored what was happening with us. We spent hours sharing our favorite memories of Hazel and remembering funny stories about the hotel. I understood why my aunt had loved him so much; he'd made her happy in a way no one else could, and he was doing the same for me. I was going to need to cling to that joy, because in less than twenty-four hours, the appearance of my family might suck it out of the hotel.

CHAPTER TWENTY-ONE

For the tenth time in the last fifteen minutes, I pressed my face to the stained glass that ran the length of the front door. The colored panes put an aqua hue over the overcast fall afternoon. I scanned the stoop for any movement and jumped back when several people pulling their luggage behind them came in view.

"They're here," I said, my voice louder than necessary.

"Right on time," Larry replied, straightening his tie before disappearing into the kitchen.

Skye walked in carrying a silver platter with glasses of wine. "Don't worry, girl. I brought the good stuff. Everyone will be relaxed and enjoying themselves in no time."

The door swung open, and my mother's cheery voice filled the lobby.

"Good afternoon, Gemma!" My nerves eased and my heart warmed at the sight of her. She craned her long neck and ran her manicured fingernails over the wreath of autumn leaves hanging from the front desk. Her artificially plumped lips curved into a smile as she locked eyes with me and pulled me into her arms.

"Hi, Mom," I grunted as she squeezed the air out of my lungs and peppered my cheek with kisses.

"You look just as beautiful as the decorations. You outdid yourself, darling."

"Thank you."

Over her shoulder, my father walked in. He pulled on his silk tie and turned up his nose like something bad wafted in the air. His scrutinizing gaze took in every square inch of the hotel that was part of his family's legacy. He wasn't impressed with the haystacks and pumpkins in the entry or the rose and thistle flower arrangements in the staircase's vases—or me, for that matter.

"Why is the parking lot empty? Fall is one of the busiest seasons up here."

"Hello to you too, Dad," I said, unable to hold my tongue.

"Hello," he said with zero joy. "Why is the parking lot empty?"

I took a deep breath; I was sure Raven wouldn't stick to her promise and tell the entire family what happened on my watch. It was a safe bet that she'd picked up her phone multiple times to call them, dying to mute the speaker and laugh as they lost their shit. But she must have stuck to her word because witnessing their disappointment and my embarrassment firsthand would be world-class entertainment during a family get-together.

With one more squeeze from my mom, I squared my shoulders, held my head high, and said, "We had a water-main break in the basement and had to close down while we wait for the insurance money to come through. It was—"

Trevor and his family burst through the door, his dark hair mussed and his eyes bloodshot as though he'd already been drinking for half the day. His wife was in slightly better shape, giving my mother a bright smile. As for my niece and nephew, they were screaming with excitement and running toward me with their arms wide. My guess was that the two-hour car ride here was the seventh-level-of-hell kind of bad.

"Hi, little friends!" I exclaimed, squatting down to shower them with hugs and kisses. I may have added an extra flair to my welcome to show my father just how his demeanor sucked the life out of a room.

High heels clicked on the tiled floor. I released my niece and nephew as Raven entered the room on Archer's arm. My stomach somersaulted, and my breakfast threatened to make a second appearance down the front of my burnt-orange dress.

"Mom, Dad, this is Archer. We met here at the hotel." Raven looked up at him and batted her eyelashes, turning her body in toward his and resting her palm on his chest. "Archer is a guest curator at the Spelling Historical Museum. He's from New York but is staying here for the duration of his exhibit."

I bit the inside of my cheek to keep from laughing as my aunt and uncle swooned all over him. That confirmed it; Raven had no idea what she was dealing with when it came to Archer. Which wasn't surprising, because if she had any idea that Archer wasn't human, she wouldn't let him touch her with a ten-foot pole.

"If only you were the owner of this hotel," Deborah was saying, her shrill voice loud and clear. "It would be streamlined, sleek, worth staying at."

Archer's eyes darted to Deborah with a flash of anger. He cared about this hotel and Hazel's legacy as much as Soren and I did. But he didn't speak up. Coward.

"This is what happens when amateurs do the work of professionals, but I'm working to change that." Raven really thought she was going to take the Reynard out from under me, and she had no qualms about mentioning it while I was in the same room. Her intentions were painfully clear; she was already planning every change that would turn it into a trendy boutique getaway. She might be restricted by the trust, but the Reynard as I knew it would be ripped apart if she got her hands on it.

That would happen over my dead body.

"Good afternoon, family," Hunter greeted us, entering the room hand in hand with Caden.

I breathed a sigh of relief. If anyone could field all my father's questions about the leak and knew more about the insurance situation than I did, it was Hunter. He would be the reason I survived this gathering.

I rolled my eyes as my mother went into her only piece of "proof" that she was all right with Hunter's sexuality for the millionth time—the story about her sophomore year in college when she had a roommate who was a lesbian. Normally, I would sit back and snicker at Caden's attempts to steer her in a less problematic direction but tonight I was too nervous to be even remotely amused.

As Caden cut short my mother's misguided tooting of her own horn, moving the conversation to the improvements to the bar, my father approached me.

"When were you going to tell me about the leak and shutting down the hotel? Didn't you think that was an important piece of information to share?" he asked, crossing his arms over his chest.

I exhaled, working through the anxiety he stirred in me and said, "Because of this."

"Because of what?"

"Because of the way you treat me, Dad! Like I'm—"

"Dad, lay off her," Hunter said, sliding in beside me. "She did the best she could. It was a shit situation, and I wasn't even here to help her. She handled it in the most effective way possible."

"Don't take up for her, Hunter. She should have told me."

I glared at my father and took a step back toward the kitchen. "Please, continue your conversation about me like I'm not even here. I have to go check on the food."

I slipped away to the kitchen, and Larry grinned as he moved the turkey from the oven to the platter. "This dinner is fit to feed royalty, if I do say so myself. It's been a long time since I've cooked a meal like this. How's it going with the family?"

"Do you think it's possible for me to reopen the portal on this property and let it swallow me up?"

"You would miss our *friends* if you did that." He opened a cabinet and stood on his tiptoes. "I can't find the gravy boat. It's probably in your kitchen; it was Hazel's and it's shaped like a turkey. Can you go check?"

"Sure." Anything to get me away from the lobby for a few more minutes.

Bypassing the elevator, both because I still hated it and because the stairs would take longer, I trudged up the staircase to my room, where I dug through the cabinets until I found the gravy boat in question. I had to laugh as I wiped it down; it was exactly the kind of thing Hazel would own—brightly painted and clunky.

On my way back downstairs, a haunting melody floated toward me from the direction of the drawing room. It wasn't unheard of for a guest who could play to show the others their talent, but no one in my family was musically gifted. Gripping the ceramic turkey, I made my way across the wooden planks and stopped short of the open French doors. Soren was sitting at the piano, fingers flying over the keys, his dark hair tousled, T-shirt stretched over his broad shoulders. Posting a picture of him like this could easily have made him famous on every social media platform known to humankind.

I didn't want to interrupt his playing. The music was magical, and I feared that if I stopped him, I would break the spell. The way his fingers danced across the keys, the dip of his head as he focused on the notes, each one waltzing and spinning through me. Everything about the scene was as though I'd been meant to stumble upon it.

When I sensed the song was coming to an end, I approached the piano and slid onto the bench next to him, our thighs brushing each other as I leaned into him and whispered, "That was beautiful."

Soren tucked his lips between his teeth and studied the piano keys. He nodded his appreciation and said, "Aren't you supposed to be hosting a party right now? I thought I heard a lot of noise coming from the lobby."

I shrugged and nudged him with my elbow. "I mean, I am, but the food probably isn't ready, and I was sent to retrieve this," I said, holding up the turkey-shaped gravy boat.

He laughed and shook his head as he said, "That damn turkey. Hazel used it religiously every Thanksgiving. I think she may have actually made it herself."

My lips tipped into a grin as I pictured Soren sharing Thanksgiving dinner with my aunt. It was good to know they had had each other and never had to spend a holiday alone. I didn't want that to change now.

"Soren, what are you doing for dinner?"

"I have some pizza from last night waiting for me."

I shook my head. "Not today you don't," I said, grabbing his wrist and tugging him to his feet. "You're coming to eat with me."

"Oh no," he said, shaking his head. "A meal with your lovely family? I think I'll pass."

I looked at him pleadingly, sticking my bottom lip out for effect. "Please? I am begging you. Raven brought your brother, and my dad is being a dick, and I just can't do this by myself. Please."

"All right, all right, stop begging. I'm sure you've kept them waiting long enough, and God knows, they can't have dinner without the gravy boat."

"Thank you," I murmured, slipping my free arm through his as we descended the stairs back into the lobby, where Larry and Skye were hustling to get the food on the table. I dropped Soren's arm and handed Larry the gravy boat before leading the way toward the double doors into the hotel's dining room.

When Soren and I entered the massive room, everyone's heads turned toward us. We inched along the back of the table, pressing our backs to the row of arched windows that ran from the floor to the ceiling. I took special pride in the scowl I received from Raven as we passed her and Archer. We reached the two empty chairs across from my mom, and her eyebrows went into her hairline as she glanced between Soren and Archer.

"Who's this, Gemma?" she asked.

"This is my friend, Soren," I said, tingles coursing through my veins as his name left my lips.

"And obviously, Archer's twin brother," Soren said, a titter of laughter flittering through the room.

Trevor cleared his throat. "You and Raven dating twin brothers? Isn't that kind of incestuous?"

"Oh my God," I mumbled. "Soren and I are not dating. We're friends. I don't know what these two are." I waved my hand in Raven and Archer's general direction. "Can we just eat, please?"

"Yes, let's. We don't want the food to get cold," Mom said, and everyone took their seats, me in between Soren and Hunter, Raven and Archer safely at the other end of the table.

Hunter leaned over and whispered, "So, Raven actually stole your boyfriend? What a bitch. When did that happen? Why didn't you tell me? Can I punch him in his gorgeous face?"

I laughed and murmured, "Halloween. I didn't tell you because it wasn't even worth it. She can have him. And yes, please. But not until after we eat the pumpkin pie; I don't want a fight to cut dinner short."

The scraping of forks against plates and the hum of conversation filled the room. Trays of stuffing and turkey were passed around for seconds, and four empty bottles of wine already sat on the table.

My dad used a homemade roll to soak up the gravy on his plate and said, "Your kitchen staff deserves an award; this turkey is to die for."

Shocked by the compliment, I said, "That was all Larry." I grinned and nodded at the old man across the room.

My dad's gaze dragged over to Larry and his nose scrunched, as if he was just noticing Larry's existence and not approving of the "help" sitting at the table.

"Absolutely. I've gained, like, ten pounds since moving in here," Hunter joked, rubbing his belly.

Raven snickered. "You'd have to be blind to miss that." She looked me up and down, her green eyes glittering with malice. "Looks like Gemma's in the same boat."

Skye's mouth fell open, and her muttered "Rude" could be heard all the way at the other end of the table.

Rage bubbled up within me, and I was seconds away from showing Raven what boat she could get on when the doors to the dining room flew open and all heads turned toward the sound. My heart leaped into my throat when I recognized the visitor.

Dressed in a tacky polyester suit was the woman who had called me two times a day and had sent me five handwritten notes since I had had to evacuate the hotel. She was personally offended that the Reynard had been shut down so long.

The Spelling town manager, Karen Roberts.

"Miss Fox? I need to speak with you. I'm so sorry to interrupt your Thanksgiving dinner, but it is urgent," she said, putting her hands on her thin hips and bobbing her head so quickly that I was surprised her blond wig didn't go flying across the room.

I pushed away from the table and gestured for her to step outside. "Of course." When we were in the lobby, I opened my mouth to speak, but Karen had lost every manner she had appeared to have in front of my family.

Her voice was loud and demanding as she said, "I wasn't planning on barging in on your Thanksgiving dinner, but some of the residents said they saw guests pulling into your parking lot, and I thought it was a holiday miracle; clearly, I was wrong. When do you plan on opening the Reynard again, Miss Fox? I've gotten complaint after complaint from business owners, and frankly, I'm sick of it. Three weeks is plenty of time to get that leak fixed and open your doors."

My heart sped up and banged against my ribs. The doors to the dining room weren't that thick, and my nosy family was no doubt absorbing every word spoken. "I'm sorry, but could I ask you to please lower your—"

"Businesses have lost vital revenue! The late Ms. Fox would have never let something like this sit for weeks. This community relies on the Reynard for their livelihood. If people can't come to your hotel, they've lost their main reason to visit our town. You've let the biggest moneymaker here sit empty for nearly a month!"

No matter who this woman was—I didn't care if she was the

governor of Connecticut—she didn't have the right to speak to me like that. "I'm not 'letting it sit.' The waterline was fixed earlier this week, and the foundation will be secure—"

"I don't want to hear your excuses. Just get it fixed before you have all the small-business owners in this town knocking down your door. Then you'll have something else to fix on your hands."

And where there was drama, my mother and Deborah were prone to inserting themselves right into it. "What is going on out here?" Mom asked as Deborah eyed Karen's cheap pantsuit.

"Who are you?" the town manager asked.

"Who are you, barging into our Thanksgiving dinner? This is very unprofessional," Deborah snapped.

My eyes widened as the three women went back and forth—they had met their match in each other. Let them go at it with their manicured claws out.

"You know what I find unprofessional? Leaving the rest of Spelling to wonder how they will pay their bills while you all feast away in a hotel that has been closed for three weeks!"

"Three weeks?" My dad's voice was a jolt to my system. "Gemma, what is she talking about, *three weeks*?"

"This hotel has been closed since right after Halloween," Karen snapped. "Like I said, it's what brings people to Spelling. If you aren't open, the rest of the businesses suffer."

"We have it under control, Dad," Hunter said, stepping out of the dining room.

"Jesus Christ, I had no idea it had been that long." My dad tilted his head to the side and looked at Hunter. "Is that why you asked me for a fifty-thousand-dollar loan? To speed up this process?"

My brother clenched his eyes shut and gripped the hair at the top of his head.

He'd gone to our dad for the money after I told him I didn't want to ask him. Even though his intentions were good, I wished he hadn't done it.

Looking at Karen with pleading eyes, I said, "Could you please excuse us? You've made your point, and I can assure you things will start moving. But my family and I need to deal with this in private."

"I want to know how you're going to fix—"

"Ms. Roberts, is it?" Raven asked, stepping out of the dining room. "I'm Raven Fox, the hotel's operations director."

Karen glared at my cousin as she accepted her outstretched hand. "I didn't know the hotel had an operations director."

"Neither did I," I mumbled under my breath.

"The Fox family has brought me in to help streamline our processes and to make the hotel more attractive to a higher-caliber clientele." Raven rested her hand on Karen's elbow and steered her through the lobby. "I would like to schedule a time with you to talk about how we can work together to . . ."

When I turned back to the dining room, everyone was out of their seat and staring at me. "Could everyone excuse us for a moment? I want to talk with Mom and Dad alone."

Hunter and Caden both squeezed my arm on their way out, and Trevor reluctantly ushered his crew onto the back porch.

My uncle and aunt planted their feet, until Hunter said over his shoulder, "Seriously. Gemma wants to talk to them alone. You can go in the bar to wait."

It was Archer who listened to my brother and motioned for my aunt and uncle to lead the way. "Skye is the best bartender in town; you have to try one of her specialty drinks."

The rest of the room followed behind them, with Soren at the end. He paused in front of me and dropped his voice as he leaned in. "Are you okay, Gem?"

My breath hitched at his proximity, and when I looked up at him from under my eyelashes, my heart skipped a beat when I met the worry in his eyes. Like he'd do anything right now to make this easier for me.

"I'm fine," I murmured. "Don't go far, though, I might need you when this is said and done."

He nodded and slid his hand down my arm until our fingers intertwined. "I'm not going anywhere." With a squeeze, he let me go and disappeared into the bar.

When I was alone with my parents, we sat back down at the dining room table, and I hung my head in shame. No matter what, Karen had been right; Hazel wouldn't have let the hotel stay closed for three weeks. "Let me—" I began, but Dad immediately started in on me.

"Gemma Diane Fox, this is exactly why we wanted you to give up the hotel. We predicted this would happen. You couldn't even commit for longer than a couple of months, and now it's turning into a money pit. You are not capable of running a business. This has got to stop. Don't you think it's time you handed things over to Raven?" he said, his voice cold and as honest as I'd heard it in a long time; he really believed what he was saying about me.

"But—"

"No *buts*," my father said, leaning back in his chair.

"Christopher," my mom said, and my attention snapped to her, praying that she would be able to calm him down. "Aren't you being a little harsh? This could have happened to Raven just as easily. Water leaks happen, and it takes time to fix things like this."

"It shouldn't have taken this long. Gemma isn't capable enough for this. You saw her with that woman. She couldn't take charge of the situation, but Raven did. This hotel needs someone who can manage every aspect; Gemma can barely function as an adult," he said, and my heart splintered.

His words held no uncertainty and no remorse. He wouldn't lie in bed tonight and question if he had been too harsh with me. In his mind, I'd proven my worth countless times. He believed I was better suited for something cozy, less complicated, something where I didn't have to think and perhaps not even show up. My dad truly believed I was a waste of space.

Mom shook her head. "Christopher, stop."

"Libby, don't tell me to stop. I'm right. And I think it's time we gave up the charade and handed the hotel over to the Fox who can run it instead of running it into the ground."

"Dad—"

"No, Gemma, listen—"

I slammed my palm on the table and stood. "No, *you* listen!" My parents gaped at me, but I kept going, the words flowing freely. "I want to keep this hotel because it's what Hazel wanted. And most of the time, I enjoy running the business, and I finally feel like I have a purpose. I can't give it up. I can't. I know I should have talked to you about it sooner, and I won't make that mistake again. But please, don't do this. You don't understand what it means to me."

What I couldn't tell them is that staying at the hotel was bigger than just me. This was the only home Soren and Archer had. What would happen to them if things went badly between Archer and Raven? Would she send them back to the shack? Would she stop paying them for all they did to keep the stories of this place alive? Would she take away the only thing that gave Soren purpose? It made me sick to think about it.

"I don't think *you* understand," Dad said, standing up and meeting my eyes, his unmoved. "You don't have a choice."

"Please don't do this," I begged my mother, knowing my father was a lost cause. He had made up his mind, and he wouldn't be swayed, but I had a sliver of hope that my mother would be malleable.

Dad's hazel eyes went dark, and his tone was decided as he said, "It's over, Gemma. The Reynard is going to Raven."

CHAPTER TWENTY-TWO

After my parents delivered the death sentence regarding my ownership of the Reynard and declared everyone would be leaving tomorrow afternoon except for them, I ran out without so much as a glance over my shoulder.

I would not let them see me cry.

This was the biggest disaster, the absolute worst-case scenario. Everything they'd predicted had come true. I'd failed, no matter how I cut it, no matter what excuses I tried to give. I had failed at running the Reynard just as I had failed at everything else in my life. It didn't matter that I'd tried my best; when it came to my father, my best would never be good enough.

Unlocking my suite, I stormed inside, leaving the door wide open. I stalked into the kitchen and pulled a soda from the refrigerator, needing some caffeine to calm my nerves. Tears glided down my cheeks as I grabbed a glass from the cabinet and set it on the counter, unscrewing the lid on the two-liter. Out of nowhere, the soda exploded, fizz and liquid spraying all over my clothes. The bottle slipped from my hands and knocked over the cup on the counter. It shattered into a million pieces, and as I attempted to set the bottle upright, I cut my hand on a shard of glass that wedged itself into my palm.

"Fuck!" I screamed, dropping to my knees, sobs racking my body as I tried to pull the glass from my skin.

"Stop, Gemma. Stop." Long fingers curled around my wrists, holding my hands apart. Through tear-blurred eyes, I found Soren squatting in front of me. "Come on, let's get you cleaned up."

He walked me to the bathroom, guided me to sit on the toilet lid, and ever so gently worked the glass out of my palm. After he tossed the shard into the trash can, he laid my hand palm up on my thigh.

"Here," he said, snatching a washcloth and wetting it, pressing it into my hand. "Put pressure on that so it'll stop bleeding, okay?" I nodded and numbly watched as he turned to fill the tub with hot water and bubbles. When the foam inched above the sides, he turned off the water and lowered his hands into the suds.

"It's nice and hot," he said, shaking the bubbles off. "If you need anything, just holler; I'll be in the kitchen. All right?"

I nodded, still trying to catch my breath as he slipped out the door.

With trembling fingers, I peeled the washcloth from my palm to find the bleeding had almost stopped before removing my clothes and sliding into the warm water. My muscles immediately relaxed, and I sank down until just my head hovered over the iridescent lavender-scented cloud. I was getting a grip on my emotions when I heard a broom swish followed by the clink of glass sweeping over the kitchen floor.

Everything I touched fell apart, and I was dependent on everyone else to clean up the messes I left behind. I fought back the tears, and my chest burned with the buildup of my grief. Hiccupping once, twice, the floodgates opened again, and I was sobbing.

A soft tap came at the bathroom door. "Gemma, are you okay?" Soren asked.

I thought about lying, trying everything in my power to sound normal, like I wasn't having the biggest breakdown of my life, but it was useless.

"No," I squeaked, closing my eyes and letting my humiliation join the rest of the emotions swirling within me.

"Hold on." He rushed away from the door, and the cupboards in the kitchen opened and closed. About two minutes later, he returned and asked, "Is it all right if I come in?"

"Yes."

The door creaked open, and Soren peeked around the frame before entering with two glasses of wine. He handed me one and sat on the floor next to the tub facing me. His hair was tousled, and his deep-blue eyes were washed with concern. "What happened after I left?"

I took a sip of the wine and inhaled before saying, "As you saw, things aren't easy with my family. I'm sure you can relate to that after living with your brother for one hundred and forty years."

He snorted at that and nodded for me to continue.

"My father completely berated me, and my mom tried to stop him, but she couldn't. And then he—he's—he's making me—" I stuttered, but I couldn't finish the sentence. I broke down into fresh sobs, the horror of what I was about to say weighing on my soul. "I can't do this, Soren," I wailed, setting the glass of wine on the floor before I broke it too.

"We'll figure something out."

"We won't. The whole town is upset with me; my dad thinks the only thing I'm good at is fucking things up. And let's be real, I'm—I'm not made for this." I buried my face in my wet palms and wept. My entire body rattled with the force of sobs that were now bordering on hyperventilation.

The water sloshed around me, and I was enveloped in strong arms. I glanced up to find Soren fully clothed in the water with me, holding me through my pain. He ran his hands over the soaked ends of my hair and pulled me tightly to his chest. I gripped his drenched T-shirt as I rested my face in the crook of his neck and cried.

"That's it; let it all out," he said, rocking me back and forth.

I nuzzled closer into him and felt his heart beating against my skin. Its rhythm was steady but quick, and I wondered what he thought of me right now. I had to look pathetic, weeping naked in the bathtub, but then it occurred to me that *pathetic* might not be the right word. *Broken* flashed through my head.

But not shattered.

Within his arms, I felt like I was being glued back together, like at least one person didn't think I was incapable, irresponsible, or idiotic. Soren cared enough about me to crawl fully clothed into a tub full of lukewarm water for no personal gain. He just wanted to hold me.

"Soren." I didn't even know how to say what I was feeling.

His hands moved to my cheeks, stroking my hair back as he kissed my forehead. "Shh. Let me get you a towel."

Holding my legs to my chest, I watched him stand and pull his shirt over his head. He tossed the soaked fabric in the sink before doing the same with his jeans. Stepping out of the tub, he kicked his discarded shoes to the side and grabbed a towel. He ran it over his lean, muscular body before securing it around his hips and taking the second towel in hand. Holding it open, he turned his head to the side and closed his eyes. I couldn't help but smile at the small act of chivalry.

Getting carefully to my feet, I stepped out of the tub and

wrapped myself in the towel. When I had it tucked safely around my chest, I pushed my hair out of my face and said, "You can look now."

His eyes flicked to my bare collarbone for a millisecond before returning to my face. "Do you feel a little better at least?"

"Yes, thanks to you. But I'm cold now," I admitted, wrapping my arms around each other and rubbing them with my palms.

One side of his mouth tilted up into that sly little smirk I'd come to adore. "I can help dress you if you'd like, and I always seem to have a lot of body heat I'm willing to share. Just let me know." He stepped out of the way and gestured at the door with a sweeping motion.

The thought of Soren seeing me naked without the bubbles *and* slipping clothes over my tingling skin had butterflies taking flight in my stomach. They flapped their wings with vigor, heating me from my cheeks to the apex of my legs. I pressed my thighs together and asked, "How about if I take you up on the second part?" I walked out of the bathroom to my room and beckoned him to follow me.

"I can do that," he said, stopping right outside my door.

"I'll be right back," I promised, walking to the dresser and rooting through the drawers for pajamas. I glanced out into the living room, where I had purposely left the door cracked. I stayed right where I was and let the towel drop to the floor, tossing the pajamas lazily on top of the dresser.

Soren was turned to the side with his arms crossed over his chest. His head jerked like he was struggling to keep it facing straight ahead, but ever so stealthily, it tilted just a bit, and he glanced at me from the corner of his eyes. I wasn't sure if he knew I'd caught him, but his gaze darted forward, and he ran his hand over his face. When he removed it, his cheeks were a warm rose.

I chuckled to myself and slipped on the pajamas—a satin tank top and shorts. They were a couple years old and about two sizes too small, but I had a feeling it wouldn't be too big of a fashion mistake. I grabbed a pair of plaid pajama pants from the drawer and opened the bedroom door.

"Okay, you can come in now." I held out the dry, clean pants. "These are my brother's; he left them here when we first moved in. I don't have any extra shirts, though. Sorry," I said with an exaggerated shrug.

Soren took the pants and turned his back to me. He dropped the towel, followed by his wet boxer briefs, and I wasn't as calculated in my attempts to look him over. Heaven help me; his backside was awe-inspiring, like something carved out of stone. The flannel slid over his round ass, stretching taut when it was in place, and I longed to discover if it was as hard as it looked.

He gathered his wet underwear and disappeared into the bathroom. I paced the room for a moment, my mind reeling with everything that had happened. Not only was dinner a disaster, but shame about the aftermath crept in. What had Soren thought when he'd found me on the floor bloody and crying? I couldn't even stand up to my own family. Not only were they stripping the Reynard from me, but I'd let them take a piece of my dignity. I had to have looked so pathetic and weak, and I wouldn't blame Soren if he was thinking about running. I'd had plenty of days when I wanted to run from myself.

I moved to the dresser and went to take off the diamond necklace I had found in Hazel's jewelry box. The longer Soren was in the bathroom, the more my worry bloomed. Was he just biding his time while he planned an escape route? No, he wouldn't do that. I'm sure my earlier episode was nothing compared to the four lifetimes' worth of acts he had witnessed in the hotel. But the guests came and went; I was a messy permanent fixture.

The bathroom door opened, and I held my breath. I only released it when the gentle pad of footsteps came in my direction. Soren stopped in my doorway and rested his shoulder against the frame. His dark hair fell to the side of his forehead, putting his cerulean gaze on full display. He studied me, setting every cell in my body buzzing. My hands shook as I fidgeted with the necklace's delicate clasp, never catching it just right to release it.

"Let me help you with that," Soren said, moving behind me and sweeping my hair over one shoulder.

I jumped out of his reach. "No, don't! I don't know if it's gold."

"Calm down, it's not."

His body against mine blanketed me with warmth, and it took every bit of control I had not to lean into him. I opened my mouth to respond, but first I had to swallow the lump in my throat. "How did you know it wouldn't hurt you?" I whispered, focusing on the way his fingertips brushed against the nape of my neck.

Soren chuckled, his warm breath caressing my sensitive skin. "Because I gave this to Hazel on her sixtieth birthday. I ate ramen noodles for five months saving the money for it, and during Winter Spirits, I rushed out the door at sundown and ran to the jewelry store on Main. It's a real diamond, but I had them set it in silver. They thought I was insane for putting such a beautiful stone in such a cheap metal. I was glad you chose to wear it tonight."

My breath caught, and I watched as he gently laid the necklace on the smooth wooden surface. I turned to face him and tilted my head to meet his eyes. "That's so sweet. I—" The lump in my throat had returned, and I gulped again before finishing. "Thank you."

"For what?"

A laugh slipped from my lips, and I shook my head. "Are you kidding? For everything. Being there for Hazel, trying to warn me about Archer, helping me figure out the book, crawling into a bathtub fully clothed to hold me while I cried. Just to name a few," I said, cutting my eyes to the left and back to his, my stomach in knots.

"You don't have to thank me for any of those things. I did it all for Hazel and y—" He clamped his mouth shut and tucked his lips between his teeth. "I wanted to do them, Gemma."

My chest blossomed with warmth, and I closed the tiny bit of distance between us. "Well, whatever the reason, I'm glad you did."

He brushed his knuckles against my forehead, capturing a rogue strand of hair and tucking it behind my ear. His fingers lingered on my neck, curling to the back as his gaze searched mine. He licked his lips and leaned in closer until his chest skimmed over my satin cami. "I shouldn't want to be so close to you, but it's so damn hard to keep my distance."

I slid my hand up his bare chest and to the side of his neck, slipping my fingers into his hair. Angling my face toward his, I whispered, "Then don't. Don't keep your distance. I like you right here."

He swept his lips over mine, sending an uncontrollable tingling sensation over my skin. "If we do this, if we give in, you have to promise me one thing."

I nipped at his bottom lip. "Anything."

"Promise you won't fall in love with me."

It seemed like an easy enough promise to make. I mean, he wasn't proposing marriage here, just a healthy make-out session. And I had a feeling I wasn't the only one desperate to know what a kiss between us would feel like.

"I promise."

Soren's fingers at my neck held me steady as his mouth slowly pressed against mine. Each soft kiss lingered like he was memorizing the shape and taste of my lips. He sucked and licked and coaxed my mouth open until he slid inside and deepened the kiss.

I was consumed with spearmint, a hint of red wine, and a hot flame low in my stomach. The burn raged through me to the tempo of my heartbeat until every inch of me was set aflame. I basked in the heat that only Soren could fuel and prayed that it would never subside.

He pulled me flush against him, and I sighed into his kiss. Slipping one hand down the curve of my back, he let his fingers drift under the hem of my shirt and rest against my bare skin. I clenched his hair in my fist and tugged, and he nipped at my lip in response. Just when I thought I would spontaneously combust, he pulled back and licked his lips, his blue eyes piercing the heart of me.

"Wow," I murmured, unable to tear my gaze away from him.

"I've never . . ." He shook his head.

"Don't tell me you've never kissed someone before."

Soren chuckled, and I pressed my palm to his chest so I could feel his joy rumble through him. "You are far from my first kiss, but I've never felt anything like that before."

My heart fluttered, and I nodded, my cheeks reddening under his stare. "Me neither. For me, kisses have always been just that— kisses. They usually led to more, but the kiss has always been forgettable. But that . . . that, I will never forget." He twirled a strand of my hair around his fingers and rubbed it against the pad of his thumb, and every single thought left my head.

Except the immediate realization that I didn't want him to leave.

"Soren, will you stay with me tonight?"

"You've gone through a lot. I don't want to—"

I grabbed his hand and pulled him toward the bed. "I was promised body heat. That's all I'm asking for."

Soren cleared his throat to conceal a laugh, and I glanced up at him with my brows furrowed.

"What?"

"I was just thinking—didn't you say you wouldn't ask me to warm your bed if you were 'sleeping on a goddamned glacier'?"

I rolled my eyes, pulled back the blankets, and sat on the bed. Patting the mattress next to me, I said, "A girl can change her mind."

"That she can." He lay down and pulled me back against him. With a kiss to my forehead, he whispered, "I think you'll agree that I'm far from glacial."

I pressed my cheek to his chest to hide my burning face. "Trust me, I know. Your kiss warmed every part of my body."

"I aim to please, Miss Fox."

CHAPTER TWENTY-THREE

I waited until the last of my family's cars pulled out of the parking lot, leaving just my mom and dad. I should have been terrified to face them alone again, worried that they would reinforce what they'd said last night, but I wasn't. I'd spent the hours after Soren fell asleep picking out small possibilities of how I could turn this around. If I could get my mom on my side, just *maybe* I would have a chance in hell of staying longer. She could at least buy me a week or two with Dad, and I would bust my ass to prove I could handle all the responsibility that came with the hotel. Until the trust was signed over to Raven, I still had hope.

When I walked into the sitting room, my parents were perched on the antique couch, my father looking like the harbinger of death and my mom his reluctant squire. "Take a seat, Gemma," my dad said firmly.

I sat across from them in a red velvet chair and folded my hands in my lap.

Dad clasped his hands between his knees and held my gaze. "I want you to understand that this isn't a total loss for you. I'll even help you with a new venture if that's what you want to do. But this hotel needs a lot of work, and it needs to be managed by someone who has experience. Raven has been successfully running hotels for years now, making her very capable. This is the right choice for everyone, including you."

I kept my composure, holding my head high even though I felt like screaming. "Dad, if you let Raven take the Reynard, it is a total loss for me. It's a loss for this town too. I understand I didn't handle the leak to your standards, but I did what I believed was best for the guests and for the reputation of the hotel. I didn't want to cut corners and risk the bad reviews. Before the pipe issue, things were going very well. People felt like Aunt Hazel was still here, and they loved that. If Raven takes over, she'll get rid of all those traditions guests love that make the Reynard special."

Hazel might not be the best selling point since everyone thought she was a little off, but they couldn't deny that she had done more for the Reynard than any of the women who had owned it before her. She wasn't about the money or the notoriety; my aunt was about the people. She didn't care if they were visiting for a night or trapped here for over a hundred years, everyone who walked through these doors was welcomed. Raven couldn't sustain that kind of customer service, but I could.

"Please don't judge me on the last month," I continued. "This is a big adjustment for me, and I was proud of everything I accomplished."

I fell silent in a feeble attempt to hear them praise me, but they just stared like they were waiting for the end of my childish rant.

I blew out a frustrated breath. "Raven hates this place; Hazel gave it to me for a reason. Every summer and Halloween when I came to stay here, I felt like I really belonged. That wasn't the norm for me." Dad opened his mouth to object, but I shook my head. "Let's face it; I'm not the daughter you hoped for. I wasn't valedictorian or the star athlete; I'm flighty and stubborn, and as you always love to remind me, I can't commit to anything. But I have committed to this. Please, *please*, don't take it away from me. Give me a chance."

If they didn't see it my way after that speech, I didn't know what else I could possibly say to change their minds. This was my heart and soul splayed out on the table, and I was waiting for them to carefully hand it back to me or demolish it until nothing was left.

Dad stood and clasped his hands behind his back as he paced the room. "I hear what you're saying," he said in a tone that very much implied that he did *not* hear what I was saying, nor did he understand. "But the responsible thing to do at this point is to give it to Raven. It's what should have happened to begin with."

My blood boiled at his blatant disregard for me, my feelings, and my abilities. How was I ever going to meet one of his high standards if he stopped giving me chances? I didn't want the bar lowered for me; I just wanted the opportunity to clear the hurdle. But he wasn't going to give me more time to better my game or find a strategy that worked. My dad was tired of waiting while I continuously failed.

"Raven has plans and solid ideas on how to execute them. She's talking about keeping the bar design Hunter created and turning everything down here into a spa. She wants to market it as a couples' getaway or a place for girls' weekends. Whatever she decides, the hotel will be better off with someone who knows what they're doing."

"That's not an option." Soren appeared at the top of the stairs, waving a yellow envelope as he descended them. "Not only is the Reynard considered by the state of Connecticut to be a historical landmark, but Hazel had stipulations in her will about altering the building."

My eyes grew wide, and I gaped at Soren, both for what he held in his hand and how handsome he was in his gray pullover and jeans.

"And who are you again?" Dad asked.

"Soren Hyde. We met last night. I work with your daughter."

"With? Don't you mean *for*?"

Soren kept his cool gaze on my father and, in a slow, deep cadence, said, "I work *with* your daughter, among other things."

I shot Soren a glare, but the flush of my cheeks surely didn't make it as menacing as I intended. I held out my hand for the envelope and asked, "Where did you get this?"

"Hazel applied for historical status a few months before she died. I found the certificate in the back office," he said, handing me the papers.

I grinned up at him and made sure my fingers brushed against his as I took the document. "Thank you, Soren," I murmured before turning back to my parents and looking at them as if silently asking, *Well? What do you have to say now?*

"Just another reason you can't afford to keep this place," Dad said, shaking his head. "Historical landmarks require a great deal of upkeep."

Soren took a deep breath and directed his frustration at my parents. "The hotel was left to Gemma. Doesn't she have any say in this?"

"Not when she needs our help to keep it afloat," Dad replied. "Hazel was barely making ends meet around here. She refused to cut the staff during slow seasons, and she was spending money left and right on things that no one can account for. Gemma had her chance to get it right, and now my brother and I are making the decision to give this place a shot with Raven."

My disappointment in my mother spread through my chest, my insides burning with it. Would it kill her to take up for me? All she had to do was tell my father that she thought it would be best if he gave me more time. He hated upsetting her and would give in. But she remained ramrod straight on the edge of the couch with her hands folded in her lap.

"It's a shame that you won't support her in something she's so clearly passionate about," Soren said, his gaze darting between my parents.

"Gemma has been passionate about a great many things in her life; her indecision is her greatest downfall," my dad replied.

Mom finally spoke up, but instead of taking up for me, she asked Soren the question I knew she'd wanted the answer to since last night. "You said you 'work with' my daughter, 'among other things.' What other things might those be?"

My cheeks burned, and I opened my mouth to scold my mom for such a blunt question. She wasn't daft and could put the pieces together however she saw fit. It wasn't necessary to hear it from Soren's mouth, but he answered.

"I was always taught that a gentleman keeps the details of his love life between himself and his partner. So, I beg your pardon if I choose to leave that at Gemma's discretion."

I pulled my lips between my teeth in order to keep from laughing. My mother's head looked like it was about to explode, and my father's eyes were wide in astonishment.

But my dad's shock didn't last long. "Well, Mr. Hyde, don't get too attached. Our Gemma doesn't have a good track record in the relationship department either."

I wanted to crawl under the couch and die. What kind of father says something like that about his own child? And right in front of her? Couldn't either of them say one nice thing about me?

Soren didn't miss a beat, holding my father's stare and saying, "And that is what makes all those details I didn't tell you about so much fun." He dipped his head toward my mom. "Mrs. Fox, it was a pleasure meeting you. I hope you will do the right thing by your daughter and not turn the Reynard over to your niece."

My breath hitched as his gaze met mine. I'd never witnessed anything as sexy as him putting my dad in his place. The authority in his voice and the set of his broad shoulders as he faced off with him—it was like the natural fear he should harbor was nonexistent. He wanted to stand on my side of the line they drew, and he showed no sign of regret.

Soren lowered his head and smiled as he walked past me toward the stairs. I had no doubt that everything he'd just done was solely for me. The countless small kindnesses he performed for me had become one of the biggest reasons I adored him. I turned back toward my parents and said, "Well? Is there any hope of you listening to me, or do I just need to give it up?"

"I don't like your tone, Gemma Diane," my father snapped.

I threw my hands in the air and paced in front of the fireplace. "Dad, you are threatening to take away—"

"It is not a threat. It is a promise. You will remain here as manager for the next two weeks while Raven takes care of business in Boston. Then, you'll step aside and let her run things."

"Dad, please—"

"You will leave the Reynard in two weeks, and that is final."

If I knew anything, I knew my father's word was his bond. He wouldn't sleep on it and come to an epiphany or realize I was the better choice for the hotel. His mind was made up, and my time at the Reynard was coming to an end.

CHAPTER TWENTY-FOUR

I asked Soren to give me the night alone. The disappointment that flashed in his eyes was crushing, and I almost changed my mind. But I needed to use the little time I had left to find answers, since I knew the book could never leave the Reynard. I had about one third left to read and only days left to do it.

I poured myself a cup of tea, settled in the armchair next to the woodstove, and dove back into Hazel's entries.

I have tried for many years to find a way to get into the kobold realm, to try to help Soren and Archer get home, but to no avail. Amity did an excellent job of closing the portal for good. But that didn't stop me from figuring out a way to combat the curse. Not reverse it entirely—there is no way I can see to actually do that. I also don't think there's any way I can truly help both boys, but I have found a spell that I think will give at least one of them a chance to go home. I think Wanda is starting to regret teaching me about magic, but I have to help them, and I really think it worked.

That being said, the boys are still stuck here for now. But I added a stipulation to the curse, a caveat that says that one brother can go back home.

Just one.

Wanda always talks about order and balance in magic. A give and take.

The debt for Robert and Gregory has been paid for generations now, and I believe magic has granted the twins this small reprieve. Unfortunately, it comes at a new cost.

Falling in love is the key, for love is a stronger force than any magic. The Reynard is handed down to Fox women. One must fall in love with one of the twins. Then one brother can go back, and the other will remain here as payment for the wrongs the kobold did to our family. Both were wrong, but decades upon decades have passed, and the Hyde brothers have paid for too long for a never-ending feud that wasn't their fault.

I cast the spell tonight, and everything seemed to line up perfectly. But we won't know for sure until the next descendant inherits the Reynard. Which means I will never know, unless I see it from Beyond.

I am confident in my decision to bypass Raven and pass the Reynard down to Gemma. Even though she's still a child, I can't think of a better person to take over after I'm gone, and what's better, I know her mind and heart will be open enough to at least entertain the notion of falling in love, thus freeing one of my boys from his prison.

I swallowed and closed the book, letting it slide from my hands into my lap.

It all came down to me.

All the unending questions that Soren and Archer refused to answer, the tidbits that kept me up at night—they all snapped into place.

Soren telling Archer he was going about things all wrong; Archer jumping from me to Raven so fast. He had only wanted to use me to free himself from the Reynard and leave Soren behind. And when I refused to give myself fully to him, he moved on to his only other chance—the other Fox woman on the property—the one with a great chance of becoming the hotel's new owner.

God, Archer was such a dickhead. He wanted me to free him over his brother, and he would stop at nothing to do it. While he was pitting me and Raven against each other, his brother was begging me not to fall in love with hi—*oh fuck.*

If I fell in love with Soren, he'd be free in his realm. Away from me. I'd be heartbroken if he left. He couldn't bear to hurt me, not like he felt he'd hurt Hazel.

I had been the key. I could've broken the spell, but now it would be up to Raven.

The thought of my frigid cousin having true feelings for anyone beyond herself or committing to anything aside from work was laughable. But I'd seen the way she'd wrapped herself around Archer in the hallway and the lingering glances she'd sent his way during our family dinner. At first, I thought her attraction to him had more to do with me than him. But now I wasn't so sure. And if she chose Archer, what would happen to Soren? Would he spend another century and a half confined to this property, his only interactions with others a series of creepy acts that had them questioning if he was real? Maybe Raven would figure out Archer's game and her feelings would shift to Soren. It was possible. She could find herself charmed by his smile or overhear him at the piano. Soren could see the good in her and bring it to the surface. Then she would be wrapped in his arms, sharing a bed with him, feeling his skin pressed against hers.

All the things that I wanted with him.

My heart squeezed as if in a vise, my feelings for Soren rising to the surface. What I felt for him was far, far more than lust. Not love. Not yet. But it was more than I'd felt for Archer. And Soren felt something for me too.

I set the book on the ground next to the chair and stood, stretching my arms high above my head. Once I'd worked every kink out, I pulled on a sweater and headed out into the hallway. I was hoping to run into Soren so I could tell him what I'd learned. What I didn't expect was to find Archer leaning against the wall outside my door.

His amethyst gaze was deadly and the expression on his face unreadable. "Gemma," he said in what could be mistaken as a growl.

I crossed my arms over my abdomen and pulled my sweater closed. "Archer. I don't really understand why you're snarling at me, considering I'm the one you pushed aside for my bitch of a cousin. *You* fucked *me* over, remember?"

"Don't be so sure about that," he said, staring at the framed landscape across from him.

"What do you mean? In what world am I in the wrong?"

Archer pushed away from the wall and stood in front of me. "I didn't take you as the kind of girl to try to put a wedge between brothers. You've moved on quickly from me to Soren."

I bristled and a laugh escaped my lips. "Oh my God, how hypocritical can you be? You're fucking my cousin because I wouldn't let you take what you wanted from me. And I know why you were doing it now, Archer, and you're an asshole for it." I walked away but then whirled around to face him. "By the way, I don't take getting involved with Soren lightly."

"Are you sure you're not taking advantage of him? He's been lonely since Hazel died, which makes him low-hanging fruit for the desperate."

"You're disgusting. And I didn't offer *anything*, and I was never yours."

Archer just rambled on as if I hadn't even spoken. "How did you two happen anyway? You just couldn't keep your hands off each other so you gave in to your whims? That's just like you, isn't it, Gem?"

I rolled my eyes so hard it hurt. Archer was almost as bad as my dad. "You have no clue what you're talking about. My relationship with your brother is nothing like whatever we had. We respect and trust each other like two mature adults."

He snorted and shook his head as he turned away from me. "That's a mouthful coming from a girl who fucked up so badly, she has to give up her hotel and can't commit to a shampoo, let alone a relationship."

Fury boiled inside me. So what if I never finished a bottle of shampoo and a collection of them graced my bathroom? It didn't mean that I was incapable of something deeper. But as far as the hotel went, I couldn't deny that I'd failed.

I stepped toward him and grabbed his arm, forcing him to face me. "You don't know what you're talking about, but to tell you the truth, it doesn't matter what you think. You burned your last bridge with me, Archer Hyde. You'll never get what you wanted from me, and I hope Raven denies you at every turn, leaving you to rot here for the rest of your miserable life."

He tilted his head and his eyes narrowed. Pulling his arm from my grip, he said, "That will never happen; I'll make sure of it."

"You're a bigger idiot than I am."

He tsked and said, "Shouldn't you be thanking me? Isn't it every girl's dream to get with two hot brothers at once? Soren and I have adapted to the times in every other way; perhaps he'd like to share before you have to go."

My palm made contact with his cheek before I realized what I was doing, the sound echoing through the empty hallway. "Fuck you, Archer."

His deep-purple eyes flashed with something I couldn't place before his normal cocky demeanor set in again. He hiked up an eyebrow and hissed, "You look just like your father when you're angry. I guess the apple doesn't fall far from the tree and all that shit. Have a good night, Miss Fox."

My stomach churned as his final words rang in my ears. I knew he'd said it on purpose, yet the remark still hurt more than I wanted to admit. So much so that I didn't fully register when he disappeared into his tiny flying form and left me alone in the hall.

As if on autopilot, I turned to my door and retreated into my suite. I couldn't face Soren after that exchange with Archer. Not only had I lost control, Archer's words had held too many painful truths. I'd failed, and now Soren could be trapped here for the rest of his life. I wasn't ready to face that possibility, so I had no choice but to go to bed and start over tomorrow.

CHAPTER TWENTY-FIVE

After spending time with Larry working on the budget, I reviewed plans for Winter Spirits with Hunter. Even though I wouldn't be around to implement them, I wouldn't stop doing what Hazel had wanted me to do until the moment arrived for me to step out of the hotel as its owner. It was the least I could do to honor her memory. But even the motivation to make my aunt proud wasn't enough to keep thoughts of Soren at bay.

Every bump in the wall and dark shadow drew my attention. I was desperate for any sign that I wasn't the only one who couldn't get our kiss out of my head. The gentle movement of his lips against mine was infused with a passion unlike anything I'd ever felt. And his body. I wanted to trace each groove his muscles made and press my skin to his. His kiss was without a doubt the best I'd ever had, and I'd kissed my fair share of boys.

By four o'clock, I left the front desk in Larry's care and strolled the hallway to my suite. I would miss the easy commute home, and the staff who'd become family, but mostly, I'd miss having a piece of Hazel in my every day.

I slipped my key in the door and looked over my shoulder at the sconce on the panel next to me. Soren was probably roaming the passages in the walls, or perhaps he was sitting in the bell tower by himself. All I had to do was pull the lever. Then I could find him and tell him about my run-in with Archer, along with the other things taking up space in my head.

Looking down at my wrinkled Reynard polo and khakis, I scrunched my nose. Not exactly how I wanted Soren to see me after two days apart. I ducked into my suite, stripping off my work clothes and putting on a pair of dark jeans and a jade-green sweater that dipped low in the front. Taking my hair down, I let it fall loose around my shoulders and dabbed on a bit of blush and mascara. Soren had seen me at my worst, whether it be vomiting at his feet or sobbing in the bathtub, but I wanted to feel good about myself when I saw him today. I wanted him to really *see* me, and I needed to know that the other night wasn't a fluke.

When I was satisfied that I didn't look like a hotel manager anymore, I took a deep breath and walked into the hallway. Before I could stop myself, I pulled on the light fixture and put my palm on the wall, pushing gently. The panel gave way and swung open. A small voice in my head told me I shouldn't be here; this was Archer and Soren's safe place. Hazel had designed it so they could have privacy and somewhere that was only for them. But I pushed the nagging feeling away and stepped inside. I was running out of time, and I wanted to spend what was left of it with Soren.

I turned on my cell phone flashlight and skimmed the beam over the narrow stone corridor. This passage looked no different from the others—the same cold gray stone walls and floors, and musty, damp air. At the end stood a winding wooden staircase that ascended into the darkness above. I gripped the railing and climbed until I reached a set of black iron double doors that featured arched windows with floral embellishments. I chewed my lip, suddenly nervous to knock. Not because I was scared to see Soren, but because I didn't want the wrong brother to greet me.

I exhaled a long breath and rapped my fist on the metal before I could chicken out. For about thirty seconds, nothing happened, and I considered knocking again, but the sound of steps stopped me. Soren opened the door, and both of his eyebrows shot up.

"Gemma, what are you doing up here?" he asked, looking behind me like he expected to see the guests lined up for a ghost tour.

I shrugged, letting my arms drop to my sides. "I wanted to talk to you, and I—I just thought I'd see if you were home." It was a stupid thing to say. If he wasn't here, then he was somewhere on the property. Technically, he was always home. "I shouldn't have come. I'm sorry, I'll go." I turned the way I'd come, rubbing my forehead with my fingers.

"No!" He grabbed my arm and ushered me toward him. "I was just surprised to hear someone knocking on our door. It's been quite some time. The last few years of her life, Hazel had trouble navigating the stairs in the dark, so we always went to her. Come in."

He stepped to the side, and I entered the only true home Soren and Archer had ever known. It was bright and open with sleek leather furniture and modern decorative pieces. A massive flat-screen television hung on the gray stone wall, and on each side were floor-to-ceiling bookshelves crammed with books. A MacBook sat open on a natural wood dining table with six high-back chairs. The kitchen area was filled with concrete countertops and stainless-steel appliances. The Hyde brothers' home was a far cry from Hazel's suite, which was stuck in the 1800s with a splash of the 1950s.

Soren gestured to the sofa and spoke over the smoky voice of Stevie Nicks playing from the stereo. "Can I get you anything to drink?"

I walked to the sofa and sank down into the soft leather. "Yes, please. Just a soda is fine."

It was strange to be in his personal space, tucked inside his safe haven. He moved more freely here, his shoulders not as tense and his walk a bit lazy. It even made the dynamic between us feel different, yet he was just as courteous as always. This was where Soren could be himself with no worries.

He returned with two cans of lemon-lime soda and cracked them both open before handing me one.

"Thank you," I said, taking a sip and setting it on a coaster on the coffee table.

He sat next to me on the couch and ran a finger through the hair falling around my face. "Is there something on your mind?"

"Yes. Did Archer tell you that we ran into each other in the hallway yesterday?"

"My brother hasn't said much to me in recent weeks. Why, what happened?"

I sighed and replayed the entire conversation for him, even the slap I'd delivered at the end of the interaction. "It just got me thinking." I stopped, drawing my bottom lip between my teeth. This was another question I *needed* the answer to but was too afraid to ask, too afraid to face the possible truth.

Soren set down his soda and turned to face me. "Talk to me."

I looked down at my hands until he put his thumb under my chin and raised my face to his. Sighing, I said, "Does it bother you that I was with your brother?"

He released my face and clicked his tongue against his teeth.

I could almost see the thoughts rolling around in his head as his eyes swept back and forth over the living room before landing back on me. "I'm really not interested in your time with Archer. He moved quickly, and his relationship with you was a game to him. There is no comparison between what I want and what he wanted. The only thing that bothers me about him being with you is that he hurt you."

Relief spread through me, and I met his gaze. "And what is it that you want, Soren?" I whispered, willing myself to control my breathing.

"I want what we have to always be simple for you. Something you look back on with fond memories." He tucked a strand of my hair behind my ear. "I just want to be near you."

One side of my mouth tilted into a smile, and I leaned forward to press my lips to his jaw right under his ear. He wrapped his arms around me and lifted me onto his lap, my legs straddling his. "Is this close enough?" I murmured, tugging on his earlobe with my teeth.

"We're getting there." His fingers inched under my sweater and ran up my spine, slowly tracing each bump.

My palms drifted to his chest, fiddling with the buttons on his shirt. "All I could think about today was your mouth."

"You weren't alone. From the moment I wake up until I drift to sleep, all I think about is kissing you."

"Really? I—" I ducked my head and blew out a breath before continuing. "I was afraid it had just been me. When you didn't come downstairs the past couple of days, I thought maybe I'd misjudged the situation."

"I know how important it is to you to show your family what a mistake they're making. I didn't want to distract you from what you need to do. But now that I have you alone"—he nipped at my bottom lip—"I plan to keep you *very* distracted."

I slid my palm from the front of his shirt up into his hair. "Being distracted by you sounds like heaven. There is nothing else I'd rather spend the rest of my time here doing." I adjusted on his lap and tightened my legs around his waist. "That kiss the other night . . ." I pressed my lips to his jawbone and over his throat. "It was the kind of kiss I daydream about. A simple rush I could easily chase after for the rest of my life."

Soren rested his head on the back of the couch, and his pulse pounded at the side of his neck. His hands slid over my ribs, stroking my skin into millions of tight goosebumps. "A kiss has never made me feel like that before, like all I want to do is give you anything you need."

I lifted my head and hooked my finger under his chin to bring his gaze to mine. "I need you. I need you to kiss me again, but this time, I don't want you to stop." I moved over him, pressing the seam of my jeans against the evidence of his desire. "I just need you."

He kissed me with the same slow passion he had the other night. His tongue stroked mine like he was savoring the taste of me. Each moment that passed, his kiss grew hungrier, his teeth captured my bottom lip, his hand pressing against my spine, demanding I move closer. My fingers gripped the hair at his nape and my hips rocked over him, creating a torturous friction that had me aching for more.

Soren turned, pressing me into the couch. Hovering over me, he asked, "Is this all right?"

My breath caught and I nodded, wrapping one leg around his hip to pull him closer. "It's more than all right. It's all I've wanted for the past two days—to be underneath you," I rasped, gripping the front of his shirt in my fist and tugging his mouth to mine, capturing his lips in another fiery kiss.

He pulled his mouth away from mine and dragged his lips down my neck. His hands had found their way under my sweater again, and he eased it up until the cool air of the room was a contrast to the heat where our bodies met. I released him and held my arms over my head, silently letting him know I wanted him to take it off.

When my top lay haphazardly over the back of the couch, Soren brought his lips back to my neck. He kissed my collarbone, the valley between my breasts and the center of my abdomen. Each kiss lingered, soaking in the feel of the new patch of skin, and I was helpless to do anything more than run my fingers through his hair and watch him explore me.

He reached the waist of my jeans, and his gaze met mine over my body's curves. "May I?" he asked, playing with the brass button.

"God, yes," I breathed, and when he unsnapped the button and tugged the denim down, I lifted my hips to make it easier for him to remove them.

He bit his bottom lip as he slid the jeans down my legs and dropped them to the floor. "My God," he said, running his palms up and down my thighs, his skin just rough enough against my smooth, freshly shaven legs. "You are exquisite."

My cheeks heated, and I pushed my hair out of my eyes. "Thank you."

He pressed his body against mine, and his mouth resumed where it had left off. My skin sizzled, and the only thing that saved me from combusting was the cool leather at my back. The tips of his hair caressed my stomach as he left a trail of kisses to my navel. He moved lower until his chest rested between my legs and his warm breath penetrated the thin fabric of my panties. He held my gaze as he dipped his head and brushed his lips against my center.

I lifted my hips to his mouth, pressing myself against him. "Oh God, Soren."

His mouth opened, and he nipped at my sensitive skin before dragging his tongue up the middle. My core contracted, and I tangled my fingers in his hair and pushed gently, letting him know how badly I wanted him. "Don't stop," I begged, my release building almost embarrassingly quickly.

He eased my panties to the side and feasted on me as if he were a starving man and only I could fill that hollow ache in him. Every lap of his tongue and kiss from his lips brought me closer. I moaned his name, which only made him more eager to please me. It was as if my happiness in that moment was his.

I chased after my release, my body tensing until it could no longer contain the pressure. I lost myself in the unrelenting strokes until I gripped his hair and pulled him away from my sensitive center.

He crawled back up my body, and I spread my legs further to welcome him before wrapping them around his hips. He nuzzled his face in my neck and said, "I can't get enough of you, Gemma."

I laughed and pushed his hair off his forehead. "Well, that's perfect, because *I* can't get enough of *you*." I sobered when I thought of the other thing that was on my mind. "Soren?"

"Yes?" He drew lazy circles over the swells of my breasts, sending shivers up my spine.

"I read more yesterday. There isn't that much left to go," I murmured, my lips against his temple.

His fingers stopped their tracing for a moment, but he recovered quickly and asked, "And what did you find?"

"I know why you don't want me to fall in love with you."

"And why is that?"

"It'll break the spell. It's what Archer wanted from me. And if I break the spell, if I fall in love with you, it's over. You'll leave, and you're scared of hurting me the way Hazel was hurt when you didn't feel the same about her. Is that why you were so nasty to me when we first met?" I asked, tears choking my voice.

He dropped his head to my chest and released a long breath. His body sank against mine like he had carried this heavy weight for too long and I'd saved him from it in the nick of time.

"During one of my last conversations with Hazel, she gave me a warning. She said that I was about to face heartache like I've never known." He swallowed and took a deep breath that pushed his chest against mine. "She told me that just as she easily fell in love with me, so would . . ."

"So would I," I finished for him. "You thought if you were a big enough asshole, you'd be able to hold me at arm's length." My lips quirked into a smile. "See how well *that* worked out for you."

He laughed and shook his head. "It worked out perfectly. I care about you, Gemma. Even if you are no longer a part of my *every* day, I need you to be part of *some* of my days."

I ran my hands over his skin, lifting his chin and placing a kiss on the corner of his mouth. "I will be. I'm not going away forever, but if you change your mind, I understand."

"Never. I'll always want you around. Always."

Always. The word echoed through the quiet living room. It was all I wanted, to stay here with Soren, to be able to lie in his arms any time I wanted, to shower his skin with kisses.

I wanted to make him feel as good as he'd made me feel, to bring him to the brink of ecstasy. He deserved that. And more.

He deserved everything.

Suddenly, I shifted and flipped us over, so I was sitting on top of him, one thigh on either side of his legs. Leaning forward, I unfastened each button on his shirt, pushing it off his shoulders. He sat up and pulled it off, dropping it onto the carpet. I trailed my fingertips over his chest, tracing every hard line of muscle, drawing my bottom lip between my teeth as I watched his eyes flutter shut.

My hand wandered down his abdomen and popped the button on his jeans. "Can I?" I whispered, my fingers dancing across the zipper.

He nodded, and I slid the zipper down deliberately, one notch at a time, and the proof of his desire for me was hard under my fingertips. I pushed the jeans off his hips, and he kicked them to the floor.

"Soren," I whispered, sliding my hand further down, my fingertips dipping just under the waistband of his boxers. "Let me touch you."

"Take, ask me to give—whatever you want, Gemma, I want it too."

I slipped my fingers further under his waistband and gripped him in my palm, shuddering at the sensation of him bare against my skin.

"So, if I wanted to"—I leaned over, the swells of my breasts brushing against his lower abdomen as I planted open-mouthed kisses on his sternum—"put my mouth on you, that's something you'd want too?"

"I haven't—I've never had a—" His eyes went wide, and he inhaled sharply. "It's been a long time since I've been touched like this, and *never* like *that*."

My lips parted in surprise. "I'm the lucky girl who gets to be your first?" A thought struck me, and my eyes widened to match his. "Surely that wasn't *your* first time giving . . ."

He chuckled. "The last time I had relations with a woman was in the fifties, and pleasuring a man with one's mouth wasn't a very ladylike thing for a nice girl to do. But they were more than willing to take whatever I wanted to give them."

"That's unfortunate and very"—I kissed down the center of his chest—"very"—down the V of his abdomen—"very"—under his navel—"selfish of them," I finished as I closed my lips over him, sliding from the tip and taking him as far in as I could.

He lifted his hips from the cushions in response to each movement of my mouth. His lips parted as he watched me take him in deep, and a string of profanities flowed out of him in a lust-filled moan. I took his hand and brought it to the back of my neck and curled his fingers around my hair. He caught on quickly, helping me set a pace that had his neck bowing back.

"Fuck. Just like that," he said, when my lips and tongue glided along the smooth length of him.

I met his gaze, thrilled with the wonder I found written on his face as he watched himself disappear into my mouth over and over again. The muscles in his abdomen flexed, and he pressed himself deeper.

"Oh God, Gemma. I'm going to . . ."

I kept my lips closed tight around him, and his moans filled the room. His body went limp, and his hand fell away from my head. I released him with a final kiss to his sensitive skin and crawled back up into his arms, lying on top of him with my head tucked under his chin.

"That was . . ." He shook his head and held me close. "Thank you."

I looked up at him, unable to stop the smile from spreading across my face. "That's all I've wanted to do for weeks now: to feel your skin against mine, to know how you sound when you're unraveling. And to be the one who makes you feel that way."

He kissed the top of my head. "Stay. Don't go back to your room tonight."

Warmth bloomed in my chest, and I nodded against him. "I wouldn't dream of being anywhere else but in your bed tonight, Soren Hyde."

CHAPTER TWENTY-SIX

When I woke up the next morning, I smiled before I even opened my eyes, remembering the night before and how Soren had made me feel. Stretching my arms above my head, I took in his room. The furniture, comforter, even the walls were crisp, bright white, which made the hints of warm gray pop throughout the massive space. The large window under the bell took up much of one wall. The sun shone through, warming my bare skin. I slid my arm to the other side of the bed where Soren slept, and my heart soared when my palm landed on his chest. He'd stayed in bed with me. I'd not even asked him to, never mentioned how important it was that I not wake up alone after spending such intimate moments together.

Rolling over on my side to face him, I soaked in every detail of his face—the slope of his nose, his dark, arched eyebrows, smooth olive skin, and his long, black lashes barely grazing the skin under his eyes. He was truly the most beautiful man I'd ever encountered, and although he was genetically identical to Archer apart from their eyes, his beauty was on another level. It radiated straight from his heart and soul, and that made him perfect.

And if he was perfect like this, not even in his natural form, what must it be like to see him as a kobold?

I brushed a stubborn piece of hair from his forehead, and he stirred. His eyelids fluttered open, his icy-blue gaze piercing me to the core.

"Good morning," I whispered, leaning forward and planting a kiss under his ear.

He stretched his arms above his head and groaned with a wide smile on his face. "Good morning. I can't remember the last time I slept that well."

I snuggled in the crook of his arm and tangled my legs with his. "Me either. Thank you for staying in bed with me. I assume that"—I glanced at his alarm clock—"11:27 a.m. probably isn't your usual wake-up hour."

"No," he said, his voice cloaked with a sexy morning rasp. "But I'm normally not completely exhausted when I go to bed either. But I really enjoyed the activities that put me in such a state. I take it that you're skipping work today."

"I have other important things to do with the time I have left. Let Raven take care of it."

"In that case, would you like me to make you breakfast?"

I sat up, pulling down the T-shirt he had lent me. "Yes. But isn't Archer here?"

"He lives here. Are you planning to hide in my room until you're sure he's gone?"

I ran my fingers through his hair and kissed the corner of his mouth. "Is that an option? Because I wouldn't mind hanging out here with you indefinitely. It's not like I'll have anywhere else to be in a week or so."

"The only problem is that your brother will notice you're missing and say something to your parents, and your evil cousin will be more than happy to turn this hotel upside down looking for you and then claim it as a total loss. Do you see where I'm going with this?" He turned his head and kissed me. "Up with you, Gemma. You can't hide your life away in here with me; I won't allow it."

"How am I supposed to go without those kisses when I leave?"

"You will just have to promise to come back and let me place them on you again and again until you tire of me."

A weak laugh rattled my lips. "That will never happen."

"I hope it doesn't. Now come on, get up so I can make you something to eat."

I sat up and swung my legs over the edge of the bed, and he moved toward the door, pulling a black T-shirt over his head.

"Wait," I said. "I want to ask you something."

"Anything," he said, looking down at me expectantly.

"Can I—I mean, will you show me your true form? I just keep thinking about it. You guys always seem to disappear, and I don't even know what I'm looking for."

Soren's laughter filled his bedroom. "It's not that impressive, to be honest."

"Can I be the judge of that?"

"Far be it from me to deny you the chance to behold the glory of a kobold."

He took a step back but kept his eyes on me. They glowed like blue lightning against the night sky, and then, he was gone.

"Soren?" A burst of blue light zipped by in the corner of my vision. I followed the glow, but it was like trying to keep an eye on a bee in flight. He zipped over the dresser, knocking over a bottle of cologne and fluttering the sheets on the bed as he flew over them.

Holding my hand out, I said, "Can you hear me?"

The ball of light slowed and drifted to my palm. I don't know what I expected to see when I leaned in closer to him, but he was nothing more than a glimmer of radiant aqua, too small to see with the human eye.

I lifted my hand to eye level and whispered, "Wow, that's incredible." I sat on the bed and crossed my legs, studying the shimmering ball in my hand. "So do you just transform back?"

Soren jetted away from my palm, and just as quickly as he'd vanished, he reappeared. "I told you it wasn't that amazing."

"It was pretty incredible, but this"—I flicked my gaze down and then back to his face—"is even better."

"I like this form better as well. This has been my real skin for my entire life. Archer and I didn't even know we could shift forms until Hazel took over and allowed us to research what we are," he said, opening the bedroom door and extending his hand to me.

I couldn't imagine living a life so void of freedom that I wasn't even allowed to learn more about such an important aspect of who I was. My parents might be overbearing and my father impossible to please, but at least they never restricted my internet usage.

"Well, as long as I'm here, I'd like for you to stay in this form," I murmured, taking his hand. "Now, you can make me breakfast."

※ ※ ※

"No! No more pancakes, Soren," I said, laughing as he placed another one on my plate. I was on the verge of bursting at the seams, and he wouldn't quit feeding me.

"Just one more." He sat on the barstool next to mine at the counter. "I like that face you make when you take the first bite. It's like you have a little piece of heaven in your mouth."

I resisted the urge to make a dirty joke and settled for a

compliment instead. "Your cooking *is* really good." I cut a piece, slathered it in syrup, and popped it onto my tongue.

The bedroom door on the other side of the suite opened, and Archer stepped out. His dark hair was combed away from his face, and the sleeves of his baby-blue button-up were rolled to his elbows. "Don't fall for that line, brother. She enjoyed my cooking as well."

I rolled my eyes and dropped my fork to the plate with a clatter. "Oh please. You were taught by the same woman, so it's not like it's that big of a stretch, Archer."

He made his way into the kitchen and opened the refrigerator, scanning the shelves. "From the sounds of it, Soren and I do some other things the same way. I could hardly sleep with all the noise coming from his room."

I blushed at the memory of Soren touching me one more time before we fell asleep. I was so caught up in him that I didn't even consider that Archer might return and hear us. Nothing else mattered but us in those intimate moments when he made me feel like the only person who existed.

The muscle in Soren's jaw ticked, and he set his fork down. "You're walking a fine line right now, Arch. Show the woman some fucking respect."

"Or what?" Archer closed the door, opened the orange juice he'd selected, and drank straight from the carton.

"Or I'll wipe this floor with your ass."

"It's a shame she didn't fall in love with you either and that the transfer-of-ownership papers will be signed next week. I bet you thought you were so close to going home."

"I am home." Soren's cheeks turned a bright red that trailed down his neck.

"What new adventure will you be off to, Gem? Maybe next time you can find a set of vampire triplets."

"It's really none of your business what I have planned." I smirked as I took a sip of orange juice from Soren's glass, as mine was empty and I wouldn't be drinking out of that carton again. "I know what you're going to be doing, though."

Archer raised an eyebrow. "And what's that?"

I inspected my fingernails and pushed my cuticles back before saying, "Good luck getting Raven to fall for you, buddy. I'm afraid that's already a lost cause. She may be fun to fuck around with, and she may be an easy lay, but she'll never fall in love with you. She's too selfish."

He crossed his arms and leaned against the counter. "I wouldn't be so sure about that. Don't let your jealousy get the better of you, Gem. It's not a good shade on you. You and I both know that all I needed was a couple more weeks with you and you would have been nursing a broken heart right about now."

Soren jumped to his feet and kicked his chair back, causing it to crash to the floor. "Get the fuck out."

"This is my goddamn house! *She* can get out!"

In four long strides, Soren stood face-to-face with Archer. "Hazel would be appalled by the way you're acting."

"Don't bring Hazel into this! She knew how important this was. She understood that I'm suffocating to death in this hotel. You're so fucking narcissistic, Soren. I bet you thought she did it for you, but she did it for me. This is meant to be my out!"

"You can have the fucking out! Go make Raven fall in love with you, but stop belittling the woman I"—he paused, clearing his throat—"care about because you didn't get what you wanted out of her."

"Fuck you!"

"Fuck *you*; you're an asshole."

Archer's gaze darted to me. "Don't be fooled, Gemma. He is just as big of an asshole as I am. Be glad you get to run away from all of this."

I scoffed and got to my feet, walking around the counter and bumping Archer out of the way. "No one is as big of an asshole as you. You won that title *all* on your own. And I have some real contenders for it in my life, but you? You take the cake. Raven will be back in a few days. Give it your best shot with her. But if she *actually* falls for you, we might just get to feel hell freezing over. So, good luck getting out of here, pal. I wish you the best."

Like my rant didn't even faze him, Archer raised the carton and said, "It was nice knowing you, Gemma. Thanks for showing me *and* my brother a good time."

Soren didn't give me a chance to stay and watch Archer gulp down the juice after his disgusting toast. He led me to his room to get dressed and out of their apartment. We didn't say a word as we walked hand in hand through the tunnels. The only communication between us was his thumb brushing back and forth over my knuckles. I took the silence to mean that he needed a moment to collect himself since I was feeling the same way. We wound down several flights of steps, and Soren nudged a wall that opened into the freezing morning air.

"Are you all right?" he asked as we stepped into the line of trees that skirted the far side of the property.

I shivered and pressed myself to his side, turning my face away from the chilly wind. "I'm fine. He's a dick, so I'm not going to take anything he says to heart. I mean, if you and I hadn't had that conversation about me having been with both of you, that whole exchange would have probably brought me to tears, just because I wouldn't have known how you felt. But I'm okay." I squeezed his hand and turned to face him, planting a kiss on the soft skin of his neck. "I promise."

"I know it doesn't excuse his actions, but he's hurting. He can't let go of the bad that happened here, and on some days, I don't blame him."

"I get it. And I wish I could do something to help you both, because I know he means the world to you. But my hands are tied. I leave in less than two weeks, Soren. That's what's bothering me right now, the idea that I won't be able to just see you whenever I want. My heart is aching; the burn in my chest and need to cry are always right there at the surface. To say—" I paused, the lump in my throat growing by the second. "To say I care about you isn't enough. You almost said something earlier that you didn't mean to say, didn't you?" I asked, chewing my lip and avoiding his eyes.

"I think I've made clear my feelings for you, Gemma."

I wanted him to say it. But I knew that wasn't going to happen. Not today. So, I just nodded and cupped his cheek in my palm. "And I hope that mine for you are just as plain to see."

"I meant what I said; don't fall in love with me. What we have is good; it's more than I could ask for. Besides, you're young and beautiful. You'll leave this place and have so much life to live, and I want that for you. I want you to be happy and free."

Tears stung my eyes, and I shook my head, trying my best to keep them at bay. "I don't *want* to be free from this place or from you. This is all I want. I wish they weren't taking it away from me, but they can't keep me from coming back here to see you. I'm not going to go away forever. Unless that's what you want me to do." The thought made my heart tighten in my chest.

He ran his thumbs under my eyes before my tears could streak down my face. "I've watched this place take so much from one woman after another. Amity lost her children. Maybell, the years of her life that should have been dedicated to grandchildren and easy living. Betty lost the life she wanted, and it turned her into a bitter, hate-filled woman. And my dear Hazel gave up everything for us and this hotel. You deserve better than this. You should have a man by your side who can take you for long walks along white-sand beaches and dine with you at gourmet restaurants. As much as I want to give you those things and so much more, I will never be able to do so."

I could see how much this meant to him, that he didn't want to hurt me, only wanted me to have everything. But right now, I just wanted to live like everything wasn't about to change. "All I want for the next two weeks is to be with you. Can you give me that?"

"Yes, it's the least I can do."

Soren wrapped me in his arms, and I rested my head against his chest, listening to the steady beat of his heart. He ran his fingers through my disheveled hair and kissed the crown of my head. Our sorrow lingered between us, reminding us of all the things we would never have. But I wouldn't let it weigh me down and steal from me the final days I had with Soren. I didn't care if it broke my heart in the end, I would give him a taste of what could have been if I could only stay.

CHAPTER TWENTY-SEVEN

A picnic next to the stream that ran along the outer edge of the property, a night of dancing to old love songs in the dining room, and a very late-night skinny-dipping session in the hotel pool that lasted for only three seconds before Soren and I were overcome by laughter and chattering teeth. We had made the most of every day, and in doing so, they had all gone by too quickly. Tonight would be our final adventure together at the Reynard, and Soren had promised that he'd saved the best for last.

He told me nothing more than to dress nicely but warmly and that he would meet me in the tunnels an hour before sunset. I spent longer than usual choosing my clothes and curling my hair into waves. With a cable-knit cardigan over my black fit and flare dress and the diamond Soren had bought Hazel around my neck, I slipped into the passage.

I was a mess of contradicting emotions passing through the narrow tunnel. The end was upon me, and I was more in love with the Reynard than I had been even a week ago. I spent hours behind the front desk listening as Larry regaled me with all his favorite stories about Hazel. Every lunch hour, Skye and I left the hotel and wandered out into the town square. We indulged in all the little niche eateries, including gorging ourselves on three doughnuts apiece from Put a Spell on You. Every evening, I grabbed Hazel's old lantern, put on one of her chunky pieces of silver jewelry, and led the ghost tour through the hotel. The thrill of watching the guests huddle together and yelp as pounding came from the walls and disembodied male voices followed us was invigorating. I loved witnessing their wonder for the supernatural. But it was the nights tucked in Soren's arms that I loved most about this hotel.

We talked until we fell asleep midsentence and laughed until our sides ached. One of us would wake the other in the middle of the night just to finish the conversation. It didn't matter that I was functioning on minimal sleep; I would give it all up to capture more moments with him.

Arms slid around my waist and a broad chest pressed against my back. "Nervous?" Soren asked, planting a kiss on my neck.

I didn't even jump; I knew his touch so well even after such a short amount of time. I lifted my hand and wrapped it around to the back of his neck, gripping the hair at his nape, tilting my head to allow his kisses to continue. "Not at all. I've been bouncing off the walls all day; between the anticipation about tonight and my ADHD, Larry was ready to shoot me with a tranquilizer dart. Can you tell me yet? Where are we going?"

"I would have hated to wrestle the old boy down to the ground for laying a hand on you. I'm glad he showed some restraint."

I laughed. Soren had a soft spot for the hotel's oldest employee. He wouldn't dare hurt him.

He continued, "And as far as where we are going, do you really think I'd ruin the surprise when we're so close to the reveal?"

I huffed and turned to face him, wrapping my arms around his neck and pressing myself to his front. "Of course not. So, let's go," I said, rubbing against him teasingly and planting a kiss on his collarbone.

He folded my hand inside of his and guided me up the staircase toward his home. When we reached the top, he moved to the side of the door. I furrowed my brows as he pushed on the wooden slats next to it and another passage door creaked open. Dust and aged oak filled my lungs, and I hesitated when he pulled me forward.

Soren glanced back at me and winked. "Trust me, you want to see this."

A flash of a memory lit up in my head. Hazel and me outside the hotel before the Winter Spirits festival, and the young man who had mysteriously vanished from the front steps. My heart fluttered as I remembered him and his beautiful blue eyes—the eyes of one of the boys in the painting above the fireplace.

I stepped inside the tunnel. Soren was right; I did want to see this. I wanted to make new memories with him that I would never forget, just like the first one we'd made ten years ago.

Stepping over the door's threshold, Soren pulled a flashlight out of the bag he carried, shining it up a steep flight of stairs. I cocked my head to the side and looked up at him. "Wait, I thought this was the farthest up you could go."

His crooked grin made my heart skip a beat. "You ought to know that there's always more than what meets the eye, especially at the Reynard."

"Touché," I said, gesturing toward the staircase. "Lead the way."

"Be careful on the steps," he cautioned as we climbed, winding up and up until finally we came to another door, and before he opened it, he looked back at me over his shoulder. "Close your eyes."

"Soren—"

He looked at me sternly. "Close them."

"Fine," I said with a playful sigh, letting my eyelids flutter shut.

He gripped both of my hands in his and pulled me forward, the door shutting with a click behind us. There was some shuffling as he put down the bag he'd been carrying.

"Okay," he said on a sharp exhale. "Open them."

I did as he asked, and when I realized where we were, my heart skipped several beats.

The circular room was covered in tall windows that had once been open but were now covered in thick glass. Wrought iron railings circled the entire room on the outside, and above our heads, the giant, long-ago-silenced metal bells hung from the ceiling.

The bell tower.

Soren had brought me to the one place in the Reynard I'd never gotten to go, the place I thought was impossible to experience.

"Holy shit, Soren," I breathed, staring out the window directly in front of us at the sky, which was streaked with pink, orange, and purple, ushering out the setting sun. "This is incredible."

"It gets better." He pushed on the glass in front of us and it swung open, letting in the late autumn air.

I stepped to the railing, and my hair floated around my face on the chilled breeze. Spelling was alive with tourists strolling the square, and live music spilled out from the most popular café. Antique light posts burned amber, and salt and pine perfumed the air, all of it set to the backdrop of the orange-and-purple sky kissing the aqua ocean.

Soren stood behind me and rested his chin on my shoulder. "This is the only way I get to see the world beyond this property."

I glanced at him from the corner of my eye as he wrapped both arms around my waist, and I rested my hands on top of his. "This is so beautiful, Soren. My whole life, I wanted to come up here and see Spelling from this height. From where I knew you two did. But I thought it was impossible." I turned to face him, staying in the circle of his arms. "How did you know I wanted to come here? I don't remember talking about it with you."

"You stare up at it every time you walk into the hotel. I'm almost jealous of the longing in your eyes. I have no question that you know how many arches circle it or what type of leaf the railing is molded to look like. And the smile on your face when the recorded bells toll is priceless. I wish you could hear what they sounded like before they were corroded."

He had rendered me speechless. When I finally was able to construct a sentence, I managed, "You are so sweet."

He pressed a kiss to my forehead and stepped backward, pulling me inside and shutting the window against the chilly evening air. "Come sit, I brought champagne and strawberries," he said, gesturing to the thick, soft blanket he'd spread on the floor of the tower.

Shaking my head in astonishment, I sat as he lowered himself in front of me, mirroring my position, our knees touching each other. "You are more than sweet," I said as he poured me a glass of champagne and handed it to me. "You are truly incredible."

Soren smiled as he retrieved a container of plain and chocolate-covered strawberries. "You don't need to win me over with flattery, Miss Fox. If you haven't figured it out yet, I absolutely adore you." He held up his glass, and I followed suit. "Here's to a night neither of us will ever forget."

I clinked my glass against his and smiled at him over the rim. He met my eyes, and something burned deep inside his electric-blue irises, igniting a fire low in my stomach. I drew my bottom lip between my teeth and set my glass on the floor. "Can I have a strawberry?" I asked, raising one eyebrow.

"I don't even have to ask; I know you want a chocolate one," he said as he plucked one out of the container and held it in front of my mouth.

"Of course," I said, parting my lips and allowing him to slip the fruit between them. I took a bite, and the juice slid down the corner of my mouth. I raised my hand to wipe it away, but Soren was in front of me in an instant, his lips hovering over mine.

"Allow me," he breathed, kissing the sweet nectar from my skin.

He consumed me, and my heart pounded out of my chest as he traced the seam of my mouth, coaxing me to open to him. It didn't take much; all I wanted was him—everywhere.

Soren eased me to the blanket and braced himself over me as we continued to kiss. His hand glided down my side and over my hip. I shivered when his cool fingers caressed my thigh and slipped under the hem of my dress. His lips moved to my ear, and he kissed the sensitive spot below it.

"I love the way you feel beneath me," he said.

"Me too," I whispered. I spread my legs to allow him room, and he settled between my thighs, pressing against me in the most delicious way. "It's like we were made to fit together."

His thumb found its way under the edge of my thin lace panties and brushed over my hip bone. "I spend more time than I should thinking about the way that would feel."

Soren peeled my sweater back and stretched the neckline of my dress down my arm. His kisses were a hot trail on my skin, working their way over the tops of my breasts. I wiggled out of my sweater and set to the task of releasing the buttons of his shirt. His teasing thumb widened its strokes, coming dangerously close to my center.

I unfastened the last button, pushed his shirt over his shoulders, and watched his muscles flex under his skin as he shrugged it to the ground. I unbuckled his belt and unsnapped the button on his slacks, tugging on the zipper.

"Soren, you're teasing me," I gasped as his thumb brushed just over the place that ached so badly for him. "Don't you feel how much I want you?"

His other fingers slid under the lace, and one moved through my wet center and eased inside of me. "Yes, you feel so good." He moved slowly in and out as his thumb pressed circles into that part of me that made my breath quicken and every muscle in my stomach coil.

I lifted my hips to his hand, the extra friction making my neck stretch back and my spine bow. "God, that is perfect." I reached between us and pushed his pants down his legs before slipping my hand into his boxers, closing my fingers around his desire. His groan of desperate need had me panting into his kiss.

"Soren, you want this as much as I do," I whispered against his lips. "Please don't hold back from me because you're trying to protect me." Lifting my hips again, I pushed down on his lower back so that he was putting just a little more pressure on my core. I needed him, needed to feel him *everywhere*.

He groaned in frustration. I questioned if it was with me or if something else had him vexed. Every move he'd ever made with me was for my protection, and here I was telling him to let go and give in to what we both wanted. I opened my mouth to urge him to relax when he lifted my dress up my body and I had my answer. He pulled it over my head and tossed it behind us before removing his shoes and socks and discarding his pants. A heavy sigh left him when his body returned to mine and heated skin touched heated skin.

He glided his hands behind my back, unclasped my bra, and lowered the straps down my arms. He took his time peeling away my undergarments like he was basking in the anticipation of seeing what lay beneath. When I was naked, he kneeled between my legs and brushed the backs of his fingers over my breasts, stomach, and thighs.

"Every inch of you is so fucking beautiful," he whispered in awe.

I shivered under his caress and let my eyes roam over his bare skin. "Thank you," I breathed, reaching for him and pulling him down to me. I brushed my nose against his as I murmured, "You are every single thing I have ever wanted. And more; I never thought there would be someone so exceptionally perfect for me, and yet, here you are. I lo—" I paused and closed my eyes briefly. Could I say those words without scaring him? But could I hold them back when they were the absolute truth? "I love everything about you."

Soren stiffened against me, and his tone was desperate as he said, "No matter what happens tonight, you can't fall in love with me, Gemma."

"I won't," I assured him, but even I could hear the certainty in my voice faltering.

"Please don't fall in love," he whispered again and pressed his lips to mine. The kiss was slow and full of raw emotion. The way his tongue sought mine was like this kiss could be our very last, and he held me so close as if he were trying to keep me from falling through his grasp. And his need ignited mine.

I wrapped my legs around him and moved my lips along his

jaw. Soren's hands slid between us, cupping my breast and running his thumb over my nipple until it was aching under his touch. I arched under him, eager to feel his mouth sucking and soothing the delicate peak. Our bodies spoke to each other in a language all their own, and he drew my nipple between his lips.

A groan escaped me, and I tangled my fingers in his hair, tugging gently as he sucked, the tightness in my core growing with every passing second. "Soren," I whispered, dragging my fingernails up and down his spine.

He trembled under my touch and pulled back, his lips popping away from my sensitive skin. I whimpered, disappointed, but just as soon as his lips left one hardened bud, they closed around the other. I sighed, sliding my hand back into his hair, grateful for how attentive he was.

Shivers ran up my spine when his hand glided underneath my hips, tilting them to invite him in. He grasped his erection and guided it through the wet apex of my legs—the head gliding over the bundle of nerves that craved his attention. He pressed into my entrance and released my nipple. His warm breath swept over me as he said, "Tell me what you need, because the moment I feel you wrapped around me, I fear I will lose myself."

I placed my palm on his face, brushing my thumb over his cheekbone. "First, I want you to kiss me again," I whispered. It must have sounded like a strange request, with all the parts of his body at my disposal, but his lips on mine made me feel weightless, like all the cares and struggles in my life were irrelevant. "And then, I want you to make love to me. Is that allowed?" I asked, my mouth quirking up into a crooked smile.

"I don't think I'm capable of showing you how deeply I care about you in any other way."

Soren kissed me as his body sank into mine, making us one. His worry about not lasting long must have dissipated, because he put every effort into sliding his tongue against mine and running his hands over every part of me that he could touch. He rocked his body in and out of mine, and with every long stroke, the tension mounting inside me grew closer to bursting into pure ecstasy.

My breath became ragged, and I rolled my hips against him, keeping perfect rhythm with his every move. "Soren, I'm so close," I whispered against his ear, kissing the soft spot where his neck met his collarbone. I slid my hands down his back and gripped his ass, pushing him harder against me. "But I never want this to end." I stretched my neck back and let my eyes fall closed with the building pleasure.

His breath sped up, and his hips thrust with more urgency. Soren held himself over me with one arm as the other gripped my thigh. "Oh my God," he moaned, and his body trembled.

I was on the precipice, ready to dive in and feel the release flow through me, and I wanted him to feel it too. "Let go, Soren. I want you to come with me," I gasped, tightening around him, urging him to find his release.

He turned his face to the vaulted ceiling, the cords in his neck straining and his lips parted. The sounds of his release vibrated through me, sending me over the edge as well. The world stopped, suspending us in our passion for one another. We didn't have to worry about tomorrow and the fear of never being like this again. Soren and I were all that existed; everything began and ended with us. And at the same time, everything moved at the speed of light, and our bliss ended too soon. Soren collapsed on top of me and gathered me to him, rolling to his side and tucking me into the crook of his arm. We basked in the aftermath of our lovemaking for some time, weaving in and out of consciousness.

"Soren?" I asked, tracing figure eights on his chest.

"Hmm?"

"Don't be angry with me, but remember when I told you I wouldn't fall in love with you?"

His eyes went wide, and his head bolted up from the floor. "Gemma, you—"

I pressed my finger to his lips and pushed his head back down, climbing on top of him and straddling his lap. "I was just going to say that's going to be very, very difficult."

"I'm not sure that is easing my worry," he said flatly, crossing his arms behind his head. "But I can't deny that it makes me happy as well."

I smiled and laid my head on his chest, whispering, "Good, let that feeling outweigh the worry."

Encircling me in his arms, he said, "You are making it impossible for me to let you go, Gemma."

But he would have to, because my time was up, and tomorrow, we'd say goodbye.

CHAPTER TWENTY-EIGHT

The last couple of hours had been hell.

My run as the owner of the Reynard was over. I had breakfast with the staff and thanked each of them for their dedication to the hotel and assured them they would be in good hands under Raven's management. The entire time I spoke, I couldn't meet Larry's or Skye's gazes; both of them were aware that my comforting words held lies. After saying goodbye to them, I signed the papers that officially turned my hotel over to Raven. That moment would live on in my nightmares for years to come.

I was packing the last box when a tapping came at my door. I jumped up, hoping against hope it was Soren. After the day I'd had, I could use the distraction from my depressing thoughts. But when I swung the door open, my heart sank, and my guard went up at the same time.

Raven stood in the hallway in her navy blue pinstripe business suit, her black hair slicked into a bun on top of her head. "Gemma," she said with that tone of superiority she had so long ago mastered. "Good evening. I thought I'd check and see if there's anything I can do to help you."

Get out faster, I completed her sentence in my head. "No. I'm fine." I stepped aside, my manners winning over my bitterness. "Would you like to come in anyway? How about a shot or a beer? Oh wait, sorry, those are only drinks for us alcoholic deviants."

"Well, at least you acknowledge it. I'll take a glass of water," she said, glaring at Hazel's belongings with a curled lip as she sat on the couch. "I can't believe you chose to stay in here. This place is"—she lifted the hand crocheted blanket next to her with two fingers—"lacking."

I didn't even bother to suppress my eye roll as I filled a glass with tap water, no ice. "Do you have to be so snobby? I mean, I realize who our families are, but Hunter and I managed to not follow in the rest of their footsteps. Why couldn't you?" I wouldn't stand quietly by as she came into what I had considered my home and spouted insults. "You never liked Aunt Hazel or anything about the Reynard. So, it isn't surprising that you wouldn't approve of her suite. Why comment on it at all?" With more force than necessary, I set the glass on the table in front of her and said, "I'm out of bottled water; maybe you can use your better-than-thou attitude to bless this glass so it won't taste like shit."

Raven scowled. "Keep mocking me, that's fine; we already know who came out on top. You were Hazel's favorite with all your little shared secrets and love for dabbling in dark practices. You two are the reason why this place isn't right. I didn't get involved in your séances and tampering with ghosts, and that made her not care for me, so I didn't care for her."

My cousin was ridiculous. Hazel would have gladly treated her the way she had me, but Raven was so disconnected. I now understood the reasons why the hotel and its history were precious to our aunt. As a child, I thought it was just because she was the owner, but it was her love for and devotion to Archer and Soren.

How could she enjoy the company of someone who despised the very thing that brought her the greatest happiness?

I couldn't help but bask in this one thing that made Raven jealous of me. It was petty, and I should have told her that Hazel had loved her just as much as me, but I didn't, because deep down I knew it wasn't true.

"What do you want, Raven? Why are you in my room? You got what you wanted: control of the hotel. You and our families successfully pushed me out. What more can I give you? You're taking *everything* I have. Do you understand that?"

She stood and a spiteful smirk quirked her lips to the side. "I guess I just wanted to gloat one last time. It's a shame you have to leave your new boy toy behind. Don't worry, cuz; I'll take good care of him. It's what a good girlfriend would do: take care of his brother's broken heart."

My palm itched to smack her right in her smug face, but I clenched my hand into a fist at my side and stalked to the door, flinging it open. "You don't need to worry about Soren; I'll be taking care of him. Now get the hell out before I knock you on your ass."

Raven laughed, the sound of it grating on my every nerve. "You couldn't kick my ass if you wanted to. Remember, while you were busy stuffing your face and figuring out which boy band you liked better, I was earning my black belt."

"Oh who cares? Get out!"

I moved back, giving her a wide berth to exit when the book on the coffee table caught my eye. I hadn't finished it. As soon as I'd signed the papers, all the words were lost to me, the pages blank. There were so many of Hazel's thoughts I'd never know, and I hated handing Raven the book, but it was necessary. This was a guidebook for the owner, and I could only hope that it would make her see how important this place was.

"Before you go, here. You're going to need this," I said, picking up the book before she walked out.

Raven stepped back and eyed it. "What is it?"

"Basically, a journal with entries from every woman who owned the hotel before us. You should read it. The key to this room will open it, and you must read from start to finish, but be careful. It can be intense, and you shouldn't take in too much at once."

I couldn't tell her it was magical; she would probably burn it in case it was possessed by evil spirits. But I could do her this one favor in hopes that it would benefit Soren and make his time with her bearable. He had already survived so much hatred from the women in our family; he didn't deserve that treatment again. And no matter how big of an asshole he was to me, neither did Archer.

Without a word, she grabbed the book and turned away, taking the last piece of the Reynard from my hands.

As soon as the door shut behind her, I sank down onto the couch and put my head in my hands. Going back to Boston was the last thing I wanted to do, especially because my lease was up on my apartment, and I'd be staying with my parents until I found another place. The idea of spending every day with my dad was almost as bad as leaving Soren.

Almost.

I picked up my last box and looked around Hazel's suite one more time. The woodstove I'd sat in front of while reading, the bed I'd shared with Soren, the bathtub where he'd held me after everything went to shit. Leaving felt wrong, like driving against traffic on a one-way street. But it was time to let go.

I locked the door behind me and walked down to the front

desk where Larry and Skye were standing, forlorn expressions on their usually jovial faces.

"Hey, now. Don't look so sad," I said, my voice strained over the perpetual lump in my throat. "I'll come back to visit. And things might change around here, but it will be all right. Raven knows how to run the business."

Larry smiled and put his weathered hands on my shoulders. "We know. But she's not Gemma," he said, pulling me into a hug.

Tears gathered at the corners of my eyes as I wrapped my arm around him and pulled Skye in next to us. "Thank you for welcoming me and helping me get my shit together. Even though I ultimately failed, you two gave me the best start I could've asked for."

Skye shook her head. "You didn't fail. If your family had given you half a—"

I put my finger to her lips. "Take care of Soren for me?"

They both nodded, and as if he'd heard his name, Soren appeared at the top of the staircase, looking down into the lobby with his hands crammed in his pockets. He jogged down the steps and stopped right in front of me, placing his palms on both my cheeks. "You weren't going to leave without saying good-bye, were you?"

I shook my head and the tears betrayed me, sliding down my face one after the other. "Of course not. I just—I don't want to go at all. Remind me again why I can't just stay?"

He offered me a smile that didn't reach his eyes and pressed his lips to my forehead. "Come on, Gemma. Let me walk you to your car."

I took his hand and intertwined our fingers, leaning into him as we walked down the creaky front steps and out to the parking lot. I wished that instead of going back to my room this morning after we'd woken up in the bell tower, I had just stayed with him or asked him to come with me to finish packing. Those were precious hours I would never get back. And now, time really was up.

He crammed my last box into his truck and shut the hatch, and I leaned against the car, pulling him to me. I ran my fingers up and down his spine, chewing my bottom lip to keep from breaking down.

"I'll FaceTime you every day. The first chance I get to come back to visit, I'll be here. It won't be that bad," I said, but I knew that last statement was a lie. It was going to be the hardest thing I'd ever done.

Soren wrapped his fingers around my upper arms and moved me away from him. His lips were set in a firm line, and the spark in his eyes was gone, leaving them dull and lifeless. "It's time to say goodbye, Gemma. I don't want you trying to fit me into every open space in your life. You deserve someone who makes you a priority, who can go out of their way to surprise you and chase after you. This is it for me"—he waved a hand at the hotel—"I'm just another fixture at the Reynard."

My brows furrowed as I searched his face, looking for any sign that he wasn't being sincere, that I was misunderstanding. "This sounds an awful lot like a breakup speech, Soren. Tell me you're not breaking it off with me, not after—" My voice broke, and I cleared my throat. "Not after what we shared last night."

"You will never understand how selfish I want to be. I spent all night watching you sleep, the way you drape your leg over mine and how you keep your palm resting on my heart." He took my hand and pressed it to his chest. "Then the sun lit up your face, and I knew I couldn't keep you hidden in the bell tower with me. You're a free spirit who needs more than what I or the Reynard can give you, Gemma."

I clutched the fabric of his shirt and slid my free hand into his hair, pulling his forehead down to mine. "That's quite possibly the sweetest and most heartbreaking thing anyone has ever said to me. But I want to hide with you. I want you with me all the time, no matter what. I don't—" I drew a sharp inhale and chewed the inside of my cheek before I said, "I don't want to live my life without you. I know you told me not to fall in love with you, but that's something that even I can't wiggle my way out of. It's inevitable, Soren."

He gripped my wrist and pulled my fingers out of his hair. "You will always be the one who consumes every corner of my mind—the one my arms ache to hold and my lips want to kiss. I will live the rest of my life with this stabbing pain in my chest and revel in it every fucking day because it reminds me that for a small moment in time, you were mine. You will heal and move on, Gemma. You won't be like the other women this place tore apart, and I won't be the reason it ruins you either."

I couldn't stop my tears now, and I knew I probably looked pathetic, but I wouldn't lose him. Not like this. "But it doesn't have to be like that, I mean, maybe one day I can break the—"

He pressed my hand to his lips and kissed it. "Don't come back, Gemma."

I vehemently shook my head.

"You made me a promise not to fall in love with me. I'm—" He swallowed and took a deep breath. "I'm asking you to keep it."

I wanted to shout, to stomp my feet, to force him to see he was wrong. I would never let this place go, or him—both were engraved into my very being. But he didn't give me the chance. Soren released my hand and walked away without looking back, leaving me to pick up the infinitesimal pieces of my heart.

CHAPTER TWENTY-NINE

I'd been gone from the Reynard for three weeks, and it had easily been the most miserable time of my life. I'd looked for a new job, but the only thing I could find was driving for a food delivery company. Every afternoon, I got in my car and went around Boston delivering cheesecake and tacos to people with actual careers. The money wasn't atrocious, but it wasn't enough to get my own apartment yet either. So, after driving for eight hours, I was forced to go home and lay eyes on the people who had betrayed me. I didn't know if I'd ever be able to forgive my parents for their part in handing the Reynard to Raven, and my father's indifference told me he couldn't care less. My mother felt sorry for me at least; she tried to cheer me up, but nothing could snap me out of the dark cloud I'd been living in since the day I left the Reynard.

After delivering my last meal of the day, I stopped at a local coffee shop for a white-chocolate mocha. When I walked through the door, my heart stopped.

A man stood at the counter—tall, dark hair, lean but muscular build, wearing the same gray pullover that Soren had worn so many times. I moved toward him, but when he turned around, his eyes were brown and his face not nearly as handsome as Soren's.

I swallowed and averted my gaze, staring at the ground until the guy passed.

Of course it hadn't been Soren. That was the whole reason for this misery; he couldn't leave the Reynard, and now he never would because I wasn't there to break the spell. Even if he did end up back in the kobold realm and I never saw him again, I'd still choose to free him. I hated the thought of him stuck in the hotel until the end of time.

I got my coffee and returned to my car, my face turned down against the frigid wind. I plopped in the driver's seat, rested my forehead against the steering wheel, and sobbed. I wanted nothing more than to hear Soren's voice, just to know that he was all right. I had tried to call him so many times, but he wouldn't answer. All my texts went ignored, and the emails I sent were unanswered. I'd called and asked Larry for news, but he said he'd only seen Archer with Raven since I'd left.

Shaking my head, I lifted my eyes to the dusky sky. Soren had told me not to come back, but he did it because he thought it was best for me. He was wrong. All of this was wrong. What was stopping me from going back? Nothing. Before I could change my mind, I threw my car into reverse and took off for the freeway. Soren's order to stay away be damned; I was going to see him tonight.

The drive felt like ten hours instead of two, and when I finally pulled into the parking lot at the Reynard, a sigh of relief slid from my lips.

"Thank God," I murmured, getting out of the car and stretching my arms over my head. I looked down at my clothes and wished I'd changed before coming; suddenly my holey jeans and V-neck black sweater seemed lacking. I brushed the lint off my torso and walked toward the hotel.

Archer strolled down the front stairs before I made it to the door, his hands in his pockets and head bowed. I stiffened at the sight of him; this was not the cocky asshole I was used to seeing. Something was off. He met me halfway to the front porch and raised his gaze to mine.

"I need you to come this way with me, please," he said, his voice quiet and monotone.

My brows furrowed, and I shook my head. "What's going on? Where's Soren? Is he okay?"

"Other than the constant self-deprecation for breaking your heart, he's all right. But you can't go inside."

"What? What are you talking about? I just drove here from Boston; you can bet your ass I'm going in."

He released a long, slow breath and combed his fingers through his hair, looking at anything but me. I shoved past him and clipped him with my shoulder, but I didn't make it far. His fingers curled around my wrist, holding me in place.

"Raven took out a no-trespassing order against you. If you step inside, she'll call the police. None of us wants to see you dragged away like that."

My heart stilled in my chest and my jaw dropped. "Excuse me? She did what? On what grounds did she order it?"

"She claimed you threatened to kick her ass. Also, the hotel is private property; she has the right to refuse anyone entry and service."

I closed my eyes and willed my racing heart to slow down. She'd taken our last exchange in Hazel's suite and used it against me. I'd meant my threat as one cousin to another, but she'd twisted it. "Why in the hell would she do that? She knows how much this hotel means to me."

"You already know why, Gemma. She's a conniving bitch. Your cousin took the opportunity to ban you from the hotel the first chance she got."

"Wait, you're calling your girlfriend a conniving bitch? Or did you break up with her?" I couldn't hide my incredulity. Raven was Archer's one chance to free himself from the Reynard. Had he given up so soon, and why?

He shifted from foot to foot and shoved his hands in his pockets. "As soon as she pulled that shit with the no-trespassing order, I wanted to break it off with her. Soren is a mess. I've never seen him regret anything as much as telling you not to come back. The sentimental idiot held out hope that you wouldn't listen and you'd come back to visit. Now he doesn't even have that. It doesn't matter what happened between you and me; no one fucks with my brother." Archer's mouth was set into a hard line, and his anger was palpable.

"How is it possible I didn't know about this? I've been gone three weeks. If someone got a no-trespassing order against me, I should have been notified."

Archer pulled a sealed envelope with a red "Return to Sender" stamp on the front from his back pocket. "She sent it to the wrong address on purpose. I guess she wanted you to endure the hurt of coming back here, of being so close to him, and not being able to see him."

My hand trembled as I took the letter. Of all the hateful things Raven could do to me, now she had permanently taken the place I loved most. Her cruelty had no limit.

A glutton for punishment, I opened the envelope and read the formal letter issued by the Town of Spelling. I crumpled it in my hand, squeezing it with every ounce of frustration coursing through my body. I hated her.

"I'm so sorry, Gem. For everything. I'm sorry I used you, and that I fucked around with Raven. I don't expect you to believe me, but I had to tell you," Archer said, running both hands through his hair.

"You really broke up with her?" I asked.

He nodded then tilted his head from side to side. "Well, I intend to. I try to do it every day, but there's one problem: I haven't seen her for more than a moment since you left. She is *always* busy. It's almost like she's on some drug that keeps her moving a hundred miles a minute. She barely eats, and she's probably lost fifteen pounds in three weeks. Just from what I've heard the others say and the small glimpses I've gotten of her, I'm wondering if she's unhinged. I haven't had a chance to have a serious conversation with her. But that means I haven't had a moment *alone* with her either. I'm done; she just doesn't know it yet."

Archer really was willing to give up his one chance to get out of the Reynard, the only thing he'd wanted for so long. It was impossible for me to continue resenting him when his concern was for Soren. "I forgive you. Besides, with everything that's going on, I don't have the energy to hate you. You're trying to do the right thing, and that's gotta count for something."

Ever since Halloween, Archer and I hadn't had a kind word to say to one another; we had both been guilty of throwing petty insults and delivering deliberately hurtful jabs. But here he was passing on this devastating news—with sorrow and compassion instead of ridicule and hatred. And his remorse was sincere.

After spending the last three weeks with my dad, who had no compassion or understanding to spare for his own daughter during her darkest days, Archer's small gesture of kindness was enough to bring tears to my eyes.

"What did Soren say when this happened? Is he angry? Does—" My voice cracked, but I pressed on. "Does he miss me?"

"He's devastated—stays in bed all day, hardly eats, and he won't talk to me very much beyond the occasional good morning. But I don't blame him. I wouldn't want to talk to him either if he treated someone who I cared about the way I treated you. But he doesn't need to say it for me to know he misses you."

The tears that had filled my eyes now fell freely down my cheeks. To think of Soren so miserable made my chest ache. "This isn't fair," I muttered, running my fingers through my hair and gripping it at the roots. "There has to be some way I can see him."

"You can't go inside. The staff is under strict orders to detain you on sight. Raven keeps the front desk open all night now. And even if I could roll him out of bed, I don't know if coming down here would be the best idea for either of you. It won't change anything. Not right now. You would both leave more torn up than you already are."

"I get what you're saying, and I don't want him to hurt more. Can you do me a favor? Will you tell him I tried to come see him? I don't want him to think I don't care about him anymore."

"He knows you do. I'm sure half of his anguish is knowing how badly this hurts you. But I will tell him, I promise."

With nothing more to say and a burning desire to drown in my sorrows alone, I returned to my car. I held it together for a moment, gripping the steering wheel until my knuckles turned white. As my rage grew within me, my body trembled, and tears streamed down my face. The fury welled inside me until I exploded, punching my horn and screaming.

Fuck Raven! She had taken everything I loved and left me with nothing but the searing hatred I felt for her.

"Gemma, are you coming down to dinner, or do you plan to hide in your room forever?" Mom called from downstairs, and I rolled my eyes so hard I thought they'd fall out of my head. Lately, even my mother was on my nerves. She didn't understand how I could possibly be so torn up over a "ratty old hotel."

Of course she didn't. No one did. Even Hunter had told me I needed to "suck it up" and move on with my life. Granted, he didn't know the whole story; I had a strong suspicion he wouldn't be so indifferent if he knew the way I felt about Soren. In fact, no one knew about Soren, and that was making it even harder.

I stuck my head out of my door. "I'm not hungry!" I yelled, my voice echoing down the imperial staircase.

Mom went silent except for the clicking of her heels on the tile floor. A minute later, she was outside my open door, knocking on the wall in greeting. "Gemma Diane, I am worried about you. You haven't eaten in days."

"I'm eating." I didn't bother to tell her that it was strictly a liquid diet; it was all my stomach could handle. Archer's words plagued me, and I couldn't get the picture of Soren alone in the bell tower out of my head. I thought about it every waking moment, sending my insides rolling like a boulder down a steep hill. I missed him, he missed me, and I couldn't think very far beyond that.

Mom came into my room and sat in the chair at my desk, crossing her legs at the ankles. She nodded at the empty protein-shake bottle on my nightstand. "If by eating you mean drinking those, then you aren't eating." She leaned forward, her elbows resting on her knees. "Talk to me, Gemma. Something is wrong, and it isn't just that Raven took over the hotel. It's something else. Let me help you."

"You wouldn't understand."

"Try me."

Anything had to be better than stewing in this pain. Maybe Mom wouldn't understand exactly what I was going through, but perhaps she could relate to the universal heartache. She had had her share of boyfriends before marrying my dad, and at least one of those had to have ended in tears.

"I met someone while I was at the hotel. His situation makes it impossible for him to leave Spelling, and he thought it was for the best that we break things off before I left."

Mom cocked her head to the side and came to sit next to me on the edge of my bed. "Oh honey, I am so sorry." She took my hand in hers and rubbed my knuckles with her palm. "I didn't know you had—" Recognition dawned on her face, and she said, "This is the boy from Thanksgiving, isn't it? The handsome one who had the balls to stand up to your father."

"There's no way to a girl's heart like telling her overbearing father that he's wrong." Mom raised an eyebrow and pursed her lips. "Yes, that's him."

"I see. Well, he was quite a handsome guy, and if his personality was even half as good as his looks, I can understand why you're torn up," she said, and her teasing tone made me crack a smile for the first time in weeks. "Why don't you go see him? If you need money to take a trip, I'll be glad to help you out."

"That's the thing, I can't. He's currently not in a position where he can take a visit from me."

"Is he in jail?"

"No!" I was trying my best not to lie to her and not say anything that would trigger her to call her psychiatrist friends. I also couldn't bring myself to tell her that Raven had issued a no-trespassing order against me. My situation was already complicated, and I didn't want to add more family drama to it.

I cleared my throat and said, "I just meant that he thought it was best to break things off, and he asked that I not come visit. I guess he thought it was easier for us this way."

"I understand." Mom sighed and put her arm around me, drawing me into a hug. "So, you're nursing a broken heart while also losing your biggest dream." She kissed me on the temple and squeezed me once before standing. "I'll leave you alone, but please, Gemma, come to me if you need anything. Promise?"

"I promise. If I think of any way you can help, I'll let you know. Thank you."

"You're welcome, honey." She stepped out the door, but she turned around and added, "It's times like this that I understand why they call it *falling*; it sure hurts when you land, doesn't it?" She gave me a tight-lipped smile and disappeared down the hall.

I stared after her, my lips parting with the sudden realization I'd been trying to avoid, trying to deny. I had fallen in love with Soren, and I'd fallen hard. But I'd never told him, and now it was too late.

"A masquerade ball is a great idea. It's probably the classiest thing that has ever happened to that place."

My ears perked up as my father walked down the hallway on the phone.

"I wouldn't worry too much about her. You know how she is, and I'm sure she's just exhausted from putting her all into the hotel."

I didn't miss the louder-than-normal volume of his voice or the overzealous praise he gave Raven. He was doing it on purpose, showing me the result of being more driven like my cousin.

Raven was turning my fun night for the entire town into some fancy soiree. It was going to be over-the-top, and she would prove that she was better than me *and* Hazel. It also sounded like, based on my father's comments and my conversation with Archer, her efforts were getting to her, and that was intriguing. The perfect Raven Fox was on the verge of some deranged prom queen–level meltdown, and I had a duty to be there to stop her from slaughtering the entire town. It was a funny thought, but enough to motivate me to move.

I threw on a pair of tennis shoes and snatched my purse from my dresser, running out the door before anyone could notice I was leaving. If the hotel was throwing a masquerade ball, I would be there with bells on. January 21 was the one night a year when Soren could leave the property, and the only chance I had to see him and let him know I loved him without ending up in handcuffs. I couldn't pass this up, and I was going to make sure I looked damn good doing it.

CHAPTER THIRTY

I parked my car in front of city hall and stepped out onto the sidewalk. The sky was spitting snow, and I was thankful I'd added a faux-fur shawl to my outfit at the last second. I brushed the front of my formal dress, the emerald satin cool and smooth under my fingertips. The skirt swished around my ankles as I walked down the streets of Spelling. It had been a tradition to stroll the long way to the square with Hazel on Winter Spirits—a moment just for us before we were drawn into the excitement of the night. I wanted to keep that up, even if it all seemed wrong.

I nervously twirled a dark-blond curl around my finger, holding my breath in apprehension; I could only hope that I'd see Soren sometime tonight. Surely he wouldn't miss out on the festival and his one night to break free from the confines of the property. He had to look forward to this night above all others and know this was our one chance to bend the rules that were keeping us apart.

My black sequin-and-lace masquerade mask hung from my index finger and swung against my leg, and I pulled the stole tighter around my bare shoulders. I smiled at the town citizens as they passed; most of them were dressed to the nines and ready for the dance. In the distance, a waltz carried on the strings of violins, cellos, and basses drifted through the night air. Everything about tonight was mysterious, elegant, and a little bit sexy, and I couldn't stop the corners of my mouth from pulling up.

I tied my mask around my face, thankful for the small bit of anonymity it gave me. Like the Hyde brothers roaming the streets of Spelling, I, too, was out of place on this magical evening. But that didn't mean I was without a purpose.

Steady footsteps came from behind me, echoing off the brick storefronts. I twirled around, the fabric of my dress rustling with the movement. A chill ran down my spine when I found nobody there. I picked up my pace and concentrated on the clicking of my heels against the cement, but each swift step was echoed by that of another.

I turned a corner, hoping to lose my invisible stalker. "Get it together, Gem," I told myself, keeping my gaze on the shadowed street. The gas lamps that lined the road led to the spooky mansion that had been the home of Gerald Spelling, a wealthy sea merchant and the town's founder. This stretch of Spelling always reminded me of some seedy dark alley where Jack the Ripper took the lives of his victims. It had been my favorite when walking with Hazel, but I couldn't say the same tonight.

My heart was pounding, and my breath escaped my mouth in plumes of fog. I was coming up on the locked gates of the estate and would reach a dead end if I didn't change course. The pillars that held up the wrought iron fencing were adorned with stone gargoyles who sneered at me as I jogged past them. River-rock alcoves housed concrete benches that were meant to give pedestrians a reprieve from the sun on a hot day, but tonight, they did nothing but creep me out. These were the hiding places for the things that go bump in the night.

No sooner did I have the thought than an arm snaked around my waist and a hand clapped to my mouth.

"What exactly are you running from, sweetheart?" The words were spoken with a breathy, deep cadence, and I had no doubt who had me in his clutches.

Spearmint mingled with the chilled sea breeze, and when I turned to face my captor, I met a striking electric-blue gaze. Those eyes. Even the black mask Soren wore couldn't disguise that stare. I'd missed it for the past six weeks, and mixed with the bewitching aura of the night, it brought out something wicked in me.

"You. I was scared of what would happen if you caught me," I whispered in a startled but flirtatious tone. "What do you plan to do with me, handsome stranger?"

Soren leaned in, brushing his lips against my ear, and said, "I plan on doing the naughtiest things to your sweet body." He slipped his arms around me and pulled me closer; he was clearly feeling the effects of being away from each other for so long as much as I was.

I reached up and trailed a finger along his jawline and down the center of his chest. "Anything naughty you want to do to me is more than welcome. It's been six weeks since I've been in the company of a gentleman, and let's just say"—I stood on my tiptoes and whispered in his ear—"I'm hanging on by a thread."

He pulled me deeper into the alcove, and I took a moment to admire the way his black suit hugged his body. Not bothering with a tie and leaving the top two buttons of his dress shirt undone made the formal attire edgy and perfectly Soren.

He removed my stole, letting it fall to the bench, and pressed me against the stone wall. The off-the-shoulder cut of my dress left my upper back bare, and the freezing rocks chilled my skin. But my discomfort was short-lived when his lips met mine. Our masks brushed together, reminding me that we were in disguise and hidden in a dark corner where we could be caught at any moment.

I rolled my head back against the wall as Soren peppered my neck and collarbone with deep, frantic kisses, and his hands shifted through the layers of chiffon until he found the slit that ran high in the front of my dress. His mouth stretched into a smile against the exposed swells of my breasts. "One might think that you had every intention of this happening tonight," he said, his fingers tracing the thin lace covering the part of me that ached for him the most.

I tangled my fingers in his hair and tugged gently until his mouth was inches from mine. "This is *exactly* what I wanted to happen tonight," I breathed, running my tongue along the seam of his lips. "I've spent far too long thinking about this moment." I nipped at his bottom lip and slid my hand between us, gripping the proof of his desire.

Soren moaned into my mouth and lifted my leg, wrapping it around his hip. "I've missed you so much. You don't know how many hours I spent locked in my room daydreaming about touching you again."

I released the button at the front of his slacks and lowered the zipper. "Oh? And did you touch yourself like this when you thought of me?" My hand slid into his pants and circled the smooth, hard length of him.

"Fuck yes," he hissed. "But it never felt as good as when you touch me."

The thought of him pleasuring himself to daydreams of me was almost too much to handle. "It doesn't, does it? But every time, I still cried out your name," I murmured against his mouth, keeping my hand wrapped around him, squeezing and pulling gently.

He slipped his fingertips underneath the lace between my legs. He pressed against the bundle of nerves at the top and glided his fingers back, sinking them into me. "You pretended it was me."

I groaned and pushed against his hand, longing for more of him. "Every time, but it's not the same, Soren. I need you right now. Please."

"I never knew just how badly I needed to hear those words from you." Kneeling before me, he lowered my panties and placed them in his pocket before kissing the smooth skin just above my sex. He stood, brushed my skirt away from my thighs, and lifted me, my legs wrapping around him.

I gripped the back of his neck, pressed my forehead to his, and whispered, "Don't hold back. I don't need sweet tonight, Soren. I need you to let go and show me how much you missed me."

"The last thing I plan on doing is holding back." He aligned our bodies, and as he sank inside me, he tilted his head back, and his eyes fluttered closed. "You feel better than I remember. Your body was made for me."

I had no time to adjust; there were no gentle strokes like that night in the bell tower, just the raw, desperate need to be one with me. His gaze wandered to the place where our bodies met, and he watched as he dipped inside me over and over again.

"I can never get enough of this, of you," he said, moving faster and thrusting deeper.

I buried my face in the crook of his neck and ran my tongue across his smooth skin. "I could let you touch me like this every hour of every day and never get tired of it," I gasped as his movements grew wild, matching my racing heart.

His hand slid up my spine and into my hair. He wrapped the tendrils around his fingers and tugged, tilting my face to meet his.

Our lips brushed as he said, "Be careful with your words, Gemma. I just might hold you to them. I'd enjoy nothing more than taking you over and over again until you beg me to stop."

I took his bottom lip between my teeth and tangled my fingers in his hair, matching his force. "I would *never* beg you to stop."

Never had I spoken truer words. I knew that now. This was the man I wanted. It didn't matter that he was bound to a hotel and not of this world. He was the one who complemented my strengths and made up for my flaws. Soren Hyde was the being I was meant to spend the rest of my days with.

I rolled my hips against him and sucked the soft skin on his neck, leaving red marks as I went. He growled his pleasure, giving little thought to those who might pass by, and the notion fueled my lack of control. I was starving, and he was the only nourishment that would fulfill my craving.

"Soren," I murmured when my core contracted. "I'm going to . . ." A moan severed the words, and I whimpered his name.

That was all it took for him to lose himself. He fisted the curls at the nape of my neck, and he pulled as he spent himself inside of me.

His lips trailed from under my ear to my jawline and then to my mouth, and he kissed me so sweetly that it was almost comical after the moment we'd just had. He held me close, giving me a second to find the strength to stand on my own. For the second time tonight, he knelt before me. This time, he removed the handkerchief from his breast pocket and cleaned me before tossing it in a nearby waste bin.

I cleared my throat and glared up at him with a cocked brow. "My panties, Mr. Hyde."

He looked like a schoolboy caught with his hand in the

cookie jar as he pulled them from his pocket and held them for me to step in.

"Thank you, sir. Now, I'm ready to dance," I said, straightening my mask and looping my arm through his.

As much as I hated to admit it, my cousin's execution of Winter Spirits was even more magnificent than I'd imagined. Firepits were scattered around the party, surrounded by wooden logs where children gathered with sticks to roast marshmallows. The dining area was in a massive white heated tent, where many of the older folks ate and conversed. White lights draped over the center of the square where the dance floor was located, and tall heaters shaped like naked winter trees glowed with bright-orange balls in the center, keeping everyone warm. Soren and I worked our way through the crowd to the dance floor. I shook my head at the full orchestra sitting off to the side and playing classical renditions of modern songs. Soren pulled me into his arms and set our bodies to a slow tempo that matched the music.

"Is it strange that the air always feels fresher and lighter the moment I step over the Reynard's property line?" he asked.

I shook my head, tightening my arms around his neck. "Not at all. It's sort of ironic, though."

"How so?"

"That for me, the air feels lighter and fresher the moment I come back here. Every minute away from this place, away from you, felt like an eternity. This is where I belong, Soren." Tears filled my eyes, and I looked down, blinking them away. I stayed silent for a moment before glancing back up at him. "Did you know Archer told me about the no-trespassing order?"

"He told me, and I beat myself up about it for days. It should have been me."

"No. I'm actually—I'm actually glad it was him. I would've broken down if it had been you, and I managed to somehow keep it together long enough to drive home."

Soren gnawed on his bottom lip and nodded. "He said it went well and that the two of you were civil to each other. He told me he apologized to you."

"He did. I was surprised, but it felt good to let go of that anger and resentment. He was really worried about you, you know. He said you weren't eating and hardly got out of bed." I cocked my head to the side and brought my palm to his cheek. "You have to knock that off, Soren."

"I know. It took every ounce of strength to get ready for tonight, but I couldn't risk missing the chance to see you." He kissed the top of my head. "And I'm glad you found the closure you needed with my brother."

"I know you have been a little bit distracted since I've been gone, but how are things going with Raven and the Reynard?"

"According to Archer, Raven barks orders and makes far too many remarks that she should just keep to herself. She might keep Skye because she's young and quick, but I don't think Larry will last long." He sighed. "I'm really afraid of the direction the Reynard is going in if your family is so set on her running things. She hates it here. The few times I ventured out of the bell tower, I overheard comments that have me questioning her mental stability."

I moved both arms back around his neck and closed the bit of distance between us. "Archer mentioned something like that too. Which is odd, considering that for all Raven is or isn't, she's always been grounded; I've never seen her slip like that. Did he break up with her?"

"Yeah, when he finally got her alone long enough. He said

she didn't take it well, but let's not talk about her anymore." He pulled me in tighter and brushed his nose along the side of my head, taking in the scent of my hair. "She's taken too much from us already, and I refuse to give her this moment too."

Nodding, I lay my head on his chest, listening to his heartbeat. In his arms was where I'd been dying to be for weeks, and for the first time since I'd stepped off the Reynard property, I felt like I was where I was supposed to be.

Soren spoke after a moment, and I loved the way his voice vibrated through him, a low rumble against my cheek. "What I said when you left, this is it. This is what I meant. I wish I could give you nights like this all the time. I would hate to think that I was just another person who held you back from everything I know you can do. You were made for bigger things than this small town, Gemma."

In that instant, a life with Soren flashed through my head. Nights in front of the fireplace, cuddling while I read and he watched football, cooking dinner together on Friday evenings, making out in the middle of a public place because we just can't keep our hands off each other, walking down the aisle, perhaps having a family, growing old together.

It would never happen. Even if I had been able to stick to *one fucking thing* in my life, I couldn't have lived out the rest of my life with Soren. I would have broken the curse, and he would no longer be here. I grabbed the lapels of his coat, emotion welling in my chest, threatening to bust it open. "Soren, I have to tell you something, and I don't want you to get angry."

He looked down and pushed a curl out of my face. "I'd never be angry at you, Gem."

"I broke my promise."

Reaching behind my head and loosening the ribbon on my mask, I pulled it away from my skin before sliding my fingers up to his temples and pushing his up over his forehead. "Soren, I'm so helplessly, desperately in love with you. I know I promised I wouldn't, but I should've never made such a futile vow. I love you"—I kissed his jawline—"I love you"—then his cheek—"I love you," I whispered, my lips finding their way to his.

Soren exhaled, and his body molded to mine, hugging me like he planned on never letting go. "Those words fall so easily from your lips."

"They do, and I will continue to say them."

"I love you, Gemma. I knew from the moment I handed you the Fox tome that I was going to fall madly in love with you. I knew I would have to let you go, but I was never, ever going to be all right without you."

I kissed him again, tears flowing freely down my cheeks, moistening our lips. "What are we going to do, Soren?"

"I don't know. We'll figure something out, but for now, just dance with me," he whispered, pulling me close.

I rested my cheek against his chest and watched the world spin around us. We were the center of it all, and this moment was all that mattered. Nothing existed outside of us, not the crowded dance floor or the lit bell tower in the distance. Everything was me and Soren— until a dark figure caught my attention. With her skeletal arms crossed over her chest, Raven stared at us with dull jade eyes.

CHAPTER THIRTY-ONE

Raven sauntered over to us in a dress that ironically looked like something straight out of Hazel's closet—high ruffled neckline, cameo brooch in the center of the lace paneling that covered her chest, and a high-waisted tiered skirt that ended at her ankles. The only thing that wasn't reminiscent of our great-aunt was the bland ivory of the fabric. Hazel would have said it gave one the appearance of innocence, which meant the wearer was hiding dark sins.

I clutched Soren's arm the closer she got, and he whispered reassurances.

My cousin raked her glare over us and spat, "You're not welcome at the Reynard, Gemma."

"And that's why we're dancing in the street," I clipped back.

"Just don't forget that if you set foot on *my* property, I will have you arrested."

Anger simmered inside me. I wanted to lose it and push her on her ass. It would have delighted me to embarrass her in front of all these people whom she'd worked so hard to impress. But I remained calm. I hadn't spent all those years learning to control my impulses just to give my cousin a reason to have me arrested. "I wouldn't expect anything less from you, Raven."

She sneered and turned her attention to Soren. "Mr. Hyde, I require your presence in the hotel."

He stiffened at her formal address and cleared his throat. "On this particular night, I'm enjoying the town of Spelling, and I'd like to keep it that way."

His words were clear to me but cryptic to someone who didn't know details about his situation. I got the feeling that he was trying to determine just how much she knew about him and his past.

"I can see that, but your brother finds himself in a precarious situation, and he requires your help."

I chuckled. "Archer in trouble; that sounds about right."

Raven ignored me and flashed my dancing partner a bright, fake smile that was fitting for a toothpaste advertisement. "This should only take a moment." Looking me up and down, she added, "And don't follow him like the sad little puppy you are. Stay out here."

I clenched my teeth and glared at her until Soren placed a finger on my jaw and turned my face up to his. "I have to make sure he's all right."

Nodding, I stood on my tiptoes and kissed his cheek, pressing my lips to his ear and whispering, "Don't take too long, please."

He put his hand on the back of my head and kissed my nose. "I'll be right back, I promise."

Raven beckoned to him impatiently, and with a sigh, he followed her inside.

I left the dance floor and grabbed a hot chocolate at the beverage cart. Sipping the steaming sweet drink, I watched as the dance floor filled with a younger crowd excited to take part in a popular line dance being played by the orchestra. The song's quick beat sounded awkward coming from the classical instruments. But those dancing made it work.

After four more songs and another hot chocolate, I was fidgeting, and my attention was divided between the festivities and the hotel.

"You should listen to the restlessness inside you, Gemma. The spirits are trying to tell you something ain't right," said a smoky voice from beside me.

Wanda Willow watched the crowd, hands on her hips, resting on the rhinestones swirling down the sides of her purple dress. Feathery fake lashes framed her brown eyes and coral lipstick painted her lips. Like the rest of the town, she was dressed to impress, or at least to make a statement.

"Wait, what?" I set the hot chocolate down on a nearby table and gave Wanda every bit of my attention. "What's not right?"

"You let your kobold boyfriend go into the hotel with your wicked cousin. Your aunt says Raven is up to no good."

My heart jumped into my throat. "You talked to Hazel? What is Raven doing? Is she hurting Soren?" My questions were rapid-fire, and my mind was racing with all the horrifying possibilities.

Wanda cocked her head to the side and gave an exasperated sigh. "Do you want to waste time waiting for me to see if Hazel will tell me more, or are you going to save the man you love? I've already told you; the spirits are beckoning you into the hotel to set this right."

Damn the consequences; I had to make sure he was okay.

I reached out and squeezed her shoulder as I walked past her toward the hotel. "Thank you, Wanda. I won't let Hazel down. Tell her that. Please."

"You just told her yourself. Now, hurry before that girl does something that can't be undone."

I pushed people out of my way as I ran straight toward the

Reynard. I took the front steps two at a time and yanked the front door open. The lobby was dark; not even the dim emergency lights were on. I flipped the switch on the wall, but nothing happened. The electricity was off.

Pulling my cell phone out of my purse, I flipped on the flashlight and hurried to the staircase. Every step deeper into the hotel set me on edge. Something about all of this didn't feel right.

The second floor was silent; all the guests were outside. My footsteps echoed throughout the hallway, setting an eerie beat. I pulled my stole around my shoulders, warding off the chill running down my spine. The stillness of the hotel was heightening my anxiety to the point that my teeth were chattering.

I didn't even know where to look for Soren and Archer, so I wandered around until the unmistakable sound of voices came from the drawing room. My fear slightly dissipated, and I picked up my pace, my dress rustling around my ankles as I ran.

"What the fuck do you think you're doing?"

Soren.

"Tonight is your lucky night, kobolds. One of you is finally going home."

"That's not how it works, Raven."

My cousin's laughter drifted down the hallway. "Isn't it? Aunt Hazel made it so that one of you monstrosities could go home. I'm simply fulfilling her wish."

Well, she read the journal.

Reaching the double doors to the drawing room, I pressed myself against the wall out of sight. My eyes scanned the room, finding Archer in a fabric chair with his hands tied behind him and his shirt halfway unbuttoned. His hair was slicked to his head, dripping with a clear liquid. And across from him was

Soren, bound to a wooden chair with blood streaming down the side of his head and onto the collar of his shirt.

Gold glinted from Soren's wrists, and the breath left my lungs like I'd fallen from the roof and hit the ground on my back. Raven had not only read how to undo the curse, but learned their weakness.

"For fuck's sake, I thought Betty was a sadistic bitch, but you just might have her beat," Soren said, clenching his jaw, an expression of pain marring his beautiful features.

Raven flew across the room and her palm cracked against his face. "Do not speak to me that way, you vile, unnatural monster. I hold your life in my hands right now; if I were you, I'd treat me with a little more respect."

He flexed his jaw and tilted his head side to side. "Do you hear yourself when you speak? I don't owe you a fucking thing."

Archer lifted his chin and lowered his voice, "You don't have to do this, baby. Come take the chains off and we can work this out."

Her eyes flared with a fiery rage I'd never seen from her before. "Baby? Don't you dare call me your *baby*. The moment I read what my aunt wrote about the curse, I figured it out. You moved so easily from Gemma to me because you knew she wouldn't be able to keep the hotel. I was falling for you. I could have done it. That is, until I realized you were using me. Other women may fall for the charming words and handsome face, but I know you're a snake."

"I'm not the only one who does whatever it takes to get what they want, *baby*," Archer mumbled, and Soren shot him a glare.

"Don't compare my determination to succeed to your deceit. You're evil, Archer Hyde! You both are, and so is this hotel. I won't let you take my life. I'm righting the curse. One of you will go home, and the other will burn with this godforsaken building. I hope it is you who goes down in flames for all the disgusting things you coaxed me into."

Burn?

A squeak escaped my lips, and I stumbled forward, giving away my position. I nearly tripped over my own feet as I ran to Soren and squatted in front of him, putting my hands on his cheeks, rubbing my thumb along the angry red welt. "Are you okay?" He nodded as I fumbled with the chains around his ankles.

"And what would this party be without our fourth member?" Raven said with a deranged laugh. "Some would say that although a disgusting tramp, her job is the most important tonight. For it was her sin that will set us all free."

"Hurry, Gemma. She's lost her goddamn mind," Archer said from the other side of the room.

My eyes bounced between Soren, Archer, Raven, and the yellow bottle in her hand. Lighter fluid.

My heart thudded against my rib cage as I said in the calmest voice I could muster, "Raven. Put that down. Please."

Her green eyes were wild, her normally perfect black hair loose from the bun she'd twisted it into, cascading over her shoulders in a mass of tangled strands. "I don't think so," she snapped, kicking me away from Soren and squeezing the bottle over his head, soaking his hair with the flammable liquid.

I scrambled to my feet and held my hands out in front of me in a gesture of surrender. "Raven. Please. Stop. You can't do this." When she just continued soaking Soren with lighter fluid, something dawned on me. "Raven, you read the book all at once, didn't you?"

She jerked her head toward me and laughed. "Yes, I'm a speed reader, not a procrastinator like you."

Oh my God. "Raven, what have you done? I told you to be careful with it; you didn't listen to me." I glanced at Soren, whose eyes had widened in horror. He had come to the same conclusion as I had.

The book had taken the ultimate toll on Raven. Forget passing out, feeling dizzy, and barfing on your boyfriend's shoes. It had brought her deepest fears to the surface, fueling them into an inferno. All reason had left her, and she was driven by the need to both correct what our ancestors had done and get back at Archer for his slight against her in the most extreme way.

I was pulled from my thoughts as Raven took a fistful of my hair and yanked my head back, dragging me into the middle of the room. "It's time to right Amity's wrongs and be rid of the abominations she released on our world. Choose—who stays and who goes."

"What?" I asked, working to break free of her grasp but unable to move. My eyes darted between the brothers, and panic rose in my chest. "What are you talking about? I fell in love with Soren, but it was too late. You owned the Reynard by the time I confessed it. I have no power here, Raven. I don't know what you want me to do, but I'm not going to let either of them burn."

She jerked my hair and hissed through her teeth, "You really are so dim-witted, Gemma. The book didn't say that the *owner* had to fall in love with one of these *things*, just that someone from the Fox line must. Therefore, your lack of standards makes you the winner. Mommy and Daddy will be so proud of you for finally doing something right."

"If Hazel's spell worked, then Soren should be gone. This isn't a choice for me."

"Did you even finish reading it, or did Hazel put too many big words in there for you?"

A yelp left my mouth as she pulled again. "I didn't have time to finish it before you took the hotel from me. Like I told you, you have to be careful with how you read it. You didn't listen and it's—"

Raven's maniacal laughter interrupted me. "Is there anything you don't do halfway?"

Anger rose within me, her mistake with the journal momentarily forgotten. I clawed at her in another attempt to escape her grasp, leaving behind angry red scratches on her skin. "Yeah, actually. I don't *halfway* hate you; I hate you with every fiber of my being. How about that?"

"She doesn't love halfway either, Miss Fox. And that's why she won't do what you're asking her to do. Not like this," Soren said, struggling against the chains at his wrists.

Mr. Cartwright's words flew through my mind, his words loud and clear. *It cannot be relocated or demolished. It comes as is, for lack of a better explanation. For lack of a better explanation*, what a strange thing to say, unless it was a hint to the spell. Raven might have read everything, but she hadn't read the stipulations carefully enough. And I prayed that would work to my advantage.

"But I can't choose. I fell in love with Soren. That's it, end of story. If this spell were real, it would've been broken already, but clearly, it hasn't been. I guess Hazel's magic didn't take after all," I said, trying to buy time.

"Lord give me strength," Raven called to the sky before speaking to me as if I were a toddler. "Gemma. You. Have. To. Pick. Which one of these demons do you want to send home? You just have to say the words *Soren or Archer, I set you free. Consider your debt paid.*"

This didn't make any sense. I thought it was clear how the spell was to be broken, and it wasn't a choice by just any Fox descendant. Was it?

But Raven was right; I hadn't finished the book. I had no way of knowing what it said at the end aside from taking her word for it.

I looked up at Soren, searching his face for the answer. If this really was the way it would end, if this was the way to set one of them free, did he want it to be him? Did he want to return to his people? It was easy to say that he wanted to stay here, but when presented with a chance to return to his homeland, would he really give it up?

"Don't you dare say it, Gemma. I would rather turn to ash with this building. You know what to do," he said, his voice low and steady.

My eyes darted between him and Archer, and it was so clear to me which brother wanted to go. But what did that mean for Soren? Would he ever get to leave these walls? I was almost 100 percent certain that the hotel was not going to burn, but could he be happy, spending his days here until the hotel was handed down to the next Fox woman?

"Gemma. Do you need me to draw you a picture?" Raven pulled something out of the pocket of her dress, and when the unmistakable flick ignited a flame, it was time to decide.

Once again, time was up for me.

I felt the heat of the lighter against my neck, and I screamed in agony as she held the flame to my skin. "Shit, Raven, please stop!"

Soren roared, "You bitch, put the lighter down, or I swear to God, I'll kill you with my bare hands." But trapped in the chains, there was nothing he could do to stop her.

His words were an idle threat; he knew it, I knew it, and so did Raven. Her cackle filled the room, and she said, "Choose, Gemma. Now. Before I burn every inch of skin off your whore body."

I dragged my eyes away from Soren and met Archer's amethyst

gaze. *Are you sure that's what you want?* I mouthed to him. *Do you want to go home?*

He shook his head and said, "You don't have to, Gemma. You can set him free if that's what you want. I've taken enough from you, and my brother deserves to be free, much more than I do."

Raven shifted the flame to the other side of my neck, and I wailed in pain. Meeting Soren's blue stare, I whispered, "I'm sorry."

"Gemma, no!" Soren shouted, but my mind was made up.

Taking a deep breath, I closed my eyes and said as strongly as I could through the pain of the burns on my neck, "Archer, I set you free. Consider your debt paid."

When the room came back into focus, Archer was gone—the golden chains discarded on the floor and his clothes draped over the chair. A bright-purple ball of light zipped across the room, charging for Raven's head. She threw me to the floor and swatted at Archer in his true form, dropping the lighter.

"In the name of all things pure, I send you back to the depths of your hellish realm. Be gone, demon!" she screamed.

I scurried to Soren and yanked on the knotted chains at his ankles. "I've doomed you; I'm so sorry."

"No. When you let Archer go, you set me free. This is what I've wanted since the day Hazel told me she found a way to send one of us home. I meant it; I would rather burn in this world than live thousands of years in a realm without you in it, Gemma."

As soon as I unknotted the last chain, I stood and pushed his hair off his forehead. "I love you, Soren. I love you so much."

"I love you with every—"

A thump sounded behind me, and I spun around to find Raven on her stomach with her lighter in hand. She twirled the flint and brought the flame to the fringed edge of the Persian rug. "Burn, burn, burn," she chanted in a crazed mumble.

Archer flew to my side and buzzed around—a perfect depiction of my racing heart. I hurried behind the chair and set to work on the binding wrapped around Soren's wrists. My hands shook as I fought the tangled metal, the delicate chains impossible to untwine.

"Go, Gemma, get out of here, now!" Soren ordered, the plea in his voice raw and desperate.

"No, I won't leave you!"

A bloodcurdling scream came from behind me. "What did that witch do? Why won't it burn?" Raven's face was beet red as she rushed to the curtains and tried to light them on fire. But nothing happened.

Relief washed over me; she couldn't do it. As long as the Reynard was Soren's home, it could never be demolished. Hazel wouldn't just set one brother free; she would keep the one left behind safe. Her intentions were always to protect them both.

I rushed to the antique desk in the corner of the room and yanked open the drawers, looking for anything that could break Soren's chains. Crayons, a pad of paper, pens, but nothing that would sever the layers of gold holding him down. I snorted when I opened the last drawer and found another of Hazel's wooden statues—an abstract man with a very large penis in his hand.

"Gemma!"

I whipped around to catch Raven slithering toward Soren, holding out the lighter. Without a second thought, I grabbed the sculpture and sprinted across the room. My cousin inched closer to Soren's chair, swatting at Archer as he buzzed around her to stop her. I lifted my weapon in the air and swung it. It hit her in the back of the head with a crack, and the lighter fell from her hand. She whimpered and crashed to the floor.

I stood stunned, panting for breath, my heartbeat so wild that it sounded like the pounding of feet against the wooden floor.

"Gemma," Larry cooed, taking the statue from my hand. "Are you okay?"

I ripped my gaze from Raven's unconscious body and looked at Soren. Skye knelt behind him, working the gold free with some sort of small tool.

"I'm fine," I whispered, squeezing Larry's arm but not taking my eyes off Soren. "How did you know what was going on?"

He lifted a brow, and at the same time, we both said, "Wanda."

Larry jerked his chin in Raven's direction. "You didn't kill her, did you?"

I laughed despite myself. "I hope not. But you should call the cops."

"I'm on it," Larry said just as Skye pulled the last chain off Soren's wrists and helped him to his feet.

I rushed to Soren and threw my arms around his waist, burying my face in his shirt. He was swaying back and forth like he'd just gotten off a carnival ride, but his grip on me was firm. Releasing me with one arm, he pulled a handkerchief from his pocket and wiped the lighter fluid from his face and hair.

Skye cleared her throat. "Gemma, Soren, why don't you two step across the hall into the library, and we'll take care of this until the police come."

"Actually, I'd rather step outside, if that's okay. I need some fresh air," I mumbled against Soren's chest.

Soren nodded and gave Larry and Skye a quiet thank-you as we left the room.

It was too much—my cousin's atrocious acts, the force I'd used to stop her, and the decision I'd made that trapped Soren here for the rest of his life. The weight of it all was crushing.

"Gemma?"

"I'm fine." I sniffled, looking up at him. "I am just so glad you're okay. I was terrified for a second there that she had won."

He leaned in and kissed the top of my head. "It would have taken more than that for her to win."

I wasn't so sure about that. What the hell had I even accomplished? I turned my attention to Archer as he flitted around our heads. I forced a smile but couldn't disguise the disappointment in my voice as I said, "You're still here. Looks like breaking the spell didn't do anything but put you in your true form."

"A new way for you to be constantly annoying," Soren grumbled, but an unmistakable playfulness laced his tone.

We walked out into the frigid night where everyone was still dancing and gawking at the grand finale of the fireworks show. I took several deep breaths, basking in the burn of the cold air in my lungs. I was still alive, and so were the Hyde brothers. It may not have ended up *exactly* how I would have hoped, but this was better than the alternative.

My time as the Reynard's owner was over, but the hotel was still standing, and my family's legacy would live on. New generations would come to this place for a one-of-a-kind experience. They would leave believing in the impossible and with happy new memories.

"Oh, Mommy, look at the bell tower," said a little girl, pulling on her mother's dress. The sequins of her tiny mask sparkled with every imaginable color in neon hues.

I followed her outstretched finger and found a stunning

sight surrounding the pinnacle of the Reynard. Hundreds, if not thousands, of orbs floated around the bell tower. They darted in and out, some zipping through the air and others drifting like they were riding the cool breeze. Together, they were breathtaking.

"It's the ghosts coming out to play," the girl's mother said.

"No, it's *your* people coming to take you home," Soren whispered to the ball of light on his shoulder. "I hope you find the happiness there that I have found here, brother."

The violet orb moved to the center of Soren's forehead and tapped it. Archer zipped away and disappeared within the swarm of kobolds.

"Thank you for letting me keep him," I whispered to the swarm.

Soren looked down at me and pushed my hair away from my face. "What'd you say?"

I intertwined our fingers and brought the back of his hand to my lips. "Just that I'm glad I don't have to say goodbye to you again." I glanced up at the orbs dancing against the dark, snowy sky. "Are you okay? I know you're going to miss him."

"I will, but he now has what he wants, and I have what I want."

"And what would that be?"

"Come on, Gemma. You know the answer to that."

I did, but I still longed to hear him say it. These were the words we never dared to speak before tonight. I puckered my lips to the side, lifted a brow, and waited.

"You, Gemma Fox. I have you."

EPILOGUE

"Are you sure you want to do this? What if you're still bound to the property? Won't it hurt to try to step away?"

Soren shook his head and pulled his lips between his teeth. "A deal is a deal. You upheld your end of the bargain and finished the tome—the book, the damn journal. And now it's my turn to follow through."

"But we're talking about excruciating pain. I'm not sure this was a fair pact we made."

I chewed the inside of my cheek. I couldn't help but think of the night Soren and Archer had touched the pages of the book. It had zapped and burned, and they both confirmed the pain was just a fraction of what they felt when they attempted to step off the property when it wasn't Winter Spirits. I didn't want Soren to experience that again, but it was clear he wouldn't be stopped.

"You're telling me that reading Hazel's final words to you wasn't painful? I watched the tears slide down your face. Besides, I have to try, Gem. Hazel wanted us to be free. I have to believe her spell did more than just allow Archer to return to our people. It's worth the risk to try."

"All right," I conceded, holding my hand out to him. "Here, hang on to me if you need to."

He hesitated and didn't take my hand, and an internal debate flashed in his cerulean eyes. Would he inch his way over or—

Soren took a huge step into the street. His eyes went wide, and his lips rattled together as he exhaled.

"I know this is a big deal for you, but it was a little anticlimactic for me," I said with my hands on my hips.

His laughter filled the square, which had returned to its normal state after Winter Spirits. "Did you want me to fall to the ground like I was being electrocuted? We could give it another try."

"Of course not!" I stepped closer and pressed my body against his. Tangling my fingers in his hair, I whispered, "This is actually really exciting. Now you can take me all kinds of places."

"You could teach me how to drive," he said.

A sly grin took up residence on my face. "We could *do it* in the back of my car."

"I could take you to the best restaurant in Boston."

"We could make out in the back of movie theaters."

"Your ideas are very single-minded."

"Yep."

Not that Soren could talk. Ever since I'd reclaimed ownership of the Reynard, my shifts had been interrupted by a certain kobold at least once a day. He wasn't going to let time with me slip through his fingers again. And neither was I.

Soren folded my hand inside his, and we started down the sidewalk. He took his time admiring the window displays of each shop and was overly excited to wave at tourists. I would have normally ducked my head in embarrassment, but his new sense of freedom looked very good on him, and I didn't want to miss a second of it.

"I read about Raven's sentencing yesterday," he said. "Her dad had to be escorted out of the courtroom when the judge ordered her to undergo psychiatric treatment."

"You know how it goes; some people in our family don't take too kindly to anyone being less than cookie-cutter perfect. Besides, I think that even after the effects of the book wear off, Raven would benefit from therapy. Her father probably could too. So could mine."

"Speaking of dads, do you think your dad is ever going to take me fishing? I'm still looking forward to winning him over."

He didn't mean it; fishing with my dad was our inside joke. I threatened him with quality time with my father whenever he got in a slump about missing Archer. It was understandable, but it tore me to pieces to see him upset. The reminder that things could always be worse seemed to snap him out of it.

"I mean, I don't know if he'll ever be able to get past the time you basically told him I was using all the skills I'd learned in the beds of different men to fuck you real good," I said with a smirk.

"I thought he would appreciate the way you were applying things you learned in the real world to your relationship."

"Speaking of our relationship, I was thinking."

"That's a dangerous thing, but enlighten me."

"Now that we're here"—I swept my hand out in front of me—"maybe it would be nice to get away. Travel to somewhere new. Maybe find a place we both love and stay for a while."

Even as the words slipped through my lips, I second-guessed them. The hotel was flourishing under my ownership, but I couldn't take all the credit. Larry, Skye, and the rest of the Reynard staff were just as responsible as I was. Their love of the hotel's history and the hospitality they extended to its guests were the reason people returned. Although my business would be left in capable hands, the thought of leaving so soon after getting it back had my stomach in knots.

It wasn't fear of my father's disapproval or worry that my family would take it away from me again that drove my anxiety. The Reynard was mine until I was ready to pass it down to the next Fox woman. What had me on edge was the thought of leaving the one place that had always felt like home.

Soren stopped walking and held my gaze. "If it hadn't worked— if I were still bound to the hotel—I would have been just as happy as I am right now. You understand that you give me something to look forward to every day. I don't care where we are as long as you're with me, Gemma."

"And if you were still bound to the hotel, you know I'd have stayed with you. I'd never go anywhere else again if it meant that I'd be without you."

He placed his palm on my cheek and rubbed his thumb across my bottom lip. "I'd never want to hold you back, though. You know that, right?"

"You wouldn't be. I'm telling you, no matter what, my life is with you."

And it was true. We didn't know exactly what the future would hold. Would we be able to have children of our own? What would Soren's aging process be like the more years that passed? The answers were mysteries to us. But it didn't matter. Not when we had each other.

"I guess we do need to stay at the Reynard, though," I said.

"Why do you say that?"

"Who will scare the hell out of the guests if you aren't there to bang on the walls and shit?"

Soren studied my face and cocked a brow. "Is that the only reason you want to stay?"

I was very familiar with that look. It's the same one he gave me every time he was fishing for information about Hazel's final entries in the book. He never pushed too hard, but his curiosity was getting the better of him. It was time to put him out of his misery.

But not before toying with him one last time.

"You know what I'm going to tell you, Soren."

He released an exasperated breath. "You know I can't read the tome. Only the owner of the hotel can do that."

I laughed and elbowed him in the ribs. "I know, but you deserved that after all the times I had to hear that line from you." I took a deep breath and continued, "Hazel always had the right words for the right time, and the last entry of the journal was no different."

He looked past my shoulder and his Adam's apple bobbed. "She was very intuitive in that way."

"I think she knew what I would need to hear. All those times I thought I'd failed—the water leak, the money we lost from sending the guests to the other hotels, the three weeks we were closed, my parents taking the Reynard from me—I thought I'd let her down. I was devastated to think that I'd disappointed her, even in death. But in the journal, she told me what she considered to be success, Soren. And you know what it is?"

He just shook his head, his eyes meeting mine, the blue in them shining with unshed tears.

"All she wanted was for one of you to go home, and for the other to fall in love. That's it. To her, that was a success." I shrugged. "So, what do you think? Did I make her proud?"

"You made her proud, Gemma. She knew you would finish what she started. The icing on her big jewel-encrusted cake is that you love the hotel as much as she did."

"Maybe she knew that I would like this commitment thing. She just needed to give me a shove toward the right person to make me realize I had it in me," I murmured, putting my hands on his cheeks and pulling him down to kiss me.

"Is this your way of asking me to marry you?" he whispered against my lips.

"I don't know—what if it were? What would you say?" I asked, sliding my fingers into the hair at the nape of his neck.

"I'd say name the time and place, and I'll be there. I'm not going anywhere without you; remember when I told you I wanted you to have the kind of life you dreamed of before coming to the Reynard?"

"Yes."

"I look forward to giving you that life now, Gemma. Whatever you want, it's yours."

My heart sped up, thumping a fast rhythm against my ribs. I should have been used to it by now, the heart palpitations and butterflies, but I wasn't. And I knew I never would be.

"You've got it easy then, Mr. Hyde. Because all I want is you."

ACKNOWLEDGMENTS

Although writing a novel is easier with your best friend, it took the support of many to place this book in readers' hands.

To our husbands, Tony and Richard: thank you for being patient with all of our goofy, late-night antics and marathon writing sessions, and for always believing in our ability to write and publish anything we want. Even though we say we want to crawl under the table when you do it, thank you for always telling our servers to read our spicy books. We love you both.

To our children, Steven, Sara, and Aidyn: thank you for not being embarrassed that your mom writes spicy romances and spends the majority of her time creating fictional, paranormal people. The best feeling as a mom is knowing you are proud of us. We love you.

To our moms and dads: thank you for instilling in us the work ethic that will never, ever let us quit and for creating loving homes that allowed our imaginations to flourish. We couldn't love you more. And no, Dad, you don't have to read it.

Sam, thank you for all you do to share our stories with new readers on social media. Every aesthetic and silly TikTok you make about our books bring a smile to our faces. Every day we remind ourselves how lucky we are to have you in our corner. Hopefully, one day, we'll be able to pay you in more than just sneak peeks of works in progress.

To Wattpad and the Wattpad Books team, thank you for believing in us and *Spellbound* and for making our dreams come true. To Deanna, thank you for leading us down this road and holding our hands from the beginning. To Fiona, our lovely editor, thank you for all of the emails, notes, suggestions, and jokes that you thought for sure we wouldn't think were funny. Spoiler alert: we did! To our copy editor, Arin, thank you for everything you caught in your copy edits; you made more of a difference than you will ever know. To Tom McGee—two words: magic book.

To our TikTok followers: we cannot begin to thank you enough for your support since we joined BookTok. It means the world to us that so many of you love our work, join our live videos just to hear us talk about nothing, and show us so much love with your creativity in the videos you make for us. We adore you.

To our Wattpad readers: it is because of you and the excitement you show toward our stories that we continue to write. Thank you to each of you who have left comments or reached out to tell us how much you enjoy reading our stories. You fuel our drive to bring you more paranormal romances with strong women in the lead and swoon-worthy men who raise them up.

And finally, to our best friends: each other.

Crystal, I could not even begin to do all of this without you. Well, I suppose I could, but I wouldn't want to. This journey together is way too much fun to do alone. Writing with my best friend is easily the best job I've ever had, so much so that it doesn't even feel like a job; it feels like a blessing. I love you more than you love pumpkin pie.

Rachel (Felicity), I'm honored to have you as my writing partner and, most importantly, my best friend. It is because of you that I continue to write and believe others want to hear my stories. I can never thank you enough for everything you do to promote our books and expand our readership. Thank you for all the late-night laughs and for always listening as I chaotically work through plot holes. There is no one on this earth I'd rather be on this journey with. You are the sparkling sprinkles on top of my salted caramel mocha frappuccino. I love you.

ABOUT THE AUTHORS

Crystal J. Johnson is an award-winning author, Wattpad Star, and half of the writing duo Crystal and Felicity. She has written and cowritten ten novels, including *Spellbound*, *Edge of the Veil*, and the Affliction Trilogy. Crystal lives in Phoenix, Arizona, with her husband, son, and a multitude of rescued animals. She is a self-proclaimed connoisseur of Ben & Jerry's ice cream and a lover of boy bands. When she is not writing, you can find her with her nose in a book or an audiobook in her ears.

Felicity Vaughn is an award-winning Wattpad Star, author, and co-author of ten novels on the platform, including *Spellbound*, *Edge of the Veil*, and *Cruel Trust*. She has almost always dreamed of being a writer, beginning with poetry in middle school, fan fiction in college, and her first novel at the age of thirty-one. Felicity is from Nashville, Tennessee, where she lives with her husband and spoiled-rotten dog and cats. When she isn't spending time with family or writing with her bestie, you can find her watching *The Golden Girls* and sipping on a Diet Dr Pepper.

Turn the page for a sneak peek of

Available now, wherever books are sold.

CHAPTER ONE

THEA

"Is that really what you're going to wear?" Candace looked at me questioningly. She tapped her perfect pink manicured nails on her desk.

"Apparently not," I mumbled.

"Correct." Her straight blond hair brushed the tops of her shoulders as she tilted her head. She was dressed to kill in a little gold cocktail number.

"Are you going to tell me what's wrong with it?" I asked, craning my neck to see my backside in her mirror. The gray dress fell to my ankles, paired with my only black flats. My hair was up in its usual messy brown bun.

"Thea, that whole dress is a disaster. The silhouette is all wrong for your waist to hip ratio, the darts in the top do nothing for your chest, and flats to a formal event?" She stood dramatically, chair legs squeaking as they slid across the tile floor. "I'm going to have to dress you."

"No."

"Yes," she insisted.

"I don't even want to go. I'm only there for you and the fancy food."

"All the more reason to look good." Her heels clicked across the tiles as she excitedly threw open her closet doors. "The Candace Lewis entourage has to be as hot as Candace Lewis herself."

"I'm your entourage now?"

"Just get your butt over here." She pulled out several things from the piles of clothes in her extensive wardrobe, pondering them for a moment before discarding them atop a nearby armchair. "Where the hell is that designer gown I just bought?"

"The red one? Candie, that has, like, no back to it."

"Yeah, that's kind of the point." She shoved herself between two large coats. "If I had your yoga-babe shoulder blades, I'd never cover them up."

"I can barely hear you through all that fabric," I said. "Isn't something backless a little too cold for December?"

"Fashion is pain and all that. A-ha!" She emerged triumphant, holding up a long red gown. "Get that monstrosity off and put this on."

"The things I do in the name of friendship." I slipped my dress off and let it fall to the floor. Candace was on me in one fell swoop, sliding the red satin over my head and smoothing it down my body. She stood back and eyed me from top to bottom.

"Gorgeous." She clasped her hands together, flashing a wicked grin. "You look absolutely *devastating*. I'll get some black pumps!" She dove back into her closet.

Turning to the mirror, I *felt* devastating. The neckline plunged, but not quite out of my comfort zone. The satin squeezed every drop of curve it could from my hips, flaring out as it brushed the top of my thighs. It was hands down the most flattering garment I had ever worn.

"Here, put these on. Match it with this ruby lip gloss, and for god's sake, Thea, run a brush through your hair." Candace checked her reflection next to mine.

Biting my tongue, I pulled a brush through my hair and slipped the hair tie back over it once it was more neatly in place. "Happy?"

She squinted at me and stuck a decorative silver hair pin in it before nodding her approval. "Yes."

With a laugh, I turned to the side and eyed the new ornament in the mirror. "What would I do without you?"

"You'd die a book hoarder in a dark basement apartment surrounded by antiques and tears. Now, let's go."

L'Atelier Rouge, or the Red Studio, was an oversized greenhouse in the middle of an elaborate garden. What was surprising was that it managed to stay that way, undeveloped as the offices and skyscrapers of Seattle went up around it. Once the workshop of the artist Marcel Dubois, it was painted—you guessed it—red. The studio had been preserved as a museum, with a modern art gallery built on its grounds. It was a classy place, for sure. Much classier than our ride anyway.

"How did you wangle an invitation again?"

I felt a little silly pulling up to a charity event in the same dented van I'd had since high school, but Candace insisted I drive so she could *drink her weight in overpriced wine.*

"I told you already." Candie reapplied her lipstick in the mirror. "My boss couldn't make it, so she gave her tickets to whoever gave her the best article this month."

"I thought you were joking; Georgina hates you."

"Hate is a strong word," Candie said, snapping her lipstick lid closed. "And I'm her best journalist." Candace opened her door and I followed her lead until we were both on the sidewalk in the frosty night air.

"Shit! It's freezing," she complained.

"Fashion is pain," I deadpanned.

Candace glared at me, then walked as quickly as her heels allowed toward the front door. Mercifully, the snow from the previous day had been cleared off the sidewalk, or I would have ended up on my butt in these shoes.

"Are you sure we're dressed appropriately?" I eyed a stylish couple walking in—they reeked of money, and I could swear they were staring as they passed.

"Relax, I work in fashion journalism. I think I can pull together a couple evening wear looks." Candace smoothed her skirt and took the last few steps to the door in excitement. She practically dragged me to the front door, where a man in a suit was collecting tickets and scratching names off his list. Candace ogled the other guests while I tried my best to turn invisible. Dying of embarrassment was starting to sound like a good option when the guy at the door stopped to rave loudly about Candie's amazing boss and her tickets. I don't know how he'd become such a fan of a magazine editor, but it didn't look like we would get out of hearing about it until the lady behind us cleared her throat in annoyance, moving the process along.

Inside, the extravagance of it all sank in. Soft yellow light cast a golden glow throughout the room. Some wore jewelry worth probably more than my whole year's paycheck. There was a champagne fountain in the center of a huge buffet table. Even the waitstaff was dressed in black tie as they glided around balancing trays of drinks. Somewhere a piano was playing seasonal music while couples danced across the marble floor.

"Candie, this is way out of my league. How am I supposed to talk to anyone here?" I whispered.

"Relax." She sauntered over to a table loaded with refreshments, and I followed close behind. "You're here for the food and the exhibits, right? Just grab a plate and enjoy the art. Actually, you should find a cute piece of ass and dance—you look absolutely delicious in this lighting." Her eyes began to scan the crowd dangerously, and the very real threat of Candace plucking a dance partner *for* me was starting to creep into play.

"Dancing is unlikely, I'll go with the food." Giving her the side eye, I did have to admit the table looked delicious. "And you're going to be where?"

"Rubbing elbows with the rich and famous." She winked. "I'll let you be a bridesmaid in my posh celebrity wedding once I land one of them."

"Of course, I'll be a bridesmaid in your very plausible celebrity wedding."

"Have fun. Thanks for driving!" She blew me a kiss, then scooped a glass of champagne from a passing tray and waded into the crowd. Taking her advice, I turned my attention to the food.

And holy hell, *the food*.

Different kinds of fruit and cheese and meat were

everywhere. Pastries with complicated decorations were stacked high on porcelain trays. I had to stop myself from breaking off the head of a carved chocolate swan—tempting as it was, it was probably meant to be a display. Even the plates looked expensive, monogrammed with gold-leafed edges.

Loading up on appetizers I'd probably never have the chance to try again, I walked over to the art. Whoever put all this together had an eye for detail that I appreciated. The food was amazing, the soft piano was perfect, and the decor was stunning, but the art was terrible. Painting after painting of tortured gray blobs lined the walls of the main gallery. Maybe I didn't know much about modern art, but this looked like something my two-year-old niece could have made at daycare.

Taking slow steps along the wall, pausing at each canvas to try to find something interesting, my mind wandered as aimlessly as my feet. After most of my snacks were gone, I looked around, trying to find Candie. From the safety of the wall, I watched her on the dance floor as she glued herself to a guy with too much gel in his hair. Between dances she socialized with anyone near enough to participate, asking them questions about their clothes in typical Candie fashion. She was reveling in the attention; I could see the victory in her eyes. Candace had two passions in her life: fashion and people. With a smile, I popped a miniature cherry tart into my mouth as I watched her. As different as we were, she was thriving in her element, and I was happy to be here when she wound down, enjoying the food and a quiet walk by myself through the gallery. Candace spotted me against the wall and winked. Laughing, I got out of there before she could pull me onto the dance floor.

Moving out of the main room, onto a different exhibit,

I pretended I was in a world-famous museum, surveying the treasures around me in the secret hours after the visitors were gone. It was the Dubois permanent collection, not one of the ever-changing special exhibitions that passed from gallery to gallery, but the namesake of L'Atelier Rouge. Most of the guests had probably seen these paintings before or didn't care in the first place, but I'd never seen them in person. So, I walked and munched on crostini, regretting Candace's choice of footwear. After a while I paused against the wall in a particularly dim corner to rest my feet, hide, and eat.

"Beautiful," said a gravelly voice just over my shoulder. The sound startled me; I whirled around to see a man in a *finely* tailored suit standing there. His dark hair was long and pulled back, his emerald eyes filled with amusement. Broad but not bulky, tall and poised enough to join the art on the walls, this creature was walking sin.

"What?" I replied, swallowing.

"The paintings. Don't you think so?"

Setting my plate on a table behind me, I hoped he hadn't seen me stuffing my face. "Yes."

His laugh was a low, comfortable sound that crawled up my back. "Much better than the gray eyesores out front, but I suppose that's what's 'in' now."

I snorted and immediately felt the heat rush to my face, slapping a hand over my mouth.

"Is this your first time at L'Atelier Rouge?" he asked, blessedly not laughing at my reaction. His low, confident tones were right up my alley.

"It is." Was this man somehow the only other introvert at this party? Maybe, since he wasn't in the main room with the rest of the guests. Or maybe he liked the atmosphere here. I know I did, that's what drew me to museum studies.

"Marvelous. Would you enjoy a private tour?" A wicked playfulness danced across his lips.

"Do you know much about art?" I asked, approaching one of the paintings. A soft smile spread across my face, cautiously interested in where this was going.

"I should hope so." His eyes glinted as he closed the distance I had just put between us. "I own the gallery. Please, call me Devin."

"That explains it. I'm Thea, it's nice to meet you. A tour would be lovely; I'm not as familiar with modern art, but this collection is beautiful."

That seemed to take him by surprise. "Should I assume that you are familiar with other eras of art then?"

My eyes shifted to the nearest painting, a forested landscape. Warmth crept up my neck in a telltale sign that I was dangerously close to becoming flustered, either from shyness or an attraction to Devin or both. "Only lightly compared to you, I'm sure. I just finished my history degree in the spring. Museum studies."

Devin's brow raised and he gave me a reassessing gaze. "How interesting, I've been giving some consideration lately to displaying more of the gallery's history."

"Considering the original studio still stands I think that's a wonderful idea," I said excitedly. "Do you have other remaining artifacts? Information about the original owner? Any surviving photographs would be an amazing addition to the displays. All of that would make an interesting—*oh*." Biting the inside of my cheek to stop the enthusiastic babble I was spouting, I cleared my throat. "A tour would be lovely."

Devin's polished composure dropped a bit in favor of an abrupt sound of amusement. "A conversation for another time, then." His eyes moved from me to the painting I had stepped in front of earlier, causing me to still as he leaned in slightly to nod in its direction. "This series contains some of Dubois's earliest landscapes, this one being one of the first uses in his entire body of work to harness this technique regarding water texture."

The tour was more of a conversation, and it flowed easily between us. There was something captivating about the paintings that made one want to keep staring into them. Magical, whimsical little details that drew your eye across the canvas in a natural flow. When my eyes weren't caught by the paintings, I found them drifting toward Devin as we went, glancing at his strong, sculpted profile as he spoke about the history of the pieces.

He led me through the exhibit, showing me painting after painting with a comfortable curiosity between us until we reached the farthest wall. It was like I was in a trance—following his every word through the quiet gallery.

"Here, you can see the difference in his later work. For instance"—he made a sweeping motion with one arm—"this was one of Marcel's last pieces. Near the end of his life, he claimed to see things in the forest. Fairy tales come to life."

The painting was a dark line of trees behind rows of gorgeous pink lilies, the sun shining on the grass. Behind the branches, a blackness contrasted against the sunny field. Eerie eyes peered out from behind tree trunks. They were so imperceptible that I almost wouldn't have noticed them had they not been pointed out to me. It struck me as odd, considering the realist nature of the other paintings.

Devin moved, and the gentle scent of his woodsy cologne brushed my nose. He stepped back and motioned to another painting. From this viewpoint, the paintings took on fantastical elements. Wings, ears, eyes, all hidden as though Dubois himself were seeing them only from the corner of his vision. And Devin was invested in each painting, knowing the history of it, where the landscape sat, and when in his lifetime Dubois had painted it. He was fascinating to listen to, and my hungry curiosity only grew as we explored the collection.

"This one is a personal favorite." The latest painting depicted a little girl holding a bouquet of wildflowers as big as she was. Her smile was missing a front tooth, and it wasn't until I looked closer that it appeared her ears were *pointed*.

"What do you think?" He took one step closer to me, not uncomfortably close but near enough that I could feel the warmth of his body in the otherwise cool gallery. Letting out a slow breath, I calmed my nervous attraction and did my best to focus on the subject matter.

"He was a skilled painter," I said, stepping back and licking my dry lips. "If perhaps a bit eccentric in the end."

Devin's low tones gave way to a burst of laughter that lit up my chest. Immediately I regretted stepping away when I could have stayed next to him instead.

"Eccentric is an excellent choice of word." He straightened his silver tie, checked his watch, and offered me a hand. "I'm afraid I've prattled on enough. I appreciate that you allowed me the pleasure of a tour; few show much interest in Marcel anymore."

"It was a pleasure."

Devin took my own outstretched hand and kissed it

gently. My arm flared to life as though it had been asleep until now, and our eyes locked. My focus on Devin and the paintings sharpened, as if I hadn't been using my senses properly before. A hot coal of attraction landed in the pit of my stomach. "I assure you, the pleasure was all mine," he mused, letting go of my hand. As my fingers fell, I clutched them absently over my beating heart.

"Thea!" Candace called from the other side of the room— wine glass in one hand, heels in the other. She was off-her-ass drunk.

"Oh no," I groaned.

Devin chuckled, taking a step back. "I sincerely hope we have the opportunity to do this again sometime; I'd love to explore your ideas on how to go about organizing a few displays throughout the collection. I'll leave you to your friend to enjoy the rest of the party."

While I would rather have watched Devin go, the short blond spectacle in the doorway shouted, "Thea, dance with me!" then slurred, "Who'sh the hottie?"

"The *owner*. You're drunk."

"His ass should be under one of these damn spotlights," she said, a little too loudly. Several heads turned our way from the main room behind her.

"How are you already this drunk? We've only been here for, like, thirty minutes."

"Psh, it's been *hours*. Look!" Candace held her phone to my face so I could see the time, and I gaped at the numbers across her lock screen.

"That's impossible." Pulling out my own phone, I swiped through to find the same time displayed.

"No, *you're* impossible." Candace swung her arm out, sharing a few drops of wine with the pristine white floor.

"Come on, Candie, we're getting you home," I mumbled, taking the wine glass from my drunk friend. "I think we've both had enough for tonight."

CHAPTER TWO

THEA

"I don't want to go yet," Candace whined, trying to push my hand away as I reached for her seat belt. "That girl with the vintage Tiffany ring let me try it on. I want to go baaack."

"Here." I took a pastry that I had pilfered from the snack table on the way out and stuck it in her mouth. "Eat that and please don't throw up in my van."

"Mm-mmhrm phff," she said, unintelligibly, as I buckled her up. "More of these?"

Smiling, I handed her another pastry, and walked around to the driver's side door.

While the van warmed up I gave the gallery one last look, seeing a silhouette in a window on the third floor, high off the ground. My fingers tightened on the wheel. Perhaps wishful thinking on my part, but I could have sworn it was Devin. We drove off, leaving the strange party and the enchanting gallery owner behind.

—

The roads were quiet, and in half an hour I had Candace inside her warm apartment building. I was digging out my copy of her key when she began swaying her arm in front of me, a series of numbers scrawled across her skin.

"Look what I got tonight."

"Are you serious right now?" I turned the key and half dragged Candace through her front door.

"One HUN-dred percent, baby!"

"Why didn't you just put the number in your phone? This isn't middle school anymore." I caught her as she stumbled and helped her over to her bed. I unzipped her cocktail dress and let it slide to the floor. "Only you would find a booty call at an art gallery."

"No, it's—it isn't a booty call." She giggled as I tucked her into bed, the bubbliest drunk I'd ever known.

"I will remind you that I knew you in high school." I moved her shoes so she wouldn't trip on them in the morning and grabbed a wipe from her bedside table. "Let me see your face."

She sputtered and pushed, fighting me as I wiped off her makeup. "Ugh, too rough."

Eventually I was able to clean her face, and then mine, before getting her in bed and turning off the light.

"Good night, Candie."

"Nooo, are you leaving? Stay with me, pleeease!" She was half out of bed again.

"Stop! Stop," I said as I rushed back. "Fine, all right, I'll stay here tonight."

Candace giggled and made room for me on the bed. I dropped the red gown next to hers with a sigh and crawled in.

"For someone so put together, you sure are a hot mess when you're drunk," I said.

"Yeah? For someone who needs to get laid . . ."

She paused. "You . . . need to get laid."

"Go to sleep," I told her flatly. She snuggled in next to me, clutching me like a teddy bear, and I pulled the covers up to our chins. "I swear, if you throw up on me . . ."

Silence.

"Hey." I looked over—she was out like a light. I stifled a laugh. I could pretend to hate dealing with her drunk ass all I wanted, but she indulged me when I wanted to peruse a bookstore or see a new exhibit with little complaint, and the occasional designated driving wouldn't kill me.

"Night, Candie," I whispered.

I considered leaving, but she'd entwined herself around my body and would probably wake up if I moved. Oh well—it was after midnight anyway and sleep sounded really good about now.

But I couldn't.

A pair of playful green eyes wouldn't get out of my head. My fingers still tingled where Devin had kissed them. Something felt significant about it but I couldn't say what. Maybe I was excited about the gallery or about Devin or both. After a while spent counting sheep and trying to get comfortable, I gave up

15

and watched the moonlight through the windows. The occasional car passed by—a soft hush whispered through the glass every time one drove through the icy slush.

He was trouble. Too smooth, too much my type.

Focus, Thea. You don't need that kind of distraction in your life. It's not like a little bit of shared interest is going to lead to your dream career. He probably wasn't serious about hearing your ideas anyway—that doesn't happen to the quiet ones like you.

He smelled wild, like cedar trees or a campfire.

Stop it.

What would it feel like to run my fingers through his hair?

Throwing off the covers, I peeled myself away from Candace, needing air. Pulling open a drawer to borrow a pair of sweatpants and a hoodie, I willed my feet to move quietly through the studio apartment. Candie had decorated her small and expensive ideal home with her favorite name brands. And the location was great—I looked out the window and could see a thin slice of Elliott Bay. I pulled on my coat and went up to the roof.

The chill hit me right away and I tightened my coat around my shoulders. A gazebo with benches and a picnic table had been built up there for the tenants. As I sat on one of the benches, my breath clouded in front of me, but the air was doing wonders to cool down any part of me trying to stay hot and bothered.

"—heard that he already picked one."

"What court do you think she'll—"

"—about time we got another—"

Curious, I stood and walked to the edge of the building.

The streetlights below glowed yellow, and another car splashed through the slush on the road.

"—another ignorant human—"

Peering over the chain-link fence that bordered the rooftop, I saw two women sitting on the hood of a Mustang. One of them was a pretty blond; the other had snow-white hair.

I squinted—was their skin a little blue? They were wearing almost nothing, despite the freezing temperatures.

"—probably another brat for Spring."

The brisk night carried the sound so well from the street to the rooftop. Suddenly, one of them, the blond, turned and stared right at me. Watching me, she grinned and whispered something to her friend. They both broke out in laughter. I jumped back from the fence like it was on fire. Embarrassed of getting caught snooping and weirded out by their odd conversation, I'd had enough fresh air. Back inside and downstairs again, I climbed back into bed with Candace and soon fell into a deep, restful sleep—eyes in the forest and glimpses of pointed ears and teeth filling my dreams.

THE ENCHANTED FATES SERIES

DIRTY LYING FAERIES

DIRTY LYING DRAGONS
AUGUST 2023

DIRTY LYING WOLVES
AUGUST 2024